The
Alchemist
Who Survived
Now Dreams of a Quiet City Life

Usata Nonohara

Illustration by OX

04

YEN
ON

New York

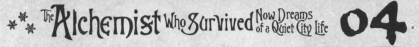

The Alchemist Who Survived Now Dreams of a Quiet City Life 04

Usata Nonohara

Cover art by **OX** Translation by Erin Husson

IKINOKORI RENKINJUTSUSHI HA MACHI DE SHIZUKANI KURASHITAI
Volume 4
©Usata Nonohara 2018
First published in Japan in 2018 by KADOKAWA CORPORATION, Tokyo.
English translation rights arranged with KADOKAWA CORPORATION, Tokyo through TUTTLE-MORI AGENCY, INC., Tokyo.

English translation © 2020 by Yen Press, LLC

Yen On
150 West 30th Street, 19th Floor
New York, NY 10001

Visit us at yenpress.com
facebook.com/yenpress
twitter.com/yenpress
yenpress.tumblr.com
instagram.com/yenpress

First Yen On Edition: September 2020

Yen On is an imprint of Yen Press, LLC.
The Yen On name and logo are trademarks of Yen Press, LLC.

Library of Congress Cataloging-in-Publication Data
Names: Nonohara, Usata, author. | ox (Illustrator), illustrator. | Husson, Erin, translator.
Title: The alchemist who survived now dreams of a quiet city life / Usata Nonohara ; illustration by ox ; translation by Erin Husson.
Other titles: Ikinokori renkinjutsushi ha machi de shizukani kurashitai. English
Description: First Yen On edition. | New York : Yen On, 2019
Identifiers: LCCN 2019020720 | ISBN 9781975385514 (v. 1 : pbk.) |
   ISBN 9781975331610 (v. 2 : pbk.) | ISBN 9781975331634 (v. 3 : pbk.) |
   ISBN 9781975331658 (v. 4 : pbk.)
Subjects: CYAC: Fantasy. | Magic—Fiction. | Alchemists—Fiction.
Classification: LCC PZ7.1.N639 Al 2019 | DDC [Fic]—dc23

LC record available at https://lccn.loc.gov/2019020720

ISBNs: 978-1-9753-3165-8 (paperback)
        978-1-9753-3166-5 (ebook)

10 9 8 7 6 5 4 3 2 1

LSC-C

Printed in the United States of America

The Alchemist Who Survived Now Dreams of a Quiet City Life

04

The Alchemist Who Survived Now Dreams of a Quiet City Life

04 Contents

PROLOGUE
Sprouting from the Scorched Earth

01

What is the source of fear?

For the Gold Lion General Leonhardt, leader of an army that faced powerful monsters with sword, magic, and his own flesh, fear was nothing but an emotion to conquer.

Leonhardt's skill, Lion's Roar, bolstered the fighting strength of the troops he commanded. If the commander of valorous and mighty soldiers was trembling in fear, it would be impossible for him to make use of that power.

For this reason, Leonhardt asked himself what he was afraid of in order to always be strong and calm.

For example, the Fell Forest. A dark place even in the daytime where fiendish monsters lived beyond the trees.

How many monsters lived there? How many powerful enemies lurked there? It was the kind of place where, even if lovely flowers bloomed at your feet, they might hold poison that would send you into eternal sleep if you took but the smallest taste of their nectar.

Another example: the Aqueduct flowing under the Labyrinth City. The vast water vein, into which the City's drainage flowed, conjured images of fearsome monsters. Even the ground underfoot there felt like it was on the verge of collapse.

Facing a powerful opponent whose capabilities can't be guessed at—the unknown—can certainly elicit fear.

This was the very reason the Labyrinth Suppression Forces had a scout unit with the task of investigating the Labyrinth. They explored new strata, ensured the safety of routes, and surveyed the types, numbers, and weaknesses of the monsters inhabiting them. Even if there were monsters that exceeded the strength of the incursion, it was possible to defeat the creatures if there was enough information to formulate an appropriate strategy.

That was what the Gold Lion General Leonhardt believed. Beyond the effects of his own skill—Lion's Roar—it was human wisdom that would overcome difficulties, quell fear, and clear a path to the future.

He couldn't have known that a being who surpassed his understanding, who would cause a paradigm shift, had just awakened from the deep, barren earth of the Fell Forest. He couldn't have known that the powerful A-Rank earth dragons had attacked the being extolled as a "Calamity," nor that this entity had recently finished turning them into charred pieces of meat as a reprisal. Leonhardt didn't yet know the Labyrinth City had caught the fearsome mage's eye, or the distance between that mage and the City was closing rapidly.

02

I am the Calamity. Now, I stand atop scorched earth.

I remember. I overslept just a little. Well, I don't really know if it was just a little. Good morning, everybody! It's a fine day for some outdoor grilling.

Mm, nothing's wrong with my magical power. In fact, it's perfect. So perfect, I overcooked three dragons with my Good Morning Fire, and now I dunno what to do for breakfast. Well, I guess it's not breakfast time. The sun's quite high in the sky. Anyhoo, I'm starving. That girl's probably awake by now, too, so I'll wish her a "bad morning" and we can eat together. I bet she'll be delighted to cook for me if I bring some tasty meat.

Oh, there's an earth dragon in the perfect spot. I may have overcooked those three from earlier, but this's a new one. Earth dragons sure have excellent technique for their size. They shoot out those stone lances real quick; makes them incredibly annoying. They're like hedgehogs. Anyhoo, I'll toss some flame blast magic into its mouth and blow its head off. Ah, this time it worked much better. The meat from the neck down is still fresh, so I've got some cooking ingredients. It's bad not to drain the blood from your prey after killing it, but that's too much trouble. I'll just carry it like this.

Mm. I thought I was gonna carry it, but turns out it's huge and heavy. I can't. I'll just cut off the back, the most delicious part, with a *wind blade, wrap that in some leaves, and carry it. I'll incinerate the rest. Too bad I have to waste it. Monsters can evolve by eating the flesh of something powerful like an earth dragon, so it's good manners to burn up the corpse and return its magical power to the ley line.*

I'll take only what I can eat and release the rest.

I was gonna sing my own praises for my exemplary deed, but I guess I shouldn't have done that. Seems like the smell of delicious cooked meat lured in a swarm of small fries from the Fell Forest. I didn't send any invitations to a barbecue party.

What the heck? Has the monster population exploded recently? Are people slacking off on culling them?

"Grant me nourishment. Consume and burn the many foes that defy me. **Flame Pillar Chaos.**"

Fire!

Every last one of the whelps facing me caught fire, and the flame pillar swept them skyward.

Ahh, they're really burning. These monsters are great to eat. They have so much fat, they burned reeeal well. I wonder if someone'll come to get me after that big pillar of fire.

I hate walking.

03

The wall surrounding the Labyrinth City was protected by the City Defense Squad.

In this City, where subjugating the Labyrinth took top priority, the strongest people were assigned to the Labyrinth Suppression Forces. As a result, the overall combat strength of the City Defense Squad was barely enough to defeat swarms led by C-Rank orc kings. To account for this, soldiers who excelled in sensing magical power would always be stationed among those keeping watch, and they were to report to the Labyrinth Suppression Forces as soon as they sensed the approach of powerful monsters.

Nevertheless, day and night they guarded the wall separating the Fell Forest from the Labyrinth City. They bore witness to the Labyrinth Suppression Forces as they took down fearsome monsters from the Fell Forest on countless occasions. Each member was a gutsy soldier in their own right, and no matter what kind of monsters appeared, they had been sufficiently trained to deal with them in a calm and orderly manner.

One of those normally staunch guards of the City Defense Squad rushed into their unit's station in a great panic and pale-faced.

"R-reporting in! We have confirmed a tremendously powerful magical reaction approximately six miles away in the southwest part of the Fell Forest!"

Kyte, the captain of the City Defense Squad, listened to the report, and although the guard's unusual behavior had startled him, he maintained an outward calm and asked for more information on the situation.

"The southwest area of the forest...... Earth dragons?"

"No, sir, it was a far more powerful response! That kind of sensation of magical power was most likely from a human......"

A person would have to train vigorously to effectively imitate the voice of a beast. Magical power was the same way, as the type of source could be discerned to some extent. But a human with more powerful magic than an earth dragon's wasn't something you encountered every day.

Understanding the gravity of the situation, Captain Kyte hurriedly reported to his boss, the colonel.

"Who could it be? A departing adventurer?!"

"That isn't possible. No adventurers above B Rank have departed today, sir!"

Nothing but thick trees filled the southwest part of the Fell Forest, and there shouldn't have been any villages or the like in that region. So if no adventurers had left the Labyrinth City, who had used such powerful magic, and for what purpose?

As Captain Kyte was making his report regarding the adventurers who departed from the City, another messenger burst into the room. This one was even paler than the last.

"Reporting in! We have confirmed another powerful magical reaction approximately five miles away in the southwest part of the Fell Forest!"

"What?! So it's getting closer... Continue to observe. I will report to the Labyrinth Suppression Forces. Captain Kyte, strengthen the southwestern gate's defenses."

"Sir!"

With a firm salute, Captain Kyte headed for the southwestern gate with his subordinate in tow.

This was no doubt the most serious incident they'd seen since the giant slime's rampage. No, even more serious than that.

The City Defense Squad wasn't especially powerful. However, the strength of their desire to protect the Labyrinth City was no less than that of the Labyrinth Suppression Forces.

Due to the low risk of the Squad's duties, many people from

good families and with lower combat strength comprised its ranks. However, if what defined the group was the idea that "the City Defense Squad consists of weak people," both the will and morale of its members would falter. In time, the residents of the City would look down on them, hindering their duties. Therefore, the City Defense Squad was defined as "a force that demands character and intelligence." In particular, the current colonel, Telluther's successor, had set forth a policy for the Squad to be "the shield of the people," and he fully enforced courteous and exemplary conduct toward commoners and adventurers alike. As a result, the City Defense Squad garnered a surprising amount of popularity.

Plus, the City Defense Squad had more points of contact with the City's residents compared to the Labyrinth Suppression Forces, who only appeared in public for the large-scale expedition parades or when something major occurred. Otherwise, they continued their expeditions into the Labyrinth in secret. Although many people couldn't read or write very well, the well-bred soldiers of City Defense treated them with respect. It was almost a task for them *not* to become well liked.

In particular, they had caught the eye of a group of young women. The salary of a soldier in their ranks was low compared to one in the Labyrinth Suppression Forces, but it was a stable job that carried few risks. Unlike soldiers in the Forces, who were immersed in vows and secrets, and who were awkward when it came to conversation, the gentlemanly Squad soldiers had a wealth of topics they could talk about. They were a real bargain.

Being well-liked by pretty young girls made things all the easier. Whether or not they were truly gentlemen or intelligent, all of them were simple at the core. If the key to popularity was gentlemanly conduct, they would strive to act in such a manner. As such, the soldiers of the City Defense Squad immediately acted as the citizens' shield in this crisis and basked in the lovely praises of those cute girls.

Under the direction of Captain Kyte, they immediately strengthened defenses at the southwestern gate, sent the gathering of young ladies assembled nearby to their homes, and observed the movements of the approaching mystery person without missing a beat.

On the opposite side of things, there was Adviser Telluther.

"The Labyrinth Suppression Forces? That's where His Excellency General Leonhardt is, right? I-I'll go, too! Take me with you!"

"......Adviser Telluther, you do understand we're in a state of emergency?"

"Of course, of course! If memory serves, at this time of day His Excellency General Leonhardt should be with His Excellency Lieutenant General Weishardt in a regular liaison council meeting at the base of the Labyrinth Suppression Forces!"

Telluther was one who latched on to the chance to meet General Leonhardt, the object of his admiration. His starry-eyed fondness for exceptional people was truly impressive, still going strong even at a time like this. Perhaps someone should have ordered him not to come in direct contact with Leonhardt?

It took a moment for the colonel of the City Defense Squad to regain his composure after Telluther's inability to read the mood. Having done so, he made for the Labyrinth Suppression Forces' base along with Telluther, who insisted, "There's no time to waste."

04

I am the Calamity. I have emerged from the river.

I recognize this river. It's a branch of the Kingdom of Endalsia's underground Aqueduct and flows into the rivers on the south side.

I'll get there soon; magic has made progress quite smooth. Well, I say I used magic, but stride length is important. I love having long legs!

There should've been a bridge across this river, but I sure couldn't find it.

Seems like people haven't been in this area for a long time.

How careless. The fruit you can get around here makes some of the best booze you'll ever have, but it doesn't look like anyone has been to harvest it. I can't believe they gave it up!

The lack of a bridge pissed me off, so I cut down several big trees nearby to make one myself. I noticed, after felling them, that the strength of the monsters around here differs depending on the side of the river. *Powerful monsters might cross my bridge and gain access to the Kingdom of Endalsia, but oh well. Surely the fruit and the alcohol you can get from it are more important.*

Pleasant drink and tasty snacks—the pickings she made were fantastic. Oh, come to think of it, I just realized something.

If powerful monsters stray onto the kingdom's side of the river, she'll be super angry. She always lectured me not to cause trouble for others ever since she was a little squirt.

Way back when, I used daidara snail mucus to make bumps appear all over my face and pretended to be sick as a little joke, but she got real mad at me afterward.

What would I do if she prepared something with those pseudo-snails as the only ingredient again? I mean, it wasn't bad, but if I ate daidara snail for every meal day after day, I'd be escar-gone.

She forgave me for that gag back then, but I bet she won't next time.

Monsters gathered around me again while I pondered such things.

They look much weaker than the ones around the scorched earth, but there sure are a lot of B-Rankers, like frenzied bears. These guys have parts that make good materials, like their livers, but beating them one by one takes a lot of time, and I've already got the earth dragon meat as a present. Mm. I'll cook them all in one go.

"Flame Pillar Chaos."

Fire!

My smoke signals are clearly visible, and I hit the bull's-eye on all of those bad boys. I pinpointed the monsters when I fired the pillars; otherwise, I might've burned down the whole forest, and then I'd have to wait on the meat. I think I deserve a pat on the back for my control. Feels good to have my intuition back, but I'm still pretty hungry.

The fire pillars should be visible from the kingdom now, though. I wonder when they'll come to welcome me.

05

"What of the unidentified person randomly firing off high-level magic as they approach the Labyrinth City?"

As Telluther and the colonel of the City Defense Squad were making their report to Leonhardt and the others, a messenger under Captain Kyte arrived to provide a progress report.

"Reporting in! We have confirmed another major magical reaction about three miles to the southwest! We've also confirmed from the watchtower at the top of the wall that a large number of fire pillars are visible near the rivers!"

"About how many?"

"Many, sir. At least a few dozen."

Normally, when attacking multiple enemies with magic, you could specify the spell's targeting coordinates. Some spells targeted in a line, like *Wall*, while others targeted an area, like *Storm*. If you didn't, the magic likely wouldn't connect. It was easy to understand if you thought of it like throwing stones at a moving target and then considering how many of the stones would actually hit. However, the wider the range, the weaker the magic's attack power.

One could say that striking enemies with perfectly aimed magic was an exemplary method of attack, but…

"Dozens of fire pillars at once?!"

Weishardt was astonished. Even if there were an adventurer

with such incredible skill and accuracy, how high would their rank have to be? Not to mention they were using fire pillars. Even casting a *Fireball* was much more difficult than launching a simple projectile because it was an embodiment of fire. Fixing coordinates ought to be necessary to activate far stronger fire magic.

And there had been dozens of those pillars all at once. If this was the work of just one person, they'd have to exceed A Rank. However, there had been no word of the likes of an S-Ranker who could control fire in the surrounding countries, let alone the Empire itself.

"Who could it be......? Are they even human......?"

Only one thing was certain: A creature in possession of truly fearsome power was heading for the Labyrinth City.

"We haven't yet determined if they're an enemy. Call the insect summoner. We'll try to use his insects to scout, and discover the identity of this person undetected. Gather the Labyrinth Suppression Forces at the southwestern gate, just in case. Have them hide and mask their presences. The City Defense Squad's station is the closest place to the southwestern gate. We'll go as well."

The Labyrinth Suppression Forces began to move immediately at Leonhardt's orders.

Telluther caught a messenger who was leaving ahead of the others to send word to the Squad of the general's visit.

"Hey, you can tidy up my room, right? Please check my toilet and water basin, too! And decorate it with flowers to make it smell nice! And then, after that......! There's some first-class tea in my room I've been saving for a special occasion, so get that ready, please!"

"......Understood."

Is he a girl inviting her boyfriend to her room for the first time? the messenger wondered, but he kept a straight face and hurried back to the City Defense Squad's station.

06

I am the Calamity. I can see the ramparts.

I've walked so far, yet I haven't even come across a single adventurer, let alone received any kind of welcome. What's the deal? No sooner had the thought crossed my mind than I realized I was looking at the protective wall.

The Stampede destroyed the Kingdom of Endalsia, didn't it?

Their lovely white wall's been repaired with stones from around the area. The barricade's been overrun by daigis ivy, too. Well, it feels a little more lived in this way than back when they were so picky just about the white wall's look.

As I pondered, I was approached by some little buzzing gnats. Magic insects.

Just when I thought I was finally receiving a proper welcome: magic insects. They stopped right in front of my eyes and nose.

Are they mocking me? This is just rude, you know? I thought I'd try burning them up a little, but I needed to be an adult about this. *Calm down, calm down. If they think I'm an enemy and won't let me inside the wall, I'd be in a real bind.*

Because she's probably in there.

I could blow away this wall no problem, but then I'd have to deal with the aftermath. And if I don't give her this meat soon, I'll miss dinner. That girl's so clueless that, even with her skills, someone might be exploiting her. She could be living in poverty, barely anything to eat. Dang, I'm hungry.

So these're probably magic insects, but I would've liked a friendlier greeting. *I'll turn on my chummy mode, smile, and address the likes of these bugs.*

"It's an honor to be welcomed. Now, lead the way."

Yet the magic insects just buzzed about and then flew off high into the sky.

Grr, so rude! As I surveyed my surroundings and wondered if I should turn the whole area into a sea of fire and kill the bugs, a pack of forest wolves gathered around. Woof, woof.

Ahh, so that's why you ran? More importantly, why are these doggies appearing so close to the City? They should be using monster-warding potions out here. She's not slacking off in her work, is she? I'll have to scold her.

Anyhoo, this barking's annoying me. Time to roast the doggies.

"Flame Pillar Chaos."

Fire!

Now, then. It's just a little farther to the City.

07

"Ack!!!"

"What is it?" Weishardt asked the insect summoner, who had broken into a cold sweat and stiffened with a start.

"I was spotted......"

"What?!"

The magic insects sent out by insect summoners were used to investigate the Labyrinth, a place crawling with monsters. At first glance they looked like normal insects, they were small, and they only made a faint sound, so they excelled at spying by blending into the scenery. Without them, the Forces wouldn't have been able to investigate the Labyrinth, which contained over fifty strata. Spotting a magic insect at first glance was no small feat...

"It wasn't merely your imagination?"

"With all due respect, sir... She turned toward my insect and asked it to lead the way, so I don't think I'm mistaken."

"I see. And what kind of person was she?" Weishardt asked, still doubtful of what he was hearing. The summoner replied, "I think it would be faster to see for yourself, sir."

I am the Calamity. I am in front of the gate.

She had trudged all this way and finally made it to the City, only to find the gate was shut tight.

Moreover, a group that appeared to be soldiers were clustered inside.

Do they think they're hiding? That I can't see them? Come on, it's not like fire pillars are that uncommon, so what's all this fuss about? Well, I miiight have made a lot of them, I guess.

Thinking it over while staring at the closed gate, a small door next to the larger entrance into the City opened, and a lone soldier stepped toward her.

"My name is Kyte. I'm the captain of the City Defense Squad. I can gather from your appearance that you're a famous adventurer, but I'd like to hear your name and the reason for your visit."

As one might've expected, Captain Kyte drew the short straw.

He didn't know whether she was friend or foe, but according to Weishardt, even if she was human, she commanded a dangerous amount of power. He'd understood what the insect summoner had said, but this was first contact with a stranger who had produced pillars of fire in the Fell Forest as she rapidly approached the City. This was an encounter with the unknown.

If she wasn't an enemy, any rudeness would adversely affect subsequent interactions, so someone who held a position suited to the occasion was required to respond to her. However, if she was an enemy, it would be a touch-and-go situation that promised sudden death.

It was quite the difficult mission, but Captain Kyte was believed capable of showing a calm response under the conditions because of the bravery he'd shown back when confronting the enormous slime. There was no doubt he was a courageous man.

But even so, the man was relieved when he saw exactly who the curious visitor to the southwestern gate of the Labyrinth City was.

If he were a soldier of the Labyrinth Suppression Forces who had fought the fake mermaids in the fifty-fourth stratum of the Labyrinth, he wouldn't have been so likely to judge someone on appearances alone, but Kyte belonged to the City Defense Squad. One could say he was still a greenhorn, in some respects.

"I'm Freyja. I came to visit my pupil. Could you let me in?"

The owner of this voice was probably around twenty-five years old, judging from her sprightly and voluptuous body.

Her golden eyes were full of strong will, and her red lips were turned up in a grin. The long hair trailing behind her caught the light and shone golden, or orange. No, it was as if red, orange, and yellow blended together like a flickering flame. This person calling herself Freyja was a beautiful woman.

"Who is your pupil?"

"Ugh, I hate bureaucracy. You don't want to let me in, do you?"

The golden eyes glinted like a carnivorous animal's as she glared at him, and for an instant the beautiful woman before him resembled an enormous fire beast. Cold sweat ran down Kyte's back.

"F-far from it. However, I assume from your appearance that you're quite a high-ranking adventurer. Our city is glad to host such adventurers. I'm simply asking questions so we may welcome you to the fullest extent possible and not be discourteous..."

Kyte's incoherent excuse wasn't a lie.

The Labyrinth City tended to treat high-ranking adventurers more cordially. Even penal laborers could be set free should they ever reach A Rank. Nothing would have been more welcome than this woman named Freyja joining the fight down in the Labyrinth.

The dangerous glint vanished from Freyja's eyes as she realized he was telling the truth, and she gave him an answer.

"I don't intend to bring harm to this city. My pupil's name is Mariela."

"Wha—? The alchemist?!"

Through the spells *Wind's Whispers* and *Telepathy*, the conversation between Captain Kyte and Freyja was being immediately transmitted to Leonhardt and Weishardt.

The mage named Freyja who'd come to the City, loosing fearsome fire pillars all the while, appeared civil enough to hold a conversation. And although seemingly short-tempered, she apparently was not inclined toward hostilities. That, at least, was a good thing, but...

"It is possible she means somebody else with the same name."

"......Do you really believe that, Weis?"

The privacy of Leonhardt and Weishardt's conversation was protected by soundproofing magic.

In a corner of the room, the adventurer-loving Telluther said to himself, "Freyja? That's the first time I've heard that name. Maybe she's an adventurer from a far-off foreign country."

If Telluther didn't know her, then there was no mistaking it. No A-Rank or higher adventurers like Freyja existed in the countries surrounding the Empire. At least, not until now.

The high-ranking mage who'd suddenly appeared at their doorstep had addressed the Alchemist Pact-Bearer, who shouldn't exist in the Labyrinth City, as her pupil.

It would be strange to believe those two weren't acquainted.

If they were truly master and pupil, there would be no problem. However, Leonhardt and Weishardt found it hard to believe such a high-ranking mage of unknown character was an alchemist's master.

"Where is Lady Mariela?"

"Today she is in Sunlight's Canopy."

"Tell her to close the shop and not to set foot outside. Lead Lady Freyja to the best lodgings and show her the utmost hospitality. Say we're looking for her pupil and try to get more information out of her."

"Sir!"

Leonhardt's orders reached Kyte immediately, and the southwestern gate of the Labyrinth City was opened to Freyja.

"Lady Freyja. The Labyrinth City is immense. We will prepare the best lodgings for you in the City, so please make yourself at home there. And we will provide you with the finest meal. We shall find your pupil, Lady Mariela, and bring her to you." Captain Kyte bowed his head very deeply.

"Thanks, but no thanks. I want to eat with Mariela today. If you don't know where she is, I can find her."

Freyja passed through the gate, turned down Kyte's offer, and chanted a spell unfamiliar to him.

"I search for thee, kin of my soul. Answer my call. **Soul Signal.**"

The man had never heard of that spell before. Captain Kyte was a shield knight, and his level wasn't particularly high. It wasn't right to say he was well acquainted with magic, but as captain he'd received basic training on its systems. Despite his instruction, this was the first time he'd ever heard of this spell. Moreover, he'd never heard of any magic that could find the whereabouts of a specific person.

"Found you. So you did wake up."

Freyja let out a laugh, and although Captain Kyte tried to detain her, she smoothly slipped away from him and began walking toward her goal without hesitation. She surveyed how the landscape of the City had changed over time, and she gave hardly a single thought to the soldiers lurking in the alleys.

The fire-haired woman's actions sent Leonhardt and Weishardt into a panic.

They'd tried to be courteous to her so she wouldn't take offense, and to ascertain if she was someone who would harm the alchemist, but they hadn't been able to buy enough time.

"I will go, Brother. I have a greater affinity with mages," Weishardt said. He stood up and hurriedly made for Sunlight's Canopy along with several mages under his command. For some reason, Telluther followed. It was reckless of him to want to get a peek at the newly appeared high-ranking adventurer, but the emergency of the situation had all but shrouded his presence.

Was the man completely unaware of what the Labyrinth Suppression Forces were dealing with?

Freyja hummed some unknown tune to herself as she appeared to glide along the main road of the Labyrinth City. Although she was taking her time and enjoying the sights, Captain Kyte was just barely able to keep pace behind her at a jog.

And following farther behind the two in a great hurry was Weishardt.

It was a mistake to travel to the City Defense Squad's station. If we were at the base of the Labyrinth Suppression Forces, we probably could have cut through underground and arrived there first.

Praying that the messenger delivering the warning had made it in time and the door to Sunlight's Canopy was closed, Weishardt's group ran through narrow alleys on their way to the shop.

08

I am the Calamity. I am in front of the door.

Far removed from the panic of Weishardt and the others, Mariela and Sieg fed off each other's sadness from the loss of Lynx, and the gloom around them dampened the mood so heavily that mushrooms could have popped up around them. No, they hadn't changed their jobs to farmer, and no actual mushrooms had grown so far.

Mariela had received a message from the Labyrinth Suppression Forces to close the shop and firmly shut the door. She'd approached the door to lock it, and she turned her head to look at Sieg with tears in her eyes.

"Sieg… Thanks to Merle, we were able to close up without any trouble, but why would they suddenly tell us to close and to not go outside? Something's probably happened… I wonder if it's something bad again…"

"Don't worry, Mariela. I'll protect you no matter what."

Drip, drop, drip, drop.

Although the rainy season had ended, it was still quite damp. It was only a matter of time before mushrooms started to sprout. No doubt some kind of fungus was taking root already. Some damp, moist kind. Mariela and Sieg needed to be disinfected, and only way to do so was with blazing flames.

Incidentally, Mariela had been so preoccupied with the weepy conversation that she had completely forgotten to lock the door.

Bang!

The unlocked door of Sunlight's Canopy flew open.

Mariela was standing with her back to the door. And behind her was...

"Marieeelaaa!"

"H-huwhaaaaaaaaaaaa??!"

Mariela panicked at the sudden hug from behind, and Sieg floundered, unable to assess the situation.

"Marielaaa, it's been so, so long. How many years has it been? Have you gotten bigger?"

"Wha—? W-wait. Could it really be?"

"H-hey, who the hell are you, lady?!"

The mystery woman was embracing Mariela and vigorously rubbing her own cheek against the startled alchemist's. In a panic, Sieg tore the woman away from Mariela. Freed at last, Mariela turned around, and both her eyes and her mouth widened in surprise and disbelief.

"M...Master???!!! How?!"

"Ah-ha-ha, I overslept a bit. Bet you did, too, right? You always were suuuch a scatterbrain!"

Her master belted out a hearty laugh, while Mariela's mouth remained agape.

Sh-she really is her master......? So that means she's the second......?! But that attack power...

Weishardt, watching the whole thing from the back of the building, was relieved at realizing there was no danger to the alchemist. However, the situation still proved to be quite puzzling to him.

"By the way, looks like you grew a bit taller. But nothing else about you has really grown, huh, Mariela? No, I don't mean your chest! Alchemy, you dunce. Well, we'll talk about all that later, I brought you a present. I'm starved. Cook it for me."

Mouth still wide open, Mariela had looked down at her chest and back up to her master's face. Freyja handed her the leaf-wrapped monster flesh.

"I-is this...earth dragon meat?! Wait, what were you thinking leaving this at room temperature without draining the blood?! What a waste. Hmm, how can we make it taste good now... Oh. I know, I know. But we don't have enough herbs. Sieg, could you go get some?"

Mariela immediately came alive at the thought of high-quality ingredients, and earth dragon meat, which couldn't even be found in the wholesale market, was among the best of the best. Excited as she was, the girl was not above feeling frustrated with her master's sloppiness; if her master had just frozen the meat, it would have made a better dish.

"U-um, understood."

Although Sieg was taken aback by Mariela' sudden change in tone, he nodded all the same. The reply came reflexively, but even if this woman was the girl's master, Mariela's escort couldn't afford to just leave her. Taking notice of the man, Freyja thoroughly surveyed him from the tips of his toes to the top of his head. Apparently pleased with her estimations, she grinned and asked Mariela a question.

"Hmm? Oh-ho-ho-ho? Is that your man, Mariela? No way! What a specimen."

"Y... Y-y-y... You've got it all wrong, Master!"

"Geez, kids these days. To think she'd choose someone so experienced and sullied. Kids really scare me."

"W-what are you talking about, madam?"

"Yeah, Master. Sieg keeps himself clean, he's not sullied."

"That's not what I meant. Ahh, but I'm so glad Mariela's still the same as ever."

Sieg understood. Mariela did not. Freyja gazed at the pair and smiled knowingly.

"Madam, please don't teach Mariela strange things......"

Sieg could tell this person was dangerous, and he gently rebuked her.

"Hmm? What're you trying to say, Dark Sieg? I'm Mariela's master. An alchemist's master is akin to their parent. You get my meaning? If so, scoot off shopping now."

"Uh! Understood, Most Respectable Mother! Off I go!" At Freyja's words, Sieg about-faced and rushed off. What happened to being Mariela's escort?

In actuality, there were guards on standby around Sunlight's Canopy, so it likely wasn't a problem for Sieg to leave the shop for a little while.

Incidentally, a heavier perimeter than usual had been imposed after Mariela was told to close the shop, but her master had slipped through all of it. She had appeared to them as an ordinary passerby. If any of the guardsmen had noticed her, it was only after she'd gone past them.

Not a one of them realized this was the effect of the song Mariela's master had been humming to herself.

Utterly ignorant of this fact, Sieg—who'd been overpowered by Mariela's master within minutes of meeting her—dashed off toward Merle's Spices to handle the impromptu shopping.

"I'm going to make this into a stew today since you didn't drain the blood, Master. But roasting it would have given it the best flavor, you know. So next time, please let the blood out and freeze it before you bring it."

"Ehh, too much trouble. Why don't you come with me next time?"

"...I think I'll pass. I'd be dead in less than a minute."

Mariela made free use of both her magical power and skills to prepare the high-class ingredient, and the resulting stew proved to be a gloriously delectable achievement. An absolute masterpiece. It was so wonderful, Margrave Schutzenwald's family chef might have even tipped his hat to it.

Despite the miraculous reunion, no one said a word as master and pupil both greedily devoured the food while Sieg served them. The night quietly wore on as the silent dinner continued.

A second alchemist, Lady Mariela's master, and what's more, a high-ranking mage...... If we can obtain her assistance, then maybe...

Weishardt lost track of time as he stood motionlessly on the street near Sunlight's Canopy, engrossed in his own thoughts. Telluther grew impatient and called out to him.

"Umm, Your Excellency Lieutenant General Weishardt, I wonder if we should go greet Lady Freyja? The young man I happened to see leave the shop a little while ago is an acquaintance of mine......"

"Hmm? Telluther? Why are you...? Well, no matter. The woman is in the midst of sharing the joy reuniting with her pupil. She has proven her connection to a citizen of the Labyrinth City. It would be uncivilized for us to interrupt. Let us withdraw."

"Oh, yes, sir... You know, it's quite interesting 'Freyja' is the same name as the 'Sage of Calamity' in fairy tales. The sage had the same name and occupation as this woman. Ha-ha, quite the coincidence."

Telluther was undeniably disappointed that this wasn't the real Sage of Calamity, but he recovered quickly enough. His innocuous statement, however, had made something click within Weishardt.

It couldn't be...

He recalled a topic of conversation from a dinner with Mariela a few days back.

It was said the Sage of Calamity had slaughtered many monsters during the Stampede two hundred years ago. Could they be one and the same? Alchemists had been sleeping in the Aguinas family's cellar under the Magic Circle of Suspended Animation. He couldn't deny the possibility.

However, the name "Sage of Calamity Freyja" was mentioned in fairy tales from far earlier than the Stampede.

I'm overthinking it. Perhaps the name of a hero from two hundred years ago merely replaced the earlier name of some fairy-tale character, Weishardt assured himself.

However, he couldn't deny the thought that had risen from the depths of his mind.

It was all no more than a guess, certainly not an assumption. The only thing he could say for certain right now was that neither Elmera's husband, Voyd, nor Mariela's master, Freyja, were people he could afford to neglect.

Telluther interjected excitedly, "I guess we'll just have to meet Lady Freyja tomorrow!" But as soon as he returned to the Labyrinth Suppression Forces' base, he was forced to make the vow, "From now on, I will not approach Freyja or Sunlight's Canopy, and I will not disclose the information I already know by any means, including by way of writing." As such, he couldn't even approach Sieg, his benefactor during the giant slime incident and whose whereabouts Telluther had discovered through sheer dumb luck, let alone Freyja. The man's despondence was unspeakable.

If this were their only issue, Mariela and Sieg's daily life in Sunlight's Canopy could have become quite peaceful, but the inquires of an overcurious man were trivial compared to the uproar caused by Mariela's explosive master.

09

"Master, you forgot to put out the lantern, too?! The almighty lantern?"

"You're saying you did, too? Such a kluuutz. Ah-ha-ha."

Mariela's master burst out laughing and mocking her pupil despite her own accidental two-hundred-year nap.

"You're impossible!" Mariela exclaimed with a pout, which served to only elicit even more laughter from her master.

Sieg had bought a stash of alcohol with his own allowance for times when Edgan came crying to him, and it was obliterated in a matter of minutes. The culprit was, of course, Freyja. She would look at a bottle and say, "Mmm, Drops of Liiife," and then promptly drain it. Although she was a disgrace to alchemists for likening alcohol to Drops of Life, it probably seemed like an accurate comparison to a drunkard.

Sieg was in charge of the household finances for Sunlight's Canopy. Watching the alcohol disappear made him think seriously about factoring "Master Expenses" into the budget as he brought in new bottles of alcohol from the storehouse. He very much wanted to support his "mother-in-law," but unfortunately his own spending money didn't seem like it would suffice.

It had been a little over two hundred years since Mariela's master departed and left the little house in the Fell Forest to her pupil.

With no advance warning whatsoever, the woman had reappeared and made herself at home, and pestered Mariela to make dinner for her.

The meat her master had brought as a souvenir was exquisite, and although master and pupil had indeed enjoyed a truly miraculous reunion after ages of separation, they wordlessly tore into their food once the cooking was done.

Even if one were to disregard the two centuries they'd slept under the Magic Circle of Suspended Animation, it had still been several years since they'd seen each other. They had so much to talk about, yet Mariela's master acted casually, as if she'd only been gone for a few days. The pair who'd been buried for more than two lifetimes carried on rambling conversations that resembled idle gossip. By all rights they should be talking about the time line of events since Mariela awakened, but Freyja's influence was too strong.

"Master, how are you here after two hundred years?!"

After eating so much of the earth dragon stew she was fit to burst (or at least rediscover Chubby-ela's waistline), Mariela finally asked the question she should have asked some time ago.

"Whoa, has it really been two hundred years? I can't believe it. Looks like the Kingdom of Endalsia was destroyed, so what country are we in now?"

"Why are you so casual about this?!"

"This is the Empire's Labyrinth City, a territory under the jurisdiction of Margrave Schutzenwald."

Mariela's mouth, once full of earth dragon stew, gaped open again at her master's feigned ignorance, so it was Sieg who had answered the question.

"Ahh, I see. The Labyrinth City, huh?"

Freyja hemmed and hmmed to herself, and it seemed like she understood everything just from Sieg's explanation.

"Wait just a second! Master! Why did you sleep for two hundred years in the first place? You said I graduated and then went and vanished, and now you show up all of a sudden! I mean, you even figured out where I was, even though the house in the Fell Forest is completely gone."

"Huh? It's because I forgot to put out the lantern and overslept."

Mariela brought the conversation back around to its initial topic, and her master responded.

Freyja acted as if she'd simply overslept and was late to an appointment. She gazed cheerfully at her interrogator as Mariela pressed further.

"Still naive, huh, Mariela? I just figured if you'd woken up, you'd be in the nearby city, because the house in the Fell Forest was probably destroyed by the Stampede. If I get close enough to you, I can find out where you are."

Apparently, her master had come straight to the Labyrinth City. If Mariela hadn't woken up, or if she had and her life had already reached its end, what would her master have done? Try as she might, Mariela couldn't picture her master being at a loss.

Oh, whatever. Master... I'm just glad I get to see you again...

This was the kind of person her master was.

No matter how inconceivable a situation, she seemed to understand everything just from the briefest of explanations, and this was completely incomprehensible to Mariela.

Mariela felt happy to see her master, relieved she was the same as ever, and just a little baffled at her way of doing things. Little had changed in the last two hundred years. This red-haired woman was unmistakably Mariela's master.

That's why Mariela decided to share some small portion of her true feelings in the same way she used to, before her master had left.

"I was kinda sad when I thought I'd never see you again, you know?"

"Oh my gosh, what's this all of a sudden? You're so cuuute!"

Mariela's master squeezed her tight.

"M-Master, that hurts. And it's hot."

Freyja had a high body temperature, so a hug from her was extremely warm, except during winter.

That's right—it hasn't rained recently... It'll be summer soon. I hadn't even realized...

As she tried to break away from her master, Mariela realized the rainy season had ended. The young alchemist felt like she hadn't been able to see anything around herself ever since they'd lost Lynx. When she looked about, even the familiar interior of Sunlight's Canopy felt strangely nostalgic, as if walking through memories rather than a solid place.

I bought that big glass vial in the corner thinking it would be cute if I put a variety of soaps in it. The colored paper I bought to make it easy to tell smoke bombs apart is still wrapped up.

And then there was Sieg, always at her side. He was waiting for an unguarded moment as Mariela's teacher continued to hold her student close. Mariela's innocent gaze exposed him, and the man turned uncomfortably as his eyes restlessly roamed around the room.

"Hee-hee..."

A completely spontaneous giggle slipped from Mariela's lips.

After Lynx had died, she was so sad, lonely, and certain it was her own fault that she thought she'd never laugh again. Mariela felt like a horrible person for laughing like this when she had lost him, and he could never enjoy himself, be happy, or laugh again.

"Master...um..."

"What's wrong, Mariela?"

Smiling through her tears, Mariela told her master about Lynx, starting with her waking up from suspended animation about half a year ago and meeting him in the Fell Forest.

Her master was an irresponsible person and normally hardly listened to what someone else had to say, but at times like this she listened intently to the very end. Even when Mariela's words caught in her throat, Freyja gently urged her to go on and stayed with her until she'd pulled out the thorn piercing her heart.

"Thaz why...*hic*, I decided I wanna kill the Labyrinth... *Sob*... Because iz my fault..."

She started crying again. Gripping a cleaning cloth that had been sitting on the table, Mariela recounted Lynx's death to her master in a mumble of a voice.

"I see. So that's what happened. Then you think Lynx's death is your fault, right?" the young alchemist's teacher asked gently. The woman softly stroked Mariela's head as if she were a small child. Sieg held a clean hand towel and fidgeted as if he wanted to join in.

"Uh-huh. Thaz why I…"

Mariela had been about to continue speaking as her instructor continued to comfort her, but that's when—

"Well, it's not! *Imprint!*"

"Gyaaah!!!"

"M-Mariela?!"

It was the young woman's first *Imprint* in two hundred years. It really, really hurt.

Sieg grew flustered at Mariela's sudden strangled shriek.

"M-Master?! Hey, what the heck? Why the *Imprint*? What is this? 'How to call your newly Pact-Bearing pupil back'?! I'm… not grateful at all, you know? The Library will open to me once I can make special-grade potions. There is no reason for you to do this! I was going to learn it really soon anyway, but this *Imprint* is stupid! And it hurts! Argh, Master!!!"

Mariela was even more flustered than Sieg.

The shock was so great that she'd stopped crying.

"It's your fault for not being able to make special-grade potions yet! And it's those guys' fault for not being able to deal with the Labyrinth even after two hundred years! Everyone bears a little of the blame. What's done is done. So it's not a matter of who's at fault. Got it? If you've got time to blame yourself and cower for that Lynx guy, then face the future and start moving forward for him, too! You've been sad long enough."

Freyja spoke with a grin as she answered her student's gaze with her own. Mariela's eyes grew as round as apriore fruit at her master's assertion.

"Master, do you really mean it……?"

"Of course. Who do you think you're talking to?"

"...Masterrr."

Mariela's quiet answer seemed to satisfy the woman. Laughing, she said, "Well? I'm right, aren't I?"

Far from merely being pulled out, the thorn piercing Mariela's heart seemed to have vanished without a trace from the shock of her master's *Imprint*.

"You are, I'll do my best. For Lynx, too."

Lynx had been a very important person to Mariela, and losing him had thrown her into a deep depression. But it wasn't as if she'd lost the time she'd spent with him. She remembered all of it. At last, Mariela had realized that Lynx wouldn't be happy to see her moping around forever.

With a determined expression, Mariela looked straight into her master's eyes.

"You're a good girl, Mariela. Now then, I bet you've been slacking off this whole time, right? You've got a lot of makeup work, so get ready to be worked to the bone!"

"Wha—???!!"

Her master smiled impishly. That wasn't a good sign.

That's just the kind of person she is...

Mariela had completely returned to normal. When she pondered the kind of unreasonable demands her longtime teacher might make, her head started to ache as though she'd been hit with another *Imprint*.

"Okaaay. I'm ready. Oh, that's right. While we're at it, there's something I've wanted to ask you. Why did you choose the Magic Circle of Suspended Animation for my graduation test?"

This was something that had tickled the back of Mariela's mind for a long time. Even she knew Magic Circles of Suspended

Animation weren't common, but if it hadn't been for that, she wouldn't have survived the Stampede. That's why it seemed so curious. Why did her master have her learn the magic circle at all? As perhaps should have been expected by now, however, Freyja's response was far from the girl's prediction.

"What? It's because the thing's a pain in the ass for me to draw myself."

"Huh?"

Mariela's master had been the one who'd Imprinted the Magic Circle of Suspended Animation on her. The woman could easily have drawn it herself.

She'd made her student do it simply because it was a bother to take care of herself.

It was exactly the sort of reasoning Freyja would employ, but Mariela wondered if this was why her instructor kept Imprinting countless magic circles on her from a young age.

"Mariela, you're good at drawing all the tiny details, you know?"

"Well, I guess, but... Is that really why you made me draw it? Because it was a nuisance to do it yourself?"

"Yup," her master answered readily.

"You're impossible..."

Mariela felt as though her knees were buckling under her, and her master proceeded to metaphorically kick her while she was down.

"I mean, you'd get it if you really thought about it. Magic circles have nothing to do with alchemy."

"!!!!!"

The shocking truth was revealed after two long centuries.

The impact was so immense that Mariela froze in place. The

red-haired teacher roared with laughter at the sight and took another brazen swig of Sieg's prized alcohol that she'd had the man pour for her.

"Please, no more…"

Mariela felt a fool for taking the words of her master so seriously. Freyja was that kind of person.

Evidently the young alchemist had over-glorified her master during the years she'd lived in the Fell Forest alone.

I haven't had a drop to drink, but my head is spinning.

As Mariela held her head, her master delivered a clean coup de grâce.

"Oh yeah, the upstairs guest room is my room now! Maaan, never in my wildest dreams did I think you'd be living in such a snazzy house, Mariela. Oh, Sieg, bring alcohol to my room later. And call me when my bath's ready."

"Certainly, Most Venerable Mother."

"Master, you're gonna live here?! And Sieg, what's with that name you're calling her?!"

In the end, that was the best Mariela could muster in trying to stop Sieg from calling Freyja "Mother."

"Yeah, nice, isn't it? I mean, you're like my daughter, after all."

"But! If I'm your daughter, how did Sieg become your son?!"

"Huh? I just thought I'd back Sieg on this one is all…"

"I am in your care, Most Venerable Mother."

Eventually, the red-haired woman had told Sieg to call her "Lady Frey" in a rather pompous tone. When Mariela had, quite plainly, informer her master that the title sounded self-important, Freyja replied, "What? I *am* important."

Sieg was conflicted, stuck between relief and loss, at seeing Mariela return to her former vigor. He felt lazy for having sunk into a deep abyss of sadness along with her. Having not yet begun to move on himself, he wondered if Mariela would leave him behind and just how far from him she would drift.

Freyja's golden eyes flickered like flame. They appeared wholly capable of seeing all the way through to the innermost thoughts of her beloved pupil and the young man who was her escort.

10

Siegmund couldn't sleep that night.

He was a light sleeper, prone to wake up at the slightest sound. He believed it was a remnant of his long life as a slave. His former master, the merchant who tyrannized him for far too long, would accost his slaves when they dared to sleep in his presence, even if they were exhausted from hard labor.

Sieg's bedroom was dim, illuminated only by the scant light of the sinking moon, but it proved enough that Sieg's single eye could discern the outlines of the handful of furniture. He sat on his bed, leaning against the wall with his arms around one knee, and he listened, without moving a muscle, to the sounds of approaching daybreak.

The night wasn't silent.

The section of the City where Sunlight's Canopy was located wasn't unsafe, but hardly anyone walked around in the middle of the night, so it made for a nice, quiet place to live. Even so, he could hear leaves swaying when the wind blew, the sounds of insects, and the fluttering of bird wings.

As daybreak neared, early-rising animals began to stir. He heard a window or a door opening from somewhere far off. Perhaps a baker was beginning preparations for breakfast? When Sieg held his breath so he could even hear his own heartbeat, sounds of the awakening City also reached his ears.

A bird's song rang from some distant place.

A *morgena...?*

A morgena was a bird that started being active before dawn. Its cry told him daybreak was near.

That's something my father taught me.

Sieg's father had been a hunter. He came from a long line of them. With bow and arrows, he stalked his prey for days at a time in the forest. He would rest in the woods exactly the way Sieg was sitting now, spending the night holding his breath. Apparently, his father even slept with his eyes open depending on where he was.

Sieg remembered the first time he went hunting with his father and spent the night in the forest. As a boy, he'd taken in everything his father taught him. His father had had no formal education, and at the time, Sieg had simply thought the teachings were easy compared to what he imagined the lectures about science and etiquette under a teacher might be like.

He understood now. Everything his father had taught him, he'd inherited through the blood coursing in his veins. That was why he took to even advanced skills with ease. Sieg's light sleeping wasn't really because of his previous life as a slave. Rather, it was more like an instinct to him.

I understand...

Sieg picked up the bow he had previously set aside.

His hands were made to hold a bow—not his knee, not even a mytrhil sword.

This was his true weapon. Holding a bow, spending the night leaning back against a tree or the wall of a cave. Now he leaned on the wall of his room and waited for daybreak.

Back then...back when he and Lynx lured away and fought the death lizards so that Mariela could escape, Lynx had watched his back. It was the first time Sieg had fought back-to-back with another, shared that mutual trust. Enemies had only ever appeared in front of him. Although he'd been fighting for his life, he'd never feared anything behind him. That was the first time Sieg had ever experienced that, and he felt he'd become the kind of person who could do that with another. That was who he'd wished to be.

If only I'd been able to use a bow back then...

If he'd just been able to use a bow, he was certain Lynx wouldn't have died. Even if he couldn't have killed the death lizard in one shot, if he could have made it flinch just a little, he had no doubt buying that bit of time would have given Lynx the opportunity to parry the monster's blade.

No, Sieg was already able to confidently wield a sword after just half a year. If he'd faced the monsters with a bow, a weapon he was confident he could learn even faster, he might have been able to protect Mariela himself.

Every time he thought back on it, his regret was never-ending.

That day, even Medical Engineer Nierenberg of the Labyrinth Suppression Forces had been absent. If only they hadn't gone into the Labyrinth.

If only they'd carried potions despite the apparent safety of the stratum. If only they hadn't taken along a baggage-carrying slave like Jay, who had no sense of loyalty.

The "if onlys" continued to pile up. Siegmund, who'd endured a harsh life as a slave, understood better than anyone that he couldn't change the past or the present circumstances born from that past.

If only he'd known back then. He'd never have guessed how many times those regrets would play back in his head.

But none of them had any meaning. Mariela had been the one who met Siegmund by chance and saved him from the brink of death. That was why he'd wanted to say farewell to his own past and never make those mistakes again. His previous self was no more. Mariela had saved Sieg's new self, and he'd wanted to continue living on using the sword she'd given him.

And he wasn't even able to protect her.

Lynx had been the one to protect Mariela. He had been Sieg's most treasured, closest friend. The one who watched his back, and Sieg had lost him. He hadn't become a "new self" at all.

Light trickled in from eastern skies. Somehow it was enough for him to make out the target set up on the wall of the rear garden. Siegmund slung his practice quiver onto his back, shifted his bow into one hand, and stood up.

If only he'd known back then. No matter how much regret he felt, he couldn't change the past. Lamentation did no good by itself.

He understood in his head that no one person was at fault, just as Freyja had said. But no matter what he tried *If I'd been able to use a bow* was the only thought he couldn't drown out.

Siegmund thought back on the half year since he'd met Mariela.

"Geez! Quit moving around! Sieg! Use a bow! Aren't you an archer?!"

That's what Lynx had said while they were fighting the needle apes during winter at the Ahriman Springs.

And it wasn't as if the bow's usefulness for fighting foes from a distance, like when they were hunting wyverns, hadn't occurred to him. Even Elmera's husband, Voyd, had pointed him out as a former archer. Sieg had made excuses for it all and kept the bow, and his past, at a distance.

I can't lose her. Even if Mariela's all that remains... I can't...

At Sieg's waist was the mythril sword Mariela had given him. And the short sword Lynx had lent him and never taken back. Lynx had entrusted Sieg with a wish along with that short sword: "Protect Mariela."

Unable to give it back, he would carry it forever. His body had been bought for no more than two large silver coins, and even after all this time, it was worth no more than that. He longed to be an escort worthy of an alchemist like Mariela, but he was physically incapable.

But even so...

He wanted to do what he could to help her, even if only a little. She'd reunited with her master and begun to move forward once more. If he could just stay by her side even a little longer...

Siegmund quietly went out to the rear garden and took aim with his bow. The target was hazy in the morning mist.

CHAPTER 1
Clearing the Way

01

"Ooh, what's that? Let's go see! C'mon, hurry up!"

"Hey, stop! If you run like that, you're gonna get lost!"

The noisy voices of a master and pupil echoed down the main road of the Labyrinth City.

Freyja looked around, regarding everything with a great curiosity and chatting away in high spirits, while Mariela followed after her, completely exhausted.

"You're so slow, Mariela. Don't you need to work on your stamina? It's because you're such a shut-in, day in and day out."

"...Whose fault is that?"

It had been a little over a week since Freyja descended upon the Labyrinth City. The week had a rocky one for Mariela and Sieg. Mariela had been hard at work making potions under her master's tutelage, while Sieg had gone out on an escort mission, also under Freyja's guidance. Today was a day off at the red-haired woman's suggestion, saying it wasn't a good idea to keep working past the point of fatigue. However, Mariela's stamina had been pushed well past its limit with her master having dragged her clear across the City all morning.

Sieg, who'd had the toughest week physically speaking, walked behind the pair. He was burdened with a large amount of baggage.

Nierenberg and others had expressed concerns about Mariela's escort having his hands so full. Freyja had quickly settled the matter by saying, "It's fiiine. If anyone shows up and starts causing trouble, I'll just burn him."

Leonhardt and Weishardt knew well the abilities of this person who'd come to the City from deep within the Fell Forest, conjuring many fire pillars along the way. They valued her almost too highly.

"No matter how foolish the ruffian, it would be excessive to turn him into cinders," Leonhardt determined, and so Labyrinth Suppression Forces soldiers hid in civilian clothes everywhere Mariela's group went in order to avert danger. Today's outing was extremely safe.

"Mariela, Mariela. Frozen dessert!" Freyja cried, running toward a street stall.

The vendor was making frozen sweets by pouring fruit juice into molds made from metal sheets and freezing it with ice magic. The molds seemed to be very well made because when the juice was poured into a single spot, it immediately and evenly spread to multiple reservoirs. They also had holes at the top for inserting sticks, and the finished frozen sweets resembled particularly aerodynamic arrows. They were small, but the juice was poured in and frozen after the fruit was minced and inserted, and the price of one copper coin each was reasonable considering the cost of the ingredients. Children who'd received their allowance sometimes went to buy one and then walked around licking it.

"Why don't you buy one, pretty lady?"

The young boy selling the sweets saw Freyja eyeing them and called out to her. She was certainly pretty, but his bold words made him seem like he had a good head for business.

"Mm, okay, I'll take three. By the way, those molds are really well made."

"The Labyrinth Suppression Forces sold them off. My dad told me it was hard to get them. He said they were the molds used to make holy arrows to defeat the King of Cursed Serpents! Mom got mad at him for buying something so silly. She said we couldn't afford to decorate the house with something like that no matter how great it was. So, I'm using it for a little business. My family owns a fruit shop, so it's perfect, right?"

Freyja lightly touched the mold as the boy spoke with pride about his little enterprise.

"The way they smelted the metal wasn't bad, either. Looks like it could be used for baked sweets, too. If you take good care of it, it'll last you a long time."

"Baked sweets! That's a good idea."

The boy was delighted at the prospect of being able to make something to sell in the winter. Freyja taught him a simple, but no less delicious, recipe. It was a type of pastry with a high-class feel, containing the minced flesh of chestnuts from the Labyrinth. It would retain a fantastic flavor and texture even if you were frugal on the quality of the other ingredients. A fruit shop could probably obtain the chestnuts on the cheap, too.

"As thanks for the idea, these are on the house!"

Holding three frozen sweets in one hand and waving to the boy with the other, Freyja walked back toward the other two. Exasperated at the sight, Mariela muttered, "Master, you got something else?!"

"Ahh, it's pretty good. Here, Mariela, Sieg, try one."

Mariela's group stuffed their faces with their respective frozen treats just a short distance away from the street stall where the red-haired woman had procured them.

It had been like this all day. They had admittedly given Freyja a little spending money, but it's not like they'd emptied their accounts for her. Rather than spend the money, the woman would teach somebody something useful and get something in return, which added to the ever-growing pile of things Sieg was carrying. There were also people who greeted her, "Oh, hey there, Frey!" as if they'd known her all their lives. She'd only just come to the Labyrinth City; it was too early for her to have good friends.

Although they were supposed to be shopping for her, they kept getting stuff they didn't need.

Freyja made Sieg defeat a giant mantis monster that had appeared near the protective wall first thing this morning. Since this saved the crops from being damaged, they'd received a bundle of freshly picked vegetables, and she made a farmer who said he wanted the monster's sickles trade a large amount of freshly collected eggs and milk for them.

When she gave some of the eggs and milk to an adventurer who said his sick child needed nutritious food, the man gave her a beautiful bird he said he'd caught, along with a cage, in recompense. She later traded the bird to a noble's servant who said his master wanted a pet. In exchange, she got a bundle of rare fruit that the servant couldn't carry home.

At lunchtime they stopped by a rather popular shop. As soon as the shopkeeper spied the three, he said, "I've got so many customers now thanks to those spices you told me about," and he gave them a free lunch. Still, Freyja gave him some of her vegetables and fruit for the freebie, and in return he gave her a few cuts of meat.

Mariela had no idea when her master had found the time to make friends with the people in the City. But similar events continued to unfold during the day, and all the girl could do was stare, her jaw hanging open.

The girl's master said, "I wonder if there's anywhere I can get some booze," as she popped another frozen dessert into Mariela's open mouth. The young alchemist looked to Sieg for help, but he seemed to misunderstand her intention. He responded, "It's fine. I've done a lot of training, so I can still carry more." Sieg oozed with mysterious self-confidence as he ate his dessert. Mariela could've done without him being so helpful in this situation.

Freyja confessed to going a little overboard after having managed to spin her various bits of luggage into bottles of spirits. The woman showed such little attachment to anything besides alcohol that it came off as disinterest. If there was anything else that truly grabbed her attention, it was asking for food. Even when it came to things like clothing, she appeared content trying to borrow Mariela's pajamas and even her spare underwear.

But then, underwear aside, she was on the verge of borrowing Sieg's shirts and tops because she said Mariela's didn't fit her chest, and Amber, quite embarrassed, went out on a hurried shopping trip for her.

In any case, Freyja seemed to not have material attachments and appeared quite fine with just the clothes on her back. For the time being, she was living comfortably with the daily necessities Amber had assembled and the adequate amenities in the house. Two hundred years ago, when Mariela lived with her master, she owned nothing, and anything she did get was from her master. That's why she'd somehow gotten the idea in her head that her instructor knew everything and had everything. However, since the two had reunited, her master amazingly wanted nothing but drink from her newly independent pupil. Freyja seemed so unconcerned that Mariela felt like she was seeing some other side of her master.

Even so, Freyja was still a woman. After two hundred years she probably wanted a new set of clothes, so they'd gone out shopping today. However, she was having an extremely good time sightseeing in the City while steadily accumulating anything but clothing.

Incidentally, although Freyja had been in suspended animation for two centuries just like Mariela had been, her clothes didn't have even a single loose thread. They could've been mistaken for brand-new. Mariela's cloak was an excellent item specially made from woven daigis fibers that absorbed faint magical power from the atmosphere to repair itself, so she'd taken good care of it. But her other clothes had been extremely worn and she'd been forced to buy new ones.

In order to make cloth from daigis fibers, you had to pick young, tender ivy that sprouted in the spring on the night of a full moon. The atmosphere contained the most magical power on such a night, so the young and weak ivy was apparently less likely to wither. Then you removed the leaves from the gathered vines, dissolved them in various types of liquid medicine, rinsed them, and removed the fibers. The fibers taken from the young ivy were thick, and when woven together, they were more like string or rope than thread. If you made them into cloth as is, they wouldn't make for a cloak that'd match well with cute clothes. Rather, they'd go well with a grass skirt and probably make for a fairly good primitive look.

Even though Mariela and Freyja were from two hundred years

ago, they'd worn normal clothing by modern standards back then, too. They weren't usually found wearing grass skirts and tearing into monster meat with their teeth.

Well, as far as monster meat, they did tear into it both now and back then, but in a slightly more modern fashion.

So in order to complete the elegant look of the cloak, Mariela had lightly tapped the removed fibers with a wooden mallet to thin them, and stretched them out narrow and wide. She splashed them with Drops of Life again and again while she hummed a mysterious song with her master, and somewhere during that and the hammer tapping, the fibers had become intertwined and made a truly impressive cloth.

"I skipped the thread-making step and made cloth! I didn't even have to weave it together!" Mariella had exclaimed when she was little.

"Looks like you're learning. We sang a song together, right? These fibers grew with your magical power, Mariela. They've adapted to it. If you sew a magic circle into it a little at a time, you'll be able to use it forever."

Her master had said something to that effect back then.

After Master left, I tried to make this kind of cloth again, but it didn't work. I wonder if the singing was important somehow?

Recalling memories from before their long hibernation, Mariela gazed at Freyja's clothes. Although Mariela's cloak was made of rare cloth, it wasn't a material that was impossible to come by. She'd never heard of singing a song to make it, but apparently it was something artisans with high level spinning and weaving skills could create. Other than the self-repair, its functions were lackluster for something made with high-grade manufacturing, and for the price, it had no dazzle, so it wasn't all that popular.

Freyja's clothes were made from a substantially different material than her pupil's cloak; that much was certain. They looked fairly high class. Freyja preferred fire magic, so doubtless her garments were made of a mysterious material that wouldn't burn up from a little heat. Even if she was satisfied with her current clothes, and desired no others, was there really nothing else she wanted?

As Mariela savored her frozen juice treat, Freyja had taken the stick from her own, having finished first, and made a pinwheel using grass from the edge of the path. She then gave it to a nearby baby having a crying fit to stop its fussing. The grateful mother gave the mage some hard candy as thanks, and so the number of things Freyja owned continued to increase with each passing moment.

Although she wondered a bit about her master's sense of values, Mariela finished her ice treat, held out her stick, and said "Master, I want a pinwheel, too," and Freyja readily acquiesced.

It wasn't as if the girl's master had no interest in anything in this world of two hundred years later. In her spare moments between the difficult training she'd subjected Mariela to, Freyja had apparently made friends with the regulars at Sunlight's Canopy and wandered around the Labyrinth City, seeing the sights.

It was great Freyja was enjoying herself, but Mariela found herself more than a little surprised at how easily she'd taken to this new world. When had Mariela awoken, it was a great shock to learn the Kingdom of Endalsia had been destroyed, two hundred years had passed, and everyone she'd known previously was long gone. She'd had to work hard to carve out a new place for herself in this Labyrinth City.

"Master, weren't you surprised that the Kingdom of Endalsia

was destroyed?" Mariela asked out of the blue as she watched the pinwheel her master made catch the wind and spin around and around. Freyja merely replied with a hum at the question, and she pondered a little before answering.

"Is the name of the country so important? People pass away eventually, don't they? They die from age, or from illness, or from injury. The fires of war take some; monsters take others. Death can come at the hands of humans or the fangs of beasts. No one, old or young, man or woman, can escape it. Many people have been born and died through the ages. Of course, the Stampede those many years ago was a great tragedy. But looking at it centuries later, there's hardly a difference between people dying off one by one or dying all at once. What's more important is that, although many people and monsters alike lost their lives that day, a human city has been built here. Mariela, look closely at the fabric of the clothes everyone's wearing. It's woven from much, much finer thread than back then. They're made from threads of uniform thickness; they're thin and light, yet far more durable. It's not just things that are easy to understand like magical tools. The thickness of glass, their way of stacking stones, the workmanship of metal. Each and every one of these things has improved. Although every individual will die someday, people as a whole have been steadily moving forward for a long time. No matter what kind of disaster has befallen them."

The pinwheel in Mariela's hand began to turn in the breeze. It spun round and round in place.

People are born, people die, and more people are born. The speech she just heard seemed like this pinwheel, but only somewhat. Although people had existed in the same place over the past two hundred years, they had made a lot of progress.

"Everything, no matter how tragic, has some kind of significance or positive aspect. The difference is whether you can see it. Yes, some of them may be too close to you to see, but you've come here from so *far* away. Look for the good all around you and enjoy the time you have."

Mariela hadn't known much about the world of two hundred years ago, and most of what she'd seen and heard since coming to the Labyrinth City was new to her. She didn't know enough to say whether this was due to the centuries of progress, but what did this world look like to her master?

Oh yeah, she noticed the structure and metal of the mold...

Mariela considered her master's sense of values, her master's gaze, and realized she only ever saw things that were already right in front of her face, missing the important things. She decided she wanted to look at the future as her master did.

"I guess you're right, Master. I need to expand my horizons more, too."

"Yeah. That's a good attitude to have, Mariela. Well then, shall we go watch the crowd lose their minds at the first potions in two hundred years?!"

"Whaaat?!"

Freyja suddenly grinned. By "going to watch the crowd," she meant rubbernecking. She'd completely ruined the mood of her own speech.

Mariela grumbled, "You're gonna be a nuisance, stop it."

Freyja answered, "We can't miss such an important event!" She pulled her pupil along and headed for the current hottest place in the Labyrinth City: the Merchants Guild.

02

The Merchants Guild was on the northeastern main road of the Labyrinth City, just a little way from the Labyrinth. While the Adventurers Guild was the hub of activity for adventurers to accept quests and sell materials, the Merchants Guild was the base for merchants and city residents.

The Merchants Guild also undertook community work from the house of Margrave Schutzenwald, such as managing residences in the Labyrinth City and prepaying taxes on goods taken out of the City. Although its product lineup was more or less geared toward merchants, the guild's shop was open to the public, so it was a place familiar not just to merchants, but to the residents of the City as a whole.

That said, normally only a few residents were there at any given time, and each staff member was busy with their own work. However, the day Mariela and the others visited, the Merchants Guild was so packed that the crowd had flowed out of the building and onto the street.

The mass of people was all heading for the Residential Affairs Division. Of course, there was no way that many people were suddenly looking for a new home. The assembled throngs forming a long line had their sights on potion vouchers that had begun to be distributed a few days ago. The Residential Affairs Division managed the census in the Labyrinth City, so the only way to distribute the vouchers evenly to everyone was to check their registers. As one might have expected, there was no way the one division alone had enough hands for this, and the guild as a whole had been busy dealing with it. The scene seemed quite chaotic.

"Vouchers have been prepared for everybody, so please don't push. You over there, please take your argument outside."

"Okay, the next thirty customers, please proceed to conference room four."

Although it was a briefing for residents as a whole, the Labyrinth City had many adventurers, who tended to be a little wild no matter their gender. They cut in line, pushed, and stepped on toes. Even when they were standing in a queue, the quarrels were endless. If this were the Adventurers Guild, whose staff members were skilled at having a "talk" with people using body language, the residents might have behaved a little better. However, the staff members of the Merchants Guild kept all communications purely verbal, which made things rather difficult to understand with all of the ambient noise.

"Whoa, it kinda looks like a festival."

Arriving at the guild with her master, Mariela stared in amazement at the great hustle and bustle. Sieg, arms still quite full, proved to be something of an obstacle for the people around them. But it was easy to guess from his sharp glare at the folks surrounding him, the way he carried himself, and the quality of the armor he wore that he was a high-ranking adventurer, so no one picked a fight. Such calculations were typical of a Labyrinth City resident.

"How long do you intend to make me wait?! I've been in line since this morning. Hurry up and let me in!"

"Can we even get potions in the first place?! Don't give us these scraps of paper; hand over the real thing!

"Yeah, that's right!"

Noon had long since passed, so anyone who'd been in line since morning was surely hungry, which would only worsen their mood. It might be inevitable for them to lose their patience and cause a scene, especially as a group that was already short-tempered and quick to resort to violence. However, one woman working for the Merchants Guild had been pushed past the limits of her patience even more than those waiting in line, and she became extremely belligerent.

"*I* haven't been able to go home! For days!!!"

Crackle-crackle-crackle!

"Ag-g-g-gh!"

The shocking electric attack came with a hoarse, reverberating shriek.

"Anyone else want to act out of line?!"

Elmera was in Lightning Empress mode, crackling from head to toe with electricity, as she forced a violent resident to pipe down.

"Ohh, I've been waiting for this!"

"That's good stuff, do it again!"

"Eee, the Lightning Empress is so cool!"

What happened to all the curses and complaints from just a moment ago? Applause and cheers broke out. Everyone was extremely happy at the rare opportunity to see the A-Rank adventurer Lightning Empress Elsee up close. A man who reached out to shake her hand in the confusion of the moment let out a scream from the intense static electricity that hit him, but after the pain faded, he smiled happily along with the man who'd been hit with the electric attack.

Incidentally, the last person to make a high-pitched shriek was Freyja. She'd already met Elmera once before, so she knew her true identity as the Lightning Empress, but she loved this kind of atmosphere.

Elsee being Elsee, she gave a conspicuous wink to Freyja and Mariela when she noticed them. The woman then withdrew into a back room, probably the Medicinal Herbs Division.

What is it with these people...?

Freyja and Elmera were both intense in their own ways. Leaving Freyja aside, it was odd to see Elmera so worked up.

At first, she had provided support as "Elmera Seele," chairwoman of the Medicinal Herbs Division in her usual attire: a blue dress and hair in a tight bun. She'd been forced into organizing everything and keeping business under control. However, no matter how much she did, the briefings on personnel organization lasted from the morning into the evening. The filing of vouchers ran from the evening onward and never seemed to end, despite everyone at the Merchants Guild working together.

At any rate, there had been a far more disputes and document falsifications than were initially expected. Thanks to the crowds that continued to loudly squabble, despite the best efforts of the guild's staff members, Elmera didn't even have the time to get to her own overtime work, let alone actually go home. So, on the second day she'd activated Lightning Empress mode and brought down her judgment on the badly behaved residents to make them pipe down. She'd followed the example of the Adventurers Guild and given them a "talk" with body language.

Every day, her husband, Voyd, came with their children to bring provisions and a change of clothes, so Elmera still went relatively easy on the residents with her anger. However, adventurers were starting fights on purpose because they wanted to be zapped by the Lightning Empress—a figure who rarely made public appearances—so there was still a show at regular intervals.

With the efforts of the Lightning Empress, it took a far less time to bring arguments under control, but it remained unclear whether the disputes themselves increased or decreased in number. Either way, Elsee's punishments were the sole form of entertainment for the residents who were tired of standing in line. Unfortunately for Elmera, the Merchants Guild's briefings looked unlikely to end for at least another week, judging by the size of the crowds.

The briefings were regarding the commencement of potion sales and the distribution of vouchers. There was no doubt that the stream of people who complained, got rough, forged documents, or tried to get more potions than others would be going on for a while.

"Since we're already here, let's give the food Master got to Elmera and go home..."

A little worried about Elmera's stress levels, Mariela when to visit the Medicinal Herbs Division with her master and Sieg like she was meeting an actor who'd come down into the green room.

"...Mariela, I'm sorry you had to see that..."

"Ohh, Ms. Elmera, that was wonnnderful. Especially that wink you did at the end. Ah, please appear on stage again in one hour."

In the Medicinal Herbs Division—which was not a green room—Leandro had taken to managing Elmera's performance schedule. Elmera was at her wit's end from her own high voltage earlier.

"Elmera, you've been working hard. Um, here, I hope you enjoy this food."

"Elsee, good job. Ooh, you looked so cool. You've made me a fan!"

"Master, please be quiet!"

"Ugh. When this work is over and done with, I'm absolutely taking a paid holiday."

While Mariela silenced her gleeful master and consoled Elmera, Sieg handed the large quantity of ingredients Freyja had been accumulating throughout the morning to Leandro.

"Ohh, this is a big help. None of us have been able to go home. Ah, the cooking? You can do it in the dining hall. You say you'll carry it for us? Ahh, many thanks. It's this waaay."

Sieg never said he would haul anything to the dining hall, but Leandro began leading the poor man anyway. Exactly as one would have expected from a person who was so pushy in their handling of people. But then, Leandro was a man who never neglected to follow through, and he let Sieg have plenty of the ingredients as his way of expressing thanks.

"We confiscated these from the people in line. We suspected alcohol was part of the reason the crowds proved so difficult to quiet. We mustn't drink it, either, so your timing is perrrfect."

Completely inexplicably, beyond all reasonable assumption, Freyja got her bottles of alcohol. Incredible. With a faraway look, Mariela watched the red-haired woman hurry home in the highest of spirits with Sieg in tow, carrying the bottles. The young alchemist reflected on the week that had passed since her master arrived.

The day after Mariela's master, also known as the Sage of Calamity Freyja, came to the Labyrinth City, a written invitation quickly arrived from the house of Margrave Schutzenwald.

Freyja, who stood out even under normal circumstances, had arrived and declared she was the master of Mariela, the sole alchemist in the Labyrinth City. Figuring the invitation included both master and pupil, Mariela saved herself the hassle of making dinner and accompanied her instructor and Sieg through the underground Aqueduct to visit the estate of the margrave.

Perhaps Nierenberg, who'd come to Sunlight's Canopy first thing in the morning as he always did, had observed the many empty alcohol bottles and sent a report to Weishardt; the spread of food and copious amounts of high-class alcohol that greeted them was even more wonderful than last time. Leonhardt and Weishardt, the leading go-getters of the Labyrinth City, personally welcomed the trio.

Three of those assembled talked about the Labyrinth subjugation and the origins of the Labyrinth City, interwoven with conversations about aristocrats in distant places. Mariela was apologetic about the money they had spent on the particularly expensive drink even though it was her second time there, Freyja partook deeply of the food without restraint, and downed the expensive spirits with reckless abandon.

"Lady Freyja. I have heard your name before. You have told us how you came to be here and that you are Mariela's master. Are you the same Sage of Calamity Freyja who incinerated the flood of high-ranking monsters from the Fell Forest during the Stampede and scorched the whole surrounding area?" Weishardt asked her, seeing that she'd had a lot to drink and guessing this was as good a time as any to ask.

"Whoa, my name's passed through the annals of history, eh?" Freyja readily confirmed she was the figure known as the Sage of Calamity two hundred years ago.

"I knew it! This could truly be an act of divine providence! Lady Freyja, we'd be grateful if you would lend your power to the Labyrinth Suppression Forces so that we may subjugate the Labyrinth!" After exchanging glances with Weishardt, Leonhardt had asked Freyja for her support.

However...

"Impossible. I can't help you the way you want me to," she answered, as if she'd discerned the nature of Leonhardt and Weishardt's request.

"I don't understand what you mean. You cannot help us the way we want you to?" Weishardt didn't appear to take offense at Freyja's rather presumptuous statement. Rather, he was more confused than anything.

"Lord Weis, was it? I can't fight the way you're expecting. You heard about my person-finding spell, right? Or did you think I didn't notice?"

Weishardt's eyes wavered just a little at Freyja's straightforward manner of speaking, though he was still not taking any insult from it. He had indeed listened to the exchange between the powerful mage and Captain Kyte through skills and magic, but Weishardt thought she hadn't noticed.

Eavesdropping on conversations and such was a common practice in aristocratic society, which was why so many people put up safeguards against it. The eavesdropping itself was obfuscated by multiple layers of magic so as not to be easily discovered. Those were the types of skills and magic he'd employed yesterday, and Weishardt was confident it was not a method that was so readily seen through. If she'd noticed but still used magic in front of Captain Kyte, that meant she was letting Weishardt hear it on purpose. The spell she'd chanted no doubt reached him.

"…That was inexcusable behavior on my part. You have my apologies. I have never heard that spell before." Weishardt met Freyja's golden eyes as he apologized. Making a false or awkward excuse to this person would be a poor move.

"I'm not trying to criticize you for the *Wind's Whispers*. It was a natural course of action. Anyway, that spell was spirit magic." Freyja's tone suggested she didn't mind the snooping. However, upon hearing her explanation, Weishardt's expression visibly faltered.

"Spirit magic?! It can't be… That art is said to be lost… However, it would explain a lot. Why there were so many flame pillars at once…"

Freyja smiled happily seeing the man wear such an expression of shock for the first time. Weishardt was a nobleman who excelled at strategy, but he was also a scholar with a deep knowledge of magic. Freyja was pleased at how quickly he took an interest in her words.

"It's because few people could use it to begin with. But that's not the problem. Spirit magic borrows the power of the spirits. So, in the Labyrinth where their power is weak, the magic wouldn't have much strength at all. Down there you'd probably be able to overpower me, Lord Weis."

Mariela glanced repeatedly at her master while muttering, "Spirit magic."

She wasn't familiar with the terms. Mariela had no idea at all her master could use such a thing. As if repelled by a shield, Mariela and Sieg found themselves unable to break into the suddenly serious conversation the girl's master had created. That was all well and truly good, however. Mariela didn't want to be involved in the first place.

Leonhardt and Weishardt sat across from Freyja and Mariela at the dinner table. Just like the last time the young alchemist had visited, the cuisine was offered buffet-style so they could enjoy the selections freely. Although a seat had been prepared for Sieg as well, he declined to sit this time, since he was Mariela's escort. Fortunately, his refusal was met with no resistance; even though it was Margrave Schutzenwald's house, they seemed to have prepared the seat with regard to Mariela's wishes. He took up a position behind her.

In other words, not only could Mariela not keep up with the conversation, she couldn't even exchange looks with Sieg, so all she ended up doing was single-mindedly devouring her dessert.

In contrast to Mariela, who didn't even show an interest in joining the conversation anymore, Leonhardt paid careful attention to the course of the discussion while also considering possible solutions.

Since Weishardt's stoic facade had been broken by honest surprise, the ability to use spirit magic probably wasn't something to be regarded lightly. However, after disclosing this fact, Freyja had said it wouldn't translate into the kind of strength they needed in the Labyrinth. Leonhardt pondered whether or not the woman was implicitly saying, "I don't want to help you."

If so, then why reveal an ace up her sleeve like spirit magic? No, this is the woman known as the "Sage of Calamity," after all. It would be rude to infer her intentions.

If the woman called Freyja sitting before Leonhardt and Weishardt truly had S Rank–equivalent abilities, they couldn't expect her to help after entertaining her just one time. Leonhardt himself had dealt many times with riffraff who wanted to be acquainted with an S-Ranker.

An S-Rank individual was said to have the strength on the scale of an entire battalion or army division. The large gap in their estimated strength was because so many S-Rankers chose seclusion over a life in the public eye. As such, the knowledge of their true strength was little more than a rumor. Now that one such person had truly appeared, in the form of the alchemist's master, Leonhardt couldn't shake the feeling this was destiny in the guise of coincidence.

Just establishing a relationship with this woman would be a substantial victory for the moment.

With that in mind, Leonhardt asked Freyja a question after watching Mariela silently pick at a confection on her plate.

"You say you wouldn't contribute much, but I've heard you're Mariela's master. If so, would master and pupil together, as alchemists, be able to offer any help to us?"

Mariela's support had already been secured, of course. Even without S-Rank fighting power, if Freyja agreed to help even a little as a master alchemist, it would probably be enough.

Considering this alternate route, Leonhardt glanced at Mariela for a moment. The girl had seemingly grown a bit overwhelmed from eating too much dessert, as she was busy drinking tea to help swallow the powerful sweetness of a cream that was overwhelming her mouth.

"Ah, about that. I can only make up to mid-grade potions."

"Pfaw! Master?!"

"What?!"

Mariela spit her drink everywhere at the shocking revelation from her master.

Leonhardt and Weishardt immediately froze, as if they'd been affected by a petrification curse. A flustered server brought out some dishcloths, and Sieg wiped Mariela's mouth while the server cleaned the table.

Pushing past her own outburst, Mariela continued. Her master's startling confession had destroyed the serious air of the conversation—it had even momentarily broken through Mariela's own common sense

"Whaaat?! Are you serious? Mid-grade... How? You're a master, right?!"

To say the red-haired woman's pupil was surprised was an understatement. Obviously, her master had taught her all sorts of things, from the important to the inconsequential, but this was the first time Mariela heard that mid-grade potions were the highest her instructor was capable of.

Of course, her explanations had been verbal, and she'd never demonstrated any of it in front of Mariela, but this was still totally, completely unbelievable.

"Hmm? Did I never tell you? Well, even if I can't make something, it's fine as long as I can teach it, right?"

"Th-that's not the problem here, you know? Ah, could it be from when I made a Pact with the ley line?"

Mariela recalled the time she'd forged the supernatural contract with the ley line and used up a large amount of her master's experience in the process, and for an instant she panicked.

"Naaah. It's always been this way. After all, with alchemy you have to make those small, fiddly potions one at a time. All that hard work doesn't agree with me. That's why my level didn't go up much."

"Huuuuuuuuuh??!"

Mariela couldn't believe it. Was she serious? That was the reason?

It was certainly in keeping with her teacher's character.

Mariela's jaw hung open, and the Schutzenwald brothers remained stiff and still.

The pair's mouths were slightly agape, and their well-groomed faces looked ridiculous. Weishardt in particular wore an idiotic expression no one had seen him make before, and his usual poker face was nowhere to be found. It was a catastrophe.

Freyja gazed with amusement at the trio's silly expressions, then drained her glass of its contents with zest. "I want to talk to the margrave about something," she said with a complacent smile.

04

Mariela's master had a completely honest conversation with Leonhardt and Weishardt about how Mariela could make four or five times the number of potions she was currently making.

Some of the problems plaguing the Labyrinth City were actually fairly simple.

Kill the Labyrinth. Even if they couldn't improve the situation in the strata, people could prevent the Labyrinth's growth by going in and defeating monsters.

Originally, this is all they'd done.

However, because the Labyrinth was a fifty-layer-plus den of evil, they were overwhelmingly short-handed. Even if the Labyrinth Suppression Forces continued to their best efforts to keep the Labyrinth under control, it was doubtful they could prevent its growth. The Labyrinth City itself had a labor shortage. No matter how much they wanted to send incursions into the maze below, they were prohibited by a simple matter of numbers.

And the Labyrinth City's lack of population, particularly adventurers, was due to the high rate of mortality and serious injury endured by the adventurers who went into the Labyrinth. The inconvenience of the main road connecting the City to the imperial capital did little to help things as well.

These two problems could be greatly alleviated with potions.

If potions were sold at the same price as in the imperial

capital, they would greatly reduce adventurer mortality rates, and even just monster-warding potions would make it easier to travel to and from the imperial capital through the Fell Forest. Both the Labyrinth Suppression Forces and the Black Iron Freight Corps, who used Mariela's potions, had proved that.

Up to now, Mariela had been supplying the Labyrinth Suppression Forces with the equivalent of a hundred high-grade potions a day. Even if all the Forces did was work to slow the expansion of the Labyrinth, there would be potions left over. Potions were used sparingly because of their value, but Mariela's potion-making abilities had already surpassed the amount used by the Forces. The young alchemist's master asserted that her pupil had the spare energy to make several times the current amount.

"That's the card you've been dealt. How will you play it?" Freyja compared her pupil to a game piece as she grinned broadly and asked her question. She and the Schutzenwald brothers exchanged looks. Leonhardt and Weishardt no longer wore the friendly expressions they'd had until now; instead, their eyes reflected the spirits of influential people entrusted with the well-being of the Labyrinth City.

If Mariela used her full power to make potions, she could supply not just the Labyrinth Suppression Forces with them, but civilians, too. With that, adventurer injury rates would decrease, and Labyrinth exploration would increase. They would probably be able to weaken the Labyrinth more than they ever had before.

Moreover, if monster-warding potions were sold on the market, people would be able to travel on the main road through the Fell Forest and trade with the imperial capital. No one would have to worry about weak but persistent monsters like forest wolves attacking in large numbers. Even regular merchant caravans would be able to travel through the forest with a comparatively small armed escort for handling larger monsters. Since materials from the Labyrinth could be transported cheaply to the imperial capital, the Labyrinth City's economic conditions would improve, and above all, low- to mid-level adventurers wanting to make a name for themselves could be readily invited to the City.

For the house of Margrave Schutzenwald that governed the Labyrinth City, it would be unthinkable to hear this information and not sell potions on the open market. The question of how to play this card was hardly a question at all: Mass-produce the potions and supply them to the citizens. It went without saying that this was an advantage they desperately needed.

However, Leonhardt carefully thought it over before answering.

"Certainly, this has the potential to greatly alter our situation, but it's not a decision for us to make."

Upon hearing Leonhardt's answer, the corners of Freyja's mouth turned up in apparent satisfaction.

"You pass. Not bad. I suppose I could let you borrow her."

I knew it...

A sense of relief washed over Leonhardt knowing he'd been able to deduce the correct answer.

The woman known as the Sage of Calamity sitting before him could use spirit magic, yet she couldn't offer any martial strength within the Labyrinth. She was the alchemist's master, yet could only make up to mid-grade potions, and she repeatedly said and did extremely thoughtless things. At a glance, she looked like a loud, imprudent young woman, and she spoke and acted accordingly. It made whomever she interacted with feel relaxed, but maligning her would invite her scorn.

She was testing me.

As far as Freyja was concerned, Mariela belonged with her as her pupil, but the house of Margrave Schutzenwald wasn't Mariela's employer and had no rightful connection to the girl. An S-Ranker wasn't going to bow down to the likes of a margrave, or even an emperor. The fact that all the S-Rankers aside from Leonhardt had concealed themselves and chosen seclusion was proof enough of that fact.

As a person with power, she wasn't going to allow the alchemist to be treated like an object. Leonhardt understood this was what she was getting at.

If he had simply treated Mariela as a card to be played by the hand of the margrave's family or that of the Labyrinth Suppression Forces, the Sage of Calamity might've spirited her away to a place beyond his reach.

To Leonhardt, the person before him seemed for all the world like a blaze in human form. If he reached out a hand toward her, the flames would burn him to a crisp. He couldn't grasp flame in his hand; blazing fire vanished in an instant once it completely consumed its fuel. The only way to keep the inferno where it was, was to offer fuel as compensation.

"What's your price?"

When Freyja had offered to lend her student, she'd probably meant, "I'll help you through Mariela." It was an unexpected but no less welcome offer. Before the fickle tongues of fire could spread somewhere else, Leonhardt asked what kind of compensation he could offer.

"Mariela's secret, the one we discussed earlier."

"Understood. I will pledge to keep her name secret."

The two signed a contract. No special techniques were used

in its forging, but breaking it would be an absolutely unforgivable course of action. At least that was the impression Leonhardt had.

"I see... In this case, could we also expect a revitalization of the economy...?"

Weishardt, who had held his tongue until Leonhardt and Freyja completed the contract, understood the significance of the "compensation" Freyja had suggested.

If Mariela made a large quantity of potions as an alchemist who didn't belong with the house of Margrave Schutzenwald, this would generate costs. Even now, the copious profits from the potions sold thus far lay in the cellar of Sunlight's Canopy. The whole City would see benefits if everyone used the money; keeping it buried would invite economic stagnation. Freyja didn't want money as compensation for the large quantity of potions that would be created from here on out. Rather, she wanted the secret that Mariela had impossibly high magical power for an alchemist and that she had the ability to make potions to remain well guarded. Likewise she desired Mariela herself to remain protected. She had probably intended to lend her aid from the start, so long as she could judge Leonhardt and Weishardt's strength of character by revealing Mariela's secret.

They didn't call her a sage for no reason... But still, this all seems just a little too convenient for us, though...

Although Weishardt felt impressed deep down, he also harbored just a little bit of doubt. Of course, this didn't mean he objected to his brother Leonhardt's decision. Weishardt would just as likely have given the same answer, as there was no other option.

Just what is your goal, Sage of Calamity?

The words of this woman enjoying alcohol in front of him

were all he had to go on; there was little else he could determine from watching her.

Currently, we have no other course but to accept her help... We should look to do so in the most optimal way.

Weishardt sought for a way to minimize the burden on the young alchemist while somehow also maximizing the number of potions made. He had no intention of simply forcing her to work, but if not even the price of a single vial was required as compensation, it would probably be better to divide as much of the labor as possible among residents of the Labyrinth City and compensate them as well. Distribute potions to citizens and return the proceeds to the Labyrinth City via the many residents in charge of the materials and interim processing. Gold coins circulating through the streets could only help the City's commerce.

"As I should have expected from one with your title, I must confess I underestimated you."

The Schutzenwald brothers praised the fiery woman. The master, in an extremely good mood, helped herself to another glass of expensive alcohol.

The three of them were in the process of forming some kind of agreement, but Mariela was the only one without a clue what they were talking about. She was utterly left out.

All I can tell is that they're talking about me, and that it's nothing good!

Mariela was fine with only understanding that much. It was the same as always. She pretended to follow along and simply nodded in agreement.

Thus, Mariela remained in the dark amid the upheaval, and the potion mass-production plan was set in place.

05

Weishardt crushed the obstacles standing in the way of potion sales one after another.

Even if Mariela could make an absurd number of potions, they were supplying the entirety of the Labyrinth City. If they didn't allocate work to other people to relieve her, they definitely wouldn't be able to put potions on the market.

Transportation of medicinal herbs, potion vials, and materials; divvying up the manufacturing process; distribution and marketing of the finished products; and above all, the alchemist's personal safety. The documents piled as high as a mountain, but with Weishardt's shrewd skill for such work, he handled them in the blink of an eye.

"An atelier will be established in the cellar of the Labyrinth Suppression Forces' base as a manufacturing site for potions. Not only is the location well guarded from the outside, but the alchemist can move to and from it safely by using the underground Aqueduct. We will secure sales channels for the completed potions through the Merchants Guild. As for the crucial matter of the alchemist's true identity, we will spread rumors that the Aguinas family has established a method of manufacturing potions. Since Robert resigned from his position as head of the household and is out of the public eye, it's perfect. Many will interpret this in a way that is favorable for us."

Weishardt explained this to Leonhardt as he handed him the approved documents. The number of guards stationed around Sunlight's Canopy had long since been increased. Almost all the troublemakers in the Labyrinth City had been crushed over the past half year, but with the arrival of Freyja, an extremely conspicuous adventurer, those who didn't exactly understand their place had begun popping up again. However, unlike Mariela, Freyja was extremely aware of the people around her and could use powerful magic to boot, so the measures taken to protect her and the others in Sunlight's Canopy were more to prevent Freyja from lighting up the City with fire pillars.

No one knew exactly how, but the red-haired woman had the habit of occasionally finding troublemakers faster than the Labyrinth Suppression Forces' intelligence unit did. She'd burn the tips of their cloaks or the hairs on their heads juuust enough. This kept the soldiers guarding Sunlight's Canopy on their toes while they blended in with the citizens or pretended to be patients. When someone smelled like they were burning, the soldiers had to quickly seize them and put out the fire. A burnt corpse in the middle of the City would be no laughing matter.

"Mariela's master is quite outrageous! To say she's lively would be greatly underselling her character. But it's thanks to her that I've grown so thin and beautiful. Intelligence work is difficult for an attractive woman."

These were the words of Merle, an agent of the intelligence unit. Incidentally, neither Leonhardt nor even Weishardt could tell in the least what part of her had gotten thinner. The amount of attention she received was exactly the same as before, too. So it didn't seem like her work was really all that hindered. Of course, as clever and capable bosses, the Schutzenwald brothers did not mention this fact. Instead, they offered a bonus to thank her: "Thanks for your hard work. We'll have special-order pastries delivered."

It was an extremely busy few days, but Weishardt finished off the mountain of documents and set his sights on potion production.

"If only the Walking Mountain of Fire could be defeated this easily…"

As he grumbled about the large difference between the two mountains, Weishardt brought the approved documents to Leonhardt, who paused while signing them to ask a question.

"Have you talked to the young woman of the Aguinas family?"

"I have not spoken to L…Lady Carol yet……"

Leonhardt stared intently at his younger brother. Weishardt wouldn't meet his gaze.

"This isn't like you. Lady Caroline is probably the one in the most danger from this plan. In any event, I'll talk to her."

"Please wait, Brother. I do not want her to misunderstand the decision as one of policy only. I will make sure to talk to her as soon as I have taken care of some urgent business, so I hope you will grant me an extension until then."

Leonhardt reflexively smiled at this human side of his brother who calmly, intelligently, and perfectly controlled even his own feelings for the sake of his objectives.

"Don't delay."

Part of him wanted to give Weishardt the leisure to nurture his budding feelings, but he probably didn't have that kind of time. Instead he only urged his sibling to hurry. Before unforeseen malice crept in and plucked the beautiful flower. Flowers that bloom in spring may fall and wash away in a sudden rainstorm.

Whether or not he knew what his brother was thinking, Weishardt calmly nodded. "Understood."

06

Medicinal herbs were the first things to be prepared. Potions that people had wanted but weren't previously available would now be sold. Chaos was expected, and they needed to distribute the potions to everyone in the Labyrinth City. Thus the potions to be sold at first would be limited to two types, monster-warding potions and low-grade healing potions, which could be mass-produced with a small amount of magical power and whose materials were easy to obtain.

Low-grade monster-warding potions would be effective for traveling along the main road through the Fell Forest, but they'd have no effect on slimes, so they couldn't be used in the underground Aqueduct that Mariela and the others traveled through. Mid-grade potions were required for that. In that respect, you could say these two types of low-grade potions were safe choices.

The needed medicinal herbs were curique, bromominthra, and daigis.

Each grew throughout the Labyrinth City and were also easy to cultivate. They had such a high growth rate that if you left just a sparse amount after harvesting them, they'd grow back in two or three days. So, by doubling the trade-in price, you could get as many slum residents and children wanting some pocket money to collect them for you as you wanted. Unlike during the uproar a while back, nobody pulled up the herbs by the roots. The buyout was such a roaring success that in the confusion, unneeded weeds were mixed into some of the bundles people brought, but a sufficient quantity of the herbs was collected.

It was the processing and quality control after the collection of the medicinal herbs that was the problem. Each plant was distinctive, but it was difficult for amateurs to distinguish them if weeds were mixed in. As for the processing that followed, bromominthra was less effective if you didn't remove its roots and flowers first, and the same for curique if you didn't remove its stems. Both the leaves and vines of daigis were usable, but the long fibers of the vines were wanted for rope and other uses.

A person with alchemy skills could use Dehydrate and Pulverize, but each medicinal herb had a different processing method, and could the chemists of this city who hadn't developed their alchemical skills at all do work like removing weeds and foreign objects?

Besides, if potions began to appear on the market, their medicine may not sell anymore. The processing price, roughly double the usual amount, and quantity of medicinal herbs Weishardt offered was enough to compensate for a decline in medicine sales, but a backlash was also expected as the medicine the chemists worked so hard to make stopped moving off the shelves.

Weishardt contacted the Medicinal Herb Division chairwoman, Elmera of the Merchants Guild, with these concerns. The reply was a curtly worded message that arrived bearing her seal: "Leave the chemists to me. I will take care of it."

*   *   *

In fact, the chemists' reactions were largely as Elmera expected.

Those who listened to the lecture in their usual seats in the study group looked at the documents handed to them about medicinal herb processing methods, then began to whisper to one another.

"Aren't these techniques exactly the same as the ones for the salves and incense we've been making?"

"From what I've heard it didn't sound like alchemists of old went to all the trouble of removing the flowers from bromominthra for cheap potions like monster-warding ones. I thought it was done for normal medicine just because its effects are weak. And I thought only our little lady could do that kinda detailed work."

"Hey, anyone ever told you how insensitive you are? That's why you can't get a date."

"Uh? What's 'insensitive' got to do with anything?"

"It's got to do with our little lady."

Realizing something, the chemists exchanged looks with one another.

"I'll do it."

"Me too."

They nodded, unanimously agreeing to take on the processing of the herbs.

Mariela hadn't shown up to the Merchants Guild's seminars since Lynx died. Caroline had been busy ever since production of the pest-control dumplings began, and she also hadn't come today.

The chemists knew Mariela had been in low spirits ever since her friend died in the Labyrinth, and they all wanted to cheer her up somehow. None of the assembled chemists seemed to object to undertaking the task.

"Anyone got a problem with it? If so, a little friend of mine will go to your shop and have a 'talk' with you."

"The guy who put daidara snail juice on himself? What a persistent jerk."

"Hey, wasn't it you who sent him?"

"Ugh, don't bring that up."

"Ohh, you were the unsung hero of the stylish tea parties, weren't you?!"

"Ha-ha-ha, you could say it was all thanks to me. Go ahead—you can praise me."

"I'm not gonna praise you, dumbass."

As the chemists exchanged idle chatter, it was clear they were of the same mind.

"Even so, our little lady is—"

"Hey, don't say anything stupid. Weren't you told that when the lady at the florist's dumped you? We don't know anything."

"Huh? But I know—"

"I *said*, shut up. If you say anything uncalled for, I'll stuff huge bugs in your medicine vials!"

"That's right. If anyone decides to be a jerk here, I'll put your label on ointment tins full of mud!"

"I'll sic a hooligan with daidara snail spots on your shop!"

Unfortunately, things quickly turned into a revelation of past misdeeds. Elmera was the one to quiet them down.

"I *certainly* don't know what you're talking about, but I will be 'speaking to' anyone who spreads unfounded rumors. I hope I have made myself clear."

"Yes, ma'am. Sorry."

Elmera, chairwoman of the Medicinal Herbs Division, wore a very cheerful smile. Lightning seemed to flash from her fingertips for an instant, and the chemists all straightened up at once.

In the end, the chemists had readily accepted the request without questioning the situation too much. They bought the three kinds of plants gathered from within the City at the normal price, processed them correctly, and delivered them to the Medicinal Herbs Division of the Merchants Guild. After the dried and pulverized herbs were inspected at the Medicinal Herbs Division, they were transported to the newly built storehouse at the Labyrinth Suppression Forces' base.

Their alchemy skills remained low, and they couldn't use their skills to distinguish medicinal herbs or process them very well. However, they could look with their own eyes, discern scents, and touch with their fingers to process the herbs correctly. They supplemented their lack of skills by using specialized magical tools. The chemists had been provided with the proper knowledge regarding the necessary bits of vegetation.

With elementary-level plants like these, each of the assembled members of the team could easily pick up on how to prepare the mixture, and they understood exactly which parts of the herbs were effective and which parts weren't.

The chemists of the Labyrinth City had improved their knowledge and skills so well that Weishardt had been worried for nothing. All they'd learned had been acquired over the past half year. The young lady alchemist "from the imperial capital" had taught them.

"You can think, 'Pain, pain, go away' as you put magic into it."

The girl called Mariela had said that as she *knead-knead-knead-knead-kneeead*ed the medicine. The simple task seemed rather fun, and it was enjoyable to watch. No doubt anyone who used the medicine she made would feel happy, too.

She'd taught them how to make medicine and become friends with them even though they'd been so cruel to her. The purpose of teaching them was to help the chemists themselves, but it had also been because she couldn't supply medicine for the entire Labyrinth City on her own.

In any case, she'd saved the Labyrinth City's adventurers and citizens alike from injury and illness.

And surely, she would this time, too.

While they had no proof, none of the assembled apothecaries thought otherwise. Having learned in the same study groups with Mariela, they wanted to help her and make her life easier, even if just a little.

Some of them probably assumed that if what they suspected was true, and they cooperated now, they could become alchemists themselves after the Labyrinth was defeated.

Whether from good intentions or self-interest, the end result of their cooperation in accordance with the Labyrinth City's objective was the same.

With a unified interest among the many pharmacists, they established their supply system without giving the Lightning Empress her chance to shine, unfortunately.

07

As for the potion vials, producing new ones was essential. The problem was the source of materials, and Mariela's treasured sandpit behind the waterfall wouldn't provide nearly enough.

The securing of a sandpit and the construction of a glass workshop were cited as indispensable.

"We received valuable monster-warding potions from His Excellency, General Leonhardt! This is an important task! Ladies and gentlemen, it's time to show what the City Defense Squad is made of! We'll clear a way through the Fell Forest and recapture the sandpit we lost in the Stampede!"

Telluther was in high spirits. His official position was as an adviser, though, and giving speeches wasn't one of his functions.

It would be problematic if the Squad heard his speech as an order, but hearing it as idle talk was somehow encouraging. There was no real harm in it, everyone let him do as he liked.

The area where Mariela and Sieg once used the remains of a glass atelier to make plate glass for the skylight in Sunlight's Canopy was near rivers that flowed into an underground water vein, and even now the place was an excellent source of sand, a deposit of large quantities of the small particles. Although the spot had long since been swallowed by the Fell Forest, it was close enough to the Labyrinth City that one could reach it by yagu within a few hours. Because much of the reclamation of the forest had been done in the interest of food production, information about the pit had been lost to time. However, armed with knowledge of the location from Mariela and Sieg, Weishardt drafted a practical plan to retake it.

Leonhardt himself had sent the order to reclaim the section of the forest up to the sandpit to the City Defense Squad.

"This is an important task. It would be no exaggeration to say the future of the Labyrinth City rests upon this operation. Clear the land leading to the site of the glass atelier as soon as possible. We're counting on you."

Telluther, who tagged along with the current colonel and Captain Kyte to receive the order, was so moved by Leonhardt's words his heart trembled. Though that was hardly a rare occurrence.

"Valuable monster-warding potions by the barrel. And several barrels, to boot. Such precious items! We will absolutely fulfill your wishes in this most important task you have entrusted to us!"

Telluther's secret desire to be worthy of Leonhardt's trust was hardly secret at all. Leonhardt had spoken true about the matter being an important mission, but these potions were a piece of cake for Mariela to craft. She'd literally made them before breakfast.

"Easy peasy squeezy in the morning. Fresh and juicy, whoo!"

The young alchemist and her master had sung strange songs together while Mariela had been working on them.

Leonhardt, who knew the truth, felt a little guilty over Telluther's excitement about the potions. "I'm looking forward to hearing the report of a successful campaign," he said by way of compensation when he issued the mission, clapping Telluther on the shoulder.

Telluther's idol had not only addressed him directly but even given him a friendly pat! The delight was almost too much for him. His face flushed with excitement, like a youth who'd just been given his first sword.

Moreover, an adventurer was dispatched as an escort for this reclamation venture.

It was the one-eyed young man who had once saved Telluther from a giant slime.

"Ohhhhhhhh! It was you! Back then! Thank you! Thank you! You've come to help me again, haven't you?!"

Telluther was on cloud nine. This was surely the beginning of his personal golden age of life. He grabbed Sieg's hand tightly and pumped it up and down. His palms were incredibly sweaty. Sieg's hand was getting wet, and he feared his grip on the bow might slip, making the weapon even harder to handle. After all, his skills had yet to fully return.

Sieg's forced smile didn't falter, however, which was exactly what one might've expected from the man Freyja had deemed "dark." It was perhaps a mature response. Personal connections were particularly helpful for an adventurer like him who was only ever called on for his sword arm. Moreover, Sieg still had the muscle memory of a slave. Understanding this, he squeezed Telluther's sweaty hands in return. Perhaps Siegmund was a little more "sullied" than Mariela thought.

Incidentally, Freyja had been the one who'd used her authority and dispatched Sieg, after seeing him practice the bow in the rear garden.

"Huh? What're you doing against an opponent that doesn't move? Well, this's good timing. If you've got time to mess around, go be an escort for the reclamation mission. You can live off the land. Don't come back until they're finished."

With that said, she promptly kicked Sieg out of the house.

Moreover, she confiscated the mythril sword Mariela had given him, leaving him with only a bow, a large supply of arrows provided by the Labyrinth Suppression Forces, and Lynx's short sword.

"I'm Mariela's—"

"I'm here, so there'll be no problems. Hey, Marielaaa. Sieg says he's going hunting for orc king meat."

Sieg had scrambled to find a foothold, but Freyja pushed him off. He tried for Mariela—his last perch before he "fell"—but Freyja had gotten there first, calling for her. The young alchemist came running from the back. Her eyes sparkled just a smidge.

"Wow, Sieg, you're gonna hunt orc kings for me?! I'm so happy! It's perfect since we just ran out! I can't wait!"

Her smile lit up her whole face. His final stronghold in this battle had already been surrendered to the enemy. Even more so because Freyja had eaten the last of the orc king meat Mariela had carefully set aside.

"By the way, he's also going to be an escort for the City Defense Squad, so he'll be out for a little while. But you don't mind, right, Mariela? He'll be in a shallow part of the Fell Forest, and the City Defense Squad will be with him, too, so he won't be in much danger."

"Okay! Be careful, Sieg! Oh, take a bunch of potions with you!" She seemed to possess no small understanding of Sieg, either. He couldn't say he disliked seeing such a lovely smile on Mariela's face after so long.

"Yeah, Mariela. I'll make sure to bring home orc king meat!"

Thus he headed for the Fell Forest with only a bow and a short sword for equipment. Sieg's difficult mission of serving as an escort for a reclamation operation while also providing meat for himself, the City Defense Squad, and any serfs that came along, began. Of course, meals were provided for those participating in the operation, but the serfs in particular had poor diets lacking in nutrients. They would need meat, even if only a little, in order to be at full strength.

Although Siegmund set out on this venture to make Mariela smile, his heart was heavy.

It was the nightmare of the Ahriman Springs all over again. He was suddenly confronted with days of training without Mariela.

However, it certainly wouldn't last a month this time. Freyja was with Mariela, but the woman's personality was worrisome. Rather than keeping her student out of trouble, it was much more likely she'd get her into it. Sieg would have to return to Sunlight's Canopy before Mariela became Chubby-ela again.

Even as Siegmund fidgeted and continued to worry, no doubt the tentacles of sugary temptation were creeping toward Mariela, and Sunlight's Canopy might be awash in drained bottles of spirits before long. It may be paradise for the alchemist master and pupil, but from the outside it would look like the very picture of hell. He resolved to return to Sunlight's Canopy at all costs before the situation could deteriorate that far.

Lynx and Edgan had both been with Sieg at the Ahriman Springs. For him, those days had deepened their friendship and were dear and glorious memories. However, Lynx was gone now, and Edgan hadn't returned from the imperial capital yet. If Sieg opened himself up now, the only one who would come and try to make friends with him was Telluther.

It was hard to hate the rather high-strung man. He wasn't a bad person, but he was much older than Sieg, and they wouldn't have anything in common to talk about. Every time he looked at the short sword Lynx gave to him, Sieg succumbed to feelings of longing for the time he spent with his late friend.

One week! No matter what I'm going home in one week!

Siegmund focused his mind. This was no time to be pondering such needlessly complicated things!

He hunted monster after monster, mostly edible ones, while guarding the group of people working hard to clear the land. He wasn't hitting much with his bow. Even when he decided to hide in the shade of a tree and aim from there, the arrows missed or merely grazed their targets. Each time, his quarry would thrash and attack, enraged. But if Sieg missed, he could just fire again. He had his short sword as well for when they got close, and he could always stab them with an arrow if he needed to. Fortunately, he had a large number of potions, and he'd also brought his basilisk leather armor. The monsters in the area weren't strong enough to pierce it, and he needn't worry about the small scrapes he got here and there.

It didn't matter whether he could hit them with an arrow, or whether he was skilled or unskilled. Thanks to the monster-warding potions, the creatures largely stayed away from the others anyway. If the man's arrows failed to strike true, the angered creatures would head for him, which was a good thing. Sieg was going to need to hunt lot of them. He had to let the serfs eat more so they got stronger.

Siegmund quickly became a hunter who didn't spare a thought for anything but the pursuit of his prey. By the time everyone in the reclamation unit began calling him "Meat Man," he was at last able to fell quarry with his bow. After releasing himself from superfluous thoughts, Sieg's body remembered the hunter style he'd learned as a child and the archery skills that his body once knew so well.

All the while, Telluther was fired up about the glorious task he'd been given. Not only had he received trust and potions from his idol, he'd also managed to reunite with his savior and high-ranking adventurer, Sieg. To work together with such a man delighted Telluther beyond belief.

Monster-warding potions were no longer scarce in the Labyrinth City. In fact, it was more difficult to gather the medicinal herbs needed than to make the potions themselves, but Telluther didn't know that. Even if he did, doubtless Telluther would still be brimming with a sense of purpose.

And his passion outstripped every other impulse he had. He shone with a light of inspiration. And this time, it wasn't the light reflecting off his head. There seemed to be an aura about the man, and it gave powerful Empathy to the people around him.

"Huuuooooooooh!"

The soldiers of the City Defense Squad were filled with a sense of motivation and purpose thanks to the skill Telluther had very conveniently evolved. The soldiers, the serfs rounded up for the reclamation operation, and even the slum residents hired for the job were uncharacteristically passionate as they cleared the way through the Fell Forest to the ruins of the atelier where Mariela and Sieg had once made plate glass.

"We've got monster-warding potions! I don't fear the likes of those Fell Forest monsters!"

"Those creatures won't dare show their faces while we've got these! The Fell Forest ahead of us is just a bunch of trees!" several soldiers of the City Defense Squad shouted with confidence. The Fell Forest was vast, and if they went into a deeper layer, they would encounter powerful monsters the warding potions wouldn't work on. But perhaps ignorance was bliss in this case.

Telluther also saw fit to greatly exaggerate Sieg's strength when he talked about the man who'd saved his life, which spurred the confidence of the group even further. Emboldened with a sense of invincibility, they downed trees, stripped them of branches on the spot, and made crude stakes to line both sides of the opened road. They wound rope made from daigis around the stakes and planted daigis and bromominthra around them. The scent of the plants would help keep unsavory creatures away. Those who could use earth magic softened the ground, and the serfs and yagus worked together to dig up stumps and large stones.

The soil was made of fine particles, so no matter how smooth and compact they tried to make it on its own, wagons would leave divots in the earth. To combat this, the company would smash large stones into gravel of a variety of sizes. They then laid the crushed stone on the soft dirt. In this way, they could construct a temporary road that, while not as good as a paved one, could withstand the passage of carriages.

No matter how much magic they could use, the City Defense Squad was below even second stringers. Although yagu could cover the total distance in a few hours, clearing the path wasn't easy work. They dispatched what few monsters did appear, and if someone ran out of magical power, a substitute tagged in. The task was exhausting, and everyone was bathed in sweat as they worked.

Although they should have been drained well beyond their

limits, everyone had smiles on their faces. Telluther's Empathy had terrifying power.

The meat they had their fill of every day was delicious, and hunger made it all the more so.

Work well, eat well. Influenced by Telluther's zealous sense of purpose and the fundamental human joy of food and manual labor, everyone cleared the way to the sandpit near the site of the glass atelier in just one week. The transportation of sand to the Labyrinth City was a success.

Incidentally, although Telluther's skill had evolved at a truly beneficial time, he was still unable to consciously control its activation. No one, not even the man himself, had even noticed the transformation of the skill. It didn't augment an individual's abilities; all it really did was enable them to tackle their work in an extremely good mood. However, the sense of accomplishment they got from finishing a great task with their own hands gave the City Defense Squad and the serfs participating in the reclamation a huge boost in confidence.

The people of the Labyrinth City admired the bravery they saw in the City Defense Squad soldiers who made for the Fell Forest with such self-assurance, and the Squad became more and more popular.

Although the actual effect was rather negligible, a Telluther-like skill may have grown within the Squad when its forces received words of praise from His Excellency General Leonhardt a few days later.

08

"Whoaaa, are all of these medicinal herbs? Wow, they're even pulverized! That's great; they're perfect!"

"Ohh. They took care of my part, too. Impressive."

Around the time Sieg and the others began their efforts in the Fell Forest, Mariela and her master were busy praising the alchemy workshop that had been established in the cellar of the Labyrinth Suppression Forces' base.

The base also connected to the underground Aqueduct, and there was a secret passage between the base's cellar and the second stratum of the Labyrinth that was paved with daigis fibers to keep slimes from approaching. Of course, because it connected to the entire underground Aqueduct, which was not paved with daigis, the Black Iron Freight Corps had carried potions through the tunnel until Mariela came forward.

The Labyrinth Suppression Forces outfitted the largest cellar near the entrance to the underground Aqueduct as Mariela's temporary workshop. It was originally a storehouse where they kept emergency rations. The shelves that had been packed with food were now packed with large quantities of processed medicinal herbs, and a great number of wooden barrels with engravings for temporary storage were stacked in a corner.

In the center of the room, a plain but well-made couch and

table had been placed on a rug, with wooden crates and barrels next to them.

It was a rather dreary setup, but it had been thoroughly cleaned. And, above all, there were so many medicinal herbs that it didn't seem like an amount that was possible to amass in just a few days. The Forces had done a fantastic job getting all this ready since the agreement was struck during the dinner with Leonhardt.

"Leave the transportation of medicinal herbs and barrels to us, Lady Alchemists. Everyone has made a vow not to pry or disclose information regarding either of you. Everything will be done in accordance with your instructions."

The three youths of the Labyrinth Suppression Forces, who were on standby in the room, greeted them politely.

In a fight, those from the Forces appointed to perform odd jobs were weaker than second-string soldiers. But youths with good manners had been chosen for the tasks. One out of the three was a woman, perhaps in consideration of Mariela and her master.

"Okay, Mariela, I'm leaving the potions to you. Hmm, you over there. The curly-haired one. You're gonna be my assistant."

After confirming her demands had been met, Freyja plopped down on the couch and invited the young man with gentle features and chestnut-colored curls to sit next to her. She took a bottle of alcohol out from a wooden crate (or perhaps a barrel?) next to the table and immediately had a drink.

This was the "my part" Freyja had referred to.

Although her curly-haired assistant was taken aback, he graciously poured the alcohol.

"Ahhh, I could get used to this feeling; it's refreshing. When you pour alcohol, do it so the label's showing. Oh, the bottle opening shouldn't touch the glass. Hold on, you do it like this. Pour it a little lower. Hee-hee, let me teach you all about it."

Mariela's master was certainly feeling pleased. Despite her appearance as a young woman, her words and actions were just like an old man's.

Despite Sieg's worries, Mariela didn't overindulge in sweets. She even tried to keep her master's drinking firmly under control, or at least limited to one bottle a day. Despite the effort, Freyja still took advantage of Mariela's ignorance of alcohol and chose to drink the strongest spirits, like whiskey and brandy. One bottle of that per day was by no means a small amount.

The way Freyja downed her drinks with the young soldier on the base of the Labyrinth Suppression Forces was mortifying and irritating to Mariela. She was quite embarrassed that such a useless adult was her master.

"Master, you're horrible. I'm gonna make potions as fast as I can and then take you home. Excuse me, please take all the curique from there to there. Oh, step back a bit more and open the bag."

Since it had come to this, Mariela put all her energy into making potions so she could finish her work and confiscate her master's alcohol. She asked the remaining two soldiers to line up large bags full of medicinal herbs.

"Form Transmutation Vessel."

Mariela created a vertical, cylindrical Transmutation Vessel with more capacity than a bathtub.

Although this cellar was large, the shelves, barrels, and her teacher were in the way, so she couldn't create a vessel any larger than this. It was most certainly an unconventional size, but a girl like Mariela didn't know what a "normal size" was. She filled the container with Drops of Life, and the soldiers' eyes widened in surprise at the faintly shimmering water gushing forth like a fountain out of empty space. Even when combined with water, Drops of Life didn't lose their characteristic pale light.

"Please put the herbs in it. Oh, the Transmutation Vessel is there, so lift them a little higher. Yeah, plop them all in. When you're done with that, line the barrels up over there," Mariela instructed, and the soldiers complied.

"Extract Essence."

Shaking was the normal way to do the extraction for a small quantity of elementary potions. Normally, the contents of an airtight Transmutation Vessel would be shaken like a cocktail, which dissolved the components more quickly.

However, both the space and magical power required to shake a bathtub-size Transmutation Vessel made that option a no go. Instead, she had to move the solvent: the water mixed with the Drops of Life. The alchemy skill Extract Essence would cause the medicinal herb components to begin to dissolve, so how the Transmutation Vessel moved was largely based on the image in the skill user's mind.

What came to Mariela's was an image of many rods with stirring blades attached to them rotating in the center of the vessel. It was like one of the contraptions she'd made with the chemists.

The shape of the stirring blades was their main attribute, and they rotated up and down in the center of the liquid to make it swirl like a whirlpool. The chemists and medical engineers had given a fervent speech about how many prototypes they'd created to develop these blades. Mariela hadn't memorized them down to the exact shapes, but she remembered well the movement of the liquid being stirred. She used this image to blend the Drops of Life–infused water and the medicinal herbs.

Her mental image wasn't of the stirring blades, but the water itself. She created an eddy at the center of the Transmutation Vessel and moved it from the top to the bottom so as to incorporate the plants into the mixture. When the swirling reached the bottom layer, it slowly spun around the outer circumference of the vessel as it floated upward. This was to break the medicinal herbs uniformly into small pieces and spread them out.

It was a large amount of liquid to mix. The Transmutation Vessel also needed sufficient strength to withstand the pressure. Thankfully, circular and spherical shapes are resistant to internal force. Compared to making plate glass however, which required high temperatures, this was far easier.

Hurry, hurry—make the current stronger.

Mariela, who had the know-how for this, rapidly intensified the water current, and churned the solvent mixture around and around as if in desperation.

When Mariela chanced glances at her master, Freyja was busy making comments like "Oh! Is this ten-year-old Otarre?! I want this one. On the rocks." Perhaps because of this, Mariela's refining seemed to grow more fervent.

When Extract Essence was finished, she used Separate Dregs to isolate the plant matter. It was fine to do this with filtration in the case of low-grade potions. The alchemist would place filter paper in the funnel and pour the mixture from the top. It was simple and easy to reproduce with alchemy skills, but the process was slower when there was a lot of the stuff. The method was the same as usual, but with a quantity like this, it seemed probable the medicinal herbs would clump up in layers even if skills were used to separate them.

It'd be better if the pressure built up.

She sealed the Transmutation Vessel and moved the filter upward to scoop up the herb dregs from the bottom. This, too, was made with magical power like the Transmutation Vessel. That way, the young alchemist could adjust the dimensions to match the size of the vessel at will. The transparent filter moved from the bottom of the equally transparent vessel to the top as it filtered out the solids. For the two guards attending Mariela, it was a mystical sight they'd never seen before.

"Hwwwwwah!"

With groans and grunts, Mariela lifted her hand. Squelching sounds issued from the invisible container in answer, as the filtration surface followed her movements up to the top. It was a surprisingly dramatic bit of action considering it came from Mariela, who always kneaded and mixed things in more unassuming ways. The vigorous exercise had seemingly squeezed the dregs of the medicinal herbs into a tightly packed clump.

"Ohhh. Even alchemy's effects increase when you put your strength into it," came the impressed voices of the two soldiers.

"Wellll, the pose doesn't really add a whole lot. It was just a spur of the moment thing," Mariela replied with an embarrassed giggle. For a moment, the guards were flummoxed. They looked at Mariela, and then glanced at the red-haired woman busying herself with drinking.

This pupil was trained by that instructor? the two were likely thinking, though Mariela took no heed.

I feel a bit better after moving around. It's kinda fun to waste a little magical power and refine potions with a "hoo!" or "ha!" every once in a while.

Mariela's mood improved just a little.

Next came *Condense* and *Anchor Essence*.

She released the pressure from the Transmutation Vessel and heated it enough to maintain the efficacy. It wasn't hot enough to boil water, but bubbles appeared within the liquid, and the volume steadily decreased all the same. She was in a cellar, so if she didn't return the released water to its magical source, the other would get damp and go bad. This was also a process unique to mass production.

And finally, after she anchored the efficacy, she would be done.

It was a large amount, but at the end of the day, they were very simple potions. Although producing so many so quickly had eaten into her magical power, the creation itself wasn't a big deal. She finished refining the potions in the blink of an eye and poured them into the barrels.

She glanced at her master and saw she'd already emptied a bottle of alcohol.

Grrr. Master, you're too fast!

Her drunken master was trying to get the curly-haired soldier to drink while he was still on the clock.

"Next! Please bring the remaining bromominthra and daigis over here, and put the curique over there!"

Mariela was getting into the rhythm of the work. Even large quantities were no problem. Now that it had come to this, she would do both groups of herbs at the same time. She wasn't going to let her master drink any more than she already had for today!

The young alchemist was on a roll, and the two soldiers ran around carrying various bags and barrels of ingredients. The curly-haired soldier either wanted to help or just wanted to get away from Freyja, because he kept glancing over at the others. Alas, he was stuck.

Hang in there, Mr. Curly. I'll take Master home soon!

With a completely different goal in mind than she should have had, Mariela completed the low-grade monster-warding potions and low-grade heal potions with astounding speed. With her magical power all but gone, she wobbled on her feet and grabbed on to Freyja for support.

"Mariela, that was greeeat. I never thought you could get it done that fast! You've really grown!"

"Ugh, Master......"

Freyja waggled her fingers as she reached for her student's head, but Mariela shook off her hands and put a slight distance between herself and her master. This was *Imprint* protection. She was happy to be praised, but she could do without the *Imprint*. Besides, her master had polished off three bottles of alcohol despite Mariela's efforts. Freyja was very drunk and very happy.

"Okaaay, see you tomorrooow. Mitchell, right? Be here tomorrow!"

Taking advantage of the distance Mariela put between them, the red-haired woman took two bottles of alcohol from a wooden crate, and then Mariela led her back toward Sunlight's Canopy.

Dang it! Tomorrow, I'll make sure she doesn't drink as much!

A crushing failure. Mariela had been utterly beaten today. Her master just drank too quickly, but she couldn't lose like this. When she got home, she would need to conduct a one-person postmortem session. The girl lamented the absence of her adviser, Sieg.

Mariela walked through the underground Aqueduct in a mood while she dragged along her flame-haired teacher, who seemed liable to tumble into a gutter at any moment.

Mariela wasn't cruel enough to hope the woman would get

swept down some waterway, but even if such a thing did happen, she was Mariela's master. And Freyja would probably make it back just fine, and then washing her sopping wet clothes would become Mariela's job.

Even at the best of times, her master fell asleep without scrubbing her face, scattered her clothes so vehemently her left and right socks ended up on opposite ends of the house, and was generally very untidy when she drank too much. Without Sieg, Mariela had the heavy responsibility of both looking after her master and doing the housework, and it was unbearable how quickly the place became a mess again after she cleaned it.

Moreover, her master was an annoyingly chatty drunk.

Mariela was just glad that the two of them safely made it back to Sunlight's Canopy. Her instructor, however, was completely sloshed while the sun was still high, and she started to strike up a conversation with Nierenberg of all people.

"Doooc, you got a huuuge crease between your eyebrows. It's a freakin' chasm. Cleavage. Butt brow?"

She cackled as she stretched her arms toward Nierenberg's forehead.

The soldier of the Labyrinth Suppression Forces—who was guarding Sunlight's Canopy under the guise of getting a medical examination—shuddered at Freyja's fearlessness in the face of this man. Perhaps Nierenberg had received a strict order from Weishardt not to be rude to Freyja in the least, because the crease in his brow deepened even further as he replied to her like an adult scolding a child. "Isn't it a bit early in the day to be drunk?"

Nierenberg's patience was in vain, as Freyja produced a toothpick and yelled "Haaah!" as she jabbed it at him.

"Look at that, Mariela! The toothpick's stuck in his brow! Wooow, it's staying put even after I let go!"

Freyja doubled over in hysterical laughter. She was gleeful. She was awful.

"Master? Didn't I tell you not to cause trouble for others? You know I did."

"Ahhh, Mariela, you're scary when you're mad."

"You haven't even seen scary yet! If you don't splash yourself with water and sober up right now, you're not getting dinner!"

Mariela angrily dragged her master to the bathroom and threw her into a cold bath, and at last, the woman returned to her senses. In her irritation, Mariela had thrown her into the water fully clothed, increasing her laundry load anyway.

Drunk Master is such a nuisance!

Two hundred years ago, her master wouldn't come home some days—where had she gone while she was being the utmost nuisance possible?

"I need more soldiers to help me tomorrow!"

Mariela made a personnel increase request to Nierenberg, who understood the situation all too well. If there were a lot of people carrying alchemic ingredients from shelves and putting them in the Transmutation Vessel or stuffing them into barrels, she could finish making the potions in a shorter amount of time.

Tomorrow's the day I won't let Master get drunk!

Mariela's determination was firm.

The next day, a total of five soldiers were deployed as Mariela had requested, including the curly-haired Mitchell. There were less of the three herbs used for low-grade potions, as expected. Instead, materials and tools for high-grade potions had been prepared.

"Mariela, make high-grade potions one at a time."

"Sure. And you can use this tiny cup, Master."

"A smaller vessel is gonna slow me down."

"Exactly."

Master and pupil smirked at each other. Their fated show-down was about to begin.

"All riiight, Mitchell, let's drink. Ah, you over there, you're cute, too. Come here and help out your big sis."

Freyja and the others immediately shifted to merrymaking mode. Although it was only the second day, Mitchell had a look on his face as if he'd achieved enlightenment. And even though they'd gone to the trouble of increasing the number of soldiers by two, Freyja had hijacked one of them.

Grrr. Mariela shot a glare at her master, then set herself to brewing potions with all her might until her magical power was nearly exhausted.

09

The efforts of Mariela and the soldiers proved to be in vain, as day after day the fire that was Freyja continued to consume the free liquors provided to her.

Sieg felled an orc king and safely returned home in a week's time, but he only had a short while to catch his breath with Mariela in front of the living room fireplace before he had to leave again.

To fulfill Freyja's dinner requests, Sieg had gone to the Fell Forest the day before. Today he went to the Labyrinth. Day in and day out it was like this. The difficulty levels of her quests seemed to be quite high. Sieg didn't suffer any serious injuries, of course, but he was run completely ragged every day, and he was lucky to come home the same day he departed.

Mariela, too, had her hands full putting out her master's fires; she was given no chance to come to Sieg's aid.

Day in and day out, Sieg went monster-hunting in the forest, and Mariela traveled through the underground Aqueduct to make potions.

"Stupid Master always wallowing in her drink, I wish she'd fall into the Aqueduct and get washed away!"

Mariela's inner thoughts slipped from between her pursed lips.

If her teacher ever was swept away in the Aqueduct, Mariela had a hunch that she would drift ashore in the deepest part of the Labyrinth and subjugate it without any trouble. That would be just her luck. Freyja loved the bottle more than anything, and down in the Labyrinth, there wouldn't be anyone to give her any drink. On second thought, perhaps she would have more trouble down there than Mariela imagined.

Setting aside that wild idea, Mariela realized Freyja must have made a deal with the Schutzenwald brothers to prepare free alcohol for her.

They were having a complicated-sounding conversation, so I had no idea! I completely fell into her trap!

Once again, Mariela wore a mortified expression on her face as she took her drunken master back to Sunlight's Canopy today.

"What's wrong, Miss Mariela? Did you eat something sour?"

Nierenberg's daughter, Sherry, quietly offered her sweetened tea.

Mariela's expression, oozing with displeasure, apparently made her look like she'd eaten something bitter. Sherry's guess at the reason for the look on her face should have been all the more embarrassing, but an offer of sweetened tea completely placated her.

"Tomorrow! Tomorrow's the day Master's going to be complaining that she didn't get enough to drink!"

Mariela tightly gripped the candy bar Sherry had given her to go with the tea and renewed her determination.

Luckily, Sieg returned before sunset, and Mariela's variety of comedic expressions helped to relieve his fatigue. While Freyja was gripping a bottle of alcohol and imitating her pupil, he approached and whispered a question in her ear.

"Lady Frey, why haven't you been offering guidance to Mariela?"

Freyja glanced at Sieg and muttered, "So protective," before giving a proper response. "But I am! Hee-hee, you don't look convinced. Being overprotective doesn't help anything, Sieg. Let me tell you something. Do you know how a person's limits are determined? Of course, their natural talents play a role, but potential is where you find the true limits."

Maintaining her mischievous attitude, Mariela's master spoke loud enough for only Sieg to hear. Sometimes, her flippant words and deeds gave way to truth.

"And people decide their own potential. Your growth stops at whatever limit you think you have. You experience a different degree of difficulty with a given job depending on whether you think it's easy or hard. So I don't tell Mariela how much she can do. She's got more than enough alchemy knowledge, but she doesn't understand how advanced it is. See, she's pouting, but she's having a lot of fun, right? Right now, she's obsessed with beating me at this game. That's the best way for Mariela to grow."

Taking responsibility for yourself to reach new heights was incredibly difficult to do. According to Freyja, that difficulty came from the fear of the precipitous road to reach those new heights.

Sieg finally understood that Mariela was unknowingly, but no less quickly, chasing her master up a steep mountain road and enjoying the climb.

"Sieg, reach the other side with your own efforts. That's the only way to move forward alongside Mariela."

After leaving him with those words, Freyja walked over toward the children and asked them, "Have all of you done your homework?"

Emily, who'd received a candy bar from Sherry; Pallois, who was helping make tea; and Elio all looked up at the sound of the woman's voice. The children had gathered in Sunlight's Canopy again today, and the acclaimed after-school daycare was open for business.

The Labyrinth City was buzzing with the sales of potions. Although a far less common topic of conversation, a school had been opened in the Labyrinth City around the same time as the potion sales announcement happened. The City's school was modeled after educational institutions in the imperial capital, but unlike those, which served the upper classes, this targeted the middle class and below.

Its purpose was to reduce the mortality rate of young people who would become future adventurers or soldiers who descended into the depths of the Labyrinth. A practical curriculum had been put together to teach not only the basics of reading, writing, and arithmetic, but the characteristics and weaknesses of monsters, and how to gather and handle materials, including medicinal herbs. The school also featured training for skills such as weapon handling and self-defense.

Three schools had been opened: the Warrior School, overseen by the Adventurers Guild and meant for children with combat aptitude; the School of Commerce, overseen by the Merchants Guild and meant for children with aptitudes for production or business; and a balanced intermediate school, which invited experienced private tutors from wealthy families to be teachers and was overseen by the house of Margrave Schutzenwald. Although there were differences in the details and distribution of the practical skills and classroom learning at each school, even the School of Commerce offered combat training. It was very characteristic of the Labyrinth City. Ideally everyone in the Labyrinth City would be able to pick up a sword and defeat at least a goblin or similarly ranked creature. This educational policy was based on the ideology of people who tended to be more brawn than brains.

The balanced intermediate school gave an impression of ambiguity. In reality however, it was meant for middle-class families so that even if they didn't have tutors, they could give their children a more advanced education. Even students of the other two schools who were found to have worthy talents could be admitted. Some children had to build their livelihood from scratch with their own abilities, while others could take advantage of their heritage, and each group needed to learn different skills. Raising skilled children and giving them a good education was the best way to solve the lack of human resources in the Labyrinth City.

Each one of the schools was in session for a short time and only during the morning. Many young children in the Labyrinth City worked, so it was necessary to provide them with the needed education in a short time. In a way, this specialized school system took the unique situations of the City into consideration.

Sherry and the other three children attended the intermediate school. Nierenberg's daughter, Sherry, had a private tutor, and Elmera's sons had received more than enough education from Elmera and Voyd, so they didn't really need to go to the intermediate school. However, there were many things to learn from interacting with children around their own age.

Emily's father was once an adventurer, but his daughter resembled her mother; she had no talent for combat, and ability-wise she was an ordinary city girl. However, she was bent on inheriting the Yagu Drawbridge Pavilion someday, and she'd been studying reading, writing, and arithmetic from Amber and regular customers since she was little; she had enough knowledge to enroll. Other than her fondness for "uni-corn," she was a ten-year-old with a promising future.

The four children, who got along well and did homework together, and the alcoholic sage made for quite a group. Freyja helped the kids with things they didn't understand by teaching them a combination of necessary, unnecessary, and advanced information. Whether she liked children or simply had a similar mental age to them, she seemed to be enjoying herself quite a bit.

Thanks for looking after Master, kids!

Mariela was grateful to Sherry and the others from the bottom of her heart. She was a little more worried than excited about how the children would turn out, but she also had to replenish ingredients for Sunlight's Canopy. She needed time to herself.

If you took the medicine out of Sunlight's Canopy, it would be a combination of a self-service teahouse, Nierenberg's clinic, and an after-school daycare. Was Mariela's presence even necessary? The status of landlady might be nice, but she already had a ton of money. She hardly needed unearned income.

"Salves, painkillers, antipyretics, stomachache medicine. After that, smoke bombs and three kinds of soap!"

Away from public eye, Mariela used alchemy to make several products simultaneously in her atelier on the second floor.

In the past, her speed would have been unthinkable, but Mariela had been too busy competing with her master to notice.

10

"At last, at last I can go hooome!!!"

At the Merchants Guild, Elmera let out a cheer.

Had it really been ten days since the briefings on the sale of potions had started?

Whenever someone forged documents to try and secure as many potions as possible, the response was to share the sales method for adventurers who didn't have a home.

"Take a voucher at the entrance to the Labyrinth, then go to the twentieth stratum to buy potions." With that, the matter was settled.

This information was released because prospects had improved for manufacturing potion vials.

Currently, people were limited to one low-grade healing potion and one low-grade monster-warding potion each, but it was a much better deal than potentially getting involved in a crime. Traveling to the Labyrinth's twentieth stratum cost magical gems, but they could use the Teleportation Circle. If they really needed to, it also wasn't impossible to get there on foot. A certain alchemist had run the distance to lose weight, so most people in the Labyrinth City could likely make the trip without a problem.

They could buy countless potions in the time they would spend in jail for forging documents or extortion, so going to the Labyrinth was much more profitable. Should they use the stairs to go back and forth, or save time with the Teleportation Circle? Since they'd gone to the trouble of traveling down to the twentieth stratum, they could also collect medicinal herbs. The trade-in price of lunamagia was going up, so it seemed prudent to collect some to diversify their investments in case the potions couldn't be sold at a high price.

Weishardt's method of solving the shortage of lunamagia, an ingredient in high-grade potions, turned out to be a successful one.

There was a safe area around the Labyrinth stairs where no monsters approached. Many people couldn't fight in the twentieth stratum but could come and go without issue via the stairs. Going all the way there for two potions was hardly worth it, but it was perfect for earning extra money if they also took on contracts to transport medicinal herbs and other materials.

In short, adventurers and chemists were also working to

collect lunamagia on the twentieth stratum because not only would it save them time transporting it, the trade-in price was high.

Incidentally, monster-warding potions were also being sold at the southwestern gate of the Labyrinth City and at the entrance to the Fell Forest. However, these were in normal, consumable vials, which were ineffective for preserving the concoctions. They were being sold solely for merchant caravans who needed them for traveling through the Fell Forest to the imperial capital and back again.

A stand selling monster-warding potions had been constructed at the entrance to the Fell Forest on the imperial capital side, and second-string soldiers from the Labyrinth Suppression Forces were stationed there to run it. The Black Iron Freight Corps had been contracted to transport monster-warding potions to this stand.

"Hiya, appreciate your business. Here's your new supply of monster-warding potions."

"Edgan, perfect timing. The Bandel Company wants an escort for travel to the Labyrinth City. They're waiting in Vantoa Village. Can you handle it? They're apparently with a customer."

"Okeydokey. You said there's a customer with them?"

"Yeah, seems to be a mediator for the Bandel Company."

"Whoa, Mr. Bandel's working hard."

While Edgan and the soldiers were exchanging information, the slaves Newie and Nick finished unloading. The barrels of monster-warding potion stacked in the three carriages were a rather large number to be unloaded by two people. Thanks to that and the early summer heat and humidity, the pair of slaves were dripping sweat like waterfalls. The soldiers, unable to just stand by and do nothing, helped them out.

The Black Iron Freight Corps had gone through big changes since losing Lynx. Dick and Malraux, who'd respectively served as captain and lieutenant, returned to the Labyrinth Suppression Forces and had handed the reins over to Edgan.

Of course, Dick had paid back Amber's debt and didn't have a reason to keep on with the Corps. Plus, over the past half year, Mariela's defense system had been strengthened, and a procedure for safely producing and selling potions had been established. So, the Black Iron Freight Corps might have ended up like this sooner or later anyway.

The other current members were the animal tamer Yuric, the healing magic user Franz, Donnino, who maintained the armored carriages, and Grandel, who was almost too thin for a shield knight. Together with the slaves Newie and Nick, the group made for a total of seven people.

Franz normally wore a mask to hide his demi-human features, and Yuric's accent and hair color were unusual in the imperial capital and the Labyrinth City. Both of them would rather live on the road with the transportation group than settle down in one place.

Donnino and Grandel originally had belonged to the Labyrinth Suppression Forces, but since their abilities weren't suited to Labyrinth subjugation, they'd joined the Black Iron Freight Corps. Simply going into the Labyrinth wasn't the way to get revenge for Lynx anyway. They chose a path for the Black Iron Freight Corps that would benefit the Labyrinth City. Newie and Nick didn't have the authority to decide their courses of action, but they seemed pleased to accompany Grandel and Donnino, who'd shown kindness to them.

And then there was Edgan.

"Without me, you guys won't have enough strength to survive."

No one saw the need to fight it, and he took over as captain.

"Grandel? Why'd Ed quit the Labyrinth Suppression Forces in the first place?"

"That's a fine question, Yuric. The Labyrinth Suppression Forces no longer needed him. He'd been making passes at the female soldiers one after another. Oh, that was a rough time."

The traveler of love, Edgan, whispered sweet nothings to many women at the same time without discrimination, from a beautiful woman too good to be a soldier, to a muscular woman rumored to be a female orc or troll. He seemed to have lost his refuge at the end of a difficult journey.

The gentlemanly Grandel told Yuric a poetic story, but the end result of Edgan's two-timing, or three-timing, or more-timing, may or may not have involved a stabbing while they were making camp.

"My soulmate just wasn't in the Labyrinth Suppression Forces. But she might be in the imperial capital, so that's why I joined the Black Iron Freight Corps."

"Has your gear of fate broken? I like making repairs."

With a sigh, Edgan's longtime friend Donnino compared destiny to a spinning mechanical part.

"My gear is spinning just fine, like any wagon wheel. Everybody loves it!"

"A wheel's not a gear. It's got no teeth, so there's no way for it to mesh with another gear…"

As a wheel, Edgan apparently had little friction and was extremely popular. His comrades of the Black Iron Freight Corps, meanwhile, supported one another as they moved forward, but unfortunately, they were not destined to complete each other.

"Edgan's soulmate wasn't in the imperial capital either, right? And he's still a wanderer."

Edgan joined Yuric and Grandel's conversation with theatrical gestures.

"Wanderer... I like the sound of that. Yeah! I'm a wanderer of love!"

"Lost child is more like it," Yuric retorted coolly. "Well, seems the preparations are complete. I hope you can make it to Vantoa Village before sunset without losing your way."

"Righto, Grandel. I may be a lost child of love, but I always know where I'm going!"

"Is the summer heat getting to him? I wish Edgan would wander off and never come back. The raptors can find their way with or without him."

"Yuric, that's enough."

Unable to simply watch, Franz stepped in with timely help to stop Yuric's overly abusive language. Yuric stuck out his tongue and then boarded a carriage with Franz.

After traveling through the Fell Forest and delivering the monster warding potions, they stayed overnight in Vantoa Village before making their return. Their cargo was a load of people bound for the Labyrinth City...along with a suspiciously large quantity of alcohol ordered by the house of Margrave Schutzenwald. It was rather obvious who the drink was for.

These days, there was work in the Labyrinth City for people who couldn't even fight, and still more for those around the strength of an intermediate-level adventurer. Moreover, monster-warding potions that allowed much safer passage to the

City than ever before were being sold. The news of this had spread not only to the imperial capital, but to neighboring villages as well.

Furthermore, the Black Iron Freight Corps had begun running stagecoaches. Impoverished people who'd caught wind of all the hearsay were likely together in Vantoa Village, the point of departure for the carriages from here on out.

Businesses that had previously only traveled across the mountain range by way of yagu caravans now began to cut through the Fell Forest instead. With merchant groups like the Bandel Company reaching the imperial capital in such a short time, word of this new revelation spread quickly.

Such was the beginning of the monster-warding potion trade. The Bandel Company, which jumped at the chance to start trade runs via the Fell Forest, was about to return to the Labyrinth City after its first transaction. Though they fully understood the effects of the monster-repelling concoction, the Fell Forest still proved to be frightening. The group was likely to prefer making the return trip in the company of the Black Iron Freight Corps.

The Black Iron Freight Corps was making a round trip through the forest again today. They transported monster-warding potions out of the Labyrinth City, then carried new immigrants on the way back. Unlike before, they weren't transporting slaves, but residents of the imperial capital. More people were starting lives in the Labyrinth City by the day. The sale of potions had radically altered the previous dynamic.

The early summer sunlight filtering through the trees of the Fell Forest slowly heated the jet-black iron carriages. This made for a very unpleasant ride for the passengers in the cargo hold, which had little more than small air holes for ventilation.

Passengers enjoyed the magical cool breezes that were conjured many times throughout the trip, but if the Corps truly wanted to be in the transportation business, they were going to need some magical tools for air-conditioning.

Along with their new sort of cargo, the armored carriages the Corps employed would need to keep up with the times as well. Though the changes the Labyrinth City would need dwarfed even those of the metal wagons.

The question was: Would all the transformations brought about by the new people moving into the Labyrinth City and the potions circulating on the market actually prove to be positive?

Edgan was reminded of a certain person in the Labyrinth City as he rode a raptor ahead of the armored carriages. Not Belisa, Yoanna, nor even Needle Ape Natasha. No, he was reminded of Sieg.

He hadn't seen the man since Lynx died.

It wasn't as if that had been Sieg's fault, of course. Edgan understood that, but for some reason he found the idea of seeing Sieg again difficult.

Sieg, I wonder how you've been doing. Maybe I'll pay you a visit some time.

The black iron carriages rolled along through the dense woods, bringing with them the immigrants heading to the Labyrinth City and the merchant caravan who had established a new sales outlet.

The thick foliage above him cast harsh shadows along the ground beneath the summer sun.

CHAPTER 2
The Spirit Shrine

01

"Pops! We've come to help!"

On the west side of the Labyrinth City, where a place called the Citadel City had once stood two hundred years ago, a group of carpenters, including Gordon, were hard at work.

It was outside the Labyrinth City's protective wall and uncomfortably close to the Fell Forest. In the past, none would have dared to order or accept work in such a dangerous location. Construction here had only been made possible because of the supply of monster-warding potions.

Gordon and the others were hard at work building a special shrine.

Clearing the road to the sandpit had yielded a large quantity of wood, and they had rapidly constructed a large building that could hold about ten carriages. The question of whether it was acceptable to build a shrine with such haste would have to wait for another time.

Gordon the dwarf was overseeing the work, while his son, Johan, and the glass artisan Ludan, assisted. They'd gathered workers from the City of course, but construction and repair in the Labyrinth City was largely stonework; there weren't many woodworkers. Though the dwarves spared no expense, they still didn't have enough hands to meet the unreasonable order of finishing this job in a week. Even if they order had come from the house of Margrave Schutzenwald.

After hearing Gordon was in a tight spot, the adventurers he'd once helped came to provide assistance. Despite their work as adventurers, not all of them made particularly good money. Many had injuries and couldn't even afford a bare bones sort of livelihood.

Gordon himself had been an adventurer in his younger days but was forced to retire due to a wound. It was only thanks to his boss, who'd given the dwarf work while he was struggling to make enough to eat, that Gordon had been able to make a successful living as a carpenter.

He couldn't repay his benefactor directly, so instead he paid it forward to the next generation. It was probably why Gordon looked after wounded adventurers by helping them find carpentry work and giving them salves he bought from Sunlight's Canopy.

The old dwarf didn't remember exactly how many adventurers he'd helped out, but dozens of people had come running to help after word spread that Gordon was in need.

Each one who hastened to the man's side was an adventurer. Gordon was grateful to have enough people to complete the work in the scheduled period of one week, but more than that, he was happy to see so many of the people he'd cared for had remained unharmed. Adventuring was a dangerous profession, after all.

Just like in the old days, hearing the name "Pops" from them moved him to tears.

"Oh! Pops, you're crying. Old people shouldn't cry so easily!"

"I'm not cryin'! This is sweat. Quit sayin' stupid things and get to work!" After barking at the adventurers poking fun at him,

Gordon rubbed around his eyes with a hand towel that had been stuffed in his back pocket.

"Wah, what's up with this towel? My eyes hurt! It stings!"

"Mm, Dad, that's a dishcloth from Sunlight's Canopy. You must've brought it by mistake."

"Whaaat?!"

Now Gordon really was crying. Though it was from rubbing his eyes with a dishrag that smelled vaguely of onions. The gathered adventurers roared with laughter.

Soldiers provided with monster-warding potions had been dispatched from the Labyrinth Suppression Forces to guard the construction site. That was why the carpenters dared to laugh so close to the Fell Forest while they worked. Perhaps the tall walls of the temple they were building allowed the workers to speak more openly; the project progressed quite well.

The workers dried the transported trees and fashioned them into posts and planks by using carpenter skills. They left the compacted dirt, not bothering to put down flooring after removing tree roots and large stones. With carriages coming and going, there was no need for floorboards.

"Say, Pops. What kinda building is this?" One of the adventurers eyeing the blueprints raised the question after the dwarf finally stopped crying.

It was strange enough to construct something in a place as potentially dangerous as this, but the building had two entrances, and just one window on the ceiling. Moreover, the door on the Labyrinth City side was big enough to let carriages through, yet the other door facing the Fell Forest was far smaller than the door of a normal house.

It provided enough space that women and children would likely be able to squeeze through, but those of larger build, like adventurers, would find themselves stuck even if they turned sideways or crouched.

The structure of the skylight was also strange. It was a double-glazed window so huge it would take the outstretched arms of three adult men to encircle it. Glass had been inlaid in an iron lattice frame to keep monsters out, but the shape of the lattice formed a magic circle. The upper and lower parts of the window were asymmetrical with each other, and a pedestal had been installed in the lower portion of the window's grating, as if something was to be placed there. The curious construction enabled something to be put between the two window layers.

"This here's a spirit shrine."

"Spirit shrine?" The adventurer, apparently a fan of gossip, latched on to Gordon's words.

"I haven't heard the full story, either, but you know how they've started sellin' potions, right?"

"Yeah, that talk about the Aguinas family inventing a way to make them?"

"That's the one. I hear the vials they go in need to be special made, too. Seems you gotta have sand containin' somethin' with the power of the ley line, like Drops of Life."

The sale of potions had become a crucial point of interest to adventurers, as they would for any other group of people. While all those who'd rushed over to help Gordon had missed the Merchant Guild's briefings, they'd heard the gist of things from others at bars, though not without embellishment. Such was the nature of gossip.

The glass artisan Ludan told the rest of the story to the adventurers, who eagerly gathered to listen.

CHAPTER 2: The Spirit Shrine

"It's common knowledge that there're plenty of places to buy potion vials in the imperial capital. In the Labyrinth City, all we got are bottles of booze that people like you drink and chuck. Doesn't matter how many potions you make if you've got nowhere to put 'em."

"You can't put them in normal vials?"

"If you use normal vials, the potions'll turn into plain old medicinal water."

"What? Potions can go bad? What a pain in the ass."

"It's different than going bad. A famous sword needs a worthy sheath, right? It's like that."

Ludan's sword metaphor proved difficult to grasp, but the likes of an adventurer had no interest in the details of how such things worked anyway. The vague understanding that potions would go bad if not put in a specific kind of vial was enough.

"And? What do those containers have to do with this shrine?" One adventurer pressed for an answer. This time, Johan took over the conversation.

"Now, calm down. The glass for potion vials needs to have Drops of Life in it. In short, it's something alchemists have to make."

"So what you're saying is the Aguinas family's been making glass, too?"

"No."

"What? Don't lead us on." An especially short-tempered adventurer heckled Johan.

"Look, I'm trying to tell you! That's why we're building a shrine. When we do, the spirits will make the sand for us!" Johan was quick to finish his explanation to the easily angered adventurer.

"Whaaat?!"

"How?!"

"Spirits will can do that? But we can't even talk to them!"

There was a great clamor among the group. Understandably so, as the explanation was rather outrageous. Such a reaction had likely been unavoidable.

"Old books and a treasure from over two hundred years ago were discovered in the estate of Margrave Schutzenwald. We're buildin' this shrine based on those ancient tomes!"

"Whaaat?!"

"Treasure?! Aha! I get it—it's that skylight, right? Right?! You put it in that pedestal up there!" As one might've expected from an adventurer, the man quickly latched on to the word *treasure*.

"Well, they call it a treasure, but that doesn't mean it's something you'd want. It's an item with a kind of curse on it."

"Huh?! A curse?!"

"That's right. As I understand it, the curse activates during the night. So, if we leave it here, the spirits will gather after dark and use Drops of Life to try and remove the curse. If someone puts sand for potion vials under the window, the Drops of Life drawn up by the spirits to remove the curse will fall onto the sand and make it usable for potion vials." Johan explained the method of using the so-called cursed treasure with a grim expression on his face. The assembled workers listened attentively with equally serious looks.

"And? What kind of curse is it?"

"It's... Such things should not be spoken of. It's that terrifying..." Johan averted his gaze, as if in fear.

"Now I have to know. Ludan, you gotta tell us!"

"No way. Even mentioning it would bring the curse upon me," Ludan hastily turned away.

"Pops! Tell us! If you don't, I won't be able to sleep tonight!"

"Enough, youngster. If you hear it, you'll wet your bed."

"The curse is dreadful enough that Dad wet himself a bit."

"Wh…wh-wh-wh-who did?! It sure wasn't me!"

"Yeah! It wasn't 'cause of the curse; Gordon's just incontinent."

"You're wrong! I may not be as sprightly as I once was, but I'm not old enough to be doin' that yet!"

His face bright red, Gordon flew into a rage, and the adventurers were quick to disperse and return to their work.

What in the world could the curse have been? Did Gordon really wet himself over it, or was that just unrelated?

Whatever the answers were, each adventurer who'd heard the story felt the chill hand of the grave down their spines as they thought what might become of them tomorrow.

02

Thanks to the efforts of the adventurers, a spirit shrine consisting of nothing but walls and a ceiling was erected in only a week. Afterward, they planted daigis and bromominthra sparsely around the structure, allowing the monster repelling plants to grow in thick.

On the final day of the shrine construction, the Labyrinth Suppression Forces carried in the "cursed treasure" under heavy guard, while Gordon and his crew all watched.

A formation of soldiers was protecting a robed man, and behind him, two soldiers carried a chest. The trunk was adorned with a great many papers and cords—seals—that gave the object a truly dark sort of aura.

The robed man wore a hood low over his eyes, obscuring his face. Judging from his outfit, he was probably someone versed in black magic.

Only the outside part of the shrine's skylight had been set, and the inner window with the pedestal attached to the interior side had been lowered to rest in the middle of the shrine. The pedestal hung by a rope attached to its four corners, with the ends of the binding running through four pulleys attached to the ceiling and connected to a winder. If the adventurers turned the winder to pull in the rope, it would lift the window frame into place.

The mysterious shaman and his attending soldiers approached the pedestal.

When the robed man raised his hand straight overhead, the two soldiers carrying the chest containing the cursed treasure lowered it to the ground and took several steps back. Round fire baskets had been installed around the pedestal in the window frame, and the two soldiers placed firewood and dried sacred tree leaves in them. After they sprinkled faintly shimmering water along the fire baskets in a circle around the pedestal, they lit the firewood.

Perhaps the shimmering liquid was holy water that had been combined with the sacred tree leaves in the burners to create some sort of protective seal. The shaman chanted a kind of spell, and one by one, the seals on the chest began to open.

Gulp.

The onlooking adventurers held their breath in suspense. At last the seals were undone, and the lid of the trunk opened.

With a horrible buzzing sound, something sinister flooded out from the container. It was a ghastly thing that resembled a cloud of dark rust or a mass of tiny black insects. Whatever it was induced an instinctual fear in all who beheld it.

Several of the adventurers had seen such a thing before in their lives of danger.

"It's a curse... It really was cursed treasure...," someone muttered, and the shrine fell deathly silent.

Fearlessly, the black mage reached into the chest full of the ghastly black stuff and took out a glass cup so large you could wrap both arms around it.

Though one might've called it glass, it wasn't a beautiful, transparent object. The cup was a deep green, almost black. The goblet color was like a blend of dark shades of green and brown. It appeared especially dull and cloudy with the black curse issuing forth from it.

The object was wholly misshapen, like the handiwork of a child. Perhaps it had been warped from the dark power? No, maybe the source of the curse was the child who made this container in the first place.

The volatile black magic writhed from within the unstable container, causing onlookers to imagine all manner of frightful things.

"It's terrible... What kind of curse could that be...?"

The adventurers and Labyrinth Suppression Forces soldiers watched from a distance as the robed man placed the cursed cup on the pedestal and secured it with metal fixtures so it wouldn't fall over. An implement of black magic with some sort of crest engraved in the center was attached to the fixtures. A sealing tool to keep the curse from breaking loose?

After installing the cup, the shaman turned toward Gordon, who stood in wait, and the old dwarf nodded solemnly.

Two soldiers sprinkled holy water over Gordon, who then moved past the barriers, inching closer until he stood in front of the cursed treasure. The baneful magic twisting and contorting within the cup seemed like it could reach out for the old dwarf at any moment.

"Raise it."

Under Gordon's direction, they turned the winder, lifting the window frame bearing him and the cursed treasure toward the ceiling. No matter what kind of evil thing was involved, affixing a window frame was a carpenter's job. This task had been entrusted to Gordon, the leader of the group.

"Pops…"

"Pops, you can do it!"

Instinctively, the many adventurers below shouted words of encouragement.

After reaching the ceiling, Gordon shifted to the scaffolding prepared in advance and quickly began to fasten the frame in place. After this was done, he attached what looked to be more sealing paper. With this, the work was complete.

Rays of sunlight cascaded through the double window with the latticework of a magic circle, creating the shadow of a complex shape on the floor of the shrine.

The cursed treasure was now set between two window frames, and there was no doubt the two overlapping shadows had some sort of special effect, too. Gordon unfastened the ropes from the frame, tied one around his waist, and was then slowly lowered to the ground.

"It's done," he said solemnly. The robed man nodded, then quietly left the temple with his escorts.

The adventurers who'd been watching the whole scene unfold suddenly broke into cheers.

"Pops! You're really something else!"

"Ahh, I knew you could do it, Pops!"

"You installed that scary thing without even breaking a sweat!"

None among them doubted the old dwarf's courage.

The adventurers had called the strange cup "scary," but they honestly had no idea just how frightful the thing was. It was better that way, however. Just knowing it would certainly bring misfortune worse than becoming "that person who wet their pants." Curiosity could, quite literally, kill the cat in this case.

It was said the treasure's curse became active at night. All who knew of the foul object would be certain to never approach the structure after sundown. Not ever.

Talking it over, the adventurers involved in building the spirit shrine struck out for a bar in the Labyrinth City and drank the night away in celebration of the building's completion.

Several days after the shrine was completed, several wagons carrying sand from the pit were brought in. It was of good quality, but it had contained impurities unsuitable for making potion vials. As such, Ludan and other glass artisans, along with some magical researchers, had used a machine to sift out the impurities before it was taken to the shrine.

Once all the wagons had been loaded into the shrine, everything but the carts and their cargo was removed. Even the animals that had hauled the wagons were taken home. The large door on the Labyrinth City side was locked tight so that no one would enter by mistake and suffer the curse. However, the door facing the Fell Forest was left unlocked. This was the door the spirits would use.

When Ludan and the others returned to the temple the next day, the sand in the wagons was shimmering faintly, full of Drops of Life.

There was no doubt the spirits had visited to try to remove the curse, just as it was written in the old books of the house of Margrave Schutzenwald. Occasionally, there would be days when the sand remained unchanged. This quickly convinced the people involved in the transport of the material that this was the work of a fickle entity.

Folks began to believe the spirit was a woman. Someone went to the temple on a dare, and heard the voice of a girl chanting something inside. When he tried to get a look at her, a sudden fireball came flying at him, and the man was forced to run for his life.

"I bet the spirit and the curse are fighting."

Rumors ran wild, and eventually people took to leaving offerings at the shrine. Everyone in the Labyrinth City believed the story of the terrifying cursed treasure that the adventurers had witnessed during the temple's construction. Reinforced patrols were deployed by the Labyrinth Suppression Forces to make sure that no one approached the shrine at night anymore.

Ludan and the other glass artisans processed the Drops of Life–infused sand into potion vials. The sudden rise in demand for the little things created a tremendous amount of work for the glassmakers. Such demand created a great many jobs alongside the emergency call for medicinal herbs.

"I'm far too busy. It's been real rough going." Ludan whined over the new workload. Gordon and Johan grinned as they helped him.

"Even so, everything's going according to Lord Weishardt's plan."

"My performance was faaantastic, eh?"

"The props were pretty elaborate, too."

"It was worth Dad getting cursed."

"I didn't get currrsed! ...I didn't get cursed, okay?"

In truth, the "spirit shrine" was a complete fabrication.

The "cursed treasure" was nothing more than a toy made by a certain drunkard sage who found it too much of a bother to throw away alcohol bottles and irresponsibly melted them instead. This explained the unusual shape of the cup.

An entrance to the underground Aqueduct sat in the Fell Forest, just a short walk from the shrine.

Gordon and the two other dwarves weren't given the details other than that they were building a "spirit shrine." The window frames did in fact resemble a magic circle of monster warding, but iron was a metal that easily lost its shape when worked with, so the magical array was highly unlikely to have any effect. Since examining it in detail would reveal the spirit shrine itself to be a fabrication, the dwarves were told everything other than the identity of the spirit when their help was requested.

"But y'know, when this work started...?"

"That's right. We found out."

"Just one pesky little mistake was all it took."

The three realized they were quite thirsty now, and only the tea at a stylish place like Sunlight's Canopy would drive away the fatigue of making potion vials. They pondered what jokes they would tell today. Even if they weren't good jokes, that girl would beam as bright as the sun. Just visiting that warm place lifted their spirits a great deal. Doubtless all three of them were thinking about heading there now.

"I'm gonna take a little break."

"Working too hard just makes it difficult to work well, after all."

"I'm gonna stink up my usual seat so Lord Weishardt doesn't take it."

The three dwarves took a break from making vials and cheerfully made for Sunlight's Canopy.

03

In the evening, Mariela, Sieg, and Freyja traveled through the underground Aqueduct toward the Fell Forest.

This was it. Freyja had finally racked up too high of an alcohol tab, and now the three were forced to go on the lam. At least, that's how it might have gone two hundred years ago.

In the Labyrinth City of today, Mariela could sell as many potions as she could make, so her master could have as much alcohol as she liked. Apparently, the Black Iron Freight Corps had been steadily bringing in good-quality stuff from the imperial capital, so even if Mariela wanted to run away, her master probably wouldn't let her.

The group emerged from the underground Aqueduct, pushed through the Fell Forest, and arrived at the rear entrance to the spirit shrine.

"Mm, no one's here again today, but just in case, I'll go check the front door. You stay here and guard her, Sieg. Mariela, get it done quickly."

Sieg and Mariela responded with an "Okay," and began to move.

Day in and day out, Mariela started work first thing in the morning. She'd make potions, replenish the goods in the shop, and keep an eye on her master. At night she processed sand for potion vials in the spirit shrine. Even with all her duties, those most exhausted were Sherry and the other three who took some of the responsibility of looking after Freyja. Amber, who was managing Sunlight's Canopy, ended up pretty tired at the end of each day, too.

So, fired up by the idea of defeating her master, Mariela went all out with her alchemy every day, ran out of magical power, and abruptly fell flat like the "sickly heroine archetype" or whatever it was that Caroline had told her about.

Mariela's master had trained her in the art of skillfully passing out, and the young alchemist turned toward a cushion she'd prepared, collapsed gracefully into its soft embrace, and slept for about two hours. The assigned soldiers knew this meant it was nap time. It was difficult for them to picture Mariela as sickly or unfortunate.

"The lady alchemist was in good health again today."

Having received reports that said things like this, Weishardt was utterly ignorant of the harsh, intensive training. Had he known, he probably would have shouted and put a stop to it immediately. However, he was currently occupied by the task of refining the spirit shrine plan. Though it had originally been one of Freyja's ideas, her original plan was crude and half-baked. Weishardt had put in a considerable amount of effort to make it a feasible idea.

Mariela entered the spirit shrine through the small back door. It was mainly for her use, so it was a bit small for Sieg. Immediately past this doorway was a device that had been installed to supply magic to a magical tool for illumination. If you poured magical power into it, that energy would flow to all the lights inside the shrine and turn them on.

Not long after the temple had been completed, Gordon and the other dwarves heard that the "spirit" had tripped and fallen in the dark, so they hurriedly installed this mechanism for it. You could say it was a gift of affection. Incidentally, the "cursed treasure" was all a trick; it posed no threat to anyone.

Around ten wagons piled high with white sand crowded the interior of the brightened shrine. Mariela went around to each one and infused the sand with Drops of Life.

It's a pain to squeeze between the wagons. I wish I could do them all at once.

Mariela wondered if, by encasing the entire interior of this shrine in a giant Transmutation Vessel, she'd be able to take up all the sand in one go. It would be as if she had grown a lot of extra limbs, or had eyes in the back of her head. Even if she couldn't touch it with her hands, she'd be able to grab the materials that way. Afterward, she could just put in Drops of Life as usual, except she would be able to do it with all the sand at once.

"Form Transmutation Vessel, Drops of Life, Anchor..."

Mariela pictured Drops of Life spilling from a hole and loaded her skill with that image. Her alchemy skill caused that vision to materialize, and once she became aware of all the sand in the shrine, it was at once instantly charged with Drops of Life.

"I actually did it..."

So much sand in the blink of an eye. She never would have been able to do this before now.

Have I gotten better at this...?

Was this a result of frantically making potions day after day, racing with Freyja?

Was Master not drinking to play around, but to force me to make potions as best as I could...?

Mariela felt an appreciation for her teacher. Perhaps she ought to show the woman more respect and kindness from now on.

Earlier that day, Freyja had shown up where Mariela was going to clean and stood in a spot where she was completely in the way, so Mariela had chased her out.

"Master, shoo, shoo, shoo!" Mariela had said while batting her with the broom. Her master had giggled, though, so maybe it was all right. Mariela didn't really understand the actions of drunks.

When the young alchemist left the spirit shrine, only Sieg was waiting for her.

"That was quite fast."

"Yeah. I think I've gotten better. I was able to do it all at once. Let's go get Master."

Mariela and Sieg circumvented the exterior of the shrine and headed for the front gate.

That's when they saw...

*   *   *

"Mmm, this's some good booze they brought. Offering drink to beg for forgiveness after I scared them off with a fireball... Spreading rumors about that was the right choice! Oh, they brought snacks, too! So thoughtfulll...!"

It seemed Mariela's feelings of appreciation were sorely misplaced.

"Master, what are you doing?! I can't believe you'd steal offerings, even if it is a fake shrine!"

"M-Mariela?! Aren't you a little early?"

"*Thanks to you*, Master. C'mon, Sieg, let's go home. Oh, but first we should lock the door so no despicable people get in!"

"Mariela, wait for meee...!"

The rumor that the alcohol offered to the spirit shrine had vanished spread among adventurers for a little while. However, the bottles only vanished at first, and that very quickly came to a stop.

"The spirit's anger was appeased," said a relieved adventurer who'd offered some drink at the foot of the temple. Even if it had been appeased, the "spirit" who sprinkled Drops of Life in the shrine probably chased the fireball generator around with a broom again the next day.

CHAPTER 3
The Changing People and City

01

The fifty-third stratum of the Labyrinth was common training ground for the Labyrinth Suppression Forces. The floor was also a great place for hunting and gathering materials.

After a Labyrinth monster was defeated, only a portion of its corpse remained. The commonly accepted theory was that magical power solidified to generate a monster, meaning such creatures weren't fully manifested when they first appeared. As time went on, their bodies incarnated bit by bit, starting with those features that best represented the characteristics of the species in question. Monsters that boasted offensive abilities yielded fangs or claws when killed, and those that boasted high defense would produce things like hides.

Someone had once put forward the idea that monsters didn't leave the Labyrinth because they couldn't, as their bodies weren't fully manifested yet. Scholars who advocated this theory reported, "If you catch a weak monster like a goblin or orc and take it out of the Labyrinth, the same phenomenon will occur as when you defeat them within the Labyrinth: The corpse will vanish, leaving behind only the portion of their bodies that had fully materialized."

Curiously, there was a reported case of the same phenomenon occurring when monsters who couldn't normally travel between strata were forced to move to a different floor of the Labyrinth.

This led to an opposing theory that proposed that the very move-ments of monsters, even from one stratum to the next, was the will of the Labyrinth itself.

Of course, things like incarnations of monsters in the Laby-rinth or the laws of their movement didn't matter at all to Dick, who today was fighting basilisks in the fifty-third stratum. The only important thing was knowing when the subjugation period was so he could collect valuable materials like the hides of those creatures.

Among the types of skins the Labyrinth Suppression Forces could currently obtain, basilisk hides were the most useful. Their slash and impact resistance could be passed on to the magical metal armor that dwarven artisans forged with, but they were also lightweight and highly resistant to spells.

Since Sieg was the alchemist's escort, he had his pick of the items the Labyrinth Suppression Forces offered on the market for fundraising purposes. Even when many of the Forces did not have such things yet, Sieg's choice came first. Those who wore light armor and attacked from a distance, or scouts who emphasized speed and skills were waiting impatiently for their turn.

"Bring it down! Don't drop your guard for an instant! **Rising Dragon Spear!**"

"Right!"

After battling with the basilisk for a few hours, Dick delivered the final blow.

Joining him in battle today were twelve people assigned under his command from the third unit of the Labyrinth Sup-pression Forces. The Forces were composed of units numbering one through eight, excluding Leonhardt's and Weishardt's per-sonal guards, as well as detachments with special tasks such as intelligence gathering. Each unit was divided in order of strength into a main force and a backup force. Below both of those was a training unit, but soldiers in that group were treated more as trainees; they weren't assigned to any unit proper.

When facing a powerful monster, numbers didn't necessarily equal power. Of course, there were large differences in strength between individual people, so numbers and fighting strength weren't proportional. However, in order to defeat a monster that was far larger than humans and superior to them in terms of strength, it was required to understand that creature's weaknesses and work together while leveraging the skills of each individual.

Even if they belonged to the same unit, there was a gap in fighting power between a backup force and a main force, and they didn't fight on the front lines together. In times of peace, the groups battled in hunting grounds corresponding to their respective levels. Casualties made the replenishment speed high, however, so the organization was divided vertically in order of strength to facilitate cooperation. If a soldier was promoted to the main force, they could fight together with those who were formerly their seniors.

When Dick returned to the Forces, he was assigned as captain of the third unit. He succeeded a former superior of his who wanted to retire from the frontline work, and a young spear user who admired him was assigned as lieutenant of the same squad. This made adapting to the new position very easy for Dick.

Did everyone in the squad admire Dick's discerning eye, the same one that had seen the true nature of the mermaids' fake breasts? The sharp rise in frequency of parties among members of the third unit ever since he'd assumed his position may have helped him earn that respect as well. The unit had the most reckless soldiers of all the Labyrinth Suppression Forces, and talking things over with them while having a few drinks proved effective.

Amber was energetically managing Sunlight's Canopy again today. Although the shop had acquired a troublesome master, and Mariela was frequently absent these days, Amber continued to put her best effort into her work. She kept saying it didn't matter whether her husband came home, as long as he was safe. If her husband was happy, so was she. Amber did her best not to believe that the reason Dick now went to so many drinking parties was because she'd said she didn't mind them. The two newlyweds had suffered many hardships to be together, and Amber didn't think her husband would do something like that.

Burdened with this go-with-the-flow situation, the third unit magnificently slew the basilisk and the victory brought Dick and the others some prized basilisk hides, magical gems, and ley-line shards, as well as the satisfaction of a job well done. These types of items were usually dropped by the basilisks of this stratum. Longer-lived ones also yielded fangs and claws in addition to hides, as well as larger magical gems, though not ley-line shards.

A great deal of time was spent subjugating the fifty-third stratum's King of Cursed Serpents, but it proved to be well worth it. By tracking the time between when a basilisk was generated and when it was defeated, the Forces could control the materials that dropped with almost perfect accuracy.

"Shall we get that one next?"

After a short break, Dick set his sights on another basilisk the soldiers had found. If they temporarily went back to the stratum stairs, the scout unit could recommend a specific target, but Dick's unit had already found one close by. Going all the way back was a bother, so this would be fine.

"Rising Drago-"

(That one's only just appeared, you know.)

A familiar voice echoed in Dick's head, just as he was about to launch his first long-range attack.

"Malraux..."

"In any case, I imagine you chose not to go back to the stairs because it was too much trouble. Think about why we were given soldier slaves for routine duties."

Dick halted his attack, and Malraux appeared beside him along with his orderly and soldier slave.

Malraux, who had returned to the Forces along with Dick, had been assigned as the lieutenant of the intelligence unit. The intelligence and scout units reported directly to Weishardt, and because of the circumstances of their work, the personnel and organizational structure of those units were not made public. That was probably why Malraux was assigned a front-facing job within the intelligence unit; he wasn't readily recognized. He was once a commanding officer in the same unit as Dick, and he possessed both combat ability and telepathic skills at the upper end of the B Rank. He, too, was once again busy day after day in both the Labyrinth and the City. The recent progression of subjugation had made it desirable for the intelligence unit to venture into the Labyrinth.

"Long time, no see. Scouting the red dragon? What's that thing up to?"

"'Long time, no see' is a fine thing to say. I do believe just yesterday you were drunk and sleeping on the road near your house. Who was it that brought you home? If a yagu inadvertently stepped on you, it would suffer an injury, wouldn't it? That's property damage. The red dragon is the same as it ever was. Just like you; for better or for worse." Dick had spoken as if regarding an old friend, yet Malraux's response was anything but.

"Oof... I thought I was sleeping in the entry hall this morning, but..."

He had no memory of what happened that night. Dick's expression told Malraux that much. He'd taken up residence in a spot near Malraux's house so the two wives could help each other, and so Amber wouldn't be as troubled during her husband's absence. Apparently, the only one who'd actually been helped by the arrangement was a drunk Dick, however.

And yesterday, Malraux had discovered Dick sleeping in an alley near his house and brought him home. Although Amber had opened the door and brought him inside despite the late hour, she'd still left him in the entry hall.

"That's just like you. Your orderly escorted you to the main road, yet you said 'Here is fine,' and parted with him on a side road because you didn't want Amber to see. Honestly. Ms. Amber was quite angry last night, you know."

Malraux spoke as if he saw the whole thing, and Dick's orderly nodded in agreement. Dick brooded about it for a bit, then said, "It's fine, she still made a boxed lunch for me today," as if trying to convince even himself.

"What is in your boxed lunch?"

"...Bread."

"Just bread?"

"Yeah."

"...She's angry."

"...You think so...?"

Since Amber had immediately come to the door when Malraux took Dick home, she'd probably been worried about her husband and had been waiting up all night for him. She had no idea he was sleeping in the street in a drunken stupor just a stone's throw from their house. Anyone would've been angry. She was probably going on a tirade about it to Freyja or Merle at Sunlight's Canopy right now.

Behind the facade of their absurd conversation, the pair's telepathic communication continued.

(*At any rate, Dick, that is your issue. Considering what happened with Lynx and the slave Jay, you probably find it difficult to give orders to the soldier slaves tasked with routine duties, yes?*)

The main force's captain and lieutenant each had one soldier slave for common tasks, as well as one orderly. The orderlies were from the backup forces, and although they were C Rank at best, they were chosen as assistants for their keen minds. The soldier slaves would carry baggage and handle odd jobs. Despite being assigned as slaves for menial errands, they accompanied their masters to the front lines, so many of them were C Rank or above and very well behaved. Each of them had their own circumstances—shouldering the massive debts of another; opposing a noble and being framed with a crime—but many among the ranks were good people at heart.

Since these types of slaves served under high-ranking individuals, they were the best workers among the penal laborers and lifelong slaves sent to the Labyrinth City, and they were treated comparatively well. They went into the Labyrinth, which was teeming with monsters, but, like Sieg, they were permitted to carry weapons, and even wear armor. Such slaves were also permitted to bring basic necessities, and provided with private rooms and salaries equivalent to an allowance. However, they were still penal laborers, the same as Jay.

(...*If they were forced to go alone and came across a basilisk, they might not make it*), Dick thought back. Malraux, with a bit of silent self-deprecating laughter, thought it a very fitting answer for the man.

The likes of penal laborers were shown no mercy. They should have clearly been treated as criminals. Malraux wondered if he was the only one swayed by such thoughts.

Dick's orderly suddenly spoke up, "Next time, I'll see you to your front door. Please let me keep watch from a distance to make sure you're let in. Rest assured I won't let your wife see me!" Then his soldier slave said, "I'll go ask for the location of the next basilisk right away!" and was just about to start running when another soldier stopped him.

This slave was still young, with a freckled face. Although he was too naive to truly resemble Lynx, the way he seemed impatient to demonstrate his worth to Dick somehow reminded Malraux of the former smiley-eyed comrade back when he'd first come to the Black Iron Freight Corps.

The assembled members of the Forces and their attendants seemed to be enjoying the story of Dick sleeping in the street. Their eyes were lit with energy. Mages and sword users may have had different roles, but they still battled side by side. Likewise, everyone assembled in the stratum had been given different tasks, but it was important for them to work together regardless of positions. Fully aware of that, Dick treated even the soldier slaves similarly to how he would treat his own subordinates.

(*You can treat the slaves as subordinates despite what happened?*)

(*Well y'know, everyone's different.*)

Malraux turned to look at his own slave. He was a large,

muscular B-Rank man who'd been assigned to be his master's shield if push came to shove. Indeed, this soldier slave with a criminal's antipathy had learned to remain silent in Malraux's cold presence, and diligently obeyed his commands.

"Dick, if you travel along the right side of the wall over there, you'll find a particularly ripe basilisk. Rhet, Taros, let's go," Malraux said and took his leave. His orderly, Rhet, answered "Yes, sir." The soldier slave Taros, whose name Malraux had called for the first time, showed slight surprise on his face, then nodded silently and followed.

(The red dragon may be the same, but the City has a slight stink to it. Dick, it would be prudent to drink in moderation.)

(Got it. You be careful, too.)

That was the end of their telepathic conversation. Malraux had probably approached Dick just to give him that warning. Dick mentally thanked his friend, musing that some truly never did change.

"Let's head right. We're gonna take down another one!"

"I'll scout ahead!"

"Make yourself scarce. Be sure not to get caught."

"Yes, sir! Leave it to me!"

Dick and the others proceeded through the Labyrinth as they watched the restless soldier slave run ahead of the third unit.

02

"A slave doesn't get to walk in the middle of the road!"

Mariela's body stiffened in shock at the sudden shouting. She'd left the shop in Amber's hands and left her master in the hands of Sherry and the others. The young alchemist was with Merle, and the two were on their way back from shopping for dinner. At a glance, the pair looked like an older woman and her daughter—easy targets—but since soldiers in civilian clothes were protecting the area, Mariela was in no real danger, even if a hoodlum adventurer caused a fuss.

"Good grief, I suppose there are more groups like this around here lately. How awful."

Merle had just been next to Mariela and chatting enthusiastically about bargain products at the wholesale market, but before Mariela knew what was happening, Merle had stepped in front of her. The older woman was both tall and wide, so Mariela was completely hidden behind her and couldn't see what was going on at all.

"There's nothing you'd want to see anyway. Now, let's hurry home and start getting dinner ready!"

Merle gripped Mariela's shoulder and pulled her into an about-face. It was a surprisingly fast spin. If Mariela hadn't been able to hear the unsettling shouts, she would have thought it was fun and asked for an encore: "Once more! Seconds! One more time!"

New people emigrating from the imperial capital because of the monster-warding potions was a good thing, but the City felt a little less safe. Around the time Mariela's master had arrived, Carol had apparently grown rather busy and stopped visiting Sunlight's Canopy. As a young lady of the Aguinas family, Carol had been accompanied by escorts since she was small, so she was probably in no danger. Even so, Mariela grew a little worried every time an incident like this occurred.

She understood from the loud voice that demanded her attention, that someone had picked a fight with a slave and was beating them. Apparently, it was all just because the slave had been walking in the middle of the road.

"Merle, we should call a guard..."

Mariela understood her own weakness, and she also understood that poking her nose where it didn't belong out of curiosity caused trouble for the people around her. What happened with Lynx had taught her that lesson to a hundred times over. Even so, Mariela was reluctant to run away without doing anything when someone who had committed no crime was suffering.

Merle cracked a smile at Mariela and said, "It's fine, I'm already contacting someone. Let's slip away now," then lightly pushed on her back.

Merle's words were a comfort to Mariela. They were about to leave when they heard a somewhat philosophical remark.

"A road is open for anyone to walk on."

"What's your problem, asshole? You gonna fight me with that weak little thing? You wanna play make-believe sword fight with an umbrella?"

"Oh, this's gotten interesting. Ela, let's sneak just a little look from back there."

The plan to escape had flown out the window. Merle pushed Mariela behind a stall and began to watch the ruckus through a gap.

"Is that…Grandel?!"

What Mariela and Merle saw from their spot behind the stall was Grandel, shield knight of the Black Iron Freight Corps, with the slave Newie following close behind. They had probably returned to the Labyrinth City after finishing their delivery. Several large baguettes protruded from the bundle Newie carried, so the pair may have been on their way home from shopping as well. Newie tried to hide behind the knight as he peeked out in a fluster, but Grandel had a slim figure like a young tree, so the slave was completely visible.

He could have hidden just fine if Grandel were as wide as Merle!

Mariela entertained the rude thought quietly to herself. Even though she'd once been called "Chubby-ela," it seemed she only thought about the present.

The slim gentleman, Grandel, with his suit that swished like a tailcoat, silk hat, thin and tightly wrapped umbrella, said to the hoodlum adventurer, "It seems you have lost your way," as he stroked his handlebar mustache.

Behind him, Newie was wearing a determined expression, despite his trembling, and in fact, he seemed ready to hoist Grandel on his shoulder and get out of there if anything happened. Maybe he was trembling with excitement? Newie had once been a fine thug himself, so he couldn't have been nervous about facing a hoodlum adventurer. At least, probably.

Believing the seemingly amusing duo to be easy opponents, the hoodlum exchanged looks with his four cohorts, left the slave he'd been kicking, and motioned for his group to encircle the upstart with the mustache.

"Sure have. We're lost and we got no money. And after we came all the way from the capital, too. So, give us all the money you got on you, old man!"

"Hrm, considering you involved an unarmed slave who did nothing wrong, I imagine you wanted to cause trouble and cheat his master out of some coin. If you think that sort of trick will go unnoticed in this city, your intellect is sorely lacking."

Without even trying to conceal his condescension, Grandel raised both hands to shoulder level and spread them in a W shape. Then he lightly lifted one leg and bent it to make a cross shape with the other, a pose that strongly implied a sense of looking down on someone.

The meaning was easy enough for anyone to grasp; even a fool could understand that Grandel was treating the ruffian like a moron.

"Y-y-y-you shon of a bitch!!!"

"Sheems like you have a shlight problem there, shonny?" Pushing further, Grandel needled at the hoodlum's error.

He never cracked a smile, even though the adventurer had tripped over his own tongue so badly one might have thought he was drunk. Grandel seemed to possess both a malicious nature unbecoming of his gentlemanly exterior, as well as quite the way with words.

"I didn't botch it up that muuuch!!!"

As one might have expected of such a man, the adventurer quickly flew into a rage and lashed out at Grandel. However...

"Heave-ho."

As if to say, "Here, borrow my umbrella," Grandel stuck out the hand holding the thing and sent the hoodlum adventurer flying in the opposite direction.

"H-how'd you do that?!"

The toppled adventurer's buddies were men of equally ill character, and after the conventional one-liner, they let out a rallying cry, drew their weapons, and stabbed at the gentleman who'd dared to rebuff their friend's attack.

Mariela was about to shout for Grandel to watch out, but with a wink Merle gently covered her mouth.

"He's not in danger, Ela. Pretty easy to see where this is headed. Even the world of ruffians has a rulebook."

What kind of rulebook? A how-to manual with easy ways to pick fights, the correct way to speak like a hoodlum, and how to make an escape without attracting attention? These hardly seemed the type to subscribe to such business publications.

Before Merle could finish explaining, Grandel undid the latch on his umbrella and opened it.

"Shield Bash."

Was that kind of thing possible? Mariela's eyes opened so wide they were near perfect circles.

When mustachioed man opened his umbrella and lightly pushed it forward, the adventurers were all blown away as if they'd been shoved by a great tempest.

"Gaaah!"

They uttered cliché screams as they fell to the ground, twitching, and then stopped moving altogether. Conveniently, they seemed to have passed out.

"No way... The Umbrella Shield Bash..."

Umbrella Shield Bash. It was a legendary special move that children longed to learn. Which meant the technique used to bring down the initial hoodlum adventurer had to have been with an umbrella sword that only a legendary hero could use. Though in the future stories about this event, it would be hard to discount the idea that it had actually been a fake umbrella sword possessed by a wandering swordsman.

"Wow, that wash incredible, Grandel!"

Even Mariela was so excited that she slurred her words. She jumped out from behind Merle and the stall and ran toward him, while Merle simply watched her warmly, content that the danger had passed.

"Grandel! That wash incredible!"

Children, feeling much the same as Mariela, came forward, surrounding the man, while the alchemist herself gazed up at the "Heroic Grandel" with great enthusiasm.

"Hoh-hoh. Oh, Mariela, it wash, washn't it?" Grandel answered, smiling.

Even if you have shield skills, their strength is bound proportionally to the shield's defensive power. A shield knight's skills also affect the equipment they wear, so all those who serve as part of a vanguard and endure heavy blows wear heavy metal armor and use shields with high defensive power.

Even if the umbrella were made of cloth woven from monster thread, at the end of the day, it was still cloth. Unlike metal or other sturdier materials, it had low physical defensive power because it easily succumbed to the cuts of weapons. Even a special umbrella was still made with a piece of fabric pulled taut. You could say it was durable all you wanted, but at most it might guard against a thrown rock. Using it as a shield to repel physical attacks from adventurers wasn't something an ordinary shield knight could do. That's why it wasn't strange in and of itself for Mariela and the children to gaze at Grandel with such reverence.

"Now wait a minute, aren't you a bit old to be spouting 'Umbrella Shield Bash' and baby talk?"

Merle interrupted as the only one who'd kept her calm, and Grandel finally returned to his senses. Tugging at his mustache in slight embarrassment, he laughed with a "Hoh-hoh" and a wink in response.

Shield gentleman Grandel. In spite of his incredibly high-ranking shield skill, he was born with a frail gastrointestinal tract; meat and fat didn't agree with him. This had left his muscles weak as a result. The giant shields that other shield knights used, not to mention their heavy armor, were too weighty for him. If he ever donned such things, he wouldn't be able to move. To compensate, his shield and armor had wheels and were pulled by raptors.

The armored carriages guarded by Grandel's shield skill had long protected the Black Iron Freight Corps from being pursued by monsters. It was, of course, impossible to use a carriage to perform a bash attack on monsters, but Shield Bash wasn't Grandel's only technique. The last carriage in the caravan—the one that was the most susceptible to monster attacks—was kept safe by Grandel's defensive skills. So long as he rode along with it, the carriage would be as sturdy as thick cast metal.

You could say working for the Black Iron Freight Corps, a company that traveled through the Fell Forest in armored carriages, was Grandel's calling.

He was a man who had found his niche.

The troupe of "legendary heroes" who kept the peace in the City triumphantly headed back toward Sunlight's Canopy. Comprising its members were Grandel, who wielded the holy shield umbrella, Newie the former thief, Merle the spice shop merchant, and Mariela the chemist.

It was a party of fabled adventurers. It wouldn't have been strange to find an alchemist among them in the old days, but it was best that Mariela called herself a chemist for caution's sake.

This party is a bit lacking in firepower, though.

Had they desired such a thing, they needed to look no further than Mariela's master. She always had plenty of that, regardless of the time or place. Mariela wanted to tell her that bigger wasn't better when it came to cooking fires, though. A swordsman or warrior would've been better choices. Sieg was out hunting, and if he wasn't at Sunlight's Canopy then the only other strong person was...

I wonder if Dr. Nierenberg would join us...

Her master definitely would, but having Nierenberg was probably asking too much. Just imagining his frigid gaze made Mariela feel like someone was looking right through her.

I wonder if there's a spare swordsman around somewhere.

Still playing her game of make-believe heroes, Mariela headed for Sunlight's Canopy.

The party of conquering adventurers was in need of more members. The usual way to gain them was to ask around in a tavern. Sunlight's Canopy wasn't exactly one of those, but Mariela's master got dead drunk there day after day, so it wasn't much different, either. You could also drink tea there, so the young alchemist figured the disparity was negligible.

Thus Mariela invited Grandel, "Would you like to have some tea at Sunlight's Canopy?" and with his acceptance, the heroes' triumphant return became official.

"This is Sunlight's Canopy."

When Mariela opened the door, she found...

"My eyes have been opened to true love! I want to convey the feelings burning in my heart! Beautiful lady, please tell me your name!!!"

"Ah-ha-ha, Fryer?"

"Fire! Is that a name?!"

"Nooo. Fryer!"

"Fire!"

"Fryer!"

The wanderer of love, Edgan, had *fallen* in love with the drunken Freyja.

He seemed to have cracked. Edgan hadn't just fallen in love. He'd tumbled all the way to the infinite depths of hell. He'd utterly lost his way in life and might never recover.

Although Mariela's master kept saying, "Fryer! Fryer!" nothing caught fire, so she seemed to still have some sense left. However, the master's good mood left her student with a feeling of unease.

From the back of the shop, Dr. Nierenberg shot Edgan a look colder than the Ahriman Springs in winter or the ice and snow stratum. The lovestruck man, however, had overcome both places in the past, and the glare seemed to have little effect on him. Maybe Sieg should have chosen his friends a little more carefully. But then, Sieg only had people like Lynx and Edgan to call friends. After Lynx's death, Sieg was given no alternative but to hunt alone in the Fell Forest or the Labyrinth every day, leaving him no time to make new friends.

If the mage joined us, the swordsman would probably come with her, but... We don't need that kind of trouble.

Mariela suddenly came to her senses. Ignoring the inebriated Freyja and Edgan, she served tea to Grandel and the others, then began preparations for dinner.

03

"This time it was just an idiot, but a lot of those types have been making their way to the City."

Merle of Merle's Spices had come to see Weishardt under the guise of a foreign merchant with tea and utensils imported from the imperial capital by the Black Iron Freight Corps. She dealt in more than just tea-related items. Merle was an intelligence operative. What she truly traded in was information.

"I see. Something to do with a noble family from the outside?"

"Maybe. We've also seen the occasional merchant keen on their own interests. It's generally what we expected. Even so, haven't the nobles been unusually cooperative? Even though the value of their assets has crashed due to the potion sales."

"The consequences of the Aguinas incident have been *cleaned up* in the City. And I've promised sufficient *compensation* to the remaining groups."

"Are you okay with that? I overheard a bit, but that promise... Hasn't the *Lady* Sage made a fuss about it?"

"It was the Lady Sage's suggestion." Weishardt provided an answer to Merle's doubts.

She was an outstanding intelligence operative, but while she knew the Labyrinth City inside and out, Merle also had a compassionate side to her, particularly where Mariela was concerned. She was well educated on the cruelty of humans, perhaps that's why she liked the naive girl better than her job.

"...In that case, I guess it's fine. Still, hearing it was that *Lady Sage's* suggestion makes me uneasy. Apart from that, the problem at hand is the groups coming in from outside the City."

The Labyrinth City was the territory of Margrave Schutzenwald's family, but they weren't the only nobles that had taken up residence there. Many noble families with official positions in the Labyrinth City had lived there for generations.

The family of Margrave Schutzenwald and the other noble families living in the City were all retainers of the Empire. However, the Empire itself had to maintain appearances as an unfaltering nation in order to stand against not only the Fell Forest, but neighboring countries as well. There were the nations of demi-humans and races prone to violence, the constantly warring family of small nations, and religious states to contend with. Therefore, the margraves entrusted with defending the borders between the Empire and these zones of conflict had been given a lot of discretionary power and autonomy within the scope of fulfilling that duty.

The noble families in the Labyrinth City were like retainers to the house of Margrave Schutzenwald.

Many of them had once served the Kingdom of Endalsia and worked tirelessly after the Stampede to restore their home city rather than abandon it. Even after the Labyrinth City became a territory of the Empire, their services were valued highly, and the noble families were given ranks in court. They were also granted small- to medium-size territories around the Fell Forest.

The lands around the Labyrinth City they once owned had been stolen by the monsters and engulfed by the forests, making them unable to reclaim. That's why the noble families were given new territories, but those new sections of land were still set close to the woods. This was said to be synonymous with guarding the Fell Forest, and it was difficult to respond to goblin and orc attacks during the harvest season in the small territories.

The reasonable solution probably would have been to cooperate and seek the protection of the strong in order to survive. However, even if they cooperated, almost no profit would remain after deducting the cost of protecting the territories from the taxes received from those endangered people. Even with the slight annual salary provided by the Empire, the noble families couldn't make decent livings for themselves. So, after two hundred years, the house of Margrave Schutzenwald had been entrusted with managing the region, from deploying governors, to furnishing and paying taxes on technology related to production, to many other areas. Most of the nobility was employed in official positions in the Schutzenwald family's lands or the Labyrinth City. They made a living from pensions or salaries and investment profits from the territories entrusted to them.

Like so many others, even the house of Margrave Schutzenwald needed assistance in manpower. So, the margrave elected to balance the cooperative noble families seeking official positions in terms of abilities and pedigree. They also used the Labyrinth Suppression Forces and the City Defense Squad for different purposes and aimed to treat them accordingly.

Even so, there were many who clung to reckless ambitions of self-importance disproportionate to their abilities. Such members of the nobility who were unwilling to compromise were purged as a consequence of the Aguinas family scandal and were now on "sick leave."

Unless they had been appointed to high-ranking positions within the Labyrinth Suppression Forces, the remaining respectable aristocratic families felt anxious about the decline in value of their assets caused by potion sales, as well as the dizzying rate at which change was coming to their City. It was perfectly reasonable that they'd harbor feelings of anger toward the house of Margrave Schutzenwald. However, due to a "certain promise," the house of Margrave Schutzenwald had presented a cooperative system to be used until the Labyrinth was defeated.

This meant that the gentry who didn't live in the Labyrinth City and held territory around the Fell Forest were more likely to be the ones to cause a problem. Many of them were wealthy, had medium-size or larger plots of land, possessed resources and yagu merchant caravan encampments within their acreages, and were only able to manage their own domains. That included matters of defense.

Claiming that they were equal retainers under the emperor and not servants of the margrave, these nobles who resided outside the City had a standardized system of cooperation to defend themselves, but they didn't hold official positions under the house of Margrave Schutzenwald.

Though prideful to the point of being a nuisance, their behavior wasn't from a sense of loyalty to the emperor, as they claimed. It was merely the result of weighing profit and loss. The fact the tax rate in their territories was, without exception, higher than that of Margrave Schutzenwald's family's territory explained it all.

As nobles and as retainers of the emperor, it would be far better to lower taxes to an equal rate with Margrave Schutzenwald's family's so the common folk could live adequate lives. Their assistance as soldiers helping to subjugate the Labyrinth and defend the area around the Fell Forest and the imperial capital would be invaluable as well.

Unfortunately, these nobles prioritized their own interests. They were bound to act after potions began to appear for sale in the Labyrinth City. So long as there were no problems with distribution channels, the Labyrinth would yield a great deal of wealth, both directly and indirectly.

Who could know what these outside nobles were they thinking, and how they would act? In these times of great change for the Labyrinth City, Weishardt was compelled to take difficult measures.

04

I will spend sleepless nights praying for your safety.

The letter was from Malraux's legal wife, who lived on an estate in the imperial capital. "A barefaced lie," Malraux spit. He tore the paper and threw it away.

The man who lived as simply "Malraux" without giving his last name was the third son of a low-class noble who held terrain at the border of the imperial capital and the Fell Forest. Since the territory was so small, there was nothing for a third son to inherit. Relying on the telepathy skill he'd had since birth, Malraux volunteered for the Labyrinth Suppression Forces and ascended the ranks all the way to a commanding officer at a young age.

It was around that time when the family of Countess Beratte brought negotiations for marriage to his parents' home.

Considering the court rank and lineage of Malraux's parents—descendants from the Kingdom of Endalsia—it was unbelievable that an old family of the Empire, one of good pedigree, and a countess's family to boot, would want him. Apparently, his appointment as a commanding officer in the Labyrinth Suppression Forces at a young age was what made this proposal possible. The family he would marry into had a yagu merchant caravan encampment in their territory, and these convoys traveled between the Labyrinth City and the imperial capital. Malraux's territory would get food, iron, and a variety of goods from the imperial capital and the Labyrinth City via the encampment. It was a proposal he couldn't refuse, even if there was someone Malraux had promised his future to.

Apparently, the family of Countess Beratte had investigated Malraux before making the marriage proposal. They had even offered him the option of having a lover and children, provided they didn't leave the Labyrinth City.

"Let's escape to a foreign country together."

That was what Malraux had declared as he took his beloved's hand, but it was she who broached the subject of parting ways and encouraged him to accept the Beratte family's marriage proposal.

Malraux didn't know until much later that a life was already growing inside the woman he loved and she wasn't in a position to flee anywhere.

Malraux's beloved, who had no social position, prestige, nor even property, believed he would be happy marrying into

Countess Beratte's family, who could provide all of those things for him.

It seemed rather suspect—why would a countess want a husband who'd become a commanding officer through his own abilities but had a low social position?

Although Malraux's beloved had doubts about someone who would offer the option of having a lover, she desired his happiness from the bottom of her heart, so perhaps she couldn't help believing that the other woman must've had those same feelings.

Malraux resigned from the Labyrinth Suppression Forces and moved into the home of Countess Beratte, where he was welcomed by his new wife, the head of the family, and a steward companionably standing by her side. Malraux immediately recognized that the steward's black hair was dyed. The chamberlain's true hair and eye color were similar to Malraux's own blond hair and blue eyes, though perhaps a bit more vivid. This attendant with suspiciously similar features made Malraux understand the reason for this marriage.

The steward was a commoner, and no matter how much he achieved or how much the two loved each other, he couldn't be the countess's husband.

So, which one of us truly has the lover in this situation, I wonder?

Just as Malraux feared, his token wife gave birth to a child who bore almost no resemblance to him save hair and eye color. The noblewoman and her attendant grew even closer, and Malraux's weak position as a man who'd married into his wife's family had gone nowhere.

Could anyone blame him for longing for his former lover?

They hadn't parted on bad terms, and not a day had gone by when Malraux didn't think of her.

His former lover, now having a hard time raising their daughter, had been the one to hire an A-Rank adventurer. She was waiting for Malraux when he arrived in the Labyrinth City.

Malraux's little girl had his exact blond hair and blue eyes. Unlike the shining golden hair of the son of Countess Beratte, her hair was a dull yellow with gentle waves.

"She has an odd habit of tightly curling her toes while she's sleeping, just like you."

At those words, Malraux said, "Please let me take care of your expenses," but she refused.

"I'm grateful for the offer, but we don't need *that person's* money."

And so, to earn money of his own...

Malraux started up the Black Iron Freight Corps and called on Dick, who just happened to need a large sum of money for Amber right around that same time; Edgan, who was searching for work outside the Labyrinth Suppression Forces; Donnino; and Grandel.

Malraux was the one who'd started the transportation group, but Dick was made captain as a preventative measure so that the Countess Beratte and her family could not exert their influence over the trade company.

Although the house of the countess showed some disapproval at Malraux's decision, they allowed him to remain in the Black Iron Freight Corps. In part because of the intervention of the house of Margrave Schutzenwald, who had a far higher social position, the only stipulation was that Malraux had to make an appearance at his secondary residence in the imperial capital once a month.

His wife had said shameless, flowery things like "It's a problem for a husband of the Beratte family not to be in the imperial capital for a single day a month," and "I'm worried about you, so I want to see you." However, Malraux was confident it was just an excuse for when she had a second child with the steward. She probably would have considered it quite convenient if her legal husband died during one of his many back-and-forth trips through the Fell Forest.

Whatever his wife expected, Malraux and the Black Iron Freight Corpse managed to pass through the forest with their lives intact. Despite it creating more difficulties, he came forward as the father of his former love's daughter, and he was permitted to live with them in the Labyrinth City for short periods.

Malraux assumed his reinstatement to the Labyrinth Suppression Forces was thanks to the strong support of Margrave Schutzenwald's family, who paid the countess a large sum of money as "remuneration."

While Malraux was away from the estate developing his new trade corporation, the family of Countess Beratte heard the business the steward was involved in had failed and their cash flow had deteriorated.

The countess had asked Malraux for money several times since the founding of the Black Iron Freight Corps, and he'd paid it on the condition that the steward's business would be reexamined, but this never came to be. The lover's business continued to accumulate debt. The Black Iron Freight Corps was doing well, and if Dick hadn't been made the captain, no doubt it would have long since been snatched up by the steward.

Malraux had planned this latest "remuneration" with Weishardt, who was familiar with the situation. As a condition, after Malraux's reinstatement to the Labyrinth Suppression Forces, a magical contract was formed stating he couldn't return to the Beratte household until he was relieved of his duties because of the secrecy involved in his occupation. While he was in the Labyrinth City, he would have no connection at all to the business of Countess Beratte's house, and he made a vow through the judicial branch of the imperial capital that he would be excluded from all interests, including debt. As this contract was functionally similar to a divorce, a proper divorce was also offered, but Countess Beratte refused to agree to it.

"Even when we're apart, I still love him."

When he heard she'd stated such a thing with a cold smile on her face, Malraux felt a chill run down his spine wondering what she was planning this late in the game.

In the course of all this, he'd received correspondence from Countess Beratte in the imperial capital.

She likely expected this to be inspected when she sent it, but what in the world is its purpose...?

A lot of people from the imperial capital were gathering in the Labyrinth City, and there had already been some fights here and there. Even members of the intelligence unit who dealt with the public were being asked to gather information.

Malraux looked up at the summer sky and saw a gathering of thick clouds. The humidity and heat only served to further agitate him.

It would be nice if some blue sky could at least make an appearance.

Malraux breathed a deep sigh at the obstructed view.

05

"Form Transmutation Vessel, Rapid Rotation."

Mariela rotated a disk-shaped Transmutation Vessel at high speed in the temporary atelier in the base of the Labyrinth Suppression Forces.

As for her master, she was partying as she had been every day, lounging on a soft and fluffy couch while four soldiers, ranging from a cute type to an intellectual, glasses-wearing type, waited on her. Daily imports of furniture and fur rugs were helping to transform the dreary cellar into a far more pleasant space. Though that was, of course, only in the party corner.

The area around Mariela remained dreary, and the soldiers who brought in bags of medicinal herbs and carried out barrels full of potion looked like they were doing disciplinary work.

Such a difference in working conditions despite being in the same room. Was this place split into some sort of heaven and hell?

Had Mariela, unable to keep her master's drinking in check no matter how hard she tried, finally gone off the rails? She kept muttering to herself as she made the Transmutation Vessel spin, and no one was quite sure why.

"Tune Temperature, then from above, Clean Water."

She dribbled water into the center of the rotating disk. It slid along the plate, then scattered and flew out toward the outer circumference from to the centrifugal force. The surrounding temperature had been lowered, so the fine drops of water froze and became tiny beads of ice.

"Mmm, it's easy to control, and I can make a lot, but the water droplets are a little big…"

The lunamagia extraction had become the bottleneck for making high-grade potions with alchemy skills alone. The solid solution dissolved very slowly in frozen water, meaning Mariela needed to find some way to make minute water droplets.

She had hit upon the idea for this method after watching drops of water scatter when Grandel spun his umbrella, and she did not wait to implement it into her own work.

"It shouldn't be impossible to make them like this, but it feels wrong somehow."

Mariela believed it possible to use this method to make even high-grade potions. Though they'd end up a little diluted, she would still be making high-grade potions using only alchemical skills.

However, there was something important she hadn't yet understood, or at least that was the feeling she had.

"Mm, either way, I've gotta think a little more about how to make a nozzle."

Reconsidering, Mariela took out the nozzle she was accustomed to using. She made high-grade potions one at a time until she'd drained her magical power and then promptly plunged into nap time, exhausted.

"I'm done for todaaay."

Mariela collapsed with a soft thud as her master, who'd appeared at her side unnoticed, caught her.

"Good job, Mariela. It won't be too much longer now until you crack it."

Mariela, unconscious after depleting her magical energy, couldn't hear her master's words of appreciation. Freyja gently lifted her student up in her arms and laid her down on the soft, fluffy couch.

All the soldiers who'd been serving her in the party corner stood and lined up near the door, and two of the soldiers who'd been helping Mariela stood waiting near the couch.

Freyja laid Mariela's hands on her stomach so that the right one was on top. Then, while chanting something, she softly touched the rainbow-colored ring on the middle finger of Mariela's right hand.

With a whoosh, a flame about the size of one's palm rose from the ring as if something were being drawn out.

It was the salamander who'd given Mariela the band.

The flame instantly took the form of a small lizard, and it alternated between looking at the woman who had called it and at Mariela when Freyja pointed to her.

Freyja brought her hand close to the salamander's nose. A bluish-white fire sprang up from her fingertips, about the size of a match flame, and the salamander eagerly swallowed it. Instantly, its entire body shook, and a bluish-white blaze burst forth from the creature. After the blaze died down, the salamander became a petite, red lizard and curled up on top of Mariela's hand.

"Keep an eye on her for a little while."

"Ma'am."

The two backup soldiers sitting on chairs complied with Freyja's instructions, and she left the room accompanied by her four hosts…or rather, her four soldiers, as if it were the most natural thing in the world.

After Mariela passed out each day, her master would always summon this small spirit and then leave the room, so the guards got used to seeing the salamander. They had been quite astonished the first time they saw it, but now it just seemed like a charming little pet to them.

The body of a spirit of flames is a flame itself, and to the guardsmen it seemed impossible for something like that to be able to lie down on someone's hand. However, it appeared no different from an ordinary lizard, save for its slight transparency. So long as you didn't look at it too closely, nothing was unusual.

While the other soldiers are busy cramming boxes with completed potions and carrying them out and disposing of the herb dregs, the two of us and this small lizard shall protect the alchemist until the Lady Sage of Calamity returns.

The two soldiers straightened their backs and steeled their nerves to carry out their heavy responsibility.

The soldiers had no idea as to the true power of the salamander that had been given enough magical power to manifest, albeit temporarily. The small fire lizard was an incendiary device capable of blowing up the entire base, apart from Mariela of course.

The magical creature opened its mouth in a yawn. One of the soldiers, an animal lover, smiled. He resolved to keep a strict watch, so that this little lizard might sleep carefree.

The salamander, which was what Freyja had actually asked to protect Mariela, looked for a good spot on the back of Mariela's hand, rested its chin comfortably, and closed its eyes, looking wholly content.

Freyja, having left behind this extremely dangerous form of

security, headed to the next venue with her four soldiers in tow. This was the after-party. A celebration in broad daylight didn't seem like it would be a very enjoyable option, though.

No one questioned the happy drunkard humming a song to herself as she made her way through the base of the Labyrinth Suppression Forces. Of course, since Weishardt had issued orders relating to the Sage of Calamity, there was no problem with Freyja strutting about the base as she pleased. However, the real reason no one took any notice of the unfamiliar outsider was because they were only vaguely aware of her presence.

This was also something that had surprised the four soldiers at first, but by now they were used to it by now. Right from the start, they could do little more than bow their heads at the unfathomable Sage of Calamity when she'd chosen only Weishardt's aides and intelligence staff as her attendants from among the soldiers provided to the alchemist. Although they had disguised their positions, the fiery sage had seen right through them all.

Freyja's chosen location for the after-party was...

A single storehouse right through the side door where food and goods were delivered to the Labyrinth Suppression Forces. A large quantity of small glass vials was stacked in carriages lined up outside the structure. Several guards were stationed at the entrance to the storehouse. After taking a few vials from the carriages, they measured their size and weight and put them on some sort of magical tool, then handed over official papers and instructed the owners to bring the vials into the storehouse.

These were potion vials.

The sand collected at the restored sandpit was carried to the spirit shrine and left there for about one night to charge it with Drops of Life. The venture up to this point was divided into several tasks ordered by the margrave's family: the collection, transportation, and fractionation of the sand, then selling it to a glass atelier. The noble families and the merchants who accepted these orders had specific interests in the sand, but its quality and price were maintained in accordance with the agreement made at the time of the order.

The sand infused with Drops of Life and used for potion vials was purchased by a great number of glassworkers in the Labyrinth City and molded into potion vials, then delivered to this storehouse.

The material for potion vials was valuable sand that took time and effort to work with. During this period, when potion vials were needed, no one processed the raw grains into normal window glass or alcohol bottles. It was sold at a higher price than normal sand, so the work itself could be privatized eventually. Of course, the potion vials themselves also had volume, weight, and other quality standards, so the artisans wouldn't be especially stingy with the glass. The prices were set so profit would be made after factoring in raw material costs and worker wages.

The soldiers at the entrance to the storehouse were performing sequential sampling inspections to check if the potion vials met the standards. The magical tool they used was the kind employed in the imperial capital when used potion vials were bought back, and it seemed to measure the Drops of Life and magical gem content within the glass.

If the sand was expensive and magical gems were used, the vials had a high material cost. The buyback price was high, so there were some people who considered foolish things in the hopes of making a bigger profit.

"Heeey, Mitchell."

Freyja suddenly hugged Mitchell's shoulder. She was drunk. Their faces were close.

Back at the start of all this, Mitchell would have been quite embarrassed, but these days he was used to it and gave a gentlemanly reply—"Please be careful." Freyja pouted a little, as if displeased, then brought her mouth close to his ear and whispered something.

Freyja's presence largely went unnoticed due to her mysterious magic, but that didn't mean she was invisible. People could see her and Mitchell flirting, but strangely, no one gave a thought to why a man and a woman had their arms around each other's shoulders in the Labyrinth Suppression Forces' base in broad daylight. The next moment when they turned their gazes away, the sight was pushed to the recesses of their memory as meaningless information, like forgetting the face of an old greengrocer.

Freyja gazed at the carriages awaiting inspection with her golden eyes, and then left for the after-after-party. Three soldiers accompanied her. Only Mitchell stayed behind. Had Freyja dumped him?

Mitchell brushed his curly hair upward and adopted a stern expression, transforming into a completely different person than the man with Freyja. He began walking toward the soldiers performing the inspections.

"Do a full check on the next carriage and the two after it. Close the entrance gate so they can't run away. Pay special attention to the last carriage in particular. Investigate its atelier. Sand was stolen a few days ago. They may be related."

"Sir!"

The soldiers followed the instructions at once. Mitchell's appearance as a cute second-string soldier who Freyja had picked out was an act; the young man was, in truth, one of Weishardt's aides.

The price of the materials and the buyback price for potion vials were both high. Inspections were done by pulling a few samples, so some people thought to "increase" the quantity of their valuable vials by putting ones made from normal glass in the center of carriages to seemingly bolster their supply. Some even took to stealing the materials for making the vials altogether.

They would take all the carriages early in the morning before the sand was carried out of the spirit shrine and hide them in the Fell Forest. Then, several days later, they would disguise the sand as crops or harvested goods and took it into the Labyrinth City. If the sand infused with Drops of Life wasn't melted and made into glass within a few days, the Drops of Life would vanish, and it would become normal sand again. This would be revealed upon inspection, but since the residents of the Labyrinth City hadn't dealt with potions in a long time, they'd be unlikely to notice.

People come up with such despicable plans.

As soon as they learned a full inspection would be done, the carriage drivers hastily tried to take their leave but were stopped by the soldiers. It was just as the Sage of Calamity had said when she whispered in Mitchell's ear.

This might not be over before the end of the day.

The soldiers recognized from Mitchell's expression of discontent that this was a matter of grave concern, and they hastened their movements.

Was Mitchell displeased that he wasn't taken to the after-after party, or was it that the work in store for him was lengthy? Perhaps he was angry at the people committing despicable fraud at a time when the sale of potions was so crucial?

The young, pretty man immediately increased the inspection personnel, and all the inspections were finished in a few hours. However, by the time Mitchell was released from work, Freyja had already taken Mariela home to Sunlight's Canopy.

06

"Lady Carol, did you spend today as you do most others? Thank you for your hard work, let's have some tea."

Weishardt thanked Caroline, who'd been working hard managing the medicinal herbs at the vault in the Labyrinth Suppression Forces' base. Ever since the decision was made to put potions on the market, Caroline had been departing her estate every morning to inspect the pest-control dumplings workshop, and then she performed medicinal herb quality control in the Labyrinth Suppression Forces' base.

Caroline herself had proposed this. She hadn't shown up at Sunlight's Canopy in a long time. It was her duty to attract attention related to potions within the Labyrinth City, so she couldn't go see Mariela.

She heard of how Mariela was doing from Weishardt. He'd never mentioned Mariela was an alchemist, but Caroline was fairly confident that she was. It had become clear to Caroline after she'd spoken with the alchemists from the imperial capital, whom Robert had forced to make the new medicine.

The alchemists from the imperial capital used many magical tools to make potions. Magical tools for medicinal use in the Labyrinth City were different from those used by alchemists, but the alchemists of this time would recognize at least some of the ones Caroline had. Besides, if Mariela was "the awakened alchemist," it would've explained the miracle of her father Royce's release from Ruiz.

It seemed to Caroline that even now, Mariela was pushing herself to the limit creating potions for the sake of the Labyrinth City. And if she was, Caroline wanted to help, even if only a little. Just like when they'd once kneaded medicine together.

With that in mind, she came forward as the person performing the medicinal herb quality control.

The base of the Labyrinth Suppression Forces was selected as the manufacturing and storage facility for potions due to having the size to store potions and materials and the fact that it was the safest place. After chemists in the Labyrinth City bought medicinal herbs supplied by the Merchants Guild, then dried and processed them, the herbs were transported to the Labyrinth Suppression Forces. At this point in time, the quality of the herbs was maintained at or above a defined level, but no one in the Labyrinth City was well acquainted with the quality control of such plants. If the valuable herbs were exposed to sunlight or managed in a place of improper temperature or humidity, they would immediately spoil.

Caroline managed things from those kinds of quality idiosyncrasies, to inventory volume and storage periods; she was an invaluable source of assistance to the Labyrinth Suppression Forces.

"Today's tea is as delicious as ever. My, this cake has an abundance of fresh fruit."

Weishardt looked at Caroline, who smiled sweetly as she enjoyed her tea, with mixed feelings.

Weishardt never thought the day would come when they would speak of things with more significance than clichéd greetings like "You look well," or "You seem in good spirits today."

He was glad to see the woman he so longed for again today. He could no longer afford to naively trust that Caroline would be safe. Weishardt visited this room every day to confirm with his own eyes that she remained unharmed.

The decision to use the Aguinas family to turn attention away from the true alchemist within the City had not been up for debate. This had made manipulating information unnecessary, as residents of the Labyrinth City, along with nobles and merchants outside the City, shifted their focus to the family that had already been managing and researching potions for a long time.

However, Weishardt hadn't intended to use Caroline as a decoy. Robert just happened to be quarantined under the pretext of "recuperation." The plan had been to manipulate information to make people think he was the alchemist. Weishardt never imagined in his wildest dreams that Caroline would come forward.

"If someone from the Aguinas family were not frequenting the Labyrinth Suppression Forces, people would begin to feel suspicious."

Caroline had a point. If she didn't act freely in the City or go in and out of the Labyrinth Suppression Forces' base, some folks would begin to suspect that the Forces had confined an alchemist within their structure and forced them to make potions. Inviting such needless resistance and conjecture within the City was undesirable. Especially these days, when so many were emigrating from the capital.

Caroline's choice was preferable and strategically correct for managing the Labyrinth City. But...

I'm just glad she's safe.

This was why Weishardt had chosen to check in on her.

To him, the fruit pastry Caroline had described as fresh was soggy, and the aroma of the black tea did little to calm his heart.

Countless people had been appointed as Caroline's escorts, and a defense system of innumerable layers had been put in place. Yet even so, Weishardt could hardly say he was confident of her guaranteed safety. He wanted to tell her to stop this dangerous activity right now and cloister herself on her estate. He wished for nothing more than for her to be secure, and at his side.

But Weishardt could never say such things.

Surely Caroline was here because she knew the danger she was in and whom she was protecting.

"I am a daughter of the Aguinas family."

The nobility in Caroline's declaration had so powerfully captured Weishardt's heart. He could not bring himself to trample on such determination, such dignity.

I will protect her without fail. And then...

He spoke of neither his own determination nor his feelings.

It wasn't yet the time for that, and there was still much to be done. The lights the Sage of Calamity had lit penetrated the shadow of the Fell Forest, casting their glow on the once dark and unnoticed Labyrinth City.

Like insects led to a flame in the night, undesirables had set their sights on the Labyrinth City and were moving ever closer.

CHAPTER 4

Alchemist Abduction

01

His thoughts churned, tumbling around and around.

Spiraling thoughts at least implied movement, if only just a little, but there was nothing in this place to drive his mind toward anything meaningful.

This boxlike room consisted of stone walls, a ceiling, a closed door, and a magical tool for ventilation that constantly fed in air of a suitable temperature. Although they were always the same, meals of a sufficient quantity were brought in through a small delivery entrance three times a day. He didn't see the face of the person who brought the food, and even if he spoke to them, a reply never came.

The windowless room had been set up to function as a bedroom, living room, toilet, and bathroom all in one. It was furnished with life's necessities, but that was all. Other than the rare letter or book delivered from his family, there wasn't anything to quell his ennui.

Letters blotted out with censoring ink and the quiet, innocuous kinds of books were insufficient for him. Even if they provided a brief diversion, he was immediately pulled back into the endless circle of thought. The temperature never changed, and he saw nothing but the room. There was little to keep one aware of the passage of time other than the delivery of three meals a day. All he had in this room, where time seemed at a standstill, were the memories of a past he couldn't go back to.

If back then, if that person, if he'd done that, if, if, if…

What meaning was there in reflecting on the past incessantly and imagining an impossible future?

"Counting grains of rock brings about no change."

However, stone would change and erode if the prisoner kept rubbing at it. Could the circle of thoughts that continued to spin around and around eventually change in that same way?

"We need someone to pretend to be a shaman."

How long had he been kept prisoner when that request fell into his lap?

What form did his thoughts take when he obediently answered that he would?

It was impossible for anyone to know.

When Weishardt received a report of the man's disappearance, it had said, "The letters from his family were inked out so that he couldn't understand what they'd written. He may have seen through that kind of censorship, however. If that's the case, there's a high possibility he understands everything about the current state of the Labyrinth City."

02

"P-Papa. W-we're f-finally here. It's the L-Labyrinth C-City."

"Yes, that's right, that's right. You did really well. Good job, Son."

A group of merchants had made it through the Fell Forest and arrived at the Labyrinth City before dusk. The guard protecting the southwestern gate frowned at their appearance.

A petite man, who looked to be the head of the merchant caravan, had a spine so bent it looked like he was carrying a load on his back. His son, whose features resembled the father's, was also rather small, but he stood up as one should. Some might've guessed he'd suffered a serious injury in the past, however. The younger man had a constant fearful look on his face as he restlessly took in his surroundings, the muscles in his face twitching as if he were having spasms.

It wasn't unusual for people in the Labyrinth City to have had serious injuries, though. The guardsman's sour expression wasn't due to the peculiarity of the pair's outward appearance.

The father-son merchant duo wore brand-new armor and helmets, unblemished by even a single scratch, along with expensive-looking cloaks. They fawned on the guard as they asked him to open the gate. Attending the merchants were men who wore tattered clothes and no shoes, save one who appeared to be a hired adventurer. It was clear from their exhausted, lifeless expressions, thin, dirty bodies, and long hair and beards that they weren't treated well.

Despite the pristine quality of the armor worn by the father and son, the slaves had been given broken weapons, and they didn't even have shoes, let alone armor. Perhaps they'd suffered injuries during their travels, because blood oozed from gashes on their bodies here and there. It was likely the only reason they were able to survive the Fell Forest at all was because the Labyrinth City soldiers selling monster-warding potions at a station near the entrance to the woods had taken pity on them, and given them plenty of the concoction to use.

Such cruel treatment was alien even to the likes of the Labyrinth City, where it was rumored that slaves who arrived never left alive. Moreover, despite appearing to be penal laborers, no slave brands were identifiable on their chests through their torn shirts.

Do they really treat debt laborers this badly...?

The guard felt the number of strange groups trying to get rich quick in the Labyrinth City had increased ever since the sale of monster-warding potions had started. But this party was especially bad.

The guard left the gate-opening formalities to one of his fellows and headed for the City Defense Squad's station to report to his superior.

"A father-son merchant pair who brought several possibly mistreated slaves and an adventurer escort?"

"Yes, sir. The adventurer looks about C Rank. Accompanying them was a man who seems to be a civil official."

Captain Kyte listened to the guard's report, while Adviser Telluther, upon hearing the adventurer was C Rank, immediately lost all interest and began cutting his nails. Ever since he'd returned from the sandpit reclamation operation, Telluther had lost his aristocratic stiffness and became a far more frank individual. Or perhaps more placid, or maybe he was simply more like a slovenly middle-aged man. It was probably just a matter of time before he took off his shoes and began cutting his toenails in front of other people, too.

"A man who looks like a civil official? A special Skill User?"

"I don't know about his skills, but he's a man in his late twenties with black hair and greenish-blue eyes. From what little I saw, he didn't seem to carry himself like someone with combat experience."

Demand was high for merchants, adventurers, and crafts-men, but currently there were few openings for civil officials in the Labyrinth City. If he had special combat skills, he probably wouldn't look any different from an ordinary person, though.

Captain Kyte was suspicious. His guardsman continued to tell him of the group's peculiarities.

"There's no reason for adventurers with valuable combat skills to come to the City during this season, right?" Telluther said as he blew off the nail shavings he'd whittled with a file. Despite a startling lack of motivation and interest, the man did manage to say pertinent things at times like these.

"Just in case, I'll report it to the higher-ups."

A man who perfectly abided by the mantra of "report, contact, consult," Captain Kyte left his seat to report to his superior, the colonel.

"If you're going to see General Leonhardt, I'll go toooo," said Telluther, and he stood as well. The eccentric man followed after Kyte to the colonel's room without cleaning up his nail trimmings.

03

From the shade of the Fell Forest's trees, a man shot a sharp gaze at the merchant's party as it disappeared through the Labyrinth City's large front gate. After the gate closed, the man finally emerged from the trees and approached the side gate next to main entrance to the City. The City Defense Squad guards stationed there seemed to be acquainted with the man, as they called out to him in a friendly manner while eyeing the large number of birds he carried on his back.

"Ah, Mr. Meat, long time no see. Got a big catch today, huh?"

"Rainy birds today? They live in suuuper high spots, right? That's our Mr. Meat."

"...I was coming here to share them since I caught too many, but..."

"Sorry, Siegmund."

Sieg had accompanied the City Defense Squad when they'd gone to clear the way to the sandpit. The one-eyed man had only served as the "Meat Man" for a week, catching and feeding game to the entire company of the expedition like a parent bird bringing food to its chicks. But the members of the City Defense Squad still seemed to think he'd come bearing food when they saw him. The imprinting was complete. Their words and actions all expressed the same sentiment: "Meat Man, I want to eat meat."

For Sieg's part, he didn't seem all that displeased with the soldiers' joy. When he caught more than he needed, he would come to the large front gate and share it, like he had today. The youths of the City Defense Squad lived in a boardinghouse, where many of them took their shift work meals. Sieg's provisions were brought into the dining hall and quickly settled into the lucky stomachs of the hungry soldiers.

Sieg wondered what he was doing feeding all these men. Was it part of some kind of friend-making practice?

Had he finally washed his hands of Edgan, who used to come to Sunlight's Canopy to complain to Sieg about his latest romantic rejection but now completely ignored him in favor of talking about "fire"? If so, Edgan might've been in a larger, more inescapable danger than he realized. Sieg was probably the only man Edgan could count as a friend.

Edgan and other members of the Black Iron Freight Corps had been staying at Sunlight's Canopy since yesterday, which meant an increase in food expenses, but Sieg had still generously given five plump rainy birds to the guards. Was the one-eyed hunter ready to forget all about Edgan?

"Whoa-ho, you sure we can have this many? This's half of your day's quarry."

"This much will be enough for my household."

"But rainy birds are high-class game, right? And these're so fat..."

The guards verbally showed restraint, but their hands gripped the birds' legs with all their might and didn't seem likely to let go. The meat of a rainy bird was tender, and it harbored no bad smells or peculiarities. It was, in a word, delicious.

Generally, even if the flavor was at a similar level, animal meat was sold at a higher price than monster meat. The cheapest of all was that of the humanoid monsters. In the Labyrinth City, where there was no land to raise livestock for food, monster meat was considered well and good to eat. But the fact that some monsters were reminiscent of humans meant it was avoided in places with a wealth of other foodstuff, like the imperial city. Ordinary citizens hardly touched such meats. In the Labyrinth City, where orc meat was a staple, a high-class item like a rainy bird would never grace the dining tables of low-class soldiers.

"Should we take it to the boardinghouse kitchen and eat with everyone?"

"Yeah! We'll have a feast! Ahh, I wish my shift would hurry up and end."

"Hey, I said 'with everyone'! That means after the guy who went to report comes back!"

Guardsmen who had been entrusted with watching over the border to the dangerous monster-infested forest, now saw nothing but the tasty birds they had been gifted.

"Anyway, were the people who came through just now merchants from the imperial capital?"

"That's right, Mr. Mea— Sieg."

"You must've seen 'em, too, right? Those merchants were the only ones wearing that fancy-pants armor, even though they were tucked away all safe in their carriage! If they've got the money to buy that kinda gear, they could at least buy shoes for the other guys!"

"Debt laborers, weren't they? I sure couldn't see any brands, even on the ones with ripped clothes. Do people really treat debtors that badly?"

The soldiers seemed to have taken great offense with the party of tradesmen who so abused their slaves.

"Looked like they could cause some trouble. I'm going to warn everyone in Sunlight's Canopy to be careful. You know where those merchants heading?"

"Well, just be vigilant. We're reporting to the higher-ups just in case, but it'd be better if you stayed away from trouble. Let's see…"

Sieg had, rather easily, obtained the information he'd wanted. The meat had proved exceptionally effective. It made suffering a nickname like "Mr. Meat" worthwhile. The insular nature of the Labyrinth City was rather strong, and it was unavoidable that word of troublesome outsiders would be passed among the City's denizens.

Sieg gave them an additional rainy bird as thanks, then passed through the side gate and headed for Sunlight's Canopy.

"Thanks for the feast. Be careful," the guards said as they saw him off. Their gazes were locked on the delicious-looking poultry, so they hadn't noticed how Sieg's eye had darkened.

The sun had long since set by the time Sieg returned to Sunlight's Canopy, where Mariela and her fiery master were waiting for him.

"Welcome back, Sieg. Wow, so much meat!"

"Thanks, Mariela. I caught a lot today, so I gave a few to the guards."

"I already made today's dinner, so I'll cook them tomorrow. Any requests?"

"Aww, c'mon, Mariela. I want to eat them todaaay. Let's prep and fry up one of them."

"Geez, Master, you just ate. Are you getting senile?"

Freyja was most assuredly not getting senile. She said a lot of stupid things, but it was still a little early for her to be cognitively impaired.

"Well, nobody's here, so can't you use alchemy and cook it up quick?"

They hadn't known when Sieg would be back, so the two women had already eaten. Today he'd gotten back after everyone else had gone home.

"Master, you're so selfish."

Mariela made a pouty face at her teacher, while Freyja reached out to grab the young alchemist's cheek. Mariela was still unaware that her master kept a thorough eye on things while she slept. Even the salamander had left by the time Freyja returned. The sage had made sure to get back before Mariela woke up, however, so her pupil would continue to only think of the woman as a drunkard.

Perhaps that was why when Freyja reached out toward her, Mariela didn't hesitate to grab her index finger and thumb and yank them in opposite directions.

"Gaaah, Mariela, you're gonna rip my hand apart!" Freyja cried while roaring with laughter. Sieg smiled slightly at the exchange and offered to assist with the cooking.

"I'll help."

"Then I will, too."

"Master, you'll get in the way. Stop complaining and wait."

While Freyja pouted at Mariela's cold remark, the other two headed into the kitchen. Mariela got the spices and oil ready, and Sieg began to prepare the rainy bird itself. Mariela said that just the leg meat would be fine for today, so he pierced it with a knife, twisted the joints backward and snapped them with a crack, and then stripped the meat from the bone. Sieg himself didn't notice that the way he used his hands today was slightly rougher than usual.

"Thanks."

Mariela took the poultry, cut it into large bite-size pieces, tossed it into a Transmutation Vessel along with some spices, and lightly mixed it while saying things like "**Pressurize** just a little. Saves time, and the flavor will soak in."

Rainy birds were medium-size creatures, bigger than a person's head. They built their nests in tall trees and had a distinctive cry. Their plump bodies were ill suited for flight. So much so that no one had seen them take to the sky. Some folks even wondered if they took sustenance purely from the air they breathed. The name "rainy bird" came from the fact that their birdsong usually preceded rainfall.

However, the reality wasn't nearly as lovely as the rumors. Their way of life was closer to that of ants or bees than most other birds. Much of the species was indistinct and possessed no gender, save for the egg-laying queens and their mates. Most of the time, the birds simply gathered food and carried it to their nests. Their distinctive voices didn't call rain, but rather soldier of their species to protect them from rain and invaders.

Unlike the queens who were so fat it seemed impossible for them to fly, the soldier birds were small and thin, no bigger than the size of one's open palm. Such distinct differences made it difficult to accept the two were part of the same species at all.

Stab.

Siegmund thrust the edge of a knife into the flesh of a queen bird, who had grown plump and comfortable from the slave labor of soldier birds. While Mariela cooked one of them, he prepared the remaining birds so it would be easy to cook them some other time.

Sieg cut open the belly and took out the internal organs, which were glistening with fat. He sectioned each body part and scraped the meat from the bones.

The feel of cutting off the pale pink flesh, the sight of the meat being torn up when he stripped the muscles from their bones, the sensation of bending the joints backward with all his might, the white color of the bones protruding from the torn flesh.

He thrust the knife in, ripping and tearing the flesh apart. What was reflected in Siegmund's lone blue eye as he prepared the rainy birds?

"Sieg? It's ready."

Mariela's voice brought the one-eyed man back to his senses.

All the rainy birds had been prepared, and some had been cut into easy-to-eat pieces.

"Cooking these will be a cinch since you sliced up so much for me. Thank you." Mariela placed the poultry in a container and deposited it in the magical tool for freezing and refrigeration.

Sieg's dinner and the deep-fried rainy bird were lined up on the kitchen table. Freyja had slipped into the room unnoticed and was now sitting in wait with a conspicuous bottle in hand right in front of the large plate of cooked bird. Just as one might expect from a sage, Freyja had understood exactly when the cooking would be done.

The food had been fried with a Transmutation Vessel rather than a pot. Temperature control in a Transmutation Vessel was Mariela's specialty, this enabled her to prepare the food much more skillfully than when she used normal cookware. The outside was flaky, and the inside was juicy. It was a dish even the owner of the Yagu Drawbridge Pavilion couldn't beat.

Perhaps as proof of how well it turned out, Freyja devoured the food with incredible gusto. The inside of her mouth was likely just as fiery as the rest of her, as she chowed down on hot food without batting an eye. Freyja could have made for an absurdly strong contender in a piping-hot-food-eating contest. If left unchecked, she might even eat everything the two had prepared.

"Master, you're eating too much. Time for some lemon juuuice."

"H-hey! Mariela! Add your lemon on your own plate!"

"It's fine; since you've already eaten enough. Sieg and I love lemon."

To keep her master in check, Mariela squeezed lemon juice onto the large plate of food. Freyja disliked the sour taste; one could say this was a method of "firefighting."

"Delicious," Sieg muttered as he watched the master-pupil dinner theater. He was having a rare drink with his dinner. The way he thoroughly chewed each bite and deliberately savored his meal called to mind the day Sieg had first joined in a toast. Mariela gazed intently at him as he partook. Finally, she said, "Sieg, your hair's gotten long. Want me to cut it later?"

There was a mirror and a magical tool for illumination in the bathroom of Sunlight's Canopy, so Mariela generally made use of them when she cut Sieg's hair at night. With a sheet wrapped around his neck, Sieg was sat in the chair facing the mirror and gazing vacantly into its reflective surface.

Mariela touched Sieg's hair with unsteady hands. She took a piece and snipped, used her fingers to untangle it, and snipped again, cutting it short little by little.

He felt her fingers gently holding his hair. When he washed and combed it himself, some of it got tangled in his fingers, causing him to tug on the knots, but Mariela had a far softer touch that never painfully pulled at his hair.

Could this be what it felt like when small, fluffy animals groomed each other?

Mariela's expression in the mirror was surprisingly serious for a girl administering a haircut. Her eyes, which tended to cross when she was doing this, sometimes widened suddenly. Her mouth, too, opened large as if she was about to say "Crap!" Her eyes would often dart to his reflection, then soften with relief as she continued her work with the scissors. Sieg did his best to stifle his laughter, pretending not to have noticed.

There was a barbershop in the Labyrinth City, and people like Edgan, who were particular about their appearance, got their haircuts done there. Mariela had skillful hands, but someone whose main occupation involved cutting hair could still have done a far better job. For that reason, Mariela had encouraged Sieg to go to such an establishment.

"It's really fine if you want to go get your hair cut somewhere else," she'd said, but Sieg had given some excuse or another to have Mariela do it. This gentle, pleasant time was precious to him.

"Hey, Sieg. Did something happen?" Mariela asked as she moved the scissors with a *snip, snip*.

I'm just an open book to her, huh...?

Mariela usually had a carefree smile on her face, but she was incredibly shrewd when it came to Sieg being worried.

"I was just a bit caught up in the past—that's all."

Sieg was positive that the man he'd seen at the gate was the merchant who used to be his master.

Sieg wasn't foolishly honest enough to tell her that the tradesman who'd once abused him had come to the Labyrinth City. Even if he needed to talk to someone about it, Nierenberg would've been more suitable. If he told Mariela, it would probably just upset her. She wouldn't be able to do anything about it anyway.

Although Sieg had ended up a penal laborer due to false accusations from the father-son merchant pair, he still had no proof of his innocence.

Above all, Siegmund had grown very accustomed to using his bow, thanks to Freyja's unreasonable demands, and although he didn't yet have perfect accuracy, he was now able to hit his targets. The day he would achieve A Rank and be released from slavery was most certainly drawing nearer. He felt it would be unwise to start seeking trouble now.

Yes, it was best not to get involved. Even if they crossed paths on the street, Sieg looked quite different from how he used to. His former master probably wouldn't recognize him, even if he stared

Sieg straight in the face. The one-eyed hunter was doubtful the men even remembered their former slave at this point.

Right, there was nothing to worry about, excepting the dark thoughts surfacing in Sieg's own heart, of course. What had he been thinking about while he prepared the rainy birds?

The moment he saw that father and son, the feelings he had repeatedly, irrationally suppressed, transformed into unbridled anger. Although he'd managed to keep ahold of those feelings, a black serpent of hatred and bitterness had coiled its way into his heart. Sieg resented not only the father-son tradesmen, but the world that had driven him into those circumstances in the first place. These days the dark hatred seemed likely to burst forth from him at any moment.

Now he understood how unfairly he'd been treated.

The merchants had brought debt laborers with them; people just like Sieg used to be. The slaves suffered atrocious treatment and appeared to be dead on the inside. Looking at them, the pain his body endured from regular beatings; the rebellious screams he'd silenced in the face of verbal abuse; and the painful death of his will to live all violently surged to the forefront of his mind in a furious eruption.

The torrent of frenzied, raw emotion threatened to overcome Sieg's very reason.

He didn't know why that father and son had made him a penal laborer, but he often thought it was to hide the abuse of their debt laborers, or perhaps to make him a scapegoat for their actions. He would shoulder the guilt of their failure as door-to-door salesmen. Maybe it was for some other, extremely self-centered, unjust reason.

Sieg never would have suffered such inhumane treatment had those tradesmen not purchased him.

No, even before that, the former comrades in his party had abandoned Siegmund after he'd lost his Spirit Eye. Sure, he'd certainly acted arrogant, but they should have been able to recognize that being with him was still their best chance at success.

It was their fault…no, it was that other group's fault, too. The frantic, contradictory thoughts spiraled in his mind, and the dark emotions grew like a rising tide in his chest until they became unbearable. Sieg wanted desperately to cry out, forgetting what others might think of him.

Just as he felt himself beginning to break…

Softly, softly, softly.

Mariela's hand stroked Sieg's head.

"I wonder if there's too much hair in this spot."

She gently grasped Sieg's hair and went to town with the scissors as she untangled his grayed locks.

There was a comfort in her soft hand and gentle fingertips that hadn't changed since the day they'd met.

Siegmund looked at Mariela's reflection in the mirror. Mariela caught sight of his gaze, and she gave him a warm, kindly smile. The cruelties the merchant father had inflicted upon Sieg probably held some manner of purpose to that man, even if he was a monster.

Sieg had suffered all that pain for another's vulgar amusement; he had been treated like any sense of self-worth was a delusion. Such an inhumane life was nothing short of absurd.

Sieg wondered if perhaps Mariela was, in her own way, trying to bury her loneliness by showing him affection.

Being by her side, protecting and being protected, supporting each other. Living with the childish Mariela might've seemed to some like playing house, but the care Sieg received was unconditional.

"I'm going to try trimming your bangs a bit."

The blackness that had taken hold of Sieg's heart was promptly vanquished from Mariela's smile, her gaze, and the touch of her warm fingertips.

If not black, then what color was his heart now? If hatred was a dark ebon, this complicated feeling that was even harder to control was accompanied by a lot of light and a little bit of gloom. Siegmund knew what this feeling was, but he decided to hold it for a little while yet. He wanted to doze a little longer in this place full of pure calmness and warmth.

I'll let things develop naturally.

That's what seemed best to him

This place was the greatest thing Siegmund had ever had in his worthless life.

If he hadn't ended up a penal laborer, if that merchant hadn't bought him, if his comrades hadn't abandoned him, if he hadn't lost his Spirit Eye, he would never have ended up here.

If Sieg were ever asked whether he'd rather have his Spirit Eye or Mariela, his answer would come without hesitation.

After all, if he hadn't lost the Spirit Eye and had continued being an adventurer, he never would have experienced a day like this.

Mariela had stretched her hand over Siegmund's lost right eye to cut his bangs. This gentle, irreplaceable hand had come to his rescue when they'd first met, and she had been picking him up when he was down ever since. Unable to control his overflowing feelings, Siegmund reflexively grasped her hand.

Snnnip.

"Agh!"

Mariela stiffened; her mouth opened with a gasp. She'd cut Siegmund's bangs drastically short.

"S-S-S-Sieg, you moved! I...I...I'm not going to cut it any-more. You can get it cut somewhere else!" Mariela's eyes filled with startled and embarrassed tears.

"I'm sorry. Mariela! Wait, isn't it nice and clean this way?! Yes, I think it's great! Look, it's fantastic! Well done, Mariela! Thank you!"

Even though Sieg was the one who'd been given overly short bangs, he issued a flurry of earnest apologies for some reason. He should've been angry, but instead, Mariela was. Why did she have to scold him? Maybe it was partly his fault, but she was being completely unreasonable.

"...Really?"

"Really! So, I hope you'll cut it for me again next time!"

After promising to get her sweet pastries, rare fruit, and the meat of an orc king, Sieg somehow managed to fend off Mariela's frown and teary eyes. It was, in its own way, quite the expensive haircut.

What an absurd and wholly nonsensical world.

Yet even so, Sieg no longer felt the sting of the barbs that had so tightly wound themselves around his heart, even if after coming across his former master again.

No matter what kind of awful treatment he'd endured before, it meant nothing compared to these silly little moments.

Sieg invited Mariela to eat honey-soaked lemons to improve her mood. Honey was a high-class item, a trump card Sieg had set aside for Mariela, who still clung to her frugal tendencies.

As soon as he brought it up, Mariela was excited. "Hurry up, hurry up," she urged.

When the two returned, Freyja was absent. She wasn't in the

living room, kitchen, or shop interior. All that remained was a note that said "I've gone drinking."

"Grrr, again?!" Mariela shouted in anger. Sieg on the other hand was wholly content to rub his short bangs between his fingertips and enjoy the first alone time he'd had with Mariela in a while.

Siegmund had caught a lot of rainy birds today. They'd been calling at the top of their lungs, signaling rain.

The movement of the clouds was hidden beneath the thick dark of the night, but a strong wind blew high in the sky.

A tempest would soon arrive.

04

That night.

Mariela and Sieg had spent an extremely wholesome time toasting with honey lemons, taking separate baths, brushing their teeth, preparing for medicine making or hunting, and saying good night because they'd both be getting an early start again tomorrow.

Edgan, the lost child of love, was crying tears of loneliness into his pillow at the Yagu Drawbridge Pavilion.

Meanwhile, the unwholesome Freyja was drinking in a bar with a casual acquaintance.

"Ah-ha-ha-ha! You understand, don't you, Snapper? It's a master's job to raise her pupil!"

"Snapper...? Ah well, no matter! If you leave something to them and they mess it up, you can just clean up after them!"

Perhaps their guiding principles aligned, because the two completely hit it off with each other. Both wore hoods to hide their faces, and neither had given their name, but one knew rather quickly who they were by their characteristic words and actions.

"Then let's go, Fire!"

"Yeah! Let's march, Snapper!"

And after that instant connection, they set off into the night. That was not to say that there was a crisis in Ha— Snapper's family. Rather, they were interested in handing out some lessons, backward though they likely were to be.

This was to be known as the march of the Nighttime Amusement and Messing Around Eradication Squad, newly formed by the pair of hot-blooded mentors.

One might quip that they were the ones enjoying nighttime amusement and messing around, but it wouldn't change the effects. As mentors, their affection was overflowing, and they were eager to rescue lambs lost in the night.

The two members of the Nighttime Amusement and Messing Around Eradication Squad descended upon a bar and sent an unruly adventurer from the imperial capital flying with a kick after the upstart had cried, "How can these people eat monster meat?! Oy!"

The squad celebrated with a few drinks.

Proceeding to another tavern, they entered just as a different ruffian shouted, "Look at me—everybody in the imperial capital knows me! Hey! I'm an adventurer! Pay attention to me!" This time they knocked out a small swarm of hoodlums before knocking a few back.

At yet another bar: "I, I—I—I have money, s-so, let's, let's, g-g-go to m-my room," a nervous-sounding man crudely propositioned a woman.

An older companion of the skittish man complained, "How can I afford a meal for my slave?! I can't. Table scraps are plenty, plenty." The squad lightly singed the father-son merchant duo troubling the inn owner before tipping back a few more mugs.

This was how the night of educational guidance unfolded.

The two members of the Nighttime Amusement and Messing Around Eradication Squad didn't have "talks" with the little lost lambs. They were content with the notion that actions spoke louder than words. It didn't seem likely for the squad to convene again, but in terms of sheer fighting power, its members were two of the top-ranked people in the Labyrinth City. These stunts of theirs also served as examples to others, and the City grew just a little more peaceful.

It made paying for the drinks of a certain red-haired, golden eyed woman all the more worthwhile for the house of Margrave Schutzenwald.

The hastily formed division was made up of an A-Ranker and an estimated S-Ranker, drunk though they were. Normally, it would've been extremely expensive to hire them.

"That was some nice diplomacy, Fire!"

"Well said, Snapper!"

Snappy! Snappy!

The pair exchanged a thumbs-up. Their infuriating energy caused even guards to run away from them.

The two staggered into a back street where a lone man was crouched. Although it was dim, they could distinguish trash bins and wooden boxes with empty bottles as their eyes adjusted to the darkness. Even so, the two couldn't guess as to the identity of the man. It was as if his figure were blotted out with black paint. There was more obscuring him than just the shadows of the alley. He was covered in a black, rust-like substance—it covered his entire body, and on closer inspection, it wriggled as if trembling slightly.

"This's a curse. But it's not because he was cursed; the recoil from overusing it probably bounced back on him."

Snapper frowned. This recoil was one of the reasons curses were forbidden. Unlike other varieties of magic, curses could be used without any skills.

Curses that weakened and confused people had great versatility as weapons against others, but their effects always returned to harm their users. That's why those who practiced black magic often learned skills to counter such things. Of course, a person's tolerance for averting, purifying, or catching curses differed from one to the next. When one's personal limits were reached, their entire body was burned and destroyed by their own curses. Such was likely to be the case with this man in the alley.

Despite the terrible risks and the prospect of surrendering completely to the black arts, there were always those who sought power no matter the price.

"Mm, this curse wasn't terribly harmful. Probably some kind of distraction- or fatigue-causing magic; the rebound seems unusually harsh."

The red-haired woman nicknamed "Fire" understood the nature of the curse at just a glance.

"You know about that stuff?" the one nicknamed "Snapper" asked.

"You could say that. This guy looks a bit like the relative of an old acquaintance of mine. Sorry, Snapper, but could you pretend you didn't see this and go home for today?"

Where was the drunkard who'd been barhopping just a few moments ago? Fire gazed at Snapper with clear, golden eyes.

"Well, that's a bit coldhearted of you, but there must've been some reason for us running into this poor man. I'll pretend I saw nothing afterward, but I'm going to see this through with my own eyes." He gave a snappy thumbs-up along with a dazzling white smile, a feat that was particularly curious as there was no source of light around. How did his teeth shine so brilliantly?

Satisfied with Snapper's smooth reply, Fire smiled as well and returned his gesture. Then she turned to the cursed man, held her right hand out toward him, and began to chant something in a low voice. Snapper had seen curse removal in his line of work before. He couldn't be certain of exactly what the fiery woman with golden eyes was chanting, but Snapper knew enough to tell it was unusual.

He'd never heard the spell before, but it seemed effective all the same, as the black, squirming, rust-like curse covering the man's entire body shivered as if in the throes of death.

This curse isn't messing around. It might be the middle of the night, but it's probably best to call the gang.

But no sooner had the man thought this than...

"Fire!"

The lady shouted her namesake with enthusiasm, and flames enveloped the accursed man.

"Wha—?!"

It was quite a blaze. Could she have grown annoyed and now intended to torch the other two occupants of the alley?

But in the next instant, the blaze extinguished itself as though it'd been doused, and all that remained was the man, huddled on the ground. He bore no scarring; the flame had left him and his clothes unsinged.

"Ugh..."

The man groaned as he opened his eyes and took in his surroundings.

"This is..."

It was Robert Aguinas, the man rumored to be recuperating from some unknown illness.

"Hiii, Rob. I can call you Rob, right? You feel like a guy with that kinda name."

"Ugh... Who are you?"

"I'm an acquaintance of the Rob from a long time ago. You really do look just like him. He treated me super-well back then, so I'll grant you one wish."

The golden eyes of Fire...no, of the Sage of Calamity, flickered as they peered down at Robert. As if to resist the light of those hungry-looking eyes, Robert looked back with great suspicion and muttered, "You some kinda demon...?"

"Who! Is a demon! You dumbass!"

Poke, poke, poke. The Sage of Calamity relentlessly poked and prodded at the man's forehead.

"Ah—ow! Ow, ow, ow, ow, I said ow. *I'm sorry.*"

Poke-poke-poke-poke, poke-poke-poke-poke. Robert didn't know if the forehead assault would stop, even if he said it hurt and apologized. It was a fierce attack. A shower of blows. Maybe the Sage of Calamity really was some kind of demon.

"H-hey, Fire, I think that's enough…"

Unable to stand by and do nothing, Snapper intervened, and the attacks finally ceased. By that time, Robert's forehead was bright red, and the man's eyes were full of tears.

"Hah, hah, phew…"

"Next time you say something stupid, I'll kick you so hard your ass'll break in four. You really are just like him, right down to the idiocy."

"Haaaah, I beg your pardon…"

As expected from the fiery master. Despite her less than exceptional alchemy skills, there were reasons Freyja chose "master" as her main job. Robert grew obedient like a scolded child in the face of such heated pressure from the mysterious woman. It may have been the first moment the Nighttime Amusement and Messing Around Eradication Squad did something resembling actual guidance.

"Well? You gonna run? You were searching for a way to sneak back to your house, right?"

"!!! How did you…?!"

A certain unexpected request had come to Robert as he sat in confinement under the guise of "rehabilitation." It was to dress up as a shaman and put a fake curse on the "treasure" of the "spirit shrine." He'd accepted the request with an admirable attitude and was plucked from his place of solitude. On his way back to detention after completing his task, Robert had waited for the moment when his escorts dropped their guard for even the slightest second. The second they did, he'd used smokescreen and fatigue curses to make an escape. They weren't especially harmful; Robert had only used them to regain his freedom. However, as one might've expected of the Labyrinth Suppression Forces, the curses required to befuddle them were beyond the poor man's limits. Robert did indeed escape, only to suffer the rebounding effects of his own black magic and wind up here in the alley.

What kind of person was this woman who had so easily purified such a powerful curse? Even if she wasn't a demon, there was no way she was an ordinary person. Even if one set all that aside, the truth about Robert's condition, as well as all matters concerning the spirit shrine, had been top secret. Those golden eyes could tell not only that Robert was on the run, but even what his objective had been.

Robert pondered if he was about to be offered some sort of infernal deal. Even if he was, he had little recourse but to accept.

If it would fulfill his objective, he would do it, even if his body burned for the decision. That's what he'd decided the moment he'd gotten mixed up in curses and this heretical magic medicine.

"Please, grant my request. Give me power." Robert bowed down to the flickering Sage of Calamity before him.

"Very well. This will hurt, but it'll guide you to your destination, unseen."

With a whoosh, hot air blew upward and swept the sage's hood off her head. The flame-colored hair that appeared from within was like a fire that had burst from the dark.

"I grant you an emblem. Ephemeral wisdom, I summon you from beyond. **Bestow Flame Seal.**"

Flames in the shape of a magic circle emerged before her. After a half rotation, it shrank to the size of a fist, and seared itself into the back of Robert's left hand.

"Gaaah!"

Robert grimaced at the acute pain and the unpleasant smell of burnt flesh.

"Don't worry. That burn'll disappear completely in about a week, along with its effects. Ah, Snapper, do you mind if I borrow some money?"

"Uh? Sure, I only have about five silver coins, though."

The startled Snapper...no, the Adventurers Guild guildmaster Haage, handed his wallet over to the Sage of Calamity.

I've seen a lot of wonders in my line of work, but this one might be in a whole different league...

Haage was so stunned, he offered the entirety of his spending money, and the Sage of Calamity happily helped herself to its contents.

"Hey, Rob. I'm sure you're broke, right? I'll lend you this. Be sure to remember that nighttime amusements have a high price."

Although it was money she'd borrowed from Haage, the Sage of Calamity offered it with a degree of self-importance, as if the money was her own.

After receiving the silver coins from the red-haired woman, Robert bowed his head very deeply and took a few steps backward before melting into the darkness of the street.

"His very presence disappeared. What's that seal do?"

"Meh, y'know, normal stuff. But the fact that he mastered it so quickly after it was carved into him shows he's as skillful as the Rob I once knew."

The Sage of Calamity chuckled. As the Adventurers Guild guildmaster, Haage indeed knew of this fiery woman, along with her cooperation with Margrave Schutzenwald, her unfathomable abilities, and the warning to never be hostile to her. However, wasn't helping the "recuperating" Robert Aguinas escape an act of hostility toward Margrave Schutzenwald, or even to the entire Labyrinth City?

"Why that seal?"

Haage would not overlook anything that boded ill for the safety of the City.

"Isn't it the duty of a mentor to make sure poor lost children who run away from home return safely?" The fiery sage grinned as though she understood it all.

Is she really doing this to rehabilitate Robert Aguinas?

The true intentions of the smiling blaze were indiscernible, but the guildmaster sensed no malice or hostility.

"Then I suppose I'll put my trust in you, Fire."

"Nice. Leave it to me, Snapper."

The pair exchanged snappy farewells and returned to their respective homes.

The next day.

"I'm really sorry my master borrowed money! I gave her a thorough scolding!"

Mariela had come to the Adventurers Guild to pay back the borrowed coins and apologize in earnest.

Behind her stood Fire, yesterday's partner in crime, who waved cheerfully. Mariela turned her head and chided, "Master! What are you doing?!"

Haage, who had lent all the money he'd had on hand, had put in a request at home for a supplementary budget. However, his wife, the house's own minister of finance, had rejected his request, so this recompense was a big to help to the man.

Similarly, his subordinates had caught word of his exploits in the various bars and taverns last evening, and today they'd confined him to desk work first thing in the morning. The man seemed very near death from the task.

Casting a glance at Freyja, who laughed as if to say "Yeah, I got in some trouble, heh," Haage felt uneasy. He wondered if it was really okay to trust her. Haage's subordinates had scolded him, too. "If you've got time to go barhopping, you should work more!" they'd said.

Haage wasn't sure.

Freyja seemed ignorant of the situation, simply thinking Robert was a troubled adult who'd run away from home and was having difficulties getting back. In her imprudence she'd given the fugitive an advanced seal, thinking he would make it home unnoticed by anyone around him and simply say, "Hmm? Why, no, I didn't run away."

Mariela had deduced to whom her master was indebted when Freyja had proudly proclaimed, "Hey, I borrowed money! Snappy! No idea from who!" and gave a thumbs-up. Mariela being who she was, she had not the slightest clue where Freyja had been wandering in the middle of the night, or what on earth she'd been doing.

As for Robert, who had been given a seal to fool the eyes of others...

"Before this seal disappears, before this life is extinguished, no matter what it takes..."

After receiving a miracle in exchange for his life, Robert proceeded to weave his way through the darkness of the Labyrinth City, en route to achieve his final objective.

05

Inns within the Labyrinth City took a variety of forms. Most of them were connected to a restaurant or bar, and adventurers crowded them in the evenings to the point where their collected voices reached up into the guests' rooms. Most adventurers and merchants stayed at taverns, pricked up their ears at conversations around them, talked with their employees, and gathered information about hunting grounds and materials being sold at nearby markets.

Of course, no small number of those staying for a long period of time disliked this kind of boisterous noise, so there were also facilities with a manager at the entrance, or those that operated strictly as inns only. If you didn't ring the bell, you wouldn't even meet the manager at those kinds of places. They charged extra to clean your room and change your sheets, and no employees entered the room while someone was staying there. Such a system was closer to renting an apartment than temporary lodging.

At one such inn, several people had gathered in a somewhat cramped room.

"The circumstances are ripe. It will be carried out tomorrow."

The figure that stood in the darkness to avoid the dim light had such a weak presence that, if they hadn't spoken, one would think them a shadow. The same was true for near everyone present, excepting a lone man who sat on the bed. Their outfits and harsh words in a foreign dialect hardly painted the bunch as a group of respectable adventurers.

"There will be no changes to the plan."

The man sitting on the bed was their leader or, more likely, an employer, if his tone and the feeling of distance between him and the others was any indication. Despite the decision, the man looked around restlessly while he chewed his nails. It seemed to one of the shadow men that his employer was wavering on his own plan. The shadow man, exasperated at his employer's foolishness, made a final confirmation of the details.

"The target is..."

"Yes, and one more person..."

"Understood. I'll do my utmost to capture them alive."

"I'll be in trouble if you just do 'your utmost.' I don't care what happens, don't kill 'em! After that, track down the vault and get rid of it! You can do that, right? I'm paying you a lot o' money here!"

"I understand. However, don't forget I have the first pick."

The shadow men were top-notch; the employer had made certain to gather only those with the ability to fulfill his request. However, he had changed the plan countless times and created needless work for them in the process. The hired shadows had very nearly run dry of patience, but they had to confirm one last thing.

"I have one last question. Just what kind of person is your target?"

At this, the employer sitting on the bed looked in the direction of the speaker for the first time as he answered.

"An alchemist."

In an instant, the shadow men vanished from the room. They were off to carry out their mission.

06

"If you want to move people, you should convince them they're on the verge of a crisis."

Anyone in a position of leadership learned that at a young age.

The family of Margrave Schutzenwald made skillful use of this sense of impending crisis and the influence it had over others. After employing it to lead the Labyrinth City and its surrounding territories, they were well educated on the method's intricacies. One could say the family led the will of the people and had built a solid cooperative system by skillfully sharing information, depending on another's position and influence, about the dangers of the Labyrinth that could affect the entire Empire.

People satisfied with their circumstances didn't want change. That was human instinct.

So, even if potions were put on the market in the Labyrinth City and the potential for traffic through the Fell Forest increased, satisfied people were unlikely to act in the uncertain initial stages. That was not to say folks were unprepared; they readied themselves to get going at any time. No doubt they were just observing the situation for now.

In other words, one could speculate that the mass influx of visitors to the Labyrinth City was because everyone had some sort of pressing matter. It could've been a financial or emotional reason, or something else entirely; what drove them was probably different for each person. This new economic bridge called "potions" existed, but it was yet to be seen just how sturdy a bridge it would be. Not all those motivated to cross were doing so calmly.

Many people, both inside the Labyrinth City and outside, sought potions, but things hadn't settled into a comfortable routine yet. If they were simply patient, a defined system of administration could be established.

The potion-seeking masses bustled about Caroline's surroundings again today like insects swarming a lamp in the evening. Countless bugs, all hurrying to snatch up potions before someone else did.

In the morning Caroline would leave the Aguinas family estate for the pest-control dumplings atelier. Afterward, she'd head for the base of the Labyrinth Suppression Forces. By the time evening had arrived, she would return to the estate by carriage.

Such was Caroline's daily routine. It was information that proved easy enough for anyone to gather after a few days of observation.

The ruffians targeting her were either squabbling among themselves, or they were cooperating and merely waiting for the right chance.

Regarding his unseen enemies as though they were pieces on a board, Weishardt eagerly lay in wait for an impatient insect to leap into the lamp.

"Reporting in! The Aguinas family's pest-control dumpling manufacturing atelier was attacked."

The report brought to Weishardt was as startling as a thunderclap reverberating from low-hanging dark clouds. However, the man had long been watching the sky. He'd predicted this, so surprise wasn't merited.

In the days to come, he would later think back on the moment this report was delivered as the lightning strike before the torrential rain began.

"What's the situation?"

"The assailants were a group of three who appeared to be D-Rankers. A merchant who happened to be present and four escort adventurers were taken hostage. According to Lieutenant Malraux's report, they were either acting independently or were hired underlings. Requesting permission to invite the slave trader, Mr. Reymond, for questioning, due to his expertise."

"Permission granted. Get to it."

Weishardt allowed himself a glance at the soldier, who'd given his report and was now leaving, before returning his attention to his documents. As always, Weishardt maintained a well-controlled expression that showed not the slightest bit of discomposure.

He'd figured out there had been people prowling around the pest-control dumplings atelier starting a few days ago. He'd expected them to make a move before too long. Both the attack and the subjugation went as he predicted; there was no reason to be surprised. He'd directed Malraux to make a flashy show of strength, and with that, the atelier's surroundings would probably grow quiet again before long.

However, as Weishardt reached for his cup of black tea, his break was interrupted before he'd even had a chance to enjoy the aroma coming from the cup.

"Reporting in! We received word from the Aguinas family's escorts! An anonymous group attacked the Aguinas house not long ago. The situation has been quelled and all responsible have been apprehended."

"Could the attack on the atelier have been a diversion? Don't be afraid to rough them up a little. Make them tell you everything."

"Yes, sir! Should we call Dr. Nierenberg?"

"Do as you like."

Cup still in hand, Weishardt remained as icy as ever, even after the second startling report in a row. However, his subordinates had served under him long enough to know him, and they sensed a slight anger showing through the man's facade. They proposed a sound interrogation method, then rushed out of the room as soon as they received permission.

Organized abduction was also among my predictions. They were all captured alive. We'll know who the principal offender is before long.

Weishardt returned the cup and saucer to the desk without taking a sip.

Caroline's welfare hadn't been discussed during his exchanges with the soldiers. Weishardt understood it wasn't worth reporting if she was safe. Even so, it tore at his heart.

Although Caroline was fine, the fact that someone targeting her had planned and executed an attack hit Weishardt hard. It was a flash of lightning cutting through the darkness, thunder that pierced his eardrums.

Weishardt glanced at the surface of his cooling tea. He hadn't even taken a sip of it yet. The man then issued another order to one of his attendants.

"Announce that I will be making a visit."

"Sir!"

At Weishardt's brief command, the attendant sensed where he needed to go and ran ahead to give notice of his lord's visit.

The attendant's destination was on the premises of the Labyrinth Suppression Forces' base. It was the only relatively high-class building on the premises and had been built as a lodging house for high officials and a facility to welcome honored guests. The estate, built close to the main entrance of the base, had a lot of soldier foot traffic, and you'd be hard-pressed to call it quiet. That meant it was safe, and it was close enough that Weishardt's office looked out on it.

The attendant had apparently returned from making the announcement while Weishardt tidied his hair a bit, as his ears caught the footfalls of someone running through the corridor.

He does not have to hurry quite that much. He's been reading into my emotions too much lately..., Weishardt thought while straightening his collar. Suddenly, the attendant burst into the room without knocking.

"Th...the guesthouse has been attacked!"

"What?! What of Carol—Lady Caroline?!"

"We were unable to confirm her whereabouts...!!!"

Crash!

Weishardt broke into a run toward the guesthouse before his chair had even hit the ground; he'd knocked it over when he jumped to his feet.

No one, not even those who had served under Weishardt for years, had ever seen him with the expression he was wearing now.

"Blockade the base's gate and find the intruders! Post men at the Labyrinth City's outer gate! Don't let anyone leave the City! Call the intelligence unit back from the Labyrinth and get them searching the streets! Question the captured assailants *now*! Don't let the intruders get away!"

The one issuing instructions to the Labyrinth Suppression Forces in rapid succession wasn't Weishardt, but rather Leonhardt, who'd also heard the news, and had come running.

Weishardt tortured the captured assailants, but he wasn't getting any information out of them. He chewed his lip and clenched his fists so tightly they started to bleed. Leonhardt did his best to assuage his troubled brother.

"Calm down a bit; this isn't like you. Clear your head," Leonhardt clapped Weishardt on the shoulder, and ordered the Forces to put the Labyrinth City on high alert.

Who could've done this...? Who the hell was it?!

Weishardt thought back on the people who had come to the Labyrinth City after potions had become available on the market.

A lot of rough-looking C-Rank and below adventurers had come to the City recently. Day after day, Weishardt received reports of the trouble they caused.

It was said many groups of merchants had visited from the imperial capital and the neighboring towns, too. Although monster-warding potions were available, the trip was still a frightening one, and traders traveled through the Fell Forest guarded by a more than a few escorts.

Weishardt also knew that craftsmen with manufacturing skills, led by glass artisans, also traveled with merchants or private transportation groups like the Black Iron Freight Corps to the Labyrinth City.

There had been many new residents as of late, and it was impossible to investigate the behavior of every single one, but the Forces had been expected to make absolutely sure to have a firm understanding of the developing situation regarding those prowl-ing around the Aguinas family. That's why they were able to pre-dict and suppress today's attacks on the atelier and the Aguinas residence without any problems.

Just in case, Caroline and her father, Royce, had been secluded in the guesthouse within the base of the Labyrinth Suppression Forces for the past few days.

Could they have had a man on the inside?

Few knew where Caroline was staying in the first place. Even during the days she'd been hidden there, a carriage carrying someone else in her place left the Aguinas house at her usual time to go to the atelier, then the base. No one other than residents extremely familiar with the Labyrinth City should have noticed.

We took good care of the main noble families in the Labyrinth City. I don't see any advantage for them to antagonize us at this point in time... Could it be Robert? He escaped after all? But the recoil from those curses should've left him broken and useless. Even if he'd managed to avoid the effects of his curses, what would he gain from kidnapping his younger sister?

Who could it have been? The man's mind was a squall of poorly arranged thoughts that left him with no definite suspect.

Even if Robert had run clear across the City, it wasn't logical to assume he'd find Caroline. However, Caroline was the daugh-ter of a noble family. Simply being taken by such a ruffian would be enough to mar her reputation.

Soldiers of the Labyrinth Suppression Forces had already run to the Labyrinth City gates and were calling members together to resolve the situation, but with the strict control of information, only a few knew the details of the abduction.

They needed to somehow rescue the kidnapped woman before

rumors had the chance to run rampant. Every second that passed in vain was a second too many.

However, the arrival of another messenger threw the impatient Weishardt into further chaos.

"Reporting in! Mr. Kunz Marrock from the Rock Wheel Autonomous Region seeks an audience. He has already departed from his territory and is scheduled to arrive the day after tomorrow!"

"Marrock, you say? Why now…? No, I know precisely why."

The Rock Wheel Autonomous Region was a city of dwarves located to the northwest of the Labyrinth City. It was the first city yagu merchant caravans reached when crossing the steep mountains.

The place was a remote area that took one week of travel by yagu to reach, following the steep mountain road out from the Labyrinth City. It took three weeks from the imperial capital, one week of which was through a mountain road that was impossible for carriages to cross.

Dwarves had gathered there due to the region's abundant ore veins. Though those veins didn't yield rare metals like orichalcum, they were full of iron and mythril. There was a wealth of other metals and water to be found as well. Moreover, monsters were a common sight on those mountains.

However, the land was infertile, so food consisted only of meat and potatoes, and because entertainment was even harder to come by than in the Labyrinth City, it was an empty place that normal people couldn't stand for very long. But for the dwarves, who were happy so long as they got to drink alcohol and strike iron, it was a pleasant enough home.

The Rock Wheel Autonomous Region was also a place

rumored by young, poor adventurers to be where one could obtain high-quality swords on the cheap.

However, information on fantastic swords for fantastically little coin was rather outdated. Nowadays, the region flourished as a place of production, putting out high-quality weapons and armor made from the abundant minerals and rare monster materials.

The prosperity of the Rock Wheel Autonomous Region was probably due in part to the regular visits of yagu merchant caravans from the Labyrinth City. The caravans carried materials from the Labyrinth and goods from the imperial capital, bringing a previously unseen level of prosperity to the inhospitable mountains.

There was one other party responsible for the land's accomplishments. The successive generations of half-dwarf lords who governed the region and managed the buying and selling of weapons and armor.

You could tell from the fact that they lived in such a remote region that dwarves took joy in crafting and had the spirits of true artisans.

The desire to make truly fine works was what guided them, they had no interest in the failed creations they made along the way. So they processed any failures back into crushed materials, or sold them for dirt cheap, if anyone was willing to make an offer. Even when peddling superior works that would sell for a small fortune in the imperial city, dwarves took little heed of money, caring only for what they needed to support their supply of drink. These were a people hardly suited for business.

That was not to say they were stupid. No amount of an artisan's spirit blinded them from noticing when a merchant came from the imperial capital, exchanged cheap alcohol for crafts they considered to be failures, and then sold those works in the imperial capital at a high price.

However, despite knowing they had leeway in negotiations, the only complaints they raised were things like "I wanna try some alcohol that's a little better than this." Even in trivial arbitrations, they had difficulty swaying another party.

Dwarves had a characteristic sensitivity to and were extremely sharp in matters related to craftsmanship, but they were wholly unsuited for debate and business. That is, so long as they were pure-blooded dwarves. The one who saved them was a lone half dwarf.

This man, who possessed both the disposition of a dwarf and a strong sense of commerce, united his people, traded their failed creative works at appropriate prices, and quickly became the lord of the autonomous region. Curiously, if a person's dwarven blood ran too thin, their thoughts wouldn't align well with full-blooded dwarves, and if their human blood was too thin, they couldn't skillfully handle matters of business or diplomacy. That's why the lords of the Rock Wheel Autonomous Region weren't chosen by lineage, but rather by who demonstrated the best balance in these regards.

The head of those half dwarves, and the current lord of the region, was Kunz Marrock. He was possessed of the greatest cunning found among his kind in generations.

It took a week to travel from the Rock Wheel Autonomous Region to the Labyrinth City. By the time the City received notice of his visit, his planned arrival was only two days away. This meant he had set out without sending the notice first.

The Rock Wheel Autonomous Region had maintained interactions with the Labyrinth City as an encampment site for yagu merchant caravans for over two hundred years. Unannounced though his visit may have been, it was impossible for Leonhardt and Weishardt not to give the man an audience.

Why now?

That was probably obvious. If people could now use monster-warding potions to go through the Fell Forest, the number of yagu merchant caravans passing through the Rock Wheel Autonomous Region would drop precipitously. For the dwarves, the launch of potion sales was something they couldn't overlook.

Could it really have been Rock Wheel that did it? No. Master Marrock is a man with an unreadable heart, but his troops are all dwarves. They'd be too easily recognized. They're also not particularly sneaky folk, either...

Leonhardt placed his hand on his flustered younger brother's shoulder.

"Don't worry, Weis. Kidnapping normally has a purpose. Miss Caroline won't be harmed right away. We'll sort all of this out." After reassuring his kin, Leonhardt requested the messenger to provide the details.

07

Caroline's atelier on the edge of the slums had been attacked in the early morning, when the Aguinas family's carriage arrived. Since more than half of the atelier's lot was used for the manufacturing building and the material storehouse, only two carriages could fit in at one time. The stagecoach was always escorted by another of its kind from the Labyrinth Suppression Forces, but there had been an unexpected visitor today. This meant that only the Aguinas carriage was able to enter the atelier's rear yard.

While the stagecoach entered, its chaperone waited outside in a location that wouldn't block the back street. Naturally, the soldiers on board disembarked and headed for the atelier on foot. Before they could make it through the gate, however, it was closed by the assailants who jumped from their hiding place within the atelier's grounds.

They were three thin men equipped with cheap weapons and armor. Their worn equipment looked ready for the scrap heap. Judging by their movements, the assailants appeared to be adventurers of roughly D Rank. They'd lain in wait for their quarry in the yard, and as soon as the Aguinas family's carriage entered, they'd sprung their trap; barring the way for the guards.

They were probably trying to take Caroline hostage, hoping to make demands for her safe release.

"Get them! Bring those guys down!"

"Awright, but you'd better pay us, Mr. Merchant!"

People raised their voices faster than the assailants laid their hands on the Aguinas carriage.

The one who issued the order to take control of the situation wasn't a soldier struggling to break through the back gate of the atelier, nor was it the Aguinas family's coachman. It was a merchant who'd just happened to be there for a discussion of trade. Four well-equipped bodyguards leaped from the merchant's own wagon. They had good physiques, and you could tell at a glance that they were stronger than the assailants.

Swords were drawn, and the bodyguards slashed freely at the attackers. The difference in rank was plain as day. Against the thin, ill-equipped, roughly D-Rank assailants, the escorts had the advantage, being around C Rank themselves. Even if they didn't kill the attackers, the difference in combat ability was such that the bodyguards could thoroughly neutralize them. The merchant's hired swordsmen were clearly eager for blood.

"E-eek, no!"

"Shaddap and die quietly."

The fearsome escorts swung their swords down at the assailants and easily struck and broke their weapons. Then they raised their swords again to cut down their opponents, but the Aguinas carriage's doors opened just a few seconds before they could.

It was unknown how many people were clearly aware of what happened in the moment after the carriage doors opened.

The figure who charged out at the same time the doors opened closed the distance between himself and the assailants so quickly that they hadn't even noticed. This new combatant used the sheath of his saber to knock out every last person with a drawn blade.

Just as did the assailant closest to the back gate heard the distant sounds of the strikes, he saw the other assailants and the escorts alike knocked to the ground by someone in green attire and sporting wavy blond hair. The next instant, that same person had appeared in front of him, and everything went black.

"I... I'm saved...," the assailant mumbled right before he lost consciousness. The blond man had taken total control of the situation all by himself. He frowned.

"Well done, Lord Malraux."

Malraux's orderly, Rhet, had been riding in the Aguinas

family's carriage along with him, and he rushed over to take orders. Taros, the soldier slave, opened the back gate and led the soldiers from the other carriage into the rear yard.

They had obtained information in advance about the merchant they'd never interacted with and the lurking assailants. The Aguinas family's carriage was a decoy; Malraux and the others were there in Caroline's place, and their counterplan went off without a hitch. The attempted crime had been so clumsy that it seemed almost unnecessary for Malraux to personally be present.

"Rhet, question everyone. Including the merchant and his escorts. Request Mr. Reymond's assistance for the three assailants. Refrain from treating them roughly."

At Malraux's orders, the soldiers moved to restrain the would-be kidnappers, the adventurers who'd tried to stop them, and the merchant.

"Wha—? We have nothing to do with this, I'm completely innocent in this matter!"

"We...w-we h-have to...return to the...i-i-i-i-imperial capital."

The hunched-over merchant and a man thought to be his son were ordered to get out of their carriage. They demanded to be released, saying they'd just happened to be visiting the workshop for business negotiations. Despite their protests, however, they were swiftly taken to a detention room with a dismissive comment: "Cooperate with the Labyrinth Suppression Forces."

"That's the end of the report from Lieutenant Malraux! Furthermore, his opinion is that they either acted independently or were hired, but with no connection to a large organization."

The messenger had recounted the events with excessive detail. It took no small amount of time, and as Weishardt was made to listen to the needless information, there was a growing unpleasantness about the man that seemed to chill the air around them.

"Next! A brief summary this time!"

As the superior, Weishardt started to lecture a rookie soldier who was unused to giving reports. Leonhardt shot a quick, but no less meaningful, look at his oddly behaving brother. Weishardt promptly silenced himself and listened intently.

"Sir! A summary of the attack on the Aguinas estate! The aggressors were thought to be C to B Rank and coordinated enough to be part of a professional criminal organization! They were brought in by the mixed force of third- and seventh-unit soldiers that had been hiding nearby. All hostiles were captured! At present, we haven't been able to obtain any information on the mastermind behind the incident! May we call Dr. Nierenberg to assist?"

Dick was captain of the Labyrinth Suppression Forces' third unit, and an A-Rank mage was captain of the seventh. The group that had attacked the Aguinas house seemed to be skilled, but they'd been up against two A-Rankers. They were subjugated without difficulty.

In truth, the drama of the arrest was so absurd that Weishardt would find it irritating. The message carrier had sensed the man's unpleasant disposition and omitted anything but the necessary facts, an exemplary adherence to instructions.

"Have Nierenberg engage in the questioning. I permit the use of potions as well! Make them tell you everything."

"Sir!"

Wasn't a questioning that used potions akin to torture? Without letting his concern about the methods show on his face, the courier soldier ran off to find Nierenberg.

"Next! I want to know the situation at the base's guesthouse!"

An attendant of Weishardt's, the first person on the scene, responded to his command.

"Sir! When I arrived at the guesthouse, everyone within was in a stupor! All were unhurt, save for one person unaccounted for. Those present are recovering comfortably. Lord Royce is safe as well. There was no sign of a break-in at the guesthouse! I was told they were all subjected to a powerful drowsiness after their morning tea, so we're requesting an investigation by the scout unit. We suspect the use of sleeping pills!"

"There were no other clues as to the culprit?!"

"Correct, sir! Unfortunately. A magical probe yielded no evidence, either..."

"Are you really saying there wasn't a single clue?!"

Bam! Weishardt brought his fist down on the desk.

The soldiers' expressions darkened at their commander's shout. These were the elite of the Labyrinth Suppression Forces, men and women well used to suffering angry shouts and the like. Feeble hearts that quivered before cruel words were ill suited to their line of work. A furious yell was as soft as a gentle breeze compared to the regular shrieks and cries of monsters.

It wasn't Weishardt's bellow itself that had caused his soldiers to scowl so. Rather, they were upset that their own inability had caused a man normally possessed of no emotion to express this much anger.

"Calm yourself, Weis. Retire to your room for a while."

"But, Brother..."

"That's an order."

"Understood..."

Leonhardt calmly ordered his flustered younger brother to

compose himself. He understood Weishardt's feelings very well. He even considered it a welcome change, given how Weishardt had suppressed all emotions. He had even grown to accept the deaths of his subordinates without so much as a flinch. However, Leonhardt knew that was not the time for his brother to show such feelings to those that served him.

There were soldiers who laid down their lives on the orders of Leonhardt or Weishardt. That's how it had been and how it would continue to be, for the sake of the Empire, the lands of Margrave Schutzenwald, the Labyrinth City, the people living in that city, and each soldier's special someone.

No matter how just the cause they touted, no matter how much they dressed it up with gallant and noble words, Leonhardt and Weishardt were the ones who ordered the soldiers into their graves.

Each guardsman had a life, a person they loved, a heart. Those who would command them to throw that all away could not afford to be swayed by emotion. Other than the slaves, everyone in the Labyrinth Suppression Forces had freely volunteered for their positions. The Labyrinth City had few jobs to choose from, but that didn't mean anyone had been forced to join the Forces. The soldiers had chosen their own path, how to walk upon it, and came here. Leonhardt, and Weishardt who supported him, had a duty to each one of those irreplaceable people they'd been entrusted with.

"Weis, don't forget the importance of what we hold in our hands." Leonhardt hoped the meaning of his words would reach his brother.

Weishardt clenched his teeth tightly. A moment later, his facial expression returned to its usual placidity, and he quietly withdrew to his office.

"Continue the search. Bring to light all information on suspicious people within the City."

At Leonhardt's command, the members of the Forces, as well as any others who witnessed the brief exchange between the brothers, hurried to their respective tasks with dauntless expressions, looking as though they were ready to face a fearsome beast from the depths of the lowest stratum.

08

Following the attack on Caroline's atelier, Malraux entrusted the cleanup to members of the Forces, and hurried to the base with his orderly, Rhet, and his soldier slave, Taros.

According to the information Malraux had obtained, the Aguinas estate—where Dick and the others had been heading—was attacked at almost the exact same time. The group at the workshop had been poorly prepared, and it reeked of a distraction. Dick had said something didn't feel quite right about the group that had attacked the villa, either.

There was no clear evidence, of course, but Dick's intuition wasn't something to be sneezed at. If both incidents were diversions, where was the main force? Malraux could think of only one logical conclusion.

I've got to hurry...

It was in situations such as these that Malraux's communication skills truly shone. Needless to say, the ability to make telepathic contact with distant comrades was beyond convenient. Dashing, the man made his way swiftly darting through the back alleys of the slums in order to reach the Labyrinth Suppression Forces' base as soon as possible.

The shanty where the pest-control dumplings atelier was stationed was not developed with any sort of eye for city planning. Its lanes were made up of complex, narrow passages. When one knew the way, however, it proved quicker to reach the Labyrinth Suppression Forces' base by running through these crisscrossing streets than to go by carriage along the main street.

Rhet's and Taros's physical abilities weren't as high as Malraux's, and although the two frantically followed him as best they could, Malraux held no qualms about leaving them behind if they could not keep up. The distance between the leader and his two followers steadily widened, all the more so when they reached a narrow straight.

Thud.

Before Malraux could say "I'm going on ahead," Rhet and Taros wordlessly pitched forward onto the ground.

"What's wrong?!"

Each of them had a short, dart-sized arrow protruding from their back. Thankfully, they were still breathing; their bodies had not completely stopped moving.

Blowguns?! And poison, too...?

This was a wholly different kind of attack than the one at the atelier. Grasping the situation in an instant, Malraux jumped in front of the motionless Rhet and Taros, pulled his saber from its scabbard, and stood ready for the poison arrows that were undoubtedly being trained on him.

We were followed... No, did they lure us into this alley?

Malraux hadn't seen the trajectory of the arrows that had struck Rhet and Taros. However, the projectiles themselves gave a clue as to the direction they'd been loosed from. This was a straight path. If the unseen attacker shot another arrow, Malraux would be ready for it with swift feet. He would likely be able to ascertain the enemy's exact location and move to counterattack.

The next poison arrow cut through the air with a whistling sound. So slight was the noise, it wouldn't have reached the ears of an average man in time. Thankfully, the metal of the arrowhead had caught the light, and Malraux was able to spot the sniper's hiding spot without much trouble.

There!

Parrying the poisoned arrow that was speeding toward him, Malraux was about to start toward the assassin. Suddenly, Taros the soldier slave rose to his feet and moved like he was going to shield Malraux from behind.

Taros?! What are you—?

The instant Malraux looked behind Taros, he suddenly understood everything.

After hurling his saber at the assassin who'd fired the poison arrow, Malraux turned back toward Taros. The slave had been ordered to sacrifice himself to shield Malraux in an emergency. A *second* poison arrow found its way to the large man whom Malraux had treated with indifference. Undaunted, Taros remained standing in front of his master to shield him from further harm.

Slipping past the slave, Malraux unsheathed the sword from Taros's waist and cut down the third arrow shot by a *second* assassin, then very easily rushed up a wall where the rocks had come loose. With the speed of the wind, Taros's sword was at the throat of the second assassin, who'd been lurking at the back of the building.

"It's over. You will come with me to the Labyrinth Suppression Forces," Malraux proclaimed.

The attacks on the atelier and the Aguinas estate had happened at almost the same time. The notion there was someone behind each of the incidents was no great leap of logic.

There had been two assassins. They probably contrived to perform a pincer attack by firing poison arrows from behind Malraux in this narrow, straight path while his attention was to his front.

Taros saved my life...

If the valiant man hadn't noticed the poison arrow aimed at Malraux's back when he did, Malraux might have been the one on the ground right now. In the brief moment of worry Malraux expressed for his slave, the assassin lunged forward onto the sword in Malraux's hand, ending his own life.

"What the devil...?"

The soldiers, adventurers, and even wannabe-bandits-turned-slaves living in the Labyrinth City coveted life. Even if they failed in their duty, even if they were seriously injured, death was hardly the preferable option. Whoever staged this attack worked with a completely different set of principles.

The saber Malraux had thrown had pierced and killed the first assassin. He wondered if perhaps this had been a separate force, different from the groups who had attacked the atelier and Aguinas estate, but there was no way to know now. Corpses could not be interrogated. If Malraux had been attacked, that meant the base sheltering the alchemist was most likely also...

"We must hurry to the base. Come with me and don't fall behind."

Malraux gave Rhet and Taros a cure potion each, and the two quickly recovered. He hurried to the base, accompanied by his two subordinates.

09

"**Fire!** Over there, too, **Fire**! And then over here, **Fire**!"

In the middle of the confusion at the base, Freyja began shouting indiscriminately at every suspicious person she saw. "State your business! **Fire!**" It was a performance worthy of her title as the Sage of Calamity. "What happened today, Mitchell? You lot let a man trespass all the way into the underground area and I almost torched him to cinders on reflex."

"Lady Freyja, please forgive us. We will arrest all the intruders and make them tell us who they work for." Mitchell courteously bowed his curly head, but his nervous sweat told a different story than his calm exterior.

Right before the attack, the young lady alchemist had been making potions with reckless abandon and then plunged into nap time, while Freyja had been drinking with reckless abandon and then plunged into stroll time. Up to that point, the day had been no different from any other. However, after leaving the temporary lab established in the base's cellar and heading through the underground passage for a little while, Freyja had turned toward a soldier who had come to transport potions and suddenly loosed her fire magic.

"What! What are you…?!"

"Look carefully. Do you recognize his face? He's an intruder. He'll come to his senses before long. Tie him up."

The fire pillar engulfing the intruder immediately vanished, and just as Freyja had said, the person who appeared from the blaze was someone Mitchell had never seen before. Mitchell thought the impostor had been consumed by the crimson heat, but his clothes and hair were only a touch singed. Despite the smoke coming from his mouth, the man's life didn't appear to be in mortal danger. Mitchell didn't know how Freyja did it; perhaps she wrapped him in a fire pillar to suffocate him into unconsciousness.

Very few should know of this place. And he's wearing a Labyrinth Suppression Forces uniform…

After Mitchell ordered the two soldiers who rushed in to restrain the intruder, suspend the transport of potions, and fortify the alchemist's escort, he had someone who'd been attending Freyja go report the situation and gather information.

"Mitchell. Do you enjoy hunting?"

Freyja smiled sweetly. Although she was a dazzlingly beautiful woman, her smile seemed to Mitchell like that of a carnivorous animal eyeing its prey.

Freyja's metaphor was in poor taste, but she didn't seem to have a grotesque plan in mind. All three of the intruders in the vicinity of the atelier and medicinal herb storehouse were captured alive.

The last one had concealed their presence so inconspicuously that even Mitchell hadn't noticed them. Freyja hadn't had that problem, however.

"And now, **Fire**!"

Normally, the fiery woman would probably have been all too eager to hunt down intruders throughout the base. However, after confirming the area around the atelier was safe, she returned to where Mariela was sleeping.

10

When Mariela awoke, she was on a couch set beside the fireplace in the living room of Sunlight's Canopy.

Huh? When did I make it back here?

The couch in the living room was soft and comfortable to sleep on. Her reserves of magical power had been completely restored, but she wanted to lie like this for a little while longer.

Mariela had made huge splurges on the house, so even though it was summer, the building was kept cool and comfortable via a magical tool for cooling air attached to a magical tool for ventilation. The tools consumed magical gems relentlessly, but the ground under Mariela's feet might as well have been paved with gold coins, so she didn't need to worry about that. Actually, the magical gems Sieg collected while hunting covered it, so Mariela hardly had to spend any money.

The life of a socialite is the bessst.

That was Mariela for you. She didn't understand how to use the word *socialite*, nor was she terribly satisfied with her life. It was like a certain guildmaster somewhere who said things like "I'm gonna blow off some steam from today's work!" while having only cold beer and snacks for dinner.

Come to think of it, there was an adventurer having beer and bread in a sandwich shop near the Labyrinth not too long ago.

It was probably around lunchtime. The sandwich shop was famous, yet the old adventurer had been eating plain bread with no ham or veggies between it. The food was not even dressed up with cheese or butter. Just beer and bread. If he could afford to drink, the man could surely afford some beef or ham, even soup. Yet for some reason, that adventurer had been satisfied with cheap bread and beer.

I wonder if he was having beer with a side of bread, or bread with a side of beer. Since it was a liquid, maybe it was a substitute for soup? That sure was an incredibly unbalanced lunch.

Mariela's blissful thoughts faded into the fogs of sleep as she muttered, "I don't really understand the minds of drinkers."

The voice of the girl's master, and that of another, woke the young alchemist. Buildings in the Labyrinth City had small windows and poor breathability. That's why every house was equipped with a magical tool for ventilation, and air pipes ran above the ceiling. In the case of Sunlight's Canopy, if the magical tool for air cooling was used only in the shop and the living room, voices in the corridor could be heard all the way in the living room for some reason.

"Well? What happened, Mitchell?"

"I was informed the young lady of the Aguinas family was abducted—"

"!!! You mean Lady Carol?!" Mariela asked Mitchell after springing to her feet and dashing out to the corridor.

"That's… You were awake? We are currently using everything at our disposal to search for her. Please keep this discreet."

"Mitchell, get out."

Freyja was astonished at Mariela's sudden appearance. The golden-eyed woman coldly addressed Mitchell, who bowed his head in respect.

Since Freyja hadn't noticed Mariela was awake, there was no way Mitchell would have noticed, either. Although Mitchell had served Freyja on the base, he was still one of Weishardt's aides, and he had an appropriately strong desire to rescue Caroline on Weishardt's behalf. The fact that Mitchell had leaked the classified information that Caroline was abducted was probably because he'd hoped to get Freyja's assistance if possible. He hadn't seen anything to suggest this woman Mariela called "Master" was an alchemist, but Freyja's ability to notice things far surpassed his ability to do so. For example, she had immediately spotted an intruder that was so well hidden even an excellent intelligence agent like Mitchell hadn't noticed, and she'd realized normal vials were concealed in the middle of a large pile of potion vials. It wasn't a stretch to suppose the Sage of Calamity surpassed Mitchell in combat, either.

Mitchell didn't have the authority to ask for help, but a powerful, capable person was in front of him, and she'd demanded an explanation of the situation. It would be absurd not to hope for the "possible."

However, this was only true for Freyja. He'd come to understand within the short period of time he'd been performing his duties that Mariela's fighting strength was nonexistent. That's why Mitchell hadn't intended to tell her. Doing so would be liable to expose her to danger.

The fact that Freyja, who normally would have gone hunting and roasting the intruders, had carried the sleeping Mariela back to Sunlight's Canopy was solid proof of that.

The sage was always, irresponsibly, relentlessly drinking in the daytime and agitating her pupil. However, one could guess at her true nature if they looked at her behavior while Mariela was unconscious. Mariela's safety was Freyja's highest priority, and she had no intention of either helping Caroline or getting Mariela involved.

Mitchell quietly bowed his head and went back to the base through the underground Aqueduct. With a slightly annoyed look, Freyja watched the pretty man leave, and then—with a look actually befitting her title—said to Mariela, "Think about your own safety first."

"Wait, Master! Hey, what's going on?! I said wait!"

"I'll tell you later, so just be patient in the meantime."

Mariela tried to chase her master, but Freyja returned to the living room to ensure she stayed and headed to Sunlight's Canopy.

"Amber, close up for the day. Sorry, but everyone needs to go home, too."

"Now that you mention it, the weather's looking pretty threatening. Eek! That was a huge bolt of lightning. It would be better to go home before a downpour starts. Everyone, hurry home before you get soaked!"

Amber could tell from Freyja's eyes that something was going on, so she took advantage of the ominous flash of lightning as an excuse. After she closed the shop, she returned home herself.

The base's temporary atelier was in the cellar, and it had no windows despite being a living room. It was because of this that no one had noticed the heavy clouds overhead, and how dim it was outside, even though it was the middle of the day. Every now and then a bolt of lightning crackled, visible through the skylight. The white arcs were doing their best imitation of the sacred tree, giving the impression of a nighttime storm passing through the gloomy Fell Forest.

No sooner had the large, distinct marks of raindrops appeared on the dry flagstone paths than the water began pouring down in buckets.

"Phew, I made it."

Siegmund returned to Sunlight's Canopy only a short while after Amber and the others had departed.

Today he had gone to the Fell Forest to collect the rare fruit he'd promised Mariela. There had also been signs of prey in the area that seemed like they could be dinner, but with the sudden turn in the weather, he simply picked the fruit and hurried back. Thankfully, he had returned home before the storm began in earnest.

Perhaps in anticipation of the heavy rain, Sunlight's Canopy was closed despite the fact that it was only just past noon. The interior of the shop, normally teeming with regulars, was deserted.

Since Sieg could sense Mariela's magical power from the direction of the living room, he knew she was safe. However, he didn't hear her usual "Welcome back." The only sound he heard came from the rain.

"Mariela, I'm back. I got the fruit I promised you," Sieg said, heading for the living room and opening the door. The once-large room had been remodeled when they moved in to divide it into a fireplace-furnished living room in the back, and a dining room in the front. The dining room was usually used as Nierenberg's clinic, but Mariela's master sat in the doctor's place today. Freyja was drinking with a sour look on her face.

Sieg wondered what had happened, but Freyja silently urged him to go to Mariela. He opened the inner door and entered the living room.

Mariela was sitting on her favorite couch, hugging her knees.

"What's wrong, Mariela?"

He rushed to her side and peered at her face. At hearing his voice, Mariela slowly lifted her face from her knees. She bit her lower lip hard and looked like she might start crying any minute.

"Sieg…"

The hunter saw more than sadness in her eyes. Her expression was a blend of anxiety, fear, impatience, and resentment. Sieg got down on his knees in front of her to be at eye level and asked again, "What's wrong?"

Mariela's pursed lips quivered. If she spoke about it, tears might spill out.

"It's okay, Mariela. It's okay. Tell me," Sieg said to her gently. In response, Mariela opened her mouth like she was going to speak, frowned just a little, closed her mouth again, and buried her face in her knees.

"Mariela…"

Instead of saying anything, she began shaking slightly.

Freyja had made her way to the entrance of the room unnoticed, and she took it upon herself to explain.

"They said that friend of hers, a young woman, was kidnapped."

"Young woman… Lady Caroline?"

"Th-they…thought she was me, the alchemist…" Mariela's face was still buried in her knees, and her voice came out muffled.

"She volunteered to play the role of the alchemist herself. She was fully aware of the risks."

"But…but, I wanna help her."

"And what would you do if you went to find her? What could you do? You can't fight—it'd only make a bad situation worse. She volunteered to be the decoy for you, and now you want to throw that away? All you'd do is put more people at risk to protect you."

"I know… But…"

"Lady Frey, please, you've said enough."

Freyja had been about to say more, but Sieg deterred her. Mariela's face remained concealed behind her legs. Her body was shaking now, and she was almost certainly crying.

Gently stroking Mariela's head, Sieg addressed her master in her place.

"Mariela already understands everything you just said perfectly. That's why she never said anything about it sooner. She doesn't want anyone else to get hurt on her account. She knows full well both her own powerlessness and that getting involved herself would make the situation worse. Even so, she can't stand the idea of losing a friend who was trying to protect her."

"…I know that," Freyja answered, sounding just a little uncomfortable.

"M-Master, when you…came here…y-you…found me……!" Mariela said, hiccupping. She was asking if there was a way to find Caroline.

"That was spirit magic. You can't use it, and I don't know this Lady Carol or whoever, so I can't locate her," Freyja told Mariela in a hushed, defeated tone.

"But I…don't want…anyone else…to die…!!!"

Mariela let out a strangled, slightly hoarse cry. Doubtless she was thinking of Lynx. Her anguished voice cut through Sieg as keenly as any knife.

"Mariela, I'll go look for her. No matter how many days it takes, I'll find her. And I'll bring her back, no matter what. So please, don't cry."

Sieg's promise was an empty one. He had nothing to go on, no means to search for Caroline. He was just one person, not an organization like the Labyrinth Suppression Forces or someone with special skills for tracking people down. But what else could he do? What else could he have said to her?

Sieg gently placed his hand on Mariela's fingers digging into her knees. Her small, warm hand had healed and saved him so many times, but now it was cold and trembling with sorrow.

"Sieg…," she said in a nearly inaudible voice. Freyja gazed intently at the two of them.

"…There's one way, and only one. You might be able to use it now," the sage said in an uncharacteristically heavy, quiet tone.

"Master, is that true?" Mariela lifted her head at her teacher's words.

As she looked at her pupil's tearstained face, Freyja's expression was unusually grim.

"Yeah. But, Mariela, if *what ties you* to this place is weak, you might not be able to come back."

Upon hearing her master's words, Mariela looked at Sieg, who still held her hand tightly in his. She closed her eyes for a short while as if recalling something, then looked at Sieg again and responded reassuringly, "I'll be fine."

"Please, let Mariela help her friend."

Sieg nodded to the young alchemist, and then the two of them stood and bowed their heads to Freyja. She seemed just a little uncomfortable and lonely at seeing them bowing with their hands still linked together.

"Come with me," she said and took them out to the rear garden where heavy rain was still falling.

"Drops of Life dwell in all things. They circulate through the world, and then return to the ley line. So just ask the ley line."

This "one way" imparted by the Sage of Calamity as she stood beneath the soaked branches of the sacred tree was certainly an extraordinary one.

"Mariela, your Nexus is thicker than anyone else's. Its connection to the roots of the world is stronger than anyone else's. A Nexus isn't simply a channel to draw Drops of Life from. It connects to both the ley line and the world."

What Freyja told Mariela was the true essence of alchemy. This was not the kind of thing written in her Library; just reading about it would not have been enough.

"Formless things are easily assimilated into the world; they fade. That's why they acquire physical bodies to anchor themselves. The world needs for individuals to grow, for living creatures to be diverse. The physical body becomes a wall, partitioning the individual from the world. It cuts them off from the voice of the world. But, even if someone is complete as an individual, that doesn't mean they're truly separate. Understand? You ought to be able to feel the will of the world, of the ley line, through your Nexus. Because the world is a part of you, and you are part of the world. Whatever it knows, you're capable of knowing, too. The Nexus connects you to the roots of all life."

Freyja's voice reached her ears through the sound of the rainfall, even as the heavy downpour grew so intense that their vision became hazy.

"My Nexus..." Mariela closed her eyes and tried to ask herself.

The Nexus was linked to her skills and rooted in her core. Searching for what made Mariela herself, she shifted her focus inward, deep within her tiny body.

"You understand that you're connected. Follow the connection that draws up Drops of Life. Trace it to the source. To the Drops of Life itself..."

The precipitation continued, relentless. Heavy beads of water drummed a rhythmic *pitter-patter* on the ground.

Normally, Mariela could clearly perceive the boundary between her own body and the world, but now, as she stood in the storm with no umbrella, her hair, clothes, and body were soaked through. Boundaries between the world and herself seemed difficult to define in the downpour.

The girl wondered if seaweed drifting between the waves had a way to sense the world and itself. Would it feel like this? No, maybe the clouds drifting in the sky had a more ambiguous boundary as they blended with the air.

Drip.

Mariela felt a single raindrop.

Large, pattering pearls of water fell on her and dripped to the

ground, passing over her hair, skin, and clothes. The drops from the sky, and from her, permeated the earth and went deeper and deeper in. They were just like Drops of Life returning to the ley line.

—Mariela, where does the rain come from?—

The young alchemist heard her master's voice from somewhere within the world of rain.

—The sky. From those big, thick clouds.

Ahh, those clouds I can see from the ground look so fluffy and soft and fun. I wanna dive into them, but they would be different if I got close. They're containers for the thunderstorms, full of raging lightning and brimming over with raindrops.—

—That's right, Mariela. They came from the sea. They're blown wherever the wind takes them, they fill with water, and look, it's too much for them to hold.

They steadily shed rain as if they were basins with holes in them.

Understand, Mariela?

Although it's only a small amount, Drops of Life has blended with the clouds and the rain. Every single drop of rain that falls outside and inside this city should feel very near to you.—

—Yes, Master. The raindrops are round; they're perfect circles. But the wind pushes them and spreads them.

Ahh, the mountains seem far below me. The planet's surface feels very near.

There are so many raindrops. Hitting the roofs of the City, bouncing off the leaves of trees.—

Although Mariela was in the rear garden of Sunlight's Canopy, it felt like she was spread wide and thin in the rain falling incessantly inside and outside the City. It showered relentlessly onto the earth, where the membranes of the raindrops stretched and flowed to lower places. It was like she was swimming on land; the rain made even the air seem hazy. Right now, it felt as though a fish could fly through the sky.

—Mariela, where is your friend?—

—Lady Carol, where is Lady Carol?—

No matter how much the rain filled the City, the Drops of Life were heavily diluted. Following the drops, Mariela felt like she was everywhere, and yet it also seemed like she was still the girl standing in the rain. She was spread both far and wide throughout the City, and yet so concentrated and near. She couldn't see anything clearly.

—Mariela, what kind of person is your friend?—

—Lady Carol is kind. She's beautiful, like a princess, but strong. She wants to make all kinds of medicine and help lots of people. We made it together.—

—With alchemy skills?—

—Yeah. She's not connected to a Nexus, but I think Lady Carol's definitely an alchemist. I bet the ley line wants to connect to her, too. She said she wants to make potions. Ahh, that's right. Lady Carol. That's who she is. Where are you?—

Mariela's magical power flowed against the current of the Nexus.

It intertwined, mixed, and melted into Drops of Life and spread far and wide through the raindrops engulfing the City.

Pop-pop.

The raindrops popped out before they hit the earth.

As if searching for something, someone, they spread out smaller and smaller, fell to the earth, and returned to the ley line.

Would anyone have noticed the dance of these bursting

raindrops? Surely such a slight change would be almost indistinguishable in such a storm, and no one would notice.

Surely the raindrops themselves were the only ones who knew.

Mariela felt weightless. Her body was still there, but it felt hollow. Through the sensation, Mariela mumbled something barely audible.

"Found her."

CHAPTER 5
Released

01

When Caroline awoke, she was in a gloomy room made of stone.

The air around her was a bit chilly for someone so used to the summer heat. Both the stone pedestal beneath her and the nearby stone wall were damp. She could hear rain from far away; perhaps that was the reason for the chill.

"I see you're awake, Carol."

The voice that greeted the young woman when she sat up belonged to someone she knew all too well.

"Brother..."

Robert sat in a corner of the narrow stone room, and Caroline wasted no time in probing him.

"Brother, I would like an explanation."

"You're remarkably composed, Caroline, given those people were after your life."

Robert's remark was shocking, but Caroline hardly cared as she took in her surroundings. It was an old room. Judging from the stonework, it may have been built around the same time as the estate where Estalia had slept. The pedestal Caroline was on seemed to be where luggage and other such things would've been placed. It was long enough for her to lie down on, but it was narrow, and if she'd turned over in her sleep, she would've met the floor.

Some sturdy boxes had been placed carelessly along the

ground, and Robert was seated on one of them. The stone pedestal might be where those boxes normally belonged.

Was this room a secret storehouse? A magical tool for illumination provided the only source of light, there were no windows, and Caroline could see steep stairs behind her brother. Perhaps this was a basement?

"I didn't know our house had a secret cellar."

"I learned about it directly from Uncle Ruiz. Father doesn't know about it."

Robert tacitly told her that no help would come. The young lady felt just a little relieved.

If this is my brother's secret place, and it's related to the Aguinas family, no one else will be here.

Caroline understood her brother's character and made this conjecture.

Although Robert was brilliant, he had rather strong fixations and a troubling disposition. For example, he was obsessed with everything related to the alchemists. Alchemists were a subject the Aguinas family had protected for generations, and Robert hated allowing outsiders to interfere with such things. Even in the development of the new medicine, he made the alchemists he summoned from the imperial capital help him bound by black magic.

This place, connected to the alchemy the Aguinas family so closely protected, was a personal space for Robert. A place he allowed only his supporters, or those he could completely control, to enter.

He said their father, Royce, didn't even know about this cellar. If this was truly such an important place to Robert, he really wouldn't have wanted to hold someone, even Caroline, here. In other words, Robert had no other place, no other person, he could depend on.

My brother has had no friends for a long time…

Caroline thought if she asked him about it, she might embarrass him and encourage him to start rambling on for an hour about his theories. She knew her brother quite well.

He was extremely brilliant, and that was probably why he was so confident in his own solutions to problems. If he thought something would work, he'd barrel ahead with his plan. Robert would likely have been open to other ideas had he talked to more people, but he was too awkward for that. Despite his troublesome pride, he was actually a very kind man.

"You saved me, didn't you, Brother?"

"You…you shouldn't simply go along with people so easily…"

Robert likely expected his sister to be upset as his words, but she only gave a gentle smile. Perhaps emboldened, he continued, "To think you were a scapegoat for the alchemist the Labyrinth Suppression Forces seized… Moreover, they're selling potions on the market. What is the house of Margrave Schutzenwald thinking?!"

"My, my. You must have read my letters," Caroline replied, gazing affectionately at her indignant brother.

"How can you be so cheerful?! Do you even understand what's happening?" Robert cried. "Forcing the alchemist to make as many potions as possible to sell on the market is exploitation! It goes too far! Doesn't the army know the alchemist isn't just some tool?! They were too quick to start selling potions in the first place. No one considered a production or sales plan. The yagu merchant caravans have created a structure of vested interests, and this upsets the whole order. Do you understand?! It's out of the question for a civilian to be in military employ!"

The alchemist herself had continued to mass-produce potions at an unthinkable rate, but she hardly saw potion-making as a problem. Mariela got mad at her master, laughed with Sieg and her friends at Sunlight's Canopy, and spent her days happy and healthy. Robert had assumed otherwise, but that was his own bias. However, as befit the former successor to a family that had managed potions for so long, he had a point about the problem of selling the concoctions on the market.

Over the last two hundred years, the Labyrinth City had entrusted the transportation of all goods across the mountain range to the yagu merchant caravans, and the cost was enormous. This had brought a large amount of profit to the many territories on the merchant caravans' route. The villages along the main road flourished as relay stations, and trade between territories prospered through the use of the established main road. Places like the territory of Countess Beratte, located at a junction of roads leading to the Labyrinth City, the imperial capital, and the family of small nations, flourished as transit points. They grew not only as spots of commerce between the Labyrinth City and the imperial capital, but for transporting high-quality weapons and armor made by Rock Wheel to the borderlands protecting the Empire from the wars of the small nations as well.

The distribution of arms by the Rock Wheel Autonomous Region, which sat closest to the Labyrinth City—and farthest from the imperial capital—would probably continue through the territory of Countess Beratte. However, if the Labyrinth City's merchant caravans were able to travel through the Fell Forest, those profits would start on a steady decrease. The sale of potions would completely rewrite the vested-interest structure brought about by distribution up to this point. Although reorganization was profitable for the Labyrinth City, it was highly unlikely that those with investments in ventures outside the City would remain silent much longer.

"The alchemist is a thorn in the side of anyone who benefits from the yagu merchant caravans, Carol. To them, both the defeat of the Labyrinth and that reborn alchemist will cause nothing but trouble."

Caroline knew that her brother was a kind man. Robert was extremely angry, but not for himself. He was indignant because the alchemist and Caroline had been put in danger.

"Yes. I agree, Brother," Caroline replied, her smile unbroken. Robert seemed hesitant as he continued.

"You wanted to protect the alchemist, didn't you, Carol? That's the true spirit of an Aguinas, and as your brother, I'm proud of you. However, it's not the alchemist you've volunteered to protect, but the image and honor of the Labyrinth Suppression Forces."

If the Forces had control over the alchemist, they would remain constant in protecting her no matter what kind of assassins went after her. Even if they shut her up in a tall tower or a deep cellar as a result. But if they did that, the house of Margrave Schutzenwald might go down in infamy for inhumane treatment. That's why they needed to make it known inside and outside the City that Caroline, who shouldered the role of "the alchemist," was acting freely and had chosen cooperation with the Labyrinth Suppression Forces.

Caroline's desire to protect the alchemist was exploited not to ensure Mariela's safety, but rather to safeguard the Labyrinth Suppression Forces' honor. That, above all else, was something Robert couldn't tolerate.

"I truly appreciate your concern, Brother. Nevertheless, I want to carry out this duty."

Neither Caroline's facial expression, nor her intentions, had changed one bit thus far. Although she was a calm, graceful, beautiful young woman, her stubbornness was reminiscent of another member of her family.

"Carol, there's no value in putting your life at risk." Robert searched for the words he needed to stop his sister. However, Caroline looked at him with eyes full of powerful intent and continued, undeterred.

"Brother. Our lineage protects the alchemists. Of course we must bear the full brunt of this. If I draw the eyes of the public, and someday the Labyrinth is destroyed, creating a new world brimming with alchemists, then the one who survived the Stampede will finally be able to live as an ordinary person."

Yes. That was Caroline's wish.

Someday, she wanted to make potions with Mariela in Sunlight's Canopy, and if it was no longer unique as the single potion shop in the City, she wouldn't mind.

No matter how many rival stores there might be, they would never make potions any better than the ones she and Mariela would make. There would never be a day when people didn't come to bask in the warmth of that place.

Mariela was a rare and special alchemist, but she was also a commoner. If she were used as a political tool and put on a pedestal to draw the public's attention, it was unlikely she'd be able to live freely.

Protecting the alchemist was the duty of the Aguinas family, of Caroline.

"Carol, you..."

For the first time in their conversation, Robert understood what his sister meant.

He knew Caroline had assembled a variety of magical tools and herbs to make medicine. When Robert was a child, his sister would follow him everywhere. He thought she'd aspired to be like him. But he'd been wrong. She'd inherited the blood, the will, of the Aguinas family, and Caroline herself was no doubt an alchemist of some fashion. Of course, she hadn't actually made a Pact with the ley line, so she had no skills to make potions. However, skills were an embodiment of one's body and soul.

If there were no potions, she would make medicine instead. It was a logical conclusion for one with the spirit of a true alchemist.

How could Robert oppose his sister's decision? Caroline seemed more worthy of being called an alchemist than anyone else.

"...I understand, Carol. If that's the case, I will help you, as a fellow bearer of the Aguinas name."

"Thank you, Brother!" Caroline was overjoyed from the bottom of her heart.

I don't have much longer to live. But at least let me protect Carol.

Robert now understood how his sister felt. Though neither had moved, the space between them felt smaller. It was time to marshal all the power the Aguinas family had acquired governing potions and alchemists over these past two hundred years. Robert gripped the flame seal carved onto his hand and prayed. The seal of the capricious sage who liked to play with fire was a useful, but time-limited item. It didn't reduce one's life span, or anything like that, however.

Unfortunately, Robert still misunderstood one crucial thing.

*   *   *

"Incidentally, Brother, where are we?"

"Our family's hidden storehouse in the forests east of the Labyrinth City."

The violent rain didn't seem likely to stop, but after Caroline insisted that she should notify everyone of her safety before the sun set, the pair crept out from their hiding place.

The top of the steep staircase leading from the basement was black and sooty like the inside of an old furnace. Emerging outside from a half-crumbled entrance, the surroundings seemed to be the ruins of a place once used for making charcoal.

The slope of the foot of the mountain had been used to build three charcoal-making kilns made of stone and mud side by side, and the interior of the rightmost kiln connected to the hidden storehouse.

All of them were ancient, and any chimneys that hadn't collapsed were choked with ash and soot. Charcoal wasn't currently used much in the Labyrinth City, but long ago, dwarven master blacksmiths had used it in the process of making steel, so it was no wonder that the forest contained the remains of a place that produced it.

Seems our ancestor was fond of tricks like the hidden door to our family's cellar and this hidden storehouse. I'd like to show Mariela sometime.

Although it was an elaborately hidden storehouse, the only things inside were some boxes, one of which Robert had used as a chair. They'd been scattered around on the floor, and he'd even sat on one, so perhaps they weren't storing anything particularly valuable.

While Caroline considered such things, she followed behind her brother along an animal trail.

The cloak Robert had borrowed from the Labyrinth Suppression Forces was waterproof, so it protected Caroline from the downpour, but the road was muddy with rainwater. It was very hard for Caroline to walk in her thin heels.

Robert had offered to carry her, and perhaps she wouldn't have minded if she were unconscious. But the idea of a mature young woman being carried by her older brother was too embarrassing. It was absolutely out of the question.

That reminds me—I became very sleepy after I had my tea...

Caroline had begun arguing with Robert as soon as she woke up and spotted him, so she'd had no time to recall what happened before she was abducted.

I am unharmed, and my brother was the one who did it, so Father and my escorts should be safe as well, but...

Perhaps due to her fatigue from the difficult trek back into the City, Caroline began to fuss at Robert, though it was against her better judgment.

"Brother, you are terribly unkind. We could have talked like we just did and settled the whole thing; there was no need to resort to something as vile as sleeping powder..."

But Robert's reply went against Caroline's expectations.

"I didn't use sleeping powder. I admit to sneaking into the base to look for you, but when I arrived; the escorts, Father, everyone was asleep."

"What...?"

"I was able to get you out of there thanks to the power of this seal. That, and my luck reaching you just a little before the bandits would have."

"Brother, is...is Father... Is he all right?!"

"I didn't confirm it myself, but I think he's probably fine. I didn't have time to take Father with me, but there were many escorts around him, and I left the door to the guesthouse open to make it easy for someone to notice something was wrong."

A young girl would be more effective than an aged man, whether she was used as a hostage or murdered as a warning to others. That was why Robert had prioritized securing Caroline's safety in what little time he'd had.

Robert had no way of locating their enemy, but he was certain someone had been lurking nearby, ready to abduct Caroline. The seal burned into Robert's left hand was strong. By putting his magic energy into it, his presence, magical power, and even his physical stature seemed to be perfectly hidden. It hadn't made him transparent, but instead he appeared insignificant to others, like a stone on the roadside. After experimenting with the seal's effects against a few street dogs and cats, Robert concluded that the magic would maintain the same effect if one was holding an unconscious person. The effect was weakened if holding a conscious body, however.

Luckily for both Robert and his sister, Caroline had been drugged and then passed out. He was able to outsmart the very people who'd schemed to kidnap her.

Someone else had drugged Caroline and was about to take her away. This revelation filled her with fear. When she'd woken up, Robert had been the one with her, so although she was surprised and confused, she had also been somewhat relieved. He had strayed from the path and turned to the dark arts, but to Caroline he was still her kind and beloved sibling. Speaking with him had allowed them to understand each other, and he had come to her rescue. There was no misunderstanding, and Robert had saved and hidden her before the real villain could close their grip on Caroline.

She should have been prepared—Caroline knew that now.

But even armed with that knowledge, the thought that someone had come after her made her chest tighten in fearful anguish.

02

"Sieg, call Mariela back." Freyja's sharp voice reverberated in
the rear yard of Sunlight's Canopy, cutting through the constant
sounds of the rain.

Sieg rushed to the young alchemist's side, put his hands on
her shoulders, and called her name.

"Mariela!"

Whether or not she heard, he was unsure. But Mariela turned
her face toward the one-eyed man with an unsteady movement.

"Mariela, come back. You found her, right? You can come
back now!"

There was no clear reaction to Sieg's plea. Her eyes were
vacant.

At that moment, Sieg became aware of something for the first
time.

Though he'd often looked into Mariela's eyes, he'd only now
realized they were the same golden color as Freyja's.

Her eyes didn't reflect Sieg's face peering into them, but
instead a faint, fleeting light shone from their depths, disappear-
ing as quickly as it had come.

Drops of Life? No, isn't it the color of the ley line Mariela told me about?!

He knew the color of Mariela's eyes, and it hadn't changed. Yet there was no reflection to them. Her body was here, but her spirit was in a faraway place.

"Mariela! Come back! Mariela! You can hear me, can't you?!"

Sieg refused to part with her, refused to let her go. He gripped Mariela's shoulders, calling louder and louder to her, wherever she had gone.

But her golden eyes reflected only a river of light with an unknown source. Sieg wasn't sure if his voice *could* reach her.

"Mariela…! I made a promise, didn't I?! Fruit, pastries, and orc king meat! I haven't gotten them all for you yet! You have to come back! Mariela! Mariela!!!"

Sieg searched her eyes for the girl he knew. He called to her with everything he had.

Perhaps his screams, his feelings of longing, reached out through the air and rain to reach Mariela before she could spread too wide and thin into the earth below.

"…Meat?"

"Mariela?!"

Or perhaps it was only Meat Man who had called her back.

In the middle of the pouring rain, Mariela, the girl Sieg knew well, giggled and stood with meat—with Sieg reflected in her eyes.

The man didn't know whether to sigh in relief or disappointment.

He could feel the deathly chill of Mariela's body. Her spirit had returned from a harsh journey beyond his comprehension. Even so, Sieg made a diligent effort to swallow his feelings and speak to her as he always did, now that her golden eyes held their familiar smile again.

"…For now, take a bath, and then you can have some fruit."

"And the meat?"

"Next time."

"But you promisssed!"

"Ahh, I'll keep the promise. Next time, I'll definitely bring some back. So for now… Welcome home, Mariela."

"Okay, I'll be looking forward to it. I'm glad to be back, Sieg."

And after that exchange of greetings, Mariela and Sieg headed back into the house. Neither of them realized that the distance between them had shrunk, ever so slightly.

After a moment of regarding the two with a warm expression, Freyja said, "All right, today we'll have orc meat roasted in oil!" and followed them into the house.

03

"I've identified the components of the sleepin' powder!"

The appraisal of the drug, which they thought would take only a matter of moments, had taken hours.

There were a variety of materials containing sleeping toxicants, but it was possible to narrow down the possibilities to a certain extent by looking at the condition of the affected soldiers and Royce, as well as the remaining tea. After that, if they tested the possibilities one by one, they could hopefully ascertain the type of sleeping powder and find a lead from there.

This wasn't particularly time-consuming work. Provided the materials in question could be gathered in the Labyrinth City.

Ghark had identified the powder as something that couldn't be found in the Labyrinth City, however—an important clue in its own right.

"This is a sleepin' powder often used in the small nations."

The substance was mixed not as a curative to insomnia, but to tranquilize people. It dissolved easily in water and was colorless, tasteless, and odorless. It also decomposed and disappeared over time. Since it wasn't a potion, its effects were slow and short lived. It was a strategic medicine that, if used repeatedly, could cause serious side effects.

If Ghark's appraisal had been just a little later, the sleeping powder would have decomposed beyond recognition.

His answer caused a small commotion in the council room.

A country somewhere in the family of constantly warring small nations, or a territory of the Empire that traded with the family of small nations, had acted to hinder the sale of potions in the Labyrinth City.

For what purpose?

Had the change in routes truly troubled them so?

Realizing the answer, Weishardt called Malraux over and whispered some sort of instructions to him. Malraux nodded silently and left the council room.

Meanwhile, Nierenberg, having been involved with the inter-rogations, wore an expression of comprehension.

The Aguinas family had been attacked three times today, and the result of the interrogations established that the crimes were by three completely different groups. After the culprits had been captured, it became clear there was a clear gap in the capabilities of the groups that attacked the atelier, the Aguinas estate, and the base. Speculation suggested that the first two attacks were by independent criminals or hired diversionary units.

First were the three thin raiders who'd attacked the atelier. They were slaves of the merchant who'd been on the scene. Given the merchant's performance in the whole charade, he was apparent thinking, "I'll save them from an attack by villains to make them indebted to me. Then I can break into the potion business." Apparently, the three slaves forced to play the role of the assailants had been promised their freedom if they acted threatening and then ran away. Of course, the merchant was not willing to leave free and living witnesses, so he'd planned from the beginning to make his unsavory escorts kill the poor trio.

Malraux had felt something was off before the assailants lost consciousness, and he designated the slave trader, Reymond, as their interrogator. Through him, the trio of slaves were coerced into breaking the Order from their merchant master.

The interrogation of the merchant father-son duo was simple. With Nierenberg's *gentle* questioning, they told him everything, and there appeared to be no falsehoods in their testimony. The only remaining uncertainty was the fact that the attacks happened one after another all on the same day. Both the merchants and their escorts said they'd decided the day of the attack themselves, and they had no acquaintances in this city to help them. The merchants were independent criminals and had no relation to the other attackers, nor had they been hired by anyone.

Next was the group that had attacked the Aguinas estate. They appeared to be a gang of thieves who'd operated out of the imperial capital.

Although they were a gang of thieves, it didn't mean they

were pros at kidnapping. As a somewhat high-caliber group, they were stubborn and resistant to pain, but according to Nierenberg, who had been a medical engineer in the Labyrinth City without potions for a long time, "The soldiers of the Labyrinth Suppression Forces have far more backbone."

Nierenberg had a thorough knowledge of the human body and could inflict very precise and acute pain, and his face as he did so was terrifying enough to bend beasts to his will. Among those who considered it common sense for injuries to be treated with healing magic and potions, Nierenberg seemed like a demon performing his dissections.

The assailants immediately revealed what they knew to Nierenberg, but they had been hired through an intermediary and didn't know anything about their true employer. Their orders had been to abduct Caroline. Negotiations were carried out in the imperial capital, and detailed instructions were delivered by letter to the Labyrinth City inn they were staying at the night before the deed. The house where they were supposed to detain her was empty, and Nierenberg couldn't gain any information about their employer.

Two interrogations had been dead ends, but the invaders Freyja had captured at the base were considered to be the best chance the Forces had. Among the three Freyja had knocked out and caught, two of them woke up and immediately committed suicide with poison they'd prepared. The remaining member was prevented from killing himself, but even with Nierenberg's questioning, nothing was revealed.

Yes, even the fearsome Nierenberg got nothing.

The intruders Freyja had apprehended were a part of some top-notch covert force accustomed to pain. Given this, it seemed probable that this faction had come from the family of small nations.

Strife was constant in that region. It was whispered that groups who made a living off war had taken root and arranged things so the disputes would never end. Professional spies with sleeping powder had snuck all the way into the base of the Labyrinth Suppression Forces. They had to have been extremely skilled—professionals who charged a high price.

As Nierenberg watched Weishardt give instructions to Malraux and whisper with Leonhardt, the doctor felt his conjectures were at least close to the truth.

However, Weishardt's expression remained clouded, and he didn't issue an order to dispatch the Labyrinth Suppression Forces.

It was safe to assume not everyone in this group of spies had been apprehended, either. Whoever put the medicine in the tea at the guesthouse and taken Caroline away hadn't been caught. The doors to the base were closed, and although they searched every nook and cranny inside, they could find neither Caroline nor anyone resembling an intruder.

Whoever they were, they'd most likely made it outside the base.

By now this mystery person could be anywhere. Hopefully Malraux would turn up something wherever he'd been dispatched to.

The room was thick with tension.

Perhaps I was too lenient in my interrogation...?

If Nierenberg did any more than he had already, it was possible the intruder *wouldn't be able to be returned to normal*, even with the use of a potion. Nierenberg hadn't been instructed to perform such severe questioning, but the clock was ticking. He should've been able to shake up the intruder with the information they just obtained about the sleeping powder and squeeze more out of him somehow.

The face of Nierenberg's daughter, Sherry, suddenly came to mind, but he deliberately shut it away in the innermost depths of his heart and left his seat, determined to make the captured spy confess.

It was right about that time when—

"Reporting in! We have a messenger from the alchemist. She said she knows where the young woman is!"

Dick had arrived, and he'd brought Sieg with him.

04

A group of cavalrymen ran through the downpour.

Even the rain pelting them parted as they charged forward. The wind did little to slow their progress. It appeared that the weather was on their side, but in actuality, they were allowed passage because Weishardt was riding in front and using wind magic to cut through the air.

He wouldn't allow the likes of a storm to stop him now.

"Weis, take the third unit with you."

Leonhardt had listened to the information Sieg brought and appointed Weishardt to lead Dick's unit to rescue Caroline.

"My master ordered me to save the young lady Caroline without fail. Please take me as well."

With that, Sieg joined the tail end of the group. Mariela had indicated Caroline was in the forest east of the Labyrinth City. She had seen worn charcoal kilns near her abducted friend, and there were a great many of those in the eastern woods. However, Mariela's vision had also provided them with the knowledge that these kilns sat at the edge of a slope that lead up a mountain. That was enough for the Forces to get a rough idea of where Caroline was.

Their destination wasn't terribly far from the Labyrinth City. Even though they dismounted at the forest entrance to walk the rest of the way, the forest was shallow. They could get there in under two hours.

However, fate would not make their task so easy. When they arrived at the place the young alchemist had described, Caroline was already gone. Fresh footprints on the muddy ground followed a trail about halfway, then turned to enter the forest and disappeared.

"Split up and search! She can't have gone far! These footprints show someone else is with her! Hurry!"

At Weishardt's instructions, the soldiers split into groups of three and pushed into the forest.

"Found you."

It was around the time Weishardt arrived at the charcoal kilns when Caroline heard the voice. Robert was the first to react. The words carried an accent from a foreign country. Robert spread a smokescreen curse around himself and his sister, grasped Caroline's hand, and broke into a run. Together they fled deeper into the forest.

If it had still been raining, the fleeing siblings would have been at least somewhat concealed. However, the downpour had since stopped, and the ground underfoot was soggy and damp, which made running even more difficult for Caroline. Her entire dress was heavy from the water it had soaked up, and the forest vegetation became natural snares that grasped at Caroline and her brother.

"It's useless, shaman."

A man in black dispersed the curse, sauntering toward Caroline and Robert in a demonstration of his superior strength. This was probably the one who'd used the sleeping powder in the guesthouse. His lightweight, black clothing and concealed face told them he was a spy or something like it. This person could have easily made himself disappear in the trees, yet he purposefully revealed himself, drawing nearer very much like an animal cornering its prey.

"Rgh."

Robert tempered a curse to try to keep the approaching hunter at bay. At the same time, he desperately sent magical power into the seal on his left hand to try and conceal his and Caroline's presence. If his sister had been unconscious, he probably could have taken advantage of the slightest opening to hide them both. After all, Robert had already slipped past this spy once when he'd taken her out of the guesthouse. However, since she was conscious, their presence would remain faintly detectable, no matter how powerful the seal was.

"Admirable concealment. That information is valuable, heir of the Aguinas family."

Had he noticed the seal? Or did he assume it was Roberts own spellcraft? The spy's hungry gaze fixed on Robert, his prey.

"The circumstances have changed. I cannot take two people. Therefore—"

"Carol! Run!"

Guessing the situation, Robert pushed Caroline deeper into the forest and jumped in front of the spy.

"I told you, your efforts are futile."

"Brother!"

Robert charged at the unknown man, but the spy sidestepped with practiced grace. The mysterious agent closed on Caroline in just a few steps and raised a sword he'd drawn from its concealed place of rest.

"Carol!"

Robert screamed his sister's name and stretched his hand out toward her. The dream the alchemists had left to him had slipped through his fingers before, and so had the love of his life, Estalia. Was this hand so stained in sin that it could not even save the life of his own sister?

Was this his true punishment for seeking the power found in dark curses?

Robert's eye caught the seal of flame emblazoned on his outstretched hand. For the briefest moment, the image of the incarnation of fire who had given him the seal crossed his mind.

He was certain she wasn't of this world. If he desired a miracle above what he'd already been given, he would have to give up not just the hope for a peaceful life, but the hope for a peaceful death as well.

Does that even matter anymore?

If he couldn't hold on to anything and simply lamented his own powerlessness, there was no meaning in life or death.

He would give his life, his soul, everything, without exception.

He pleaded with anyone who might hear him for the life of his sister.

When he was ensorcelled by the black arts, dropped from the family inheritance, and shut away in that place where the world had frozen, Caroline's letters had been the only things that made time move forward for him.

Even after she'd seen him in his current state, she still saw him as the same brother she'd always had.

Fwsh.

Just then, a single arrow was loosed.

It was half by accident that Siegmund found Caroline and Robert. Freyja had summoned Sieg frequently—every time the alcohol was gone, or when she wanted a snack, or when they were out of toilet paper, or when other extremely inconsequential chores needed doing—but instead of using a bell, she used magical power. Over time, Sieg felt like he could sense the direction from which Freyja sent the magic signals.

Mariela was insensitive to the magical power of others, and no matter how much Freyja sent to her, the girl took no notice. So the master would simply call to her pupil in her own voice. If Mariela couldn't hear her or wasn't around, Freyja would signal for Sieg to relay the message. It was something that had progressed beyond a simple manipulation of magical power. The lady sage made heavy use of advanced magical skills for utterly pointless things.

The other half of the reason Sieg had found Robert and Caroline was his skill as a hunter. Being thrown into the Fell Forest day after day at Freyja's decree had forced him to remember his former huntsman ways without even realizing it. So as soon as he turned his attention in the direction of the magical power he had sensed, Sieg was able to find Caroline and Robert despite how far away they were.

When he saw the spy approach Caroline, Sieg drew his bow on reflex. It was a fluid movement as natural as breathing.

Ever since he'd taken up archery again in the Labyrinth City, Sieg thought back to when he still had his Spirit Eye with each pull of the bowstring. Back then, he'd always made the best possible shot, as if an invisible hand were guiding him on where to aim and how to nock the arrow.

I want to shoot like how I used to. I want to be as skilled—more skilled—than I was back then.

Every time he thought like that, the correct stance, the correct movements, it all became unclear to him. It got harder to tell what he was doing wrong. Sieg's archery became a reflection of his own hesitation, and his arrows missed their mark.

When Freyja made him hunt in the forest, he'd had no time to think about things like hitting or not hitting, skillful or unskillful. He secured meat by throwing stones or even by killing with his bare hands if it was necessary, then returned home to Mariela. Perhaps it had been good for Sieg to lurk in the grass, or to hide in the canopy of the trees, and fire his bow at prey without the luxury of second-guessing himself.

His body remembered the correct motions and postures he'd repeated countless times in the bygone days of his Spirit Eye. Sieg hadn't lost the hunting knowledge he'd carried with him since he was a child; it had been lurking within him this whole time.

The Spirit Eye was powerful. It showed him his prey's weaknesses, taught his body the correct movements, corrected the trajectory and power of his fired arrows, and strengthened Sieg himself. It covered his own failings.

But he didn't need the likes of the Spirit Eye anymore.

His hesitation, mistakes, and weakness had been laid bare many times over, but Sieg had overcome them all.

I won't let anything else important to Mariela be taken away!

Siegmund readied an arrow. The correct posture, the correct movements, and his steadfast heart would lead his shot to the target.

The arrow flew straight and true.

A shot like this would have been impossible even with magic, but Siegmund's arrow pierced the spy's arm.

"Gaaah, where did that come from?!"

An arrow had struck the spy from so far away that he couldn't even detect its origin. He dropped his sword and scanned the area.

The forest was dense and thick; the idea that there was an opening an arrow could weave its way through was already a miracle, and that was to say nothing of the actual aiming. Had the trees themselves made way for the projectile?

Whatever it was, it wouldn't happen again. There was no path an arrow could possibly travel here.

The trees had provided the spy with cover, protecting his vital areas from the first missile. It was his right arm that had been pierced, meaning the spy was victorious. The man yet lived, and still had use of his left arm. The assassin was confident he had time enough to kill the young woman and take the shaman away.

Moving to draw another of his weapons, the assassin suddenly found his body no longer moved.

I'm being frozen...?! Where is that coming from?

Assessing that the mysterious archer wasn't his only cause for concern, the spy immediately surrounded his body with magical

power. If he used magic to force his steadily freezing body to move, it would probably result in injury, but that was acceptable as a temporary solution. Failing his mission meant certain death anyway; injury was a preferable alternative.

Finding the source of the cold that had crept up unnoticed, the spy threw three needlelike daggers at the same time. They had been dipped in poison many times over, and their surfaces were corroded so as not to give off a visible shine. The little things were almost indistinguishable from the shadows of the trees in a forest like; they were nearly impossible to see.

For most opponents, at least.

"Ice Shield."

All the deadly projectiles were parried effortlessly, and a young noble with an icy look in his eyes appeared from between the trees.

For Weishardt, who had fought higher-ranking monsters in the dim light of the Labyrinth, dealing with this assassin slowed by the cold was simple. Batting the knives away was like swatting a bug.

"Did you really think you could buy time with such an amateurish attack?" Weishardt asked, voice as chill as the grave. The noble's outline appeared blurry to the black-robed spy, who had prepared to launch his final attack the instant he sighted Weishardt.

"…Contemptible vermin." It was unclear whether the nobleman's voice reached the assassin.

Weishardt's magic Ice Field, encased the spy's body completely, leaving him transfigured into a statue of pure ice. Weishardt threw a hateful glare at his enemy, then rushed over to Caroline.

"Carol! Are you unharmed?!"

"Lord Weis..."

After running through an unfamiliar forest on a rough animal trail and being threatened with a weapon, Caroline understood that she was safe at last now that she could see Weishardt's face. As if all the strength suddenly left her legs, the young lady of the Aguinas family began to collapse to the ground.

"Carol!"

Flustered, Weishardt reached out and caught her in his arms.

"U-um, Lord Weis. I... I am sorry you must see me like this..." Caroline bashfully averted her gaze.

Although her cloak had warded off the rain, it had done little to stave off the rest of the day's miseries: She'd been drugged, taken to a hideaway in the forest, and traveled along an unpaved path in the middle of the forest during a storm. Water dripped from the tips of her hair, and her thinly applied makeup had long since come off. Both her shoes and the hem of her dress were in terrible shape from rain and mud. Even her face was stained with wet dirt.

For a young lady who experienced emotional upheaval over the thickness of her lashes, the length and curliness of her bangs, and every single one of her freckles, Caroline hardly considered herself presentable at the moment.

But from Weishardt's point of view, Caroline's alabaster skin was beautiful, no longer concealed beneath makeup and now even paler after her ordeal. The rain dripping from her long lashes and bangs seemed to sparkle more radiantly than any jewel. Caroline's cold hands on Weishardt's arm as he supported her trembled gently. Even though they both lived in the Labyrinth City, her life was so very different from his own. Weishardt confronted monsters and felt death breathing down his neck every day. How terrifying facing that must have been for a young lady who saw the future as full of hope and promise.

Caroline's quivering hands, buckling legs, and pale face were proof enough of that. No one would have judged her for clinging to Weishardt and crying in relief at being saved. However, without shedding tears or losing her composure, Caroline put what strength remained into her shaking legs.

So strong and beautiful...

The sight of her standing by herself without clinging to anyone touched Weishardt's heart.

"Carol, you don't need to stand alone. You don't need to bear the burden alone. I would bear it with you. I will stay by your side."

"Lord...Weis...?"

Weishardt firmly grasped both of Caroline's hands to hold her up, then went down to his knees on the muddy earth.

"Caroline. I will be your support. I will remain with you for as long as I draw breath. I wish to be with you."

"Lord Weishardt..."

They were not beneath a beautiful starlit sky, nor in a beautiful rose garden. The rain had stopped, but the ground was muddy, and they were surrounded by decaying plant matter and moss-covered trees. What stood in this "garden" wasn't a beautiful marble statue, but an assassin, frozen in ice.

It would be hard to say the scene was romantic, but the two saw only each other. Nothing else mattered.

"Yes... Yes! Lord Weishardt. I..."

Caroline's cheeks were a rosy shade of red as she accepted Weishardt's proposal.

After it had been decided Caroline would be the Aguinas family's heir, she had been prepared to welcome someone connected to the family of Margrave Schutzenwald as her husband. The Aguinases were an ancient line and had once held rights to potion-related matters. Now that their potions had run dry, they had neither land nor much income, and they became a family valuable only for their political influence.

Robert's disgrace only complicated matters further. No matter what kind of person she was to be married off to, Caroline was not in a position to rebuke them. Even her previous fiancé had been an alchemist from the imperial capital more than twenty years her senior whom she'd never met. For her, a political marriage was the only option that there had ever been.

But, as Weishardt came to Sunlight's Canopy time and again bearing sweets or bouquets of flowers, Caroline eventually found herself thinking, *If only it could be him.*

It wasn't that she was drawn to Weishardt's appearance or lineage. For Caroline, Weishardt's high popularity among women and his good looks were offset by the fact that he was a soldier. Caroline had worked as a chemist for a long time, and she felt soldiers were more stubborn than adventurers, and couldn't use healing magic and potions properly because they thought they could solve anything simply through blind effort alone. However, Weishardt understood the one advantage medicine had over potions was that they could be used anywhere. He endorsed Caroline's view that even regular medicine had its uses, even if it wasn't as powerful as an alchemical curative.

Besides, Weishardt supported his older brother and had a strong sense of purpose in his desire to defeat the Labyrinth. He and Caroline both hoped for a similar kind of world after the

Labyrinth. To her, Weishardt walked a similar path, and he was a person she could respect. She couldn't have wished for a better person to be her spouse.

"Let us protect the alchemist together, Lord Weis!"

Caroline accepted the proposal with a smile that lit up her entire face, and although Weishardt's expression remained unchanged, his heart crumbled at her answer.

...I... I see. At the end of the day, this is nothing more than a political marriage of convenience for Carol. Of course she would think of it as a measure to protect the alchemist and the potions...

Weishardt's had captivated ladies of both the Labyrinth City and the imperial capital, but he was not prepared to find his princely advances meant nothing in the face of sheer obliviousness. A feeling of dejection washed over him. It was as if Weishardt were gazing up from the bottom of the earth at a high peak far above him. He shifted his focus, following Caroline's glance to the frozen assassin who had taken an arrow.

If that single shot hadn't bought him time, would Weishardt have made it...? His thoughts strayed to the one who had loosed the arrow and that hunter's master.

Well, Caroline and I have made more progress than those two. I've passed a hurdle. I just need to be patient as things move forward.

Weishardt's thoughts were as one might have expected of the lieutenant general of the Labyrinth Suppression Forces. He'd overcome many hardships that had tempered his spirit like steel. He quickly recovered, and after getting up off the muddy earth, he offered Caroline his hand.

"Now then, Lady Carol. Actually, would it be all right if I called you Carol? Let's return to the Labyrinth City." Weishardt gave a kind smile, and in her eyes, he was more attractive than ever before. As if slightly bewildered by this, Caroline spoke with hesitation.

"Um, Lord Weis."

"Yes?"

"Um...my dear brother rescued me. He may have committed a crime by escaping, but...if he had not rescued me, surely you and I could not have met again."

"Ahh, is that right? So everything he did was to save you."

"Yes, that's why—" With her head down, Caroline swallowed hard. Clearly having focused her resolve, she continued, "Would you release my dear brother? He's frozen over there."

A few steps behind the assassin, Robert, too, had become an ice statue. He was frozen in a pose that seemed to say, "If you want to kill my sister, you'll have to go through me first!"

It was an extremely dangerous position for Robert to have taken. Despite the bravery of the stance, Robert's physical abilities didn't even come close to being enough to block the assassin. He hadn't been a wall at all. His position relative to the spy made this very clear. The assassin had pushed well past him by the time the two had been encased in ice.

And that wasn't even the worst part.

Although Weishardt had trapped the two, it was just to stop them from moving. He needed them alive for interrogation. In particular, Robert was hardly a threat in a fight, and he had only needed a thin layer of frost to halt his movements. Stuck in that extremely awkward pose, Caroline's brother had heard—with perfect clarity—the entire proposal.

What manner of hell is this?!

No one heard Robert screaming thoughts of discomfort. All

he could do was cry internally and alone. Was this his penance for making a deal with the flame devil? Could this have been the result of giving up a peaceful life and death? His sister was safe of course, but...

After Weishardt freed him, and Dick and the others came running to take him away, Robert looked like his soul had left his body.

"I can summon a carriage to the edge of the forest. Can you walk that far?"

"Yes, Lord Weis."

Following Weishardt, Caroline moved leisurely through the forest.

"Lord Weis......"

"Hmm? What's wrong? Am I going a bit fast?"

"No, no. It is nothing."

Caroline turned her eyes away and didn't see Weishardt's caring expression as he looked back at her.

What's the matter with me?

Despite being known as an ice user, Weishardt's hand clasping hers was large and warm. As a daughter of the Aguinas family, Caroline had to conduct herself with resolve, yet all she could think about was their linked hands. Her heart pounded in her breast.

Lord Weis proposed to me as a political partner... But, I...

One could only wonder when Caroline would realize the true nature of the feelings that had taken hold of her, or if Weishardt ever noticed that the heart of the girl gazing passionately at his back, was pounding.

The forest remained slick and swampy after the storm, and the steps of the pair walking hand in hand were awkward.

The sunlight shining through a gap in the clouds cast glittering shades on the droplets clinging to the branches. Others who saw Weishardt and Caroline on their journey home seemed to be wishing the best of luck to the pair.

05

"Thank you for coming, Lord Kunz Marrock."

Kunz Marrock—master of the dwarven Rock Wheel Autonomous Region—arrived in the Labyrinth City precisely two days after Caroline's attempted abduction, just as his message had said.

Leonhardt, who welcomed him, had prepared a two-person feast for the man. Marrock was known to dislike formal gatherings.

"I'm grateful you're sparing me some of your time despite my sudden visit. Dwarves don't pay any attention to details unless they're making something. I only realized a few days ago that I'd failed to send notice of my visit. Good gracious, I'm honestly ashamed."

"Don't worry about it, we've maintained a good friendship with the Rock Wheel Autonomous Region for over two hundred years. Its lord has graced us with his presence, so I'd like to offer a heartfelt welcome. I've prepared plenty of alcohol. I hope you'll greatly enjoy yourself."

"In that case, I'll avail myself of your kind offer. Only half of the blood running through my veins is dwarven, but it's no less a nuisance. I've got a weakness for a good drink. Good gracious, I'm truly embarrassed. Ohh, this is an eight-year-vintage that the imperial capital just started offering for sale. The merchant caravans going through the Fell Forest must be doing extremely well if you were able to get your hands on this."

Marrock grinned and picked up the bottle.

He may have been using words like "embarrassed," but his behavior didn't hold the slightest bit of humility. If anything, he was rather brazen. Marrock's blood was half dwarven, so he had the characteristic solid, short build and thick beard and eyebrows of a dwarf. Though a little taller than the average dwarf, his race was still immediately obvious; he was a very dwarven man in his fifties. However, most dwarves grew out their beards as a source of pride, but Marrock had trimmed his short, and even his eyebrows had been kept neat. His hairstyle was clean as well, giving him a gentlemanly, fresh appearance.

His tone, too, was calm and shrewd, giving whomever he spoke to the impression that he was a noble who had been doing business for a long time. Above all, his large eyes gave off a sense of noble birthright to others. Even as he laughed happily and relished his drink, they betrayed nothing of his true feelings to any observers.

A half-dwarf lord whose heart of hearts was well-hidden—that was Kunz Marrock.

"Every bottle of alcohol from the imperial capital is a quality item. I'll make arrangements to have the merchant caravans who travel along the mountain roads transport it," Leonhardt said to Marrock, who tilted his cup back in an elegant motion.

Leonhardt had broached this subject to say that the merchant caravans who traveled through the mountain roads would still exist even after people began using the road through the Fell Forest. It was likely that the only reason for Marrock's visit at this stage was that the Fell Forest had become traversable now that potions were offered on the market.

"That's very kind of you," Marrock replied, his expression unchanged. "However, the sentiment is enough. Well, the part about sending the alcohol, that is. Good gracious, the alcohol makes it a terribly attractive proposal. Honestly, I almost forgot my original reason for coming. That *is* also one of the reasons I came here, of course, but what I want is something different."

He got to the point faster than I thought he would. Does this frankness mean he's already accepted the reality of what's happening...?

As he gazed at Marrock's large, unreadable eyes, Leonhardt's expression remained neutral as well, and he urged him to continue.

"I see. Then what is your request?"

"Oh, it's nothing big. With merchants far and wide going to the imperial capital, our Rock Wheel Autonomous Region has also started its own company. We can't presume upon other people carrying goods for us forever. So we'll transport them to the imperial capital ourselves and sell them. Good gracious, dwarves involved in the likes of business—it must seem like child's play to you. Go ahead, you can laugh at how slow we are to catch on."

"No, not at all! There's no need to be so humble. It's a joint venture with the Bandel Company. Nothing escapes our notice."

Grin, grin.

Though the mouths of the two men mouths smiled, their eyes didn't at all.

The Bandel Company was a major medicinal herb distributor in the Labyrinth City and specialized in exporting via yagu merchant caravans traveling along the mountain roads. They had the foresight to quickly switch to the Fell Forest route once the sale of potions promised to reduce the flow of medicinal herbs from the Labyrinth City. It was probably a natural outcome for the Bandel Company to have its eye on Rock Wheel weapons and armor as goods to replace medicinal herbs.

"Good gracious, just as I'd expect from the renowned general. Honestly, you have sharp ears. Well then, we'll establish a branch in the Labyrinth City. I take it you won't mind."

"Of course, Lord Marrock. I believe the Bandel Company has already prepared a location for it."

Grin, grin.

Leonhardt had a general idea of the goings-on in the City. At his response, Marrock continued.

"You could say the sale of potions is a revolutionary turning point for the Labyrinth City, couldn't you? Good gracious, bearing witness to such a historic moment is more of an honor than I deserve. You'll be inundated by crowds of people, and you'll never have enough artisans. Rock Wheel is willing to offer its support. Changing our traditional sales outlets to go through the Labyrinth City is proof enough of that. However, we dwarves are inexperienced in business matters. We won't last if we don't have *some sort of help.*"

"What are you talking about, Lord Marrock? It takes one week to travel from the Rock Wheel Autonomous Region to the Labyrinth City, and six days from the Labyrinth City to the imperial capital for someone familiar with the route. Going to the imperial capital from the Rock Wheel Autonomous Region through the mountain roads takes three weeks. Traveling to the capital by first coming here is the faster route. I have nothing but the greatest admiration for your keen insight in seeing the opportunity to make profits along the way."

Dry laughter reverberated in the room. Even if Leonhardt and Marrock were having an entirely unenjoyable conversation, adult laughter shouldn't have been so dry. At this rate, their throats would be left parched.

After gulping down his drink, Marrock flashed a smile at Leonhardt and said, "Ohh, this really is some good alcohol."

In the end, all Marrock was requesting was for people from Rock Wheel to be allowed to travel to the imperial capital via the shorter Fell Forest route.

Of course, Marrock was meticulous enough to insert himself into a company that had roots in the Labyrinth City so he wouldn't be refused. He also brazenly made mention of preferential treatment, if possible. Though he probably already knew that would be turned down. Since even the Labyrinth City couldn't refuse Marrock's proposal, he'd settled for "good alcohol."

This discussion was just one of the possible scenarios Leonhardt had anticipated, one of the most reasonable at that.

The Rock Wheel Autonomous Region was located far from the imperial capital and was much smaller than the Labyrinth City. Despite all its residents being dwarves who devoted themselves to craftsmanship, Marrock had acquired information on alcohol that had just begun to be sold in the imperial capital.

Although Leonhardt wasn't able to obtain any intelligence suggesting that Marrock was involved in the kidnapping of the Aguinas woman in the Labyrinth City two days ago, it was very doubtful the half dwarf, who had paid a visit to the Labyrinth City right around that time, knew nothing about it.

Dwarves may have spoken the same language as humans and possessed the ability to bear children with them, but they were, ultimately, a different kind of people.

They found meaning in craftsmanship itself, not in where those crafts ended up. They didn't care if their own weapons spread both to the Empire and to the countries that opposed it at the same time. Dwarves operated under different morals. Understanding each other's differences was the way to coexist with them.

Knowing this, Leonhardt had said something very specific to Marrock. It was a magic phrase that had been passed down from the head of the family for generations: a kind of friendship spell.

"We, too, look forward to the day when Rock Wheel achieves 'the ultimate sword.' When that day comes, I would like to ask for a swing."

The ultimate sword.

That was the only thing the dwarves of the Rock Wheel Autonomous Region sought. The home of the dwarves didn't produce orichalcum; they wanted to cast steel that surpassed it in order to forge the ultimate sword.

How many artisans, how much time, and how much money would be needed for such a blade?

Marrock sold dwarven weapons and armor on a large scale for no other reason than to see that goal fulfilled one day.

The half dwarf was an unparalleled lord. He'd been blessed with both business ability and an aptitude for politics. His heritage also ingrained in him the fundamental desire for the ultimate sword.

However, his blood also left him ill suited for smithwork. He himself was unable to work toward the ultimate sword. Although he understood that, his desire for the weapon was like an obsession.

Marrock knew the dwarven ideal and acted accordingly as best he could. Leonhardt wanted to be a good neighbor, and his words made him an individual in Marrock's eyes for the first time.

He was no longer one person in a multitude of humans, but "Leonhardt."

"By the way, I believe your younger brother, Lord Weishardt, got engaged recently. What a happy occasion. We haven't yet achieved the ultimate, but the next time I come here, let us celebrate the best sword of the present age."

That was only two days ago… Marrock truly is a shrewd one…

Leonhardt was astonished at the speed of the half dwarf's information. The engagement was still largely unknown, even among the nobility.

"To the ultimate sword."

"To the prosperity of the Labyrinth City."

The toast didn't taste too bad to either of them.

06

After much work, it was determined that the mastermind behind Caroline's abduction was from a merchant clan. The clan had acted independently of any other larger groups. The execution of their crime had been clumsy and amateurish. If there had been any other points of contact, the scheme likely would've been exposed rather quickly.

The greedy merchant father-son pair charged people wanting to go to the Labyrinth City a travel fee to take them there. Of course, it was common for merchant caravans to transport people and items if they had the space in their wagons. Likewise, visitor inspections were easily conducted in the Labyrinth City. No one except extremely suspicious people were monitored, and once they entered the City, it was unknown where they went.

"There's no reason for adventurers with valuable combat skills to come to the City during this season, right?"

Telluther had made this comment as he cut his nails. He was referring to a man with black hair and greenish-blue eyes in his late twenties with the air of a civil official. Normally, this man would have been overlooked, but thanks to Telluther's remark, the Labyrinth Suppression Forces had become aware of him as a person of interest.

A number of territories suddenly attracted great importance to the Forces because the people who'd attacked their base were spies from the family of small nations. Malraux was well acquainted with one of them, and he had a clue as to who the man with black hair and greenish-blue eyes was.

"It has been a while. Is my wife doing well, Steward?"

Right around the time Weishardt had set out to rescue Caroline, Malraux, his orderly Rhet, and soldier slave Taros were visiting a room where a man with the air of a civil official was staying.

"M…my lord. It has been a long time. I was just thinking I might come to visit you tomorrow…"

Doubtless he hadn't expected Malraux to come calling. Although the steward of Countess Beratte's family was taken aback by a visit from his master, whom he should have been serving, he offered a token show of manners.

"Enough with the facade. You certainly made a profit from smuggling weapons to the smaller nations, didn't you? I can't imagine hiring so many spies could've been cheap."

"Wh-what are you—?"

"We captured a spy who snuck into our base. He'll tell us everything before long."

Malraux's attitude was indifferent. There was no sign he was agitated or that he desired remorse from the steward, who was a member of the family in a way. The glimpse of Malraux's heart visible in his blue eyes showed resignation, and a most profound anger. To Rhet and Taros, who had come here with him, the silent rage in his eyes also appeared somewhat sad.

"D-damn it, if you had just...if you had just died on the road in the Fell Forest...!! Do you know what it's like to watch another man claim my own child as his?!"

The steward, having guessed the situation from Malraux's words and actions, flung off his pretense and drew his sword. Countess Beratte's husband was his master, but the hostility he felt was clear in his words and his blade. This was what Malraux had expected. Why would this man expressly visit the Labyrinth City? Why had Malraux's group been attacked on their way back to the base from Caroline's atelier?

Malraux thought the man's remarks were selfish. He stared down the steward of Countess Beratte's family as the man slashed desperately at him.

This steward had an immoral relationship with the countess, and she'd taken Malraux, who had similar blond hair and blue eyes, as her husband in order to continue that relationship behind closed doors. His hair had been dyed black in an attempt at disguising their association.

If he hadn't been dragged into such a foolish trick, Malraux would have been able to live peacefully in the Labyrinth City. This man probably didn't even try to imagine the grief and hardship Malraux and his love had been forced to endure from being used and separated.

His sword is terribly slow.

The blade of a steward possessing no combat ability was mere child's play to Malraux. Even if he didn't dodge the blow, the extra armor he was wearing under his clothes would probably have prevented any serious injury. Surely he could afford to allow the man a single blow.

"No!"

"Taros…"

It was Malraux's soldier slave, Taros, who stood in the way and caught the steward's attack.

Malraux hadn't known this taciturn giant for very long. Ever since what had happened to Lynx, Malraux had started treating slaves as such, and one couldn't say he was an especially good master. But serving and protecting one's master in and of itself goes without saying for some, and Taros naturally came to his master's defense as he had in the previous attack. Malraux wasn't an especially bad master, either. After all, he'd allowed the steward to carry on as he did despite the impropriety of his behavior. Taros's words and actions quelled his reckless thoughts and returned him to his senses.

"Let me go, let me gooo!" the steward screamed as Taros pinned him to the floor.

What it's like to be unable to claim his own child…

Malraux could understand that much. But then, the steward's current situation was something he'd brought on himself.

Considering what he'd put Malraux through, there was little room for sympathy now.

"If your only purpose was to hinder the sale of potions, there was no reason for you to come to the Labyrinth City. Did you want to take my place that badly?"

The steward remained silent at the question, but the answer was clear. He had indeed come to kill Malraux.

"If so, then I can at least grant you that."

Malraux was calm as he had the last word, and the steward lost consciousness.

Once Malraux knew the facts, the matter was extremely simple.

In order to rally the family of Countess Beratte, who had fallen into financial difficulties due to a string of reckless political endeavors, the steward had smuggled weapons and armor to the family of small nations by diverting them to the Rock Wheel Autonomous Region's sales channels. Not only was Countess Beratte's territory on the way from Rock Wheel to the imperial capital, but it was also a crossroads that led to the family of small nations—the perfect setup for such a business.

However, the family of small nations was hostile to the Empire, and selling Rock Wheel weapons and armor to them on a large scale was treasonous in the eyes of the Empire. The steward had to have understood the risks. He may have intended to rally the territory's government as quickly as possible and then stop smuggling.

But the sale of potions in the Labyrinth City began before Countess Beratte's territory had recovered.

The Rock Wheel Autonomous Region would probably also

transport weapons via the Labyrinth City due to the cheaper cost. Which meant the number of yagu merchant caravans would drop sharply, and even the profits brought by merchant caravans would be lost. The smuggling could be done inconspicuously only because of the large volume of goods in circulation. If the main flow of merchandise went through the Fell Forest instead, continuing the illegal trading would be near impossible.

So the steward employed spies and assassins from the family of small nations and planned to abduct the alchemist to stop the sale of potions. The spies were talented, but in the worst-case scenario, the mastermind would be easy to surmise. In an attempt to cover himself, he'd hired a gang of thieves from the imperial capital at an exceptional price, and they weren't given any information as to who they were working for. The merchants' attack itself was merely a fortunate coincidence. The steward had realized the merchants' plan when he slipped into the Labyrinth City during their visit, and had analyzed their movements so that he could set his plan to be executed on the same day.

He'd hired spies from the family of small nations for no small fee. Whether or not the steward of Countess Beratte's family was in the Labyrinth City probably wouldn't have changed the outcome of that operation.

The steward had indeed come to the Labyrinth City in the hopes of taking Malraux's place.

If Malraux suffered an injury serious enough that he could no longer serve in the Labyrinth Suppression Forces, he could be brought back to the house of Countess Beratte. Likely confinement, or death, awaited him on his return. Afterward, the steward would return his dyed hair to its original blond color and live openly as Malraux. After a wound so severe, no one was likely to be suspicious of abnormalities in his face, voice, or memory. Countess Beratte had even sent Malraux a letter to act the part of a loving wife. Perhaps it was sent only for the expectation that multiple people would notice it during inspections, lending strength to the alibi.

It was for this personal reason that Malraux and his two followers had been attacked in the alleyway.

Two groups of visitors came to the house of Countess Beratte a few weeks after the attack on the Aguinas family.

The first was a group of soldiers from the Labyrinth Suppression Forces bringing Malraux, who they'd reported had suffered a grievous injury. "Malraux" had been injured so badly that only his sparsely remaining hair and greenish-blue eyes could distinguish him, most likely a result of intense pain. His injuries had been treated countless times with healing magic and potions, and reports claimed that it hadn't been possible to heal this "Malraux" any further than this in the Labyrinth City.

Countess Beratte started insisting this man wasn't her husband after seeing that he wasn't eating enough or even speaking. Walking unassisted was impossible for the so-called Malraux. However, a soldier that accompanied the broken man took a potion from his breast pocket and used it on the man and Countess Beratte's son to prove they were related by blood. This was a blood relation potion used to expose faithlessness. Up until recently, it hadn't existed in this ley line's region. It was an item that became available after an alchemist had appeared in the Labyrinth City.

"Father? Are you really my father?"

Although he'd been away from home for a long time, the father was very dear to his son. The young boy cried in sympathy for his so thoroughly altered parent. After the blood relation potion was used, Countess Beratte seemed to understand the situation.

Offering only the words "If you use several special-grade potions, you might be able to expect some amount of recovery," the Labyrinth Suppression Forces soldiers promptly departed.

Soon after, came the second group of visitors.

"Countess Beratte, we wish to speak with you about the smuggling of weapons to the family of small nations." It was a group of inquisitors from the Empire.

"The territory of Countess Beratte's family was seized, but she and her family apparently escaped capital punishment. It's clear Malraux had nothing to do with the smuggling, and the steward, the principal offender, is *unaccounted for*. Your house has been acquitted. It seems that three people are now barely scraping by on 'Malraux's' pension," Dick commented to the blond-haired, blue-eyed man.

"Hmm, is that so?" the man answered with a distinct disinterest.

"There's a rumor that, despite the treason toward the Empire, the emperor was deeply moved by the countess's devotion to her paralyzed husband and saw fit to show them mercy, Malraux."

"Mercy, huh...?"

The steward's wish, to be called "Father" by his own son, was sure to be granted now. However, could a mother and child so accustomed to luxury really be happy in a life of poverty with an unsightly man who could no longer move? How would the man who lived with such a wife and child feel?

The pension given to the other Malraux was three gold coins a year. The best they could do with that amount of money was have enough to eat. Buying new dresses was a thing of the past for them now.

Then there were the words the Labyrinth Suppression Forces soldiers had left with them, "If you use several special-grade potions, you might be able to expect some recovery."

If there had been no possibility, they probably would have accepted it. But would a wife who didn't work really arrange for special-grade potions for her husband when his pension was barely enough to feed her?

No matter how much his wife and child might come to loathe him or were cruel to him, the pension would only be paid to "Malraux." They wouldn't be able to send the man away.

"It's a vicious punishment," said Malraux, now just a commoner, before parting ways with Dick and heading for home.

If you worked in the intelligence unit, your existence would need to be erased sooner or later, so Malraux had no regrets in handing over his name. In return for turning in the information he'd gotten from the steward to the imperial capital, no fault was found with Malraux's parents or his family. For him, it wasn't a bad way to put an end to things.

Considering the crimes the family of Countess Beratte had committed, one might've said the emperor's judgment was unusually lenient.

However.

"Welcome home, dear."

"Welcome home, Father."

Warm light shone through the Labyrinth City at dusk. Malraux returned to the home where warm food, his wife, and daughter waited for him.

The husband earned good money, and though the wife and

daughter weren't furnished with expensive attire, they were happy and waiting for him. It was a comfortable house where steam rose from well-prepared meals and the cleaning was scrupulously done. The home welcomed Malraux as a gentle, respectable husband and father who did honest work. It was the life Malraux had made for himself. He deserved to enjoy it.

But if—

He shut the thought away as quickly as it had come. Any more than that would be an affront to the wife he loved. The wife who'd given birth to and raised their daughter in poverty, alone.

"I'm back," Malraux said, and quietly closed the door to his home behind himself.

07

"I realized something," Mariela muttered after Sieg had left to rescue Caroline.

"What's that?" Freyja asked, more quietly than usual.

"Hmm. A lot of things. But I guess the biggest thing is about Drops of Life," Mariela said, and headed to her atelier on the second floor of Sunlight's Canopy with her master.

She picked out dried lunamagia. Then curique, mandragora, and ogre dates; the usual materials she was familiar with.

"Form Transmutation Vessel, Water, Drops of Life."

Without saying anything, Mariela expanded a Transmutation

Vessel and dissolved Drops of Life into magically created water. At the same time, she expanded another Transmutation Vessel and joined the two with a thin tube. The shape resembled the ordinary vessels she'd used many times to make high-grade potions.

"Nozzles are easy, so that's good."

Up to now, Mariela had ordered a great number of nozzles to make high-grade potions.

The simplest type that sprayed only water had a small hole at the end of the tube, and the hole had a distinct shape. When they got a little more complicated, the path of the water zigzagged and the water pooled right before the nozzle, or there were several pathways for the water that created whirlpools through different water speeds. For the types that sprayed water and air together, a water tube ran through the very center and an air tube ran along the vessel's circumference.

Mariela had reproduced nozzles with Transmutation Vessels, but quickly discovered the water was being stirred up by water and air from other channels and scattering near the nozzle's outlet. So if the young alchemist changed the current of the water and air and scrambled the nozzle's outlet, she could probably create a finer spray.

However, that method used too many controls, and Mariela felt like it wasn't the correct way to go about it.

That day, she made a straightforward and familiar nozzle in the Transmutation Vessel that simply sent water and air in the proper way. As she sent the water in a free fall, she blasted it with air. With this, she could freeze the water droplets while easily mixing it with finely powdered lunamagia. However, the water droplets were too big and created a diluted extract.

"There was...no need to approach it from only the outside,"

Mariela muttered and put magic energy into the Drops of Life dissolved in the water. Drawing up Drops of Life used magical power. There was no reason she shouldn't be able to work on it after the Drops had been drawn up. Mariela wondered to herself why she hadn't noticed something like that earlier.

With a popping sound, the water droplets spraying from the nozzle burst open and scattered, finer than mist.

Since they were very small drops, their bursting wasn't very loud. But Mariela's attention was fixed on each and every little liquid bead. To her, the little sounds of bursting water were as lively as bells.

Pop, pop, pop. Tinkle, tinkle, ring-ring.

The mist shrouded the interior of the Transmutation Vessel that Mariela had created in the blink of an eye. She cooled and stirred it, turning it into something like fine powder moving in a high-viscosity liquid. It was as if the mist was gathering together with a mind of its own. Then the now pure white mist touched the lunamagia powder, turned slightly yellow, and then collected at the bottom of the vessel like light rain.

"...I did it. It was so easy."

Although Mariela would have neither thought of it, nor had the skill to make it possible until now, she had finished the lunamagia extraction with so little effort it seemed absurd that she hadn't been able to do it before.

"Mariela. Don't stop until you're completely done."

"Okay, Master."

The obstacle in making the high-grade potion had been the lunamagia extraction. Having accomplished that, the rest was easy. Carrying out multiple processes at the same time, Mariela completed a high-grade potion using only alchemical skills.

*   *   *

The Library opened.

To an alchemist, the feeling was like noticing a door that had always been closed was now suddenly open.

Some had also regarded it as abruptly being able to see color in a world of only black and white. In a world without blue, after all, you wouldn't be able to read words written in ink of such a color.

Mariela followed the newly opened knowledge and was about to search for the one potion she wanted.

"Don't be impatient, Mariela. Start with the basics first: a normal special-grade potion," Freyja reminded her pupil, who had immediately started searching for a potion to heal eyes.

"...Okay."

Mariela knew how to make special-grade potions, though that knowledge had come to her only recently. But although she vaguely understood how to make a special-grade specialized potion for the eyes, the instructions became blurry and nebulous as soon as she tried to read them. As her master had said, the ability to make basic special-grade potions was her first priority.

"Oh, Master, the materials."

"Yeah, we'll have the Labyrinth Suppression Forces prepare them tomorrow. There's no one who's been using them anyhow. They probably have about a hundred years' worth stockpiled. Mariela, you did great today. You learned something else, too, right? It's something very important. You can start working on special-grade potions tomorrow. In any case, you won't be able to make them right away. Today you should just take it easy."

At Freyja's unusually tender demeanor, Mariela finally realized her master had sensed her intentions. Her teacher really was an incredible person.

08

Several days after the attack on the Aguinas estate, Sieg officially became a free man.

It was in recognition of his exemplary deeds as an adventurer and his service in rescuing Caroline. Sieg was happily released from the bonds of slavery and became recognized as an A-Rank adventurer at the same time.

Since his master was the alchemist, several conditions were added to the terms of his release, including continuing to serve as Mariela's escort. However, they were all what Sieg wanted anyway, so the formalities were carried out without issue.

The day of the contract annulment ceremony that would free Sieg, Mariela ran around like a chicken with its head cut off starting first thing in the morning. Although they were just going to the slave trader Reymond's company, she showered Sieg with different clothing. He was forced to change every five minutes as Mariela changed her mind about what he should wear. She polished his shoes and armor until they sparkled, wondered if he'd forgotten anything, and pulled snacks from her bag to pack for him until he stopped her and told her she didn't need them. Then Mariela stuffed Sieg's bag with every kind of high-grade potion imaginable for any worst-case scenario until he turned them down. "There won't be any danger," he reassured her.

Naturally, it wasn't a day Mariela could spend making potions, so today was a break for her in that regard. She wasn't able to make normal special-grade potions yet, let alone a special-grade specialized potion for eyes, and Mariela apologized to Sieg countless times, saying, "I wasn't in time, I'm sorry."

Despite Mariela's restlessness as she awaited Sieg's release, the slave liberation ceremony was surprisingly simple.

"Ahh, it's just about undone. *Contract Annulment.* There, we're finished."

"Huh? That's it?"

"...I don't feel any different, but..."

Mariela had assumed it would be similar to when they'd formed the contract and Reymond would make fire dance, wind swirl, earth heave, and water drip from a cup while shouting things like "Your blood is now your own!" However, Reymond merely touched the slave brand on Sieg's chest over his shirt like a button and then—yup, all done.

There weren't any spectators. Sieg and the one he escorted, Mariela, passed through a room that seemed to be a reception office, and after they signed a document, Sieg was released as easily as pressing a stamp on paper.

One might've suspected Reymond of being unwilling, but that wasn't the case. The man looked back and forth at Mariela and Sieg with a happy smile the likes of which the two had never seen before.

"The fact you felt no different was most likely because the Contract of Servitude was almost gone. I could feel very little of Mariela's magical power in Siegmund's slave brand. I wonder, did you refrain from giving him many Orders?"

"Um, yeah."

Come to think of it, Mariela had only given one Order to Sieg way back in the beginning: "Don't tell anyone I'm an alchemist." Mariela and Sieg's daily life had never needed things like Orders. That was a matter of course for Mariela, but to Reymond, and most others, it was a rare thing.

"Ohh. That's wonderful. A mark of subordination is artificially conferred. It's not natural. Therefore, if the master's magical power isn't periodically transferred into it, its effect will dilute and weaken. If you make holes in your ears to put earrings in but then don't wear earrings, the holes will eventually close, right? It's the same as that."

Was it really okay for a Contract of Servitude to be that simple? If you didn't give Orders and it weakened, couldn't the slave liberate themselves or run away and cause practical issues?

Reymond continued as if to answer Mariela's unspoken question.

"The binding forces in a Contract of Servitude doesn't only function when the master consciously puts magical power into Orders. The everyday words you speak have magical power in them, too, albeit just a little. Words released to make the other person obey or make them listen to what you say pass through the mark of subordination and bind the slave's words and actions. The more out of character the words are for the slave, the more powerful they are. And the Contract of Servitude becomes more deeply rooted."

Reymond paused for a moment. He wore a look that seemed to suggest he was staring at something off in the distance, then returned his gaze to Mariela and Sieg and continued.

"This is my theory: Orders don't just bind words and actions. I think they distort the slave's will itself, aligning their heart to their master's to change their actions. Little by little, it distorts who they are."

Reymond's tone was calm, but Mariela felt the powerful feeling behind it. Perhaps they, too, were infused with magical power. When Mariela happened to glance at Sieg sitting next to her, she saw that he was listening intently to Reymond's words. Likely Sieg had his own thoughts on all this.

"But there's nothing of that in Siegmund. With all due respect, when I enacted the Contract of Servitude, I could feel considerable distortion from the influence of his previous master, but I can no longer sense that. Probably because the relationship between the two of you is filled with mutual affection. If you're joined by a far stronger bond than a Contract of Servitude, the likes of that magical bind has no meaning whatsoever."

Although a slaver by profession, Reymond perhaps had some good in him. He seemed extremely happy to see Mariela and Sieg formed a connection stronger than the Contract of Servitude. Mariela was somehow very embarrassed at being told it was filled with affection, but when Sieg answered, "Yes. I will continue to protect Mariela from here on out," she went bright red all the way to her ears and looked down at her feet.

After casting a gentle look at Mariela, Reymond said, "By the way…," and his expression stiffened as he faced Sieg. "Here. This is a copy of the record of charges against Siegmund's previous master, the merchant."

Siegmund took the document offered to him and quickly began to scan over it.

The merchant father and son, Sieg's previous masters, had attacked the Aguinas family atelier in the Labyrinth City and were arrested. That alone was a serious crime. Moreover, due to the condition of the debt laborers they'd brought with them, many other infractions had come to light after an investigation of the abuse of the merchant father and son's slaves. Other offenses were discovered as well.

Specified among the other crimes was a false claim brought against the slave who'd rescued the merchant's son. The fraudulent accusation asserted that the slave was responsible for the failed merchant caravan plan to travel through the Fell Forest as well as for putting the merchant's son in danger.

The plan of going through the Fell Forest without potions had resulted in the death of a large number of debt laborers. Despite their positions, they still had rights as people. The botched attempt had jeopardized the merchant's position.

"One of our slaves tricked us. We're victims, too. Because of that slave, even my son suffered serious injury."

A large sum of money helped grease the right palms for their laughable excuse to pass. Most would have raised an eyebrow at conveniently pinning the crime on a dead slave, but fortunately for the merchants, one had survived. To improve matters for them, the slave was stricken with a high fever and dim consciousness.

That slave had been Siegmund.

"The charge against you has been verified as false. Reparations were going to be paid from the merchants' own funds, but their cash flow seems to have deteriorated significantly ever since the failed merchant caravan plan, and even their visit to the Labyrinth City was meant as a get-rich-quick scheme. Since there were many other victims, such as the slaves who were almost forced to die in the recent assault, I wouldn't expect much in the way of satisfactory payment."

The news about the charges was likely more important to Reymond than the money.

A-Rank adventurers earned good money, but honor and reputation couldn't be so easily bought back.

"Don't worry about my reparations. Please divide them among the slaves who were almost killed. It's enough that my innocence was proven," Sieg replied calmly.

"Is that so? By the way, that father-son merchant pair became penal laborers and are here at my business as we speak. Would you buy them? Take your revenge? You can return all your sufferings onto them. The humiliation, terror, and the unmanageable resentment." Reymond's words sounded like a test.

The fact the record of charges against the merchant father and son was prepared here; that Reymond offered to sell Sieg's former owners to him; that the merchants' other crimes were investigated; and that Sieg's name had been cleared may have all been planned by Weishardt. Rewards for Sieg saving Caroline, no doubt.

However, Sieg's reply was decisive.

"No, thank you. I've wasted too much of my time on them already. I don't want to give them another thought."

"Is that so? I apologize if I overstepped my bounds suggesting it. If you ever require manpower, by all means, make a request here."

The slave trader courteously bowed his head. Sieg was no longer a slave. He was an A-Rank adventurer, which was more than sufficient to be a customer at Reymond's establishment.

"Let's go home, Mariela."

"Okay!"

Free at last, Sieg said the same sort of thing he always did to Mariela, and the young alchemist happily gave her reply.

"Ah, but there's somewhere I want to drop by first." Mariela cast a few quick glances at Sieg. Her attempts at feigning nonchalance were distinctly unnatural.

"The Yagu Drawbridge Pavilion?"

"Y-yeah. That's right, but...?"

Mariela mumbled as she made a terrible attempt at being sneaky. Sieg had found out she was planning a surprise party for him at the Yagu Drawbridge Pavilion to celebrate his release. What had cemented it was when Freyja, who always stuck close to Mariela, left with a cheery expression while saying, "I'm going on ahead, so hurry up!" It was so obvious that there would've been something wrong with him if he hadn't noticed.

Reymond saw the two off with a "We'll be awaiting your next visit" as he warmly watched the pair return home. The two still had the same distance between them as when they'd arrived.

Sieg spoke to Mariela on the way to the Yagu Drawbridge Pavilion. The sun had started setting since they'd left to join the surprise party, and the pair's shadows stretched along the road.

"Mariela... You know, Lynx..."

"Mm..."

Mariela gazed at the long shadows as the pair slowly walked side by side. It was just like when she'd first come to the Labyrinth City and she and Lynx walked together.

"Lynx loved you, Mariela."

"Mm..."

Lynx had said that when he became an A-Ranker, he would tell Mariela how he felt. So as the one left behind, and an A-Rank adventurer himself now, Sieg felt the time was right to tell her. Mariela stared fixedly at the shadows at her feet. He couldn't tell what her reaction was.

"Mariela. I...also love you." Sieg laid out his own feelings as well. Surely, he had to tell her now.

"Sieg...um. You know, the day I followed the Drops of Life to find Lady Carol..."

In response to his confession, Mariela hesitantly strung her own words together, bit by bit.

"After I looked and looked for Lady Carol, and found her somehow, you know, I...sank into the ground with the raindrops." Since she'd achieved her goal of finding Carol, she hadn't needed to keep returning to the air anymore. Mariela had fallen with the pouring rain and soaked into the earth, like Drops of Life returning to the ley line.

"Right then, I thought something. I wondered if I could meet Lynx if I went to the ley line."

Sieg quietly gasped in hushed reply. "...Did you meet him?"

Mariela had so wanted to see him again—someone precious to her, someone she'd lost. It was a beautiful sentiment.

"No. I didn't. But, when I thought maybe I could, I kept sinking down, down, down toward the ley line."

Mariela had spread her existence thin, and both her memories and emotions had grown extremely hazy in that state. Distinct intentions and thoughts, such as not being able to return if she had continued like that, or that she had to save Carol, were far from her mind as she'd plummeted deep into the earth. They had been left behind with her body, and she'd hardly felt aware of them anymore. The only thing filling Mariela enough for her to sink deep down was a floating calmness like being on the verge of waking from a nap.

"But you know, then...I heard you."

Sieg's voice had reached her in that deep place.

"I thought, 'I want to go home.'"

That was probably the best answer Mariela could muster right now. For some reason she felt extremely embarrassed for having said "meat" back then, but...

Mariela had realized how she felt in that moment. However, she didn't know what she wanted to do about it yet.

Sieg thought Mariela was still looking down at the shadows, but the alchemist had turned to look at him. The evening sun illuminated her embarrassed, smiling face.

"Really?"

"Yeah."

Perhaps Sieg was satisfied, even with that answer. The two of them resumed their walk to the Yagu Drawbridge Pavilion.

They could see the door in the distance, and it was wide open. Freyja, Haage, and Captain Dick drunkenly staggered out and waved with bottles of alcohol in their hands. Even though the man of the hour hadn't arrived yet, they had apparently been unable to wait to start drinking. It was a predictable outcome.

"Whoa, they already started! Sieg, let's hurry! The food's gonna run out," Mariela said, and the two of them broke into a run. The setting sun shone warmly on the pair.

09

A little while later.

A piece of information was brought to Sieg, who was still happily enjoying the same life in Sunlight's Canopy. Seemingly, there were meddlesome people in this city who were concerned about him.

It was a report about the merchant father and son who had attacked the Aguinas family's atelier. Detailed within was an account of how a man who used to be their slave had bought the father and son who were now slaves themselves. The man, who had been ordered to attack the Aguinases' atelier, had been kept in slavery longer than his original term thanks to the merchants' wicked designs. He was said to have been freed thanks to the crimes of the merchants being exposed.

"There's nothing left for me anymore," the man had said as he departed from the slave trading company. No one knew what on earth had happened to him for him to say such a thing.

People said the man took the merchant father and son he'd bought into the Labyrinth. Thereafter, not a single person saw any of them ever again.

CHAPTER 6
True Awakening

01

Once upon a time.

A very, very long time before human countries were built in this land.

In a certain forest, the queen of the forest spirits lived with monsters and animals.

The forest was plentiful, the animals were very kind, and the monsters were much gentler than in other regions. The queen of the forest spirits ran among the trees with the beasts and monsters, sang with the birds, danced in flower beds with the spirit children, and lived a peaceful and happy life.

One day, the spirit children summoned the queen of the spirits to a flower bed where a lone human had fallen.

This human was a hunter who survived by felling beasts with his bow. The hunter had escaped to that flower bed after a monster had grievously wounded him.

In the forest, small beasts ate nuts and insects, and large beasts ate small beasts to live. Monsters eating humans was just the way of the forest.

"Human, I eat you now. You are my food," a monster said, and it was about to eat the hunter when the queen of the spirits turned to the monster and spoke.

"Give him to me. It just so happens that I'm in need of extra help."

The queen of the spirits saw the blue eyes of the hunter, barely still open, and immediately took a liking to him, healing his wounds.

There was something the queen of the spirits didn't know. The creatures known as humans were smarter, kinder, and richer in emotion than any living thing in the forest.

"Ah, what a beautiful person," said the huntsman when he awoke and saw the queen of the spirits. His eyes were a deep, deep blue. In those eyes, deeper and more beautiful than the sky or the lakes, glittered a reflection of the queen.

"My, what beautiful eyes. What a lovely person."

The queen of the spirits became fascinated with the hunter's gorgeous sapphire eyes, his smiling face when he spoke happily, his constantly changing emotions, his kindness in the way he treated her, and his wisdom in the thinking of many things.

The queen had never known a living thing could be so sensitive. Before she knew it, the queen of the spirits had grown to love the hunter, and he felt the same toward her. The two fell in love and lived together happily in the deep forest.

02

"Oh, Emily, are you reading a book?"

"Yeah, Sherry. I looove this story!"

"Let's have a story about a hero. One who vanquishes a dragon."

"I want to keep listening to this one."

Sunlight's Canopy was noisy with the sounds of the children who'd come by again today.

Each of them blurted out what they wanted to say, and their conversation didn't quite mesh, but that hardly seemed to matter to them. Even if what the children said went in different directions, they all laughed at the same time for some reason, and they appeared to be having fun. Likely, it was a good example of language and communication skills being two different things.

The school the children attended had a library, albeit a small one, where they could borrow books donated by nobles and wealthy merchant families. Emily, who had memorized a few difficult words at school, borrowed an old children's book from the corner of the library and was now reading it aloud.

Freyja would normally seize upon a chance to pop in on such a place from seemingly nowhere and offer her great wisdom, but she was nowhere to be found within the shop section of Sunlight's Canopy. She was in the middle of something. Her favorite pupil, whom Freyja teased and put through grueling training, was battling heavy odds in the second-floor atelier while receiving lavish praise.

"Urgggggh!!!"

"Hey, Mariela. One more try! You can do iiit!"

Mariela let out a groan as if she'd been constipated for days while her master provided her with adequate encouragement. Freyja said, "One more try," but a hundred or a thousand more wouldn't have been enough, never mind one. Even so, Mariela groaned *urrrgh* and *aaaagh* with tremendous effort as she compressed a Transmutation Vessel containing Drops of Life and a ley-line shard tighter and tighter.

"Nnnnnnnnngh...!!!!!!"

Even though Mariela strained herself so much she cried out and her face turned red, none of that had anything to do with the actual handling of a Transmutation Vessel. Still, Mariela couldn't help but vocalize her efforts. At any rate, it wasn't simply because of the pressure.

Pop.

At last, the thin part of the Transmutation Vessel burst, and the Drops of Life and ley-line shard within shot out.

Cla-cla-cla-clang.

Because of the high pressure within the Transmutation Vessel, the impact was like an explosion. The Drops of Life jetted out of the Transmutation Vessel and immediately unraveled and disappeared into the atmosphere, but since the volume became nonexistent, the blast itself wasn't a big deal. However, the ley-line shard that flew out like a speeding arrow had the power to easily penetrate a human body. So Freyja had created a Transmutation Vessel as a barrier around the outside of the one Mariela was handling. The ley-line shard bounced off the invisible barrier Freyja created and ricocheted violently, and perhaps because a lot of Drops of Life had dissolved, it soon cracked and disappeared as though it had been unraveled.

Why did her master's Transmutation Vessel so easily repel the dangerous ley-line shard that Mariela's own couldn't hold? Was her master's barrier really a Transmutation Vessel in the first place? Mariela had asked her once, but Freyja had only tilted her head to the side and said "Who knows?" Maybe it was something unconscious on Freyja's part. Whatever it was, it was something Mariela wasn't yet capable of.

"Another failure..."

"Ha-haaa. What a shame! Well, don't lose heart! We've got all the ingredients in the world. Try again!"

"Grr, Master! Give me some master-y advice, here! We might have a ton of ley-line shards, but they're expensive!"

How many times today had Mariela made that mistake? Countless buckets with ley-line shards as small as the tip of Mariela's pinkie were strewn about the atelier. All of them had been purchased from the Aguinas family.

Over the last two hundred years, the Aguinas family had been buying ley-line shards under the pretense of investigation and research. Some of the alchemists who woke up in the Aguinas family's cellar in the past had possessed the ability to make special-grade potions, but it didn't mean all of them were that high ranking. In fact, not a single one who'd awakened in the last hundred years or so had been able to make special-grade potions.

The Aguinas family had set some odd conditions for themselves, and among them was "Buy out all ley-line shards and store them," so the strangely honest household bought out ley-line shards generation after generation and continued to diligently stash them away in a cellar like squirrels storing food for the winter.

As it happened, the box Robert had been using in place of a chair in the hidden room beneath the eastern forests was a treasure chest packed full of ley-line shards.

Caroline's kidnapping was officially reported as Robert escorting her to the secret stash. He had handed over stewardship of the family to Caroline in order to tell her about those hidden assets behind closed doors. Officially, Caroline hadn't been kidnapped, but rather went out of her own free will. It was just poor communication of her departure that had caused some mild alarm.

The Labyrinth Suppression Forces and Mariela bought the majority of the inherited ley-line shards at a small markup. After generations of collecting ley-line shards, the Aguinas family finally earned a profit on them.

In the imperial capital, ley-line shards were expensive items sold for one large silver coin each. You could buy a high-grade potion with one. However, in the Labyrinth City, with no alchemists, they were little more than pretty stones. The price of one in the City was one-tenth of a silver coin each. The sum was poor compensation for the hardships of subjugation, but considering the stones had no use without anyone to use them, just about all of them had been sold to the Aguinas family because they offered a slightly better price.

All told, the Aguinas family had about a hundred years' worth from a city with a Labyrinth. Tens of thousands of ley-line shards had been stockpiled, and no matter how exceptionally low the price per stone, Mariela couldn't afford even half of them after spending around half the fortune she'd accumulated.

Conversely, the Aguinas family enjoyed an incredible, and unexpected, wave of income from Mariela's and the Labyrinth Suppression Forces' investments. Since the family had decided on Caroline and Weishardt's engagement and expected to spend a considerable sum to welcome Weishardt as the husband to the head of the family, the income was a lifesaver. With passage through the Fell Forest now a possibility because of monster warding potions, the new couple would need to visit Margrave Schutzenwald's territories and the imperial capital to pay respects. That wasn't something they could just have a few dresses made for and be done with, like in the Labyrinth City. The Aguinas family was expected to prepare items befitting their family status. This meant things from clothing—and not just for Weishardt and Caroline, but for the family members accompanying them—to the carriage they rode in on, and the belongings they brought with them.

Even after Weishardt and Caroline got married, there would be no income from potions like there had been previously, so they were going to need investment funds to support and maintain an adequate livelihood, whether that involved obtaining land or starting a business.

So Mariela did as her master told her and improved the economy by spending gold coins to buy ley-line shards. The young alchemist worked hard at special-grade potion training, using up almost a hundred ley-line shards every day. It seemed terribly extravagant.

When Mariela failed, the ley-line shard vanished like a bubble bursting or smoke in the wind. One might be tempted to call it a literal bubble economy bursting.

Seeing the way her gold coins were flying from their coffers, Sieg worked hard to catch and bring home meat every day. A feat that caused Mariela's respect for him to rise an astonishing amount. This might have been a bubble, too. One could only pray it didn't burst, too.

"Waugh! Another failure!"

Just as the hardest part of making high-grade potions was extracting the base ingredient, lunamagia, the hardest part of making special-grade potions was dissolving a ley-line shard into Drops of Life.

Despite this, Freyja's simply said things like "Well, let's try it anyway" and made Mariela perform alchemy using skills alone without questioning whether that was actually the best way to do things. Mariela's habits from childhood were hard to break. If her teacher said, "You can do it," the young alchemist believed she could.

If Drops of Life touched a substance outside of a Transmutation Vessel, the liquid would unravel and vanish like smoke, but if you handled it within a Transmutation Vessel, then its properties were almost the same as ordinary water. The only exception was that it was soluble in water and oil. When water reached a certain high temperature and pressure, it shifted to a state between gas and water. It dissolved and decomposed objects that normally didn't dissolve in water. However, when Drops of Life were in this state, they dissolved ley-line shards.

Of course, even if the temperature and pressure weren't raised that high, the ley-line shards would melt bit by bit into Drops of Life, like sand dissolving, solidifying, and turning into hard rocks over time. If you took this kind of slightly melted ley-line shard out of the Drops of Life, it would burst open with a *pop* and vanish. Incidentally, if you smashed a ley-line shard, the entire thing would burst into fine grains, and in the next instant they'd dissolve into the atmosphere again. There was no way to pulverize them and make them easier to melt. That was why Mariela had been tightly compressing Drops of Life with a ley-line shard in it every day as of late.

Mariela thought if she were only compressing Drops of Life, it would be fine not to put a shard in it, but for some reason Freyja wouldn't let her do that.

"Ahhhhh! This is hard!"

"...Of course it is." The reflexive retort had come from a man standing behind Freyja, looking not unlike a servant. It was Robert.

"First of all..."

"Rooob, don't interrupt Mariela."

Poke-poke-poke-poke, poke-poke-poke-poke. Freyja launched a forehead poke assault.

"Ah—ow! Ow, ow, ow, ow, I said ow. *I'm sorryyy!*"

"You said you'd be my manservant until you paid back the money you owed, right? You understand?"

"Y-yes. However, if it's money you're after, my father..."

"That's your family's money, isn't it? Carol's money. It's not yours anymore. Don't you at least have the decency to pretend to be embarrassed about making your sister repay your debt?"

"B-but, how long..."

"Hmmm? You've accrued interest, you know? If you say anything stupid, I'll burn you."

"I—I beg your pardon..."

Mariela watched Freyja and Robert's exchange with astonishment. For some reason, the fiery woman had brought Robert here several days after Caroline's abduction.

At the time, Freyja had said something like "I'm putting you to work for that money I lent you."

The money she'd lent to Robert was borrowed from Haage. What's more, Mariela was the one who'd paid back Haage. Freyja shouldn't have gotten even one copper coin out of it...

The day he was first brought here, Robert looked worse than when Mariela had seen him in the Aguinas cellar. He had dark circles under his eyes, and he gazed at a specific spot of no discernible importance while muttering something. Mariela got a slightly unpleasant vibe from the man, as if he could no longer control his black magic very well. At times he would get a glazed look in his eyes and whisper fragments of curses here and there, regardless of where he was, like a dog marking its territory. Every time he did, Freyja would go *"Fire!"* and rebuke him with an explosive forehead poking attack. The noise was unbearable.

Incidentally, every time Freyja's *"Fire!"* burst forth, Robert was engulfed in a pillar of flame, but for some reason he wasn't burned; his hair didn't even get frizzy. Occasionally Robert's skin reddened slightly, and his clothes were a little scorched, but that was all. Mariela didn't think it particularly mattered if his sleeves or hem were singed. Though perhaps he found it difficult to bear, as every time it happened, he changed into new clothes of identical make. Freyja would yell, "That'll add to your debt!" Interest was accruing, too, so the whole thing was snowballing.

Robert returned to the Aguinas house every day. Despite having lost his right to be the head of the family, he was still considered a part of it. Therefore, his clothes were provided by his family and hadn't actually cost him anything, yet Freyja raised his debts like a loan shark.

However, every time Freyja scorched him, it was a bit longer before the next incident. His unpleasant atmosphere seemed to be diminishing as well. So both Mariela and the regulars of Sunlight's Canopy let Freyja do as she pleased. More than anything else, however…

"Hup! Ah, I missed the trash bin. Rob, put it in for me."

Mariela was extremely thankful she didn't have to deal with her master's absurdities herself anymore. Like when Freyja tried to throw trash into the wastebin and caused the whole thing to fall over and spill its contents. It was worse than if she'd just missed the target to begin with.

All right, I'll leave my master to Robert and try a little harder!

Leaving her bothersome, difficult instructor to someone else was just fine in Mariela's eyes. She resumed the practicing the dissolving of ley-line shards.

Mariela hadn't noticed what Robert had started to say, or her master stepping in before he could.

In the imperial capital, the process of melting a ley-line shard into Drops of Life required more than just a Transmutation Vessel alone, because the pressure was too high.

By simply setting up a Transmutation Vessel inside a thick metal container, one or more alchemists could remain near it. These containers were like a lump of metal with a hole about the diameter of a finger, and you put Drops of Life and ten ley-line shards inside. Next, you pushed in a metal piston with the exact same diameter as the hole above, and applied a weight of several hundred kilograms. Then you heated the metal container from the outside.

The two hundred years Mariela slept through had seen a lot of progress in materials for such canisters, pressure-increasing methods, and heating methods. However, the practice of using the container and mechanically applying pressure had remained unaltered.

Even with two centuries' worth of progress, a temperature and pressure that would completely dissolve the ley-line shards couldn't be controlled in Drops of Life. So, although theoretically one ley-line shard would be enough, you needed to dissolve ten to get one potion's worth. In other words, processing shards using pure alchemy skills was an act of sheer madness whether two hundred years ago or now.

Despite such a steep challenge, Freyja had ordered Mariela to do it.

Hmm, this was the case when I extracted the lunamagia, too, but I feel like it would be fine if I just held it down from the outside...

With a clack, Mariela flicked the ley-line shard with the tip of a finger.

The way it glittered was very pretty. On a closer look, the shape, size, color, and luster of each one was ever so slightly different, unique. They were like raptors or yagus. At first, every one of the animals looked the same, but when you got to know them better, you became able to distinguish what made each one an individual.

Ahh, I see...

Mariela realized she might have given herself a hint, and she grasped a ley-line shard tightly in her hand, enclosing it in her fingers to completely envelop it.

03

Before long, the hunter's family and friends, gathered in the forest where the queen of forest spirits and the hunter lived, and they built a small village.

All of the hunter's family and friends were kind, good people. They didn't bite like the forest monsters, and they worked more than the forest animals to build comfortable houses.

Even in the winter, fire spirits happily danced in their nice, warm fireplaces, and sometimes water spirits peeked from wells filled with clean water.

The fields the humans tilled were soft, and the earth spirits were delighted at the loosened soil.

Humans taught the queen of the spirits more songs than the birds knew, and she and her dear forest animal friends had great fun singing along with the wind spirits' chorus.

The many spirits and animals who lived in the village loved the humans, and everyone worked together to make the place like a paradise. The wonderful things didn't end there, however.

Surrounded by many friends, the queen of the spirits and the hunter were blessed with a darling baby boy, and the two were filled with happiness.

The people, spirits, and animals of the village hoped their joyous feelings would last forever.

Unfortunately, that was not to be the case.

When the humans decided to create a place where they could live, there were those they did not tolerate in that village.

The monsters.

It was very, very unfortunate, but monsters and humans couldn't coexist.

"But we'd been living so well with the queen of the spirits and everyone else in the forest!"

The monsters held an unbearable hatred toward the humans who now resided happily with the queen and the others. A part of the forest where the monsters had once roamed freely was now a village they couldn't enter.

The town was just one part of the vast forest, but to the monsters it was an insufferable insult. One day, the monsters, fed up with humans shunning them, attacked the village in great numbers to take back their home.

04

"I wonder what happened to the village…?" mumbled Elio, who suddenly remembered the story as he began to doze off in bed.

"Village?"

"Yeah. The spirit village. The one the monsters attacked."

"Emily read us a book today about the queen of the forest spirits, Mom."

"Ahh, that story. Then would you like me to tell you the rest of it?"

"Uh-uh. That's okay. I promised I'd go back again tomorrow."

Elio answered Elmera's question, and Pallois had chimed in, a trifling conversation between parent and children before bed. After enjoying the moment with her sons, Elmera returned to her husband, Voyd, in the living room.

"How are the children?"

"They're asleep."

Elmera sat next to Voyd and nestled up to him. Written summons directed toward each of them sat on the desk. They were from the Labyrinth Suppression Forces, requesting their participation in the second red dragon subjugation. Last time, written summons had been delivered only to Elmera, but this time there were two: one for her and one for Voyd.

"What's written in the summons?"

"The same as last time. They're asking us to help for the sake of the Labyrinth City's future. The soldier who brought the summons was courteous; he neither threatened nor coerced me," Voyd recounted.

The previous red dragon subjugation attempt had ended in failure. Thanks to Voyd's help and Leonhardt's bitter decision, no one had died, but they'd felt thoroughly powerless in the face of an airborne opponent. It had been over a month since then, but they still hadn't found a reliable way to pull the dragon to the ground.

Ever since that failed attempt, the red dragon hadn't come within the range of their magic. Thanks to the pull of gravity, the red dragon's breath attack had far greater range than that of magic. Even if the Forces sent for a ballista from the imperial capital that was capable of firing long distances, the dragon's breath would burn the thing to ashes before the siege weapon could even take aim.

"This time, I'm going, too."

"You can't, darling! If you did..."

At Voyd's declaration that he would participate, his wife tried to dissuade him.

"It's all right, Elmera. I'll never *forget* you. Because I remember well every moment we've spent together since we first met."

Voyd embraced Elmera's shoulders and spoke gently to her. Elmera's expression betrayed the slightest bit of unease as she leaned against her husband.

The first time Elmera had met Voyd was in a deep and dangerous stratum in the City's Labyrinth. She'd come across a man sitting absentmindedly on a rock, seemingly unaware he was in a place that was crawling with monsters.

"It's dangerous to stay for so long in a spot like that."

As soon as she'd said this, Elmera felt very foolish for doing so. They were deep in the Labyrinth, far from the stratum stairs where the safe zone was located. Meaning, this wasn't a place some incapable weakling would idle about. Her words should have been insulting to a powerful person who understood and knowingly faced such danger.

However, the man had replied like he was speaking to a child in a park at sunset: "You're right. You should hurry home, too."

The next day, and the day after that, the man was sitting in the same spot. Elmera had grown rather curious about him and came to see him every day.

"Hey, just how long do you intend to sit there?" she'd asked him, to which he responded, "Maybe until everything has disappeared."

When Elmera asked his name, he scratched his chin for a moment. He then answered, "Voyd."

The unusual response made Elmera wonder if it was a pseudonym. This man had eyes that were unusually, utterly vacant. They even seemed to say he had come this deep into the Labyrinth to die. Elmera worried for him and returned to visit often, but the strange man remained seated there in exactly the same way.

He was so calm, he didn't look like he belonged in a Labyrinth crawling with monsters, and for some reason he didn't engage in conversation, either. Although Elmera had seen him the previous day, he always spoke with a facial expression like it was the first time they'd met.

She began to grow fond of Voyd's calm presence. She felt extremely safe just being by his side, despite how deep they were in the Labyrinth.

Elmera, blessed with a thunder god's divine protection, was

constantly enveloped in a small amount of electricity, and strong static electricity would shoot through whatever came into contact with her bare skin. The only ones she could touch without worry were family members who'd gotten used to it over time. So ever since she was little, Elmera never showed any skin except during battle, and she spent her life taking care not to harm the people around her. Still, Voyd welcomed Elmera and didn't seem the least bit bothered by static surrounding her.

It didn't take much time for Voyd's secret to come to light.

This was a deep stratum of the Labyrinth. Powerful creatures constantly wandered around. Sometimes, monsters stronger than the usual ones for a stratum even sprung up. When Elmera was in danger, Voyd would cover her—literally, with his own body. After the monster was defeated, the man looked like he'd suffered a fatal wound, yet it closed up and vanished in the blink of an eye. Voyd's skill, Hollow Rift, erased every attack from the monsters.

After casually defeating a monster, Voyd would look back at Elmera with a gentle smile and speak to her like one would to someone they'd just met.

"Are you all right, *young lady*?"

Yes, he had completely forgotten both Elmera and the days they'd spent together.

Elmera had heard of the S-Rank adventurer called Isolated Hollow. He was said to be an invincible shield boasting defenses like an impregnable fortress and a superhuman recovery ability.

"You see, every time my body recovers, my memories vanish. I don't forget things like language or social norms, though..."

Voyd answered Elmera's urgent questioning in the same calm manner he always spoke with. The man held a book in his hand with small, densely packed words written within. It was his diary.

To say he "forgot" presumed the possibility of remembering again, but Voyd's memories were completely erased. A new page of the diary, which he said he began to write in so he could preserve the things he felt were even the slightest bit important, was packed with writing about Elmera.

"Don't tell me... You've forgotten your own name, haven't you?"

Voyd had never thought he'd lose his own name of all things, so he hadn't bothered to write it anywhere in the diary. The man laughed as he admitted the fact.

"There seem to be a great many people in the imperial capital who claim to be my relatives." This was written in a page with a mark on it.

Tricked, cheated, deceived.

Voyd had even forgotten the times he'd been tricked.

Even if he was praised as invincible, an impregnable fortress, the ultimate shield, Voyd remembered none of it.

This was the other side of Hollow Rift. It swallowed all of Voyd's enemies' attacks, but also its bearer's feelings, memories, the things that made him who he was, everything.

That being the case, it would've been better for everything to be swallowed. At least, Voyd thought as much when he'd written such feelings in the journal. That was why he'd come here to the Labyrinth and sat. He would sit here until his words, his way of fighting, even the knowledge that he was a person—everything—disappeared.

"Don't cry, Elmera. I'm all right," Voyd reassured Elmera as she wept. "Because I've forgotten both joy and sorrow. Everything."

Elmera could tell he was a kind person. She'd gleaned from Voyd's journal that he'd been deceived and hurt many times, but he seemed the sort of man who felt glad he'd been the only one to suffer through it all.

"Don't cry, Elmera. None of you recover quickly like I do. Neither in body, nor in mind. So please don't be so sad."

She disagreed. Surely losing even the memories of getting hurt caused sadness worse than whatever had hurt him. Isn't that why Voyd was sitting alone in the depths of the Labyrinth to begin with?

"You're wrong!"

Overcome with emotion, Elmera embraced Voyd.

He said It didn't bother him, but to her, it was sadder than anything else. Sensitive as she was, her emotions spilled over into tears, and her control over her own electricity began to weaken...

C-c-c-c-crackle, crackle, craaackle!

"Ah! I-I'm so sorry!"

It wasn't the kind of voltage that could be waved away with a simple apology. However, since it was Voyd who'd been electrocuted, he merely smoked for an instant before turning back to normal. Had it been anyone else, this would have been a disaster. Elmera would have had to go running to find someone who could use healing magic. This was exactly why she'd distanced herself from others since she was young and worked diligently to control her electricity.

"Don't worry about it, I'm fine. You are quite stimulating, Elmera."

But Voyd smiled as if it were nothing and accepted her apology.

"What? You...remember my name?"

"Huh?"

After this curious event, Voyd left the Labyrinth with Elmera, assumed a false identity, and began to live with her. Because

Elmera stood out—whether as the chairwoman of the Medicinal Herbs Division or as the Lightning Empress—Voyd became a househusband in her shadow, living quietly up to now without attracting attention or suspicion from anyone. He never forgot the time he spent with Elmera.

Old man Ghark, who'd heard the tale later, offered unromantic suggestions like "He doesn't forget how to talk, y'know? Isn't him rememberin' from the electric shock similar to that?" However, the young Elmera—well, maybe even the older Elmera of today—considered it a miracle of love.

There was no basis for it having happened, or for it happening again. Just imagining a situation that might force her to test the theory again was terrifying. She dreaded to think of the man she loved losing the time he spent with his family of two. A family that soon grew to three, and then four.

Voyd didn't even know how long he'd been alive. According to the information Elmera gathered, he didn't seem to be an abnormal age. However, it was possible Voyd's ability cured even his aging. After they began living together, Elmera felt happy every time she found a tiny wrinkle around Voyd's eyes or a hair that was just a little gray. She believed that if they lived together over the same period of time, Voyd wouldn't end up being left behind by himself in a dark place like the bottom of the Labyrinth.

Up to now, Voyd had fought only for the sake of others. That's why Elmera took it upon herself to fight on his behalf. She wanted Voyd to live quietly and peacefully.

Elmera recalled the previous attempt at subjugating the red dragon. She'd left without telling Voyd, yet he came running when she was in danger. Somehow, he'd found her out. He had saved Elmera from death, but back then, there had been some curiosity in his eyes when he looked at her afterward.

As if he'd forgotten who she was.

Thankfully, Voyd retained his memories, but there was no guarantee he'd be able to recall things the next time.

"You don't need to worry so much, Elmera. If they just want me to absorb attacks without any kind of actual plan, I'll turn them down. But, according to these summonses, they've found an attack method that should prove effective against the red dragon. And, if it's what I'm thinking of, it will be a very fascinating plan indeed."

Voyd drew his beloved wife close to him, reassuring her.

"After all, I don't want to lose these days I've spent with you and our children."

Elmera met Voyd's gaze and found that her husband's eyes, which had once been so tragically vacant, now reflected a clear future.

The creatures known as monsters were very, very strong.

No matter how many beasts of the forest gathered together, they wouldn't stand a chance against them.

Each person in the hunters' village used their ingenuity,

teamed up with the beasts and spirits who had become their friends, and fought with all their might to protect the village.

The humans with dexterous hands built a fence to keep the monsters from invading. A spirit transformed into an ivy that would conceal the humans from the invading creatures protect the village.

The humans who could fight took weapons in hand, ready to face the fiends. The animals, too, joined the effort. They carried wood for the fence, ferried the humans around, even fought alongside them.

Not to be outdone, the spirits assisted with the humans' magic. If a human called a flame, a wall of fire would appear; if they called ice, many icicles would rain down around them. When a human was in danger, a wall of earth would protect them, and when they swung their swords, a blade of wind would fly to strike distant monsters.

It was a very fierce battle.

In the middle of the fight, the compassionate queen of the spirits tried to persuade the monsters to return to the forest. The monsters may have been ferocious, and quick to torment the beasts and spirits of the forest, but even so, they were her forest comrades. The queen didn't wish to fight them. It pained her to think anyone might be injured. The humans only lived in one part of the forest. The queen believed they should be allowed to live there in peace.

The queen of spirits pleaded to the monsters with all her might. The forest was vast enough to comfortably accommodate one small village. She begged the fiends to reconsider.

Alas...

The more the beasts and spirits helped the humans, the angrier the monsters became. Until the humans arrived, it had always been the monsters who lived there with the queen of the spirits.

The monsters insisted that they had been here first. Why had everyone been so eager to make friends with the humans? Why did they have to be the only ones who were left out?

If the queen of the spirits didn't want them to be hurt, as she claimed; why did she choose the humans and not them? The creatures howled in anger.

06

Mariela could hear the voices of the children reading a book.

Since they were far away, she didn't understand what they were saying, but most likely they were reading huddled together in a corner of Sunlight's Canopy's shop.

Mariela mused that the ley-line shard in her hand wasn't all that different. She didn't know the details of what kind of monster it used to be, but she sensed by holding the tiny object that it was the type of monster that lived with a pack. After she put it into a Transmutation Vessel with Drops of Life, she slowly raised the pressure before doing the same with the temperature. Although, it might have been more accurate to say she brought the Drops of Life closer together, than saying she raised the pressure. She squeezed them like children shoving their bodies against each other in a silly game.

Her master's Transmutation Vessel was extremely durable and seemed like it could withstand significant duress, but that was unusual for such containers. Transmutation Vessel wasn't a skill to be used in combat. You could easily break one with a powerful strike at a single point, and even with the amount of magical power Mariela possessed, there was no way for one to hold pressure high enough to dissolve a ley-line shard.

That's why she didn't force the Transmutation Vessel on the ley-line shard, but brought it closer to the Drops of Life. She didn't warm the Transmutation Vessel itself, but the Drops of Life near the shard. The Transmutation Vessel was only there to ensure the Drops of Life didn't touch the air and thus return to the ley line.

A ley-line shard was a physical crystal; the Drops of Life dwelling in a monster given solid form. If magical gems were crystals of magic that embodied the world's energy itself, you could say ley-line shards were crystals of life force. They were formed inside the bodies of monsters, and one could sense a vague feeling of residual consciousness within them. It wasn't anything complex or clear, more like hazy desires of wanting to be in a pack, or wanting to run, or enjoying a certain temperature. Matching that made it easier for the shard to adapt to the nearby Drops of Life.

Mariela didn't expect it to be easy after realizing such a thing, but somehow, she became able to successfully extract a ley-line shard about once in every ten attempts.

The shard dissolved in the Drops of Life retained its liquid state even after she removed it from the Transmutation Vessel. The light of the solute was greater than that of the Drops of Life it had been dissolved in, though the glow was fleeting.

"Next, the curique."

Up to now, Mariela would have pulverized and extracted the

curique with water containing dissolved Drops of Life, but now she could extract it more easily. When she diffused Drops of Life through the curique she'd just picked from her rear garden, she could feel its medicinal components collecting in the leaves and veins.

She dissolved Drops of Life into those components and used *Separate*. Then the young alchemist loaded the drops directly into the healing components. She sensed the kindness of the earth in the medicinal herb's healing power. She believed the world wished for, not just humans, but for all the animals living in the forests to be healthy.

When she charged the curique with Drops of Life to bring it close to that wish, that ideal state, the curique's mesophyll changed into particles of pale light—like fine, free-flowing sand—and streamed out, leaving the veins.

"Crystallize Medicine."

The healing particles that streamed out were very small. They would slip between one's fingers no matter how tightly they were clenched. Dissimilar from Drops of Life, they had a tangible existence. Perhaps the nature of the Drops of Life "surrounding" them was powerful, as they disappeared at some point even if you transferred them to a vial. There was no way to stop this; thus it was necessary to connect particles together with magical power and anchor them to this world at the same time. These linked processes were collectively called *Crystallize Medicine*.

Mariela had become able to use it after she searched for Carol and almost melted into the world. The name *Crystallize Medicine* as well as a simple explanation titled *How to Crystallize the Power in Materials*, were the only things added to the Library.

These medicinal crystals could only be used by the alchemist who made them, perhaps because they were secured with magical power. However, if you put them in potion vials, they lasted longer than dried medicinal herbs, and a crystal about as big as a grain of sand could be used to make a single potion, making them very space efficient. Moreover, they sparkled. Each material had a different color, and if you put them in vials and lined them up on a shelf, they could be very pretty. Mariela was very happy with them. When she used *Crystallize Medicine* on all her materials, from the ones she'd been amassing to the ones she'd only recently purchased, both the atelier and the cellar ended up very tidy.

Surveying the cleaned room, Sieg nodded in approval, but Mariela had gotten used to the mess and felt a tiny bit unsettled. However, Mariela's master was always putting something or other wherever there was free space, and left things without cleaning them up, so it would be messy again before long.

"This is so convenient. I wish the Library had a more detailed explanation," Mariela said, hoping to learn faster.

"You won't be able to do something just by reading about it, y'know?" Freyja laughed as she answered.

Indeed, that might've been true. Even if Mariela had been told to bring medicinal herbs or materials close to their ideal state, she probably wouldn't have grasped the concept.

"The dead dragon shrooms, the dragon blood, and the viscous liquid from Slaken have all been crystallized already..."

Perhaps Mariela should have expected the ingredients of a special-grade potion to be equally extraordinary.

Dead dragon shrooms, as their name suggested, were mushrooms that grew on the remains of dragons. Despite growing on corpses, they apparently didn't get nutrition from flesh and blood. Instead, they fed on the magical power dwelling in the dragon's hide and bones. Any dragon species was fine, and some sage somewhere had recently scorched a large number of earth dragons right at the end of the rainy season, which had made their bodies the perfect seedbeds. There were still earth dragons roaming the area, however. So a joint unit of Labyrinth Suppression Forces and Adventurers Guild members held a B Rank and Above Training Camp, which doubled as dragon-blood collection. Many special-grade potion materials would be needed going forward, so apparently the collection was made a regular event to also help strengthen soldiers and advanced adventurers.

Naturally, Sieg was recruited and—equally naturally—the person who knew about the area, Freyja, didn't participate.

Dead dragon shrooms were dried at a high temperature that would make even live trees burst into flames, and were then finely crushed and extracted with water colder than ice.

Since dragon blood contained toxins, one had to mix it with three types of oil, each with a different melting temperature, and repeat the separation process to carefully remove the toxins. The remaining materials were face tree fruit and hot sand scorpion poison.

These were obtained from the stores of the Labyrinth City's Merchants Guild. Both were materials that could be collected in the Labyrinth. The monsters weren't as dangerous as earth dragons, but the guild was planning to raise the trade-in price of these materials to encourage their collection.

Mariela couldn't use the Crystallize Medicine skill on materials like those yet. It appeared to be impossible to do so on any material she hadn't processed many times over and thoroughly understood. That said, Crystallize Medicine wasn't required for making potions. Mariela thought it might be a useful technique for alchemists who were sufficiently familiar with the materials to easily extract and store them for long periods of time.

A face tree was a large, mobile tree with a human face. Several types of trees with human faces had been identified, and a face tree was one of those. It was the most active tree monster among those identified in the Labyrinth. It walked on its own by nimbly moving its roots, and the face on its trunk made different expressions. The monster's defining characteristic was its fruit that ripened at irregular intervals. When it did, one could cut it to reveal a shape like a baby's face. Although the fruit bore a gentle, sleepy expression when it was ripe on the branch, the eyes and mouth opened wide when plucked. Drying the fruit gave it a creepy face that resembled an old man with an anguished countenance. The ripe fruit held medical potency as well, but special-grade potions called for unripe fruit. The produce bore no face at that stage. Seeds were enclosed within a large pod beneath the thin, tough flesh. The inside of these seeds was the required material for potion-making.

Inside the seed of the unripe fruit was a liquid, and one would have to bore a hole to extract it. This liquid contained the magical power of a variety of living things that nourished the face tree. Pickling it, along with daigis fibers rolled up like a sponge to draw out the excess magical power, helped remove side effects.

As for hot sand scorpion poison, the essential part of preparing it was how one removed its impurities. These scorpions attacked from within hot sand and had B-Rank strength, so taking them down was easy enough. However, the amount of poison that could be extracted from one was low, and it deteriorated if it came into contact with the air. Often by the time it was delivered, over half of it had decomposed and only a few drops were usable. Moreover, the decomposition advanced in stages, and the material used to isolate the undecomposed poison could also be troublesome.

The ashes from coal used by dwarves to forge steel was suitable as a separation material obtainable in the Labyrinth City, and after mixing it into a slurry with a caustic slime's acidic liquid, it became possible to cure it for a few hours under high temperature and pressure. The time and temperature were essential, and it was possible to make holes in the particles of ash tiny enough that only the undecomposed scorpion poison could penetrate.

All the materials were complicated to process, let alone obtain. Exactly as one would have expected from special-grade potions. Just assembling all of the materials took time, but the more potions Mariela made, the less harm would come to both the Labyrinth Suppression Forces and the Labyrinth City, so she got first priority in receiving the ingredients.

Despite their processing difficulty, these other ingredients were still a piece of cake compared to ley-line shards. The process was complex, but they could be finished by following the necessary steps. All Mariela had to do was recite the directions over and over, and repeatedly go through the motions to memorize what to do.

Mariela didn't perceive issues that could be overcome with hard work alone as actual obstacles. Every time she learned new information, she could feel her world expanding. It was too fun to be tiring. In particular, after she became able to use Crystallize Medicine, she understood the materials much deeper than before, perhaps because of her increased proficiency. Engrossed in her repetitious tasks, Mariela began to feel a curious sensation. It was as if points of information she'd known up to now had started connecting to other points, organizing systematically.

Thanks to this, it took less than a month for Mariela to become able to make special-grade potions. Her success rate wasn't 100 percent yet, but specialized potions were at last within reach.

"And finally, the crystalline lens of a gazer." Mariela produced the lens, securely wrapped in a damp cloth, from a large vial where it had been stored with ice.

A gazer was an eyeball monster also referred to as an observer. This giant monster levitated via inborn magic and unleashed advanced magical attacks—so of course a special-grade potion would use a part of its body.

The enormous lens, its circumference roughly that of two open hands, was clear and translucent, yet it remained soft to the touch. After taking out a knife, Mariela sliced the crystalline lens as thinly as she could, then carefully dehydrated the pieces one by one. Since they would deteriorate if she raised the temperature or changed the pressure, she dried them in thin pieces before grinding them into a fine powder. She mixed the finished powder with a custom-made vinegar she'd prepared in advance.

As far as processing the lens went, tuning the vinegar was more difficult than the lens itself. The vinegar was made using lynus wheat as a base and combining several varieties of grains and fruit, as well as dozens of different nuts. Through the process, the mixture would take on a deep brown color. Its flavor was extremely harsh, making it completely inedible. The particular batch of vinegar Mariela was using had only just been made, so it was intensely sour, and simply opening the lid was enough to make your eyes sting and tear up.

Apparently, filling a container with this vinegar and aging it for about ten years resulted in an extremely delicious luxury item. Doing so would mean that the properties necessary for processing gazer crystalline lenses would disappear, however. Making it no longer viable as a material for potions. While she'd been preparing vinegar for the lens, Mariela had also made a considerably large batch and stored it in the cellar. She was looking forward to it in ten years' time.

The recipe for this vinegar was also recorded in the Library, but she didn't have to memorize all the ingredients when handling foodstuff. Even for Mariela, memorizing the dozens of types of vinegar ingredients would have been quite a hassle, so it was a relief she didn't need to.

Mariela combined the processed materials in the proper order, in the appointed quantity, at the exact temperature. She couldn't afford to let her focus slip at any point during the procedure. This was something she'd wanted to make for a long time.

"...It's done."

It had been a year now since Mariela had first met Siegmund.

At long last, she had completed the special-grade specialized potion for eyes.

07

"Is Sieg here yet? Is he here yet?"

Now that Mariela had completed the special-grade specialized potion for eyes, she restlessly paced around and around the shop interior of Sunlight's Canopy.

It was still too early for dinner, but she'd already finished preparing the meal.

She'd covertly put her alchemy skills to use to make a huge feast, because Sieg's eye was going to be cured. Special-grade potions hadn't been put on the market yet, so he would have to continue wearing his eye patch for a little while to keep it a secret. However, even if it was just with their friends, Mariela wanted to celebrate.

Today, Mariela felt she could forgive her master even if the Freyja completely splurged and drank every last bit of the alcohol Mariela kept stocked.

Yet, today of all days, Sieg had been recruited to subjugate earth dragons and wouldn't be back until dusk. Mariela wanted to have him drink the potion as soon as he returned, but her master had butted in with a comment that actually made sense for once.

"This is the first use of a such a potion. He should drink it in front of an appropriate audience."

Freyja did have a point. Knowing how long it would take for an eye injured in battle to heal by using the potion would be valuable information. It wasn't like the concoction was easy to make.

Mariela still found it frustrating. She just wanted to give it to Sieg already. Why had her master chosen *now* to say something so wise?

With a backward glance at Mariela, who was pouting, Freyja wrote something on a piece of paper and handed it to Nierenberg. Scribbled on it were the words "Doc, give this to the brothers."

Indeed, *Nierenberg* of all people was being made to run errands. As per usual, the Sage of Calamity boasted an imperviousness to the statuses of those around her.

Mariela had given up on complaining to Freyja, who seemed

to be comfortably situating herself at the top of the hierarchy within Sunlight's Canopy, when the children gathered in the corner of the room called out to the young alchemist.

"Mari, wanna read a book with us? I'll read it to you!"

What a kind child. So much so, Mariela wanted to boil the kid's essence and make her master drink it. She wondered if such a potion existed as she went to join Emily and the others.

"Thanks, Emily. What book are you reading?"

"It's called *The Legend of Endalsia*. We're already in the middle of it, though!"

Emily gave a simple summary of the story so far, then continued to read.

08

The monsters kept coming and coming no matter how many he defeated, and in the end the hunter lost his life in the battle.

Oh no!

The queen of the spirits called, cried, and screamed, but the hunter would never look at her again with those beautiful blue eyes. The queen of the spirits was filled with grief.

But she couldn't just cry.

The queen had a son who was very precious to her. Her child had the same blue eyes of the man she loved. She needed to protect their newborn child. The queen of the spirits left her baby in the care of the hunter's younger sister and left with the words "I am going to become one with the ley line. If I borrow its power, I can protect this land from the monsters. So long as I watch over this place, the monsters will bring no harm to it."

After the queen of the spirits held her darling son close, she gave him to the hunter's sister.

"I will watch over you always, my dearest child."

She said no more, and the queen disappeared into the earth.

No one knew exactly what she had done, but the moment the queen of the spirits vanished, the monsters returned to the forest as if an invisible hand were driving them away. The child of the queen and the hunter, as well as the other humans, were saved.

From then on, just as the queen of the spirits had said, a mysterious power protected the hunters' village, and the monsters never drew near it again. Many humans came to this safe, plentiful land. Before long, the village grew into a town, and the town into a country.

The people of this land held an everlasting gratitude for the queen of the spirits, and they raised the child of the queen and the hunter with great care.

Eventually, the boy with the blood of spirit and man took up the throne as king. The country became known as "the Kingdom of Endalsia," named so after the queen that had birthed its ruler.

The Kingdom of Endalsia prospered for a long, long time, and the hunter's descendants had long and happy lives.

"Wonderful, wonderful."

After Emily finished reading, she gave a satisfied exhale of accomplishment for having finished an entire book, and closed it. Watching, Freyja said, "You did a good job" and stroked Emily's head. "But actually, that story got something wrong." The sage began flipping through the pages of the book.

"Which part is wrong?" Emily asked, curious. The other children seemed to want to know, too.

That was Freyja for you. She was good at capturing the hearts of children.

The sage looked around at them and then spoke in a hushed tone, quite unlike herself.

"This is what the queen said when she left her baby with the hunter's sister: 'I am going to become one with the ley line. If I borrow its power, I can protect this land from the monsters. An object representative of the protective power is required make it manifest. So I shall bestow my right eye to this child. So long as this Spirit Eye remains, the monsters will not be able to assail this land.' What happened after is the same as in the book. The village was protected and eventually became a human country through Endalsia's power. It seems the boy's right eye—the one inherited from Endalsia's Spirit Eye—was a deep green like the trees of the forest. His left eye—the one inherited from the hunter—was a beautiful blue. Even after the boy died, another boy with the green Spirit Eye on the right, and a blue eye on the left, was born in the Kingdom of Endalsia. This continued whenever the previous one with those eyes passed on. So the queen of the spirits upheld her promise to protect the kingdom."

"Wooow! That story's way more interesting!"

Emily's eyes sparkled, and Elmera's son Elio nodded in agreement.

Elio's older brother, Pallois, thought for a moment, then asked Freyja, "But wait, if the spirits were protecting it, why did the Kingdom of Endalsia get destroyed?"

"That's 'cause the spirits' protection was lost." Freyja paused before continuing. "Nooow then, it's time for kids to go home before it gets dark," and she took the four children home.

"Master, that story just now...," Mariela mumbled while rereading the book. Her teacher had told her all sorts of stories, but this was the first time she'd heard this one. As she wondered vaguely why her master had never told it to her, a memory from two hundred years ago came to mind. She had been looking at the sparkling royal castle of the Kingdom of Endalsia from a distance when her master explained that it shone because spirits protected it.

Master wasn't just making that up. That means Endalsia's king is the one who inherits the blood and protection of the spirits. The cornerstone itself of the spirits' power is—

"I'm back. Hmm? What's wrong, Mariela? You seem so serious. Look, I got a share of the earth dragon meat today."

"Welcome back, Sieg! Whoa, earth dragon meat! You even got fruit, what a great catch!"

Sieg's return interrupted Mariela's train of thought. To be precise, the arrival of meat was what brought her mind to a halt.

Could Sieg really have thought bringing meat was the best thing to delight Mariela? She was a girl at a marriageable age, after all. However, if Sieg had given Mariela flowers, her happiness would have depended on whether they could be used as alchemical materials. Thus a decision to present her with meat, which would make her happy no matter what, wasn't a poor one.

"We've already got a ton of food for dinner, but maybe I'll roast just a little," Mariela said as she cheerfully took the foodstuff and headed to the kitchen.

Freyja told Sieg to wash off his sweat, then detained Robert as he was about to return to the Aguinas estate and told him to close the windows in Sunlight's Canopy.

After cutting the meat into pieces to make them easier to cook and shutting them in the magical tool for refrigeration, Mariela was going to reheat the dishes she'd made earlier for dinner, but then Nierenberg returned from an errand he had run for Freyja. Apparently, dinner was going to be put on hold for just a little longer.

"It seems both of them will be coming. I'll open the cellar," Nierenberg said before setting about his work. Before long, he returned to the shop of Sunlight's Canopy with Leonhardt and Weishardt in tow.

"Huh? Lord Leonhardt too?" Mariela finally realized by his arrival that something unusual was underway. Sieg, who'd returned from washing himself off, was also suspicious of what was going on.

"I hear the special-grade specialized potion for eyes has been completed."

"Y-yes."

Mariela nodded in response to Weishardt's inquiry. Her master had said that it was to be in front of an appropriate audience, but she couldn't believe even Leonhardt had come.

All the windows of Sunlight's Canopy's shop, apart from the skylight, had been closed to make sure no prying eyes would see in. Mariela, Sieg, and Freyja were now joined by Robert, Nierenberg, and the general and lieutenant general of the Labyrinth Suppression Forces—Leonhardt and Weishardt.

What was Freyja thinking, summoning these two? If it was necessary to show them Sieg drinking the potion, Mariela's group probably should have gone to them, not the other way around!

Leonhardt and Weishardt cut impressive figures, but the pair didn't seem to be offended by having been made to travel to her. Sieg, the only person who didn't understand the situation, was doubtful of what was going on, but he moved to stand next to Mariela, assuming his usual position as her escort.

"Please begin," Leonhardt prompted the young alchemist, and everyone's gazes settled on Sieg. After nodding to the general, Mariela offered a single potion vial to her bewildered bodyguard.

"Er, um. Sieg, this…is a special-grade specialized potion for eyes. I finally made one. I'm sorry you had to wait so long. Everyone's here to see your eye heal."

A potion that would heal his eye.

Sieg froze at hearing the girl's words. His one good eye opened wide and stared at the vial Mariela held out to him.

Why now…? Siegmund wondered as he gazed at the little vial. This thing, this potion, was something Sieg had desperately wanted.

After losing his Spirit Eye, Sieg had fallen and fallen as if he was tumbling down a slope. The ground had collapsed beneath his feet, and he'd desperately craved such a potion as he clawed his way back to the surface. His yearning, his desire, his wish had long since given way to despair, and then Sieg found himself in this city.

After Mariela had saved him, the hunter had lost count the number of times he imagined how things would have gone differently if only he hadn't lost his other eye.

Mariela was an Alchemist Pact-Bearer of the Labyrinth City, and there were days Sieg clung to the faint hope that maybe someday he could get the Spirit Eye back. But before he knew it, he'd completely forgotten that ray of hope.

Even today, he'd pierced the eye of an earth dragon with an arrow from afar and finished it off with the mythril sword Mariela had given him. He'd worked with the members of the Labyrinth Suppression Forces to defeat a powerful enemy and bumped fists with them in celebration of their victory.

Sieg was no longer a slave to anyone, and he had a home he willingly returned to. Mariela was a bit of a handful, but her smile was irreplaceable.

Siegmund had never been more fulfilled. He'd already attained everything that had meaning and value to him. Before he knew it, he'd even started to feel deep down that losing his Spirit Eye was a necessary sacrifice that allowed him to have everything he did now.

Why now...?

He'd thought that if he obtained a special-grade specialized potion for eyes, he'd accept it and be overcome with the emotion that his long-standing wish had come true and his unwavering determination had finally borne fruit.

Sieg's heart was uncannily calm. Instead, the one overcome with emotion was the delighted girl offering him the potion.

"Thank you," Sieg said, and he accepted the little glass vial.

Mariela watched him, her face full of anticipation. Her feelings were simple. Healing injuries was a good thing, a happy thing. That was all. It was an expression full of affection, like when she had wanted to give him something good to eat.

Sieg surveyed the shop interior of Sunlight's Canopy with his single eye to ensure he remembered her expression, and every other detail of today's event. It wasn't a small shop, but seven people together filled the area by the entrance.

Sieg hadn't expected Leonhardt's sudden arrival, and even

Mariela probably hadn't counted on it. Now that the sun had completely set, Sunlight's Canopy was a bit dim because the only lights that were lit were those around the assembled group. Where the light of the sun usually shone to make bright spots, the light of the moon now cast pale rays that painted the room in an almost fantastical glow. Everyone's eyes remained on Sieg, however. They were eager for him to hurry up and drink the potion. Sieg removed his eye patch so everyone could see his wounded eye, then opened the lid of the potion he'd accepted from Mariela with a *pop*.

The first time Mariela made a potion for me, she crammed it into my mouth, vial and all...

He'd been so astonished his mouth dropped open, and she'd thrust it in with a "Hup!" Although she was normally clumsy, she displayed outstanding dexterity when forcing people to drink potions. Feeling nostalgic for that unusual moment in his life, Sieg downed the special-grade potion.

It was a very strange sensation. Not as strong as energy, nor as dazzling as light. It had no shape or substance, yet it existed inside him. This source that moved his hands, his feet, and his muscles, that circulated his blood, felt like it was swelling, teeming.

This torrent spread through his flesh and seemed like it would burst out of him in a fountain. Yet it also felt like it was whirling, following the current of Siegmund's fixed body, and gathering at a single point as it circulated throughout him.

The sensation filling him was akin to a hole having opened at the bottom of a giant lake; it was as if the stars in the entire sky were piercing a dark space. All was being absorbed by his right eye.

More and more, more and more.

He was falling through something with no bottom.

Strangely, the inside of his very being seemed to be connected to something primordial; no matter how much the source filling his insides streamed into his right eye, it never ran out, it simply flowed into that single point.

More and more, more and more.

It was like the gathered light acquired a tangible density and emerged.

"Sieg?"

Upon hearing Mariela's worried voice, Siegmund opened both eyes.

One was deep blue, and one was forest green.

"Sieg, I'm so glad!"

"Hrm, so it can be restored this quickly?"

"Is this what they call the Spirit Eye...?"

Mariela was overjoyed, Nierenberg observed the effects of the potion with intention, and Weishardt was taken with the Spirit Eye. Then there was...

"Ah..." Siegmund parted his lips, and let out a small gasp in wonder. "Was the world always this full with the light of the spirits...?"

He hadn't seen in this way since he was a child. Weak little primordial drops of light were everywhere. On the counter Mariela polished so carefully, on the chairs where the regulars relaxed. They gathered in places like the tea utensils where the stylish, shining tea was poured, as if to imitate the liquid. All were dazzlingly beautiful.

Sunlight's Canopy, which was so dim before, overflowed with brightness. It was a warmth like the inside of the shop during a day when it was bustling with customers. Sieg sensed the spirit's feelings—*this is fun, I'm happy, this place is cozy*—being transmitted to him.

The brilliant world he had lost as he had grown more arrogant, now spread out around him as if blessing the restoration of his Spirit Eye.

They've come back to me, they're with me. The warm, sunny spot Mariela built must be a warm place for the spirits, too—

Siegmund couldn't hold back the tears. Mariela, began crying herself, and the light of the spirits diffusely reflected through the little droplets dampening his eyelashes, making them as beautiful as the world of dreams.

In the middle of that beautiful world...

In the center of the moonlight pouring through the skylight shaped like the branches of the sacred tree...

A single girl with green hair and green eyes appeared.

The green girl simply stood as if she'd alighted with the lunar glow. Sieg stared at the girl in astonishment, and in response, everyone shifted their gazes from him, and finally took notice of the strange phenomenon.

"Who...?"

"This light is...?"

Leonhardt and the others, experienced in battling monsters, appeared to understand that the girl standing in the moonlight didn't carry any ill intent. They were curious as to her true identity, but looked around at the tiny lights dancing and soaring in the shop.

Mariela took no notice of the shop's appearance. She stared at this person in the moonlight, then took a step toward her and mumbled something.

"Illuminaria...?"

Illuminaria. It was the name of the spirit who had taken Mariela to the ley line two hundred years ago. Why had Mariela forgotten it until now? Where had the spirit been all this time, and why had she come here now? Although Mariela was full of questions, the rest of the group, still unsure who this person actually was, prevented her from asking any further.

The girl standing in the moonlight, the spirit Illuminaria, stared at the girl who knew her name. She smiled happily but didn't make a motion to speak. The curious woman didn't appear to understand the many questions of the others.

However, she quietly held out her hands, which had been clasped together at her chest, and showed Mariela what she had been carefully holding. It was a bowl-like object in the shape of a flower, but all the tips of the petals were chipped. So many cracks ran through it that it was a wonder the thing hadn't broken.

"Is that the seven-petaled flower bowl...?"

Mariela recalled the vessel. It was the flower she had found with Illuminaria back when she went to the Spirit Sanctuary to make a Pact with the ley line. Although it had definitely been a plant when Mariela found it; when Illuminaria had cupped it in both hands and lifted it up, it became a flower-shaped vessel.

Illuminaria didn't seem to understand Mariela's question, however.

"Mariela, you can't communicate with her. She probably survived the Stampede thanks to that vessel. She was able to hide in it because she was a newly sprouted seedling."

Freyja had taken it upon herself to explain the situation in place of the silent spirit. Mariela didn't know what kind of meaning the seven-petaled flower vessel had to spirits, but if it had saved Illuminaria, then Mariela was thankful she and Illuminaria had found it together. Perhaps the flower-shaped object was precious to the mysterious spirit—battered and cracked though it was—as she carefully enfolded it in both hands once more, and then she turned toward the young alchemist and the others, spreading her hands. The seven-petaled flower vessel became particles of light that danced and wafted lightly, like dandelion fuzz, and spread out from Illuminaria's hands into the room. The diffused drops of light softly and slowly drifted downward like sparkling, dancing snow.

Although Mariela and the others should have been in Sunlight's Canopy, they suddenly found themselves floating in a place as dark as the sea at night.

"This place... When I was going toward the ley line..."

When Mariela separated from her body two hundred years ago, she had followed Illuminaria and dived into this place.

Back then, the light of the ley line could be seen from far away. This time, however, Mariela and the others didn't dive into the ley line. The biggest difference was that everyone was complete and still in their own bodies.

"This is the world Illuminaria sees..."

At Mariela's mumblings, Sieg, Leonhardt, and the others, grasped the situation and calmly surveyed their surroundings.

Seeing it for the second time made it no less beautiful. Mariela took in the scenery with the others. Even now, free-flowing particles of light rose up from and returned to the ley line.

Far below their feet was a gentle light that had once welcomed the young alchemist as if enveloping her up.

...*Huh? What is this? I feel a little uncomfortable...*

Mariela experienced a slight sense of unease. This was supposed to be a warm place that welcomed one and all without discrimination. Yet she somehow had a sensation of estrangement. It was a discomforting atmosphere, like being surrounded by a crowd that was keeping their distance, or ostracized. When she looked at Illuminaria with an expression asking what it all meant, the green-haired spirit pointed to a spot deep in the ley line.

That's where I made my Pact...

Mariela stared in the direction of the light. Sieg and the others also stood motionless, eyes fixed at that single point in the ley line. When she was young, Illuminaria had led Mariela to that innermost place. There, enveloped in light, she'd met a certain someone.

She wasn't sure, but the young alchemist got the feeling that the "someone" wasn't an embodiment of the ley line, but rather something like a warden. An existence that served as a go-between for the ley line and the surface. The ley line was energy itself, and no consciousness existed there.

But when that person had told the young alchemist their name, she'd felt they held humans, animals, the world—everything—dearly. When she connected her Nexus, warm thoughts had flowed into her.

Mariela sifted through her mind to recall the name of the being she'd encountered. Almost on reflex, the story she'd overheard Emily and the other children reading came to mind.

Mariela finally understood who she'd encountered two hundred years ago.

Curiously, once the Mariela realized who she'd met in the ley line those many years ago, she could almost see a woman's figure where she had only ever seen light before.

It was her.

The feeling swelled in the girl, and the image of the previously unknown being came into focus. That beautiful form belonged to...

"How... Why... Endalsia is..."

When Mariela called the name, she and the others promptly found themselves standing back in Sunlight's Canopy.

The light of the moon had vanished back behind the clouds. The inside of Sunlight's Canopy was dark, save for the sparse magical tools for illumination and the light of the small, formless spirits. Illuminaria had vanished as well. The gathered seven stood in silence, as if nothing had happened.

"Freyja, Sage of Calamity, I take it you called us here to show us that. However...I believe we are owed an explanation." It was Leonhardt who first broke the silence.

There were many questions he felt needed answering. What was this Spirit Eye that had summoned the mysterious dancing spirits? Who was this Illuminaria, and where had she disappeared to?

Those things were trivialized by the question Leonhardt really should have been asking. He and his brother were the sovereigns of the Labyrinth City, part of a family that would defeat the Labyrinth, and there was something the two needed to know.

Freyja calmly smiled, then turned to the formerly one-eyed hunter.

"Sieg, you could probably see it well with your eye. Someone with a Spirit Eye like you probably knows who she is. Go on, enlighten them."

Now the subject of the conversation, Sieg had turned a bit pale with all the things his eye had laid bare before him so quickly. He looked at Mariela, then faced Leonhardt.

"That… The presence in the ley line was most likely the spirit, Endalsia. She…"

The man paused, as if he was afraid to continue. Mariela took his hand. Perhaps she, too, was afraid to hear what the hunter had to say. Leonhardt and Weishardt listened intently. Nierenberg had been silent throughout the entire ordeal. Robert was quiet as well. All of them had seen Endalsia's condition with their own eyes. Even if Sieg didn't continue, they knew what he would say.

They just didn't want to accept it.

"She… Endalsia…was devoured."

That which swallowed the queen of the spirits—and tried to replace her entire existence as the guardian of the ley line—was likely the boss of the Labyrinth.

On the day of the Stampede, now two centuries past, the monsters who slaughtered and ate the Kingdom of Endalsia's people then partook of one another. The single monster remaining at the end swallowed the spirit of the ley line. The Labyrinth was born from the ruins of the kingdom. This story of the fall of the Kingdom of Endalsia had been passed throughout the years as a children's fable. However, the seven had just been presented with evidence that suggested the fairy tale was far more factual than anyone had ever suspected.

Endalsia was a spirit, and moreover, the guardian of the ley line. Being eaten by a monster wasn't enough to erase her existence; her life wasn't so easily snuffed out like that of a human's.

The fiend that had devoured the queen of the spirits and become the boss of the Labyrinth had been eating its way farther and deeper underground for two hundred years. The growth of the Labyrinth wasn't just a physical increase in the number of strata. It was an incursion into the ley line to fully absorb the existence of its previous guardian and supplant her.

Endalsia wasn't yet entirely gone. She'd gazed motionlessly at Sieg with her single left eye. There was so little remaining of her that it looked like she could disappear at any moment, but her gentle face seemed full of love and even joy at the growth of her beloved child.

However, if the master of the Labyrinth achieved its goal...

"So this is why the Labyrinth exceeded fifty strata...?"

Weishardt was at a loss for words.

"If the Labyrinth boss becomes the guardian..."

Endalsia loved every living thing equally. People, animals, even monsters.

In their vision of the ley line, Mariela and the others had felt uneasy. It was the remnants of hatred against humans. Monsters couldn't coexist with humans. If that thing took control then, surely...

"People won't be able to live in this land anymore." Freyja quietly spoke the words no one else could bring themselves to say. Endalsia was on the verge of being consumed, her existence barely more than a candle flame before a storm.

Leonhardt, Weishardt, and indeed all who dwelled in the Labyrinth City no longer had the luxury of time. It was a revelation that weighed heavy on all their minds, overshadowing the beauty of the miraculous vision they'd all been granted.

Sunset Over the Kingdom

01

"Listen, and I'll tell you an old story."

Freyja turned and spoke to the others, all of whom were still in shock at their grim situation.

The red-haired woman's tale proved to be an old one for anyone who'd grown up in the Labyrinth City. For Mariela, however, it was a story about the world she'd spent so much of her life in. However, it held far more connection to the others in the room.

The Kingdom of Endalsia.

Monsters never drew near to the country the spirits protected, not even the parts near the Fell Forest. This safety brought great wealth and prosperity. Nowhere was this more evident than in the royal castle.

It is said that fruit is ripest just before it falls. Long-standing peace fostered pride in the kingdom's people. They forgot to whom they owed their successes.

The extravagant folk in the royal palace served and lionized the power that was attached to lineage and fortune. To them, these were rights within their fabricated rules of society, passed from one generation to the next. This was the same for noble families or royalty. If one were to forget lineage, those who clawed after glory in the kingdom had only grown fat from their complacency.

However, people proved to be foolish and arrogant, growing

more conceited every time someone bowed to them. They thought they were of a chosen lineage and had special abilities.

A man was born with the right to succeed the throne, but he was forced to surrender it to his younger brother and take the position of chancellor because that man wasn't born with the Spirit Eye, a trait that was considered to be the eye of the queen of the forest spirits. The man was unwilling to sit by and accept that he'd lost the right to the throne simply because his eye was the wrong color.

The chancellor had always desired the power of the king's seat. On the day his grandfather, who had the Spirit Eye, passed away, the one to take the throne was the chancellor's brother. His brother was a far younger man than he. The ascendancy had even skipped over the chancellor's father, who had abdicated his position to serve as an adviser to the chancellor's grandfather.

The chancellor's father ordered him to support his younger brother and guard the country, but the chancellor could not accept his position.

His younger brother was kind, and he excelled at hunting and singing, but he was too foolish and mediocre a person. His personality and skills were unsuited for ruling a kingdom.

"Moldy old traditions are out of date. Having some special eye doesn't mean you should govern a country."

From the time he was a child, everyone had served and bowed to the chancellor. This was, of course, because of his former position as the crown prince, not any abilities of his own. However, the chancellor had never known any other life; he was blind to the reason.

The chancellor spent time scheming to claim the crown for himself. If outdated customs were the problem, he would erase them from history.

"Offering power to a spirit's eye is a contemptuous affront to the authority of the king. The Kingdom of Endalsia is a country that prospers *by the hand of the king.* All glory to his majesty."

Extolling the power of the king, the chancellor worked to abolish the reverence of the Spirit Eye from history. He even went so far as to expunge it from the fairy tales that children read.

Slowly and steadily, the chancellor rewrote the memory and history of the people. Those who'd lived in peace for so long had already begun to think of the story of Endalsia's founding to be just a myth. If official records were altered and rewritten, the next step was simply to wait.

Fortunately for the plotting chancellor, his father passed away before long. The stress of overwork and his own frustrations at not inheriting the Spirit Eye had finally caught up with him.

It was said the foolish, kind young king who possessed the Spirit Eye came up short when it came to dealing with matters of national politics. So the chancellor often offered his assistance. In time the king came to rely on the counsel of his older sibling. People praised the pair's close relationship, unaware of their chancellor's designs to snatch his brother's life and the kingdom. They grew intoxicated on the luxury of what they saw as the kingdom's preordained prosperity.

When the young king wanted the most celebrated princess in the imperial capital to be his queen, the chancellor showed a kind and cooperative attitude and pressed him to make a young, enthusiastic nobleman the go-between.

"Many desire the hand of the beautiful princess, but she rebukes them all. Better to employ a keen youth to convey the feelings of the king than a qualified matchmaker."

"I see. You are clever as always, Brother. The princess has enough dresses and jewels to be tired of them. Presents would hardly earn her affections."

It was an absurd conversation. There was no way for a young noble without an appropriate position or extravagant presents to catch the interest of a beautiful princess whom everyone wanted to marry. The chancellor silently mocked the foolish young king for failing to understand even such a simple matter.

The scheming elder brother saw no opposition to his plan, save the possibility of the king siring an heir. In order to ensure the failure of the marriage, he arranged to move forward with talks that existed in formality only. Even the messenger he'd chosen for the job was meant to be ineffective; a serious young noble with a strong sense of justice, the kind of man who was more a dull nuisance than anything else.

However, the imprudent plan proved to backfire. Miraculously, or perhaps disastrously, the youthful nobleman managed to finalize the marriage between the princess and the king.

"To think he gave me a full room's worth of such valuable rainbow flowers. Such passion, such beauty. They're more precious than any jewel. I gratefully accept the king's feelings."

The nobleman who happened to catch the chancellor's attention turned out to be an alchemist. Apparently, he'd had some connection that afforded him a number of rainbow flowers. Just a single bloom was a valuable treasure, but the princess now had a large room overflowing with them.

The young noble who served as matchmaker, Robroy Aguinas, was appointed as head alchemist in the Kingdom of Endalsia. On an autumn day, after a five-year engagement period, the princess was joyously married into the Kingdom of Endalsia.

"So the engagement can no longer be extended? It will prove most troublesome should an heir be born. I will have to go forward ahead of schedule," the chancellor decided.

The king was grateful that his brother had won him the woman he desired, but even that sentiment was unpleasant to the chancellor.

Heedless to the chancellor's plot, people all over the country were thrilled at the marriage of the young king and beautiful queen. The winter days in Endalsia passed by amid great enthusiasm. On one spring night, as joy still lingered amid the people, the queen had a strange dream.

A spirit with a single green eye told the queen to flee the land. Monsters from the Fell Forest were closing in. The mysterious entity who appeared in the dream and the destruction she showed were as vivid as reality. The queen trusted it was more than just a construct of her own thought, and she tried to tell the king it was a vision from the spirits. But the king, so drunk from prolonged supping at the cup of peace, merely laughed it off.

The dream became more vivid by the day, and the queen's anxiety worsened. Only the head alchemist, the king and queen's matchmaker, paid any heed to the story.

"Lord Robroy. Please, take me away from the Fell Forest." The newlywed queen's request was inspired by what the spirit in her dream had said

"Please, protect the new king growing within you." The spirit's words had meant that the queen was pregnant.

Thus, the queen fabricated an excuse. "I'm going to visit my sick and bedridden mother," she'd said. She fled the Kingdom of Endalsia with the alchemist Robroy and the few attendants she'd brought with her when she married into the royal family.

The day the queen traveled through the Fell Forest was the day the chancellor usurped the throne. The moment the life of the king possessing the Spirit Eye was snuffed out, the divine protection of the spirits vanished, and the era of safety for the Kingdom of Endalsia safe was over. It was then that the monsters of the Fell Forest began their attack…

"This is the reality of the Stampede two hundred years ago. After that, I went into my sleep. If there's anything else about that time that made it through the years, you'll know more than me." Freyja gave a nod as she finished reciting the old story.

This was the truth of the Stampede, unknown to even Leonhardt and Weishardt. The story had contained some monumentally important facts. Even Robert, who seemed somewhat uncomfortable in this gathering, looked at Freyja with surprise at what her story revealed about the origins of the Aguinas family. Freyja's tale was consistent with the state of the ley line seen a short while ago, and the young man with a Spirit Eye standing before them.

Leonhardt pondered for a moment, then hit upon a question for the golden-eyed sage. "There's something that doesn't make sense about this story behind the Stampede."

Weishardt seemingly shared his brother's concerns, and he picked up the thread of conversation by recounting the history of the Stampede's immediate aftermath.

02

The Stampede that swallowed the Kingdom of Endalsia was on a large scale, and it was certain that the monsters that had invaded were responsible for the creation of the Labyrinth.

Left to its own designs, the subterranean structure would eventually grow to an unmanageable scale, and sooner or later both the Labyrinth monsters and those of the Fell Forest would probably surge all the way to the imperial capital.

Up until its collapse, the Empire viewed the Kingdom of Endalsia as a wealthy, amicable neighbor that was difficult to attack, but that also was very unlikely to attack the capital due to its isolation in the Fell Forest.

The differing ley lines also strengthened their mutual independence. The wars of humankind tended to be ones of attrition, if powerful recovery methods such as healing magic and potions were available. The side that invaded its opponent's ley line was forced into a considerably tough fight if it didn't capture a fair number of that ley line's alchemists to ensure its own methods of recovery.

Moreover, the Fell Forest lay between the Empire and the Kingdom of Endalsia, so no matter how many monster-warding potions were used, an army would have a difficult time moving through it.

Furthermore, only the Kingdom of Endalsia had the special

circumstances of being under the divine protection of the spirits that repelled monsters. The kingdom was small but very wealthy due to fertile soil, mineral resources from the nearby mountains, and monster materials gathered from the Fell Forest. As such, there were no plans to make serious sacrifices to cross the Fell Forest and expand the kingdom's domain.

That was why the Empire built its capital close to the kingdom, about a week away by carriage. It was the safest place for the Empire among the enemy nations surrounding its borders.

However, two centuries ago, the Kingdom of Endalsia was engulfed by the Stampede and became a territory ruled by monsters. It was a catastrophe that none had seen coming.

Even if the Empire wanted to destroy the Labyrinth and take back the country, the Fell Forest and the different ley lines—once perfect demarcations for different nations—now stood in the way like an impregnable fortress. If they didn't at least establish a base near the Labyrinth for subjugation, it would be an utterly impossible task.

Without a way to keep the Labyrinth in check, monsters could easily swarm from there and the forest again. Another stampede would spell doom for the imperial capital, and by extension, the entire Empire.

Under these circumstances, Margrave Schutzenwald, who bore the responsibility of protecting the country against the Fell Forest, guarded the escaped queen of Endalsia. The margrave also accepted the entreaty of the kingdom's head alchemist—whom the queen had brought with her—to raise an army for the purpose of taking the kingdom back from the fiends who had stolen it.

Margrave Schutzenwald's troops charged through the Fell Forest without rest. When they finally arrived, the place they found was not a city with a beautiful protective white wall, nor a dazzling royal castle, but an uninhabitable ruin where innumerable people had perished and monsters scavenged for corpses.

The collapsed protective wall, the destroyed structures, and the state of the trampled, broken, and exposed pavement told a story of a terrible force that had crashed onto the unsuspecting kingdom like an avalanche. The country was in such ruins it seemed a miracle that any had survived. Some people had held on to their lives by sheer coincidence, traveling to foreign lands before the attack.

The monsters from the forest were thought to have devoured every single person who was too slow to get away or hide, and then the creatures resorted to eating one another. Legend had it that the last remaining monster dove into the earth, creating the Labyrinth.

Evidence supporting this came from the number of monsters present when Margrave Schutzenwald's forces arrived at the ruined kingdom and found the Labyrinth in its place. There didn't appear to be many more of the fiends than there could've been in the Fell Forest before the Stampede. For such an unbelievable atrocity, they expected the lands to be overflowing with the vile creatures.

However, even with only the same number of monsters as in there were in the Fell Forest, a considerable amount of time was needed to secure a place where people could live. Plus, there was this new problem of the Labyrinth.

The theory proposed by scholars of the imperial capital was that there was a correlation between the number of Stampede victims and the scale of the Labyrinth. Based on this conjecture, the Labyrinth in the ruins of the kingdom was thought to have been on an extraordinarily large scale.

This great maze of underground tunnels had to be destroyed to ensure another event like the Stampede would never happen again. It was a task of utmost importance for the safety of the Empire.

A base for subjugation was constructed near the Labyrinth to someday return this land to human hands. Overtime, this bastion grew into a city.

"Thus the Labyrinth City was created. Even now, two hundred years after the Stampede, the fact that we have not defeated the Labyrinth makes it clear that it was never going to be an easy journey. Even the emperor freely offered his support due to the extremity of the situation. It was not a venture that would last under the weak cause of merely 'taking back the Kingdom of Endalsia.' A more definite and just cause was required. That was why the emperor had the princess of the ruined country marry into the house of Margrave Schutzenwald."

The queen, who'd fled from the Kingdom of Endalsia just before the Stampede, had been pregnant. The house of Margrave Schutzenwald welcomed the newborn princess, and the Empire proposed they undertake the moral duty of recapturing their homeland and incorporate the former site of the Kingdom of Endalsia into the margrave's territory.

The Labyrinth City, having lost the divine protection of the spirits, was a dangerous place. Monsters came and went freely, and food supplies were scarce. Even if the territory were to be reclaimed for humanity, it wasn't worth the resources the Empire would have to spend taking it in the first place. The reason the house of Margrave Schutzenwald agreed to such an undertaking was because they also held territory in the place that would be the first to fall prey to another Stampede. The margrave's family also could not abide the damage that would befall the neighboring countries.

The house of Margrave Schutzenwald was a direct descendant from the Kingdom of Endalsia and its rightful successor. For this reason, they continued to shed their blood and challenge the Labyrinth for two hundred long years. All for the dream of reclaiming their homeland.

However, if their lineage truly could be traced back to the old royal family, why had no proof that they were worthy of the throne materialized? Not a single person belonging to the Schutzenwald family had the Spirit Eye.

"The princess descended from the royal family married into our family. Our house should have inherited the blood of the spirit Endalsia," said Weishardt. This was both an assertion of facts and a question of its truth. His statement was directed at both the Sage of Calamity Freyja and at Siegmund. He was asking why Sieg had the Spirit Eye.

"The Schutzenwalds are indeed of the same lineage of the Endalsian royal family," Freyja said with a look in her golden eyes that suggested a deeper knowing than any had suspected.

The way Freyja's gaze pierced the two brothers suggested that she had more knowledge of the blood in their veins than they did. What she said next removed any doubt they'd ever held about the fiery-haired woman being a sage.

"But you know, the child that the spirit Endalsia gave her eye to was a boy."

Everyone present followed Freyja's gaze over to Sieg.

"...Inheritance through the male line only?" Leonhardt muttered. His own Lion's Roar possessed an identical quirk.

Skills were mysterious things, generally considered to be passed through bloodlines, but some could only be inherited by men, and others only by women. There were even some skills—referred to as "divine protection"—that made themselves known only in one person per era, while others manifested only in those who satisfied particular requirements.

If Freyja spoke the truth, Sieg's Spirit Eye was probably the same way. Only male offspring could inherit the skill's gene, and when the previous skill owner in the family died, only one person would be chosen from among those who satisfied the conditions and possessed the gene.

Although the Schutzenwald family intermingled with the blood of the Endalsian royal family by way of the princess, they hadn't inherited the skill gene for the Spirit Eye. Meanwhile, multiple other people had been confirmed to possess the Spirit Eye during the intervening centuries; Sieg being the most recent.

"In your tale just now, the spirit said, 'protect the new king.' In other words, you're saying the queen of the ruined country had twins...?"

It wasn't an impossibility. A prince of a ruined land would only be a nuisance to a family so devoted to sacrificing everything for the sake of subjugating the Labyrinth. No matter who he was, it would be impossible for someone with no country, no people, and no funds to offer compensation equaling those sacrifices.

Did they pretend from the beginning that the queen had only given birth to a girl? Was the prince snatched from his cradle just as he was about to be killed? No one knew the answer.

Thanks to the efforts of a certain chancellor, nearly everyone had forgotten the significance of the Spirit Eye. The prince preserved his bloodline, hidden as a commoner with an unusual eye coloration, in a remote region near the Fell Forest.

"Your parents never told you anything of this?" Weishardt asked Sieg. The hunter, still at a loss for words, shook his head.

"I was raised to 'become a man worthy of the Spirit Eye.'" These were the words Sieg's late father had left him with.

Likely his father hadn't known any of this, either. Without even knowing the significance of his own words, Siegmund's father respected the divine protection of the Spirit Eye and imparted its importance to his son.

"Become worthy." Worthy of being Endalsia's king.

"Phew..."

Leonhardt breathed a deep sigh. He couldn't overlook this. A legitimate successor to this ruined country...

However, Freyja dispelled his concerns.

"That isn't something to worry about. The Kingdom of Endalsia is long gone. What is a country? A plot of land? A ley line? Two hundred years isn't a short amount of time, y'know. What have you been fighting to protect all that time? Money? Land? No. It's the people who live here, right? If so, ask them. 'What is this place?' This place has long since been the Labyrinth City, governed by the Schutzenwalds. His Spirit Eye is certainly Endalsia's eye, but spirits don't understand human constructs like kings and countries in the first place. People can put the owner of the Spirit Eye in whatever position they like; it's for humankind's own convenience. The spirits don't care."

Mariela, who had been quietly holding Sieg's hand the whole time, looked at the floating particles of light around the man. When she went to the Spirit Sanctuary as a child, the spirits were much larger and took the forms of butterflies, birds, even people. Now their shapes were frail, barely visible.

However, every one of the lights playing in Sunlight's Canopy repeatedly danced around Sieg. Somehow, they seemed very happy.

"The spirits really love Sieg, and I think if he's happy, that's enough for them."

Freyja laughed and nodded at the words that slipped from her pupil's mouth.

"That's right, Mariela. To be exact, the spirits probably sense their own ruler, Endalsia, in him. The Spirit Eye is a catalyst that strengthens the power of the spirits. That's why even these weak, formless spirits can manifest themselves here. These ones are simple, so they're plenty happy so long as this place is comfortable and the owner of the Spirit Eye is nice. A kingdom that's long since been destroyed doesn't make any difference to them."

"In other words, what's important is to destroy the Labyrinth before the spirit Endalsia is completely consumed." Weishardt communicated the obvious while holding in a sigh. It was easy to put it into words. But how much time and effort had they spent just to get where they were now?

"Yep. There's not much time left."

"Lady Sage, you have put it so simply, but..."

Nierenberg, who'd been careful with his words up to this point, admonished Freyja's light tone. The crease between his eyebrows was much deeper than it had ever been before.

"Oh, what was that? Your butt brow's gotten real bad, Doc. I'm telling you, it's fine. You understand the gist of the *arrangement*, don't you? Potions appeared on the market and people started coming to the City. People should go into the Labyrinth nonstop.

Even killing just one goblin weakens the place. Throw the entire City in there if you have to."

"That's certainly true, but even people from beyond the City won't be nearly enough. A great many people here have injuries that prevent them from going into the Labyrinth."

Carefree Freyja and cautious Nierenberg were two polar opposites. The red-haired sage didn't seem to care, but the doctor's harsh verbal assault seemed to slowly fall apart.

"That's why you have special-grade potions, isn't it?"

"However, the only specialized ones we have right now are for eyes. If someone lost an arm or a leg, no potion would be able to heal something like that."

Potions had limits on their restoration potential, and if too much time had passed since someone lost a limb, it was said that the body might prove unable to grow it back, even with magical assistance. Freyja was quick to laugh down that concern.

"What're you saying? Of course you can. You've healed bad wounds with high-grade potions before when you didn't have special-grade ones, right? Surely you have both the skills and the knowledge. Rob has the knowledge you lack, Doc."

Nierenberg had no response for her irreverence. People feared him as though he were a monster himself, and they avoided his bloodstained hands. Despite being more than accustomed to looks like that, Nierenberg wasn't sure what to do when face-to-face with someone like Freyja, who didn't care about his perceived reputation and recognized his abilities and accomplishments.

Freyja shifted away from the doctor, who had fallen silent again, and looked at Robert.

"Rooob, you heard me. This is your job. Work with Doc here to treat everyone in the slums. You've done a lot of this kinda thing, too, so if you have special-grade potions, I bet you could do almost anything, yeah? Ah, make suuure they pay the doctor's fee, okay? At least earn enough to feed yourself on your own coin. When you're done treating everyone, I'll forgive your debts."

"Uhhh…"

Robert grimaced after being so suddenly addressed. Understandably so, given the task he'd just had foisted upon him. What happened next is no surprise.

"Rooob."

Poke-poke-poke-poke, poke-poke-poke-poke.

Freyja unleashed her forehead poke attack on Robert's sullen face.

"Agaaain? Ow, ow, owww, I— Ow, *I get it alreadyyy!*"

The master was, well, the same as ever, but Robert hadn't learned at all. He even looked happy about the forehead prodding. The tense atmosphere of the previous conversations was completely ruined.

"Phew… I guess you didn't call me here to tell me about the glorious history of the Aguinases, huh…?"

Robert hung his head and walked away from Freyja, and toward Nierenberg. The doctor muttered, "It's more surprising you'd harbor such illusions in regard to the Lady Sage," kicking him while he was down.

"Doc and Rob are total opposites, but they make for a good pair."

This was the moment that would come to be known as the birth of the Mad Medical Duo among the Labyrinth Suppression Forces. The personalities, or rather, the preferences of the two were different, but both had outstanding talent. Nierenberg and Robert also shared a penchant for adopting methods with no concern at all for what were considered accepted practices in the world.

Leonhardt was a bit bewildered at bearing witness to this new, unusual, piece of the Forces—no—the Labyrinth City, but he quickly recovered.

"First, we must defeat the red dragon."

"Indeed, Brother. The Spirit Eye has returned. Even if you don't take Endalsia's divine protection into account, I have heard it improves the accuracy and power of a bow." After answering Leonhardt, Weishardt turned to face Sieg and asked, "Siegmund, will you lend us your aid?"

"Of course," the hunter answered with a firm nod. Why had the Spirit Eye returned now? Siegmund had his answer. This Spirit Eye was Endalsia's prayer for the peace and happiness of all people. Even if it dwelled in Sieg's eye, it wasn't a power that belonged just to him.

It was something that would see the wish of a commonplace girl fulfilled. A wish like wanting to live carefree and happily in the Labyrinth City. It was the divine protection of the spirits, given to Sieg to protect the world where she lived. The seven gathered in Sunlight's Canopy were united in purpose.

"We'll go over the particulars tomorrow."

Perhaps to start working out a plan, Leonhardt and Weishardt returned to the base through the cellar the same way they'd come. Nierenberg took Robert with him in a carriage back to the base as well.

03

After everyone else had left, and the room was silent, Sieg dared to ask Mariela a question.

"Mariela, you weren't really surprised, were you?"

"Yeah, somehow I kinda already knew. Right after I met you, I made potion vials at the riverbed, remember? Back then, I made such a small stove, but a salamander answered my call. It even gave me a ring afterward. It's because you were there, Sieg. When the firewood was about to run out, you added more to the stove, right? It was just normal firewood, but that salamander was so happy it twirled around. The spirits completely understood."

Mariela went out to the rear garden and approached the sacred tree. Its branches looked worn and tired. Its leaves were drooping as if it hadn't been watered in days.

"This was Illuminaria once." Mariela spoke to the ancient plant as she spread plenty of water mixed with Drops of Life at its roots.

"Seems like Illuminaria used up all the power she'd saved. That's probably why she was able to appear for a little while," Freyja added.

Mariela gently stroked the trunk of the sacred tree as she nodded at her master's words.

"I'm glad I got to see you again."

Illuminaria was a sacred tree spirit. She'd probably chosen to appear in Sunlight's Canopy through the skylight that mimicked the shape of a tree to convey who she was.

"But don't you think it's a little mean to give way more leaves to Sieg than me, your friend?"

Just like the salamander, Illuminaria was likely drawn to Sieg. After all, she had dropped many more leaves for him compared to how much water Mariela had given her.

"You play favorites." Mariela laughed. Even if the young alchemist's friend could hear her voice, she couldn't understand her. This place was still the domain of the monsters. However, a single leaf dropped from the tree and landed on the top of Mariela's head, as if to stroke her hair.

"Oh yeah, Master. I had something I wanted to ask you," Mariela said as she laid out the feast she'd prepared in advance.

Despite the long and rather weighty conversation, Freyja had wasted no time pestering her student.

"I'm starved—I want dinner," the sage had demanded.

Mariela's celebratory mood had wilted in the face of the unforeseen event, but the fact that Sieg's eye had been cured remained. Luckily, her teacher was the type of person who was always in the mood to party, so it was still a celebration. Even if it was only for three.

"Mm?"

Freyja's cheeks were already stuffed with freshly roasted earth dragon meat by the time Mariela asked her question.

"In that story from earlier, you said the ancestor of the Aguinases gave rainbow flowers to the princess, right? Were those—?"

"Yeah, those were the ones you went to all that trouble to make when you were little. Maaan, they really helped me out. Rob, too, uh, I mean the Rob from two hundred years ago. I sold them to him and made him promise he'd repay me in installments with a high interest rate after he succeeded. I didn't have to worry about paying for food or booze for about five years!"

"I knew it..."

Mariela had never been aware of it as a child, but started to have doubts after her master had showed up and started living with her in Sunlight's Canopy.

Mariela couldn't imagine her master working and had wondered how in the world she'd covered her living expenses back in those days.

"I guess I should just be glad you didn't cause any real trouble. Oh, Master, today you still only get one bottle of alcohol!" Mariela said, then confiscated the second bottle her master had excitedly brought and poured water in her glass instead.

Siegmund quietly watched the trite, everyday spectacle through both of his eyes.

SIDE STORY

The Road Home

"A blood relation potion? The potion itself isn't hard, but the 'twin seeds of curly sky grass'… Master, is there a good way to identify those?"

Several days after Caroline had been rescued, Mariela received a request for an unusual potion.

A blood relation potion wasn't something that common folk were familiar with. It didn't heal injuries or illnesses, nor did it have any special effect on the body. It was a very expensive potion that was regularly used among nobles when their children were presented to the public.

To prove the blood relationship of a child who had been newly announced to the world, the offspring's blood was dripped into the blood relation potion, followed by that of a different person. The potion turned deep crimson for parent and child, orange for siblings, yellow for grandparent and grandchild. The color was lighter the more distant the blood relationship was. It was a very important potion for nobles, who prided themselves on their lineage, to prove without a doubt that a child was theirs.

Although the concoction was a type of high-grade potion, it was extremely expensive at a gold coin per bottle. This was ten times the price of a normal high-grade potion.

Despite being so expensive, the difficulty level of making a blood relation potion was no different than other high-grade potions. The reason for the high price was half because of an added surcharge and half because one of the ingredients—twin seeds of curly sky grass—was extremely expensive.

Curly sky grass itself wasn't rare. It was a legume planted in autumn and bore fruit ripe enough for eating right around this time of year. The vines coiled into spirals and, for some reason, stretched toward the ground and hardened when they reached the soil. They were not meant to coil around anything. Rather, the vines became a support for the main plant. Hence its name, curly sky grass. They were like self-supporting beans, bearing only one bean per pod. In exchange for the low quantity of beans, the pods were soft, and pod and bean could be boiled and eaten as is.

On extremely rare occasions, two beans could be found in a single pod. These were aptly called "twin seeds". If you took them out after they were ripe enough to be planted, they became an ingredient for blood relation potions.

They were highly valuable because they were a very uncommon find when the beans were examined one by one for those that could be planted.

Freyja, who had been looking high and low for a bottle of alcohol first thing in the morning, responded to Mariela's question with seemingly no interest at all.

"Twin seeds just take hard work. We're right in the harvest season. You can dooo iiit... Ah!!!"

The sage paused for a moment after her exclamation.

"That's right—I buried twin seeds under the hut in the Fell Forest for safekeeping. What a coincidence, huh?" Freyja said as she abruptly turned around. She must have remembered something stupid because a forced smile appeared on her face. She had been so uninterested before, yet now she was like a different person. "C'mon, let's go, right now," Freyja urged, leading Mariela and Sieg toward the ruins of the little house in the Fell Forest.

This is my master we're talking about. I know what's buried under there with those seeds...

Mariela had never been told of this storage location. She hardly needed to guess what her master would have secretly buried there. Even so, Mariela was glad to revisit the little house for the first time in two centuries, and she followed briskly behind her master.

"Looks like this place was totally destroyed, huh?"

With her usual cheeriness, Freyja gazed at the site where the house she and Mariela used to live in once stood.

The house, which had been filled with memories of Freyja and Mariela, was so devastated and swallowed by the forest that you couldn't even tell where the walls had been, save for the barely perceptible remnants of the stone floor connecting to the cellar. Even the floor had been reclaimed by a large clump of grasses and herbs. No one but Mariela and her master would've ever been able to notice that a small house had once stood here.

"Ahh, isn't this the medicinal herb garden you made way back when, Mariela? Curique is incredibly fertile, but you planted it without space between each plant, so they competed with each other, leaving even sturdier ones behind. Bet these ones here now are really potent. And this huuuge tree is from the fruit seeds you planted. It's got male and female varieties, but the one you planted was male. You diligently watered it day after day and then said, 'Master, when can we eat the fruit? Maybe next month?' I couldn't bear to tell you there wouldn't be any because it was male."

The sage spoke with nostalgia about things that had happened a long time ago, perhaps picturing how the little house looked before the Stampede.

"Oh yeah, I guess that did happen..." Mariela had forgotten that precious memory until now.

She reminisced about those bygone days of so many years ago. Behind her, Sieg cracked a smile as he imagined a younger Mariela. She'd probably been adorable. To another, the hunter's expression may have looked a little suspicious, but since Freyja didn't shout "**Fire!**" it probably wasn't anything to worry about.

"Now for those indispensable s—twin seeds."

"'S'? Is there something you need that begins with 'S,' Master?"

Freyja clearly ignored Mariela's pressing and said, "Now, the twin seeds are...," and nimbly jumped down into the cellar where Mariela had slept in suspended animation for two hundred years.

"Huh? But there was nothing in that cellar." Mariela was puzzled as she laboriously and carefully climbed down into the basement after her instructor. The place was so small that when Freyja, Mariela, and then Sieg were all inside, their shoulders touched.

"Let's see, yeah, right here. Sieg, move this stone out of the way with your sword."

The spot Freyja pointed to was the exact center where Mariela had spread her magic circle and slept in suspended animation.

"This was the safest spot in the whole house. I put valuable stuff in there. Hey, there it is."

Despite its appearance, the flagstone she pointed to was actually a thin plate. It came loose quite easily after Sieg forced the tip of his sword beneath it. When it was moved aside, it revealed hole big enough to fit an armful of items. Secreted within this hidden spot was a leather bag.

The contents of this secluded satchel included curly sky grass seeds soaked in honey, and several bottles of alcohol.

"Ahh, I knew it, 'spirits'!" Mariela exclaimed. The identity of the *S* her master had uttered was alcohol after all.

The contents of the bottles had turned strange colors in the intervening years, even then there was hardly any liquid content left in them. Were they even drinkable anymore?

The curly sky grass seeds soaked in honey were probably a snack to be eaten with the drink. They, too, had rotted so badly that Mariela couldn't even tell what they'd originally looked like. They'd long since dried out, and their shape suggested that eating them now was ill advised. However, there was one other small bottle next to the honey, and the twin seeds within were steeped in a particular substance called "time-cheating nectar." This was a preservative that prevented its contents from experiencing the flow of time.

Whenever Mariela's master had made or bought the honey, she'd probably put the twin seeds she found by chance in the time-cheating nectar and took the opportunity to store them when she'd hidden the alcohol and snacks.

There was still one more thing in the bag, however.

"Ah, so the alcohol's no good—guess that figures. But these still are."

"Huh?"

The spirits were in poor condition and looked sour and undrinkable. But, if that's what Freyja had expected, then what was the object beginning with *S* that the alcohol-loving sage had so been looking forward to?

"Heh-heh-heh. Mariela, whaaat do you think these are?"

"A-are those...?!"

Freyja retrieved several tattered scraps of paper from the bottom of the bag. The ink on them had run, and it was difficult to read what was written. However, Mariela had made them when she was little, and remembered exactly what they were.

"Service voucher. I will help Master with one thing."

Those worn-out scraps of paper were premium tickets the young Mariela had given to her master on some anniversary or other such special day.

"Heh-heh-heeeh. The time to use these has finally come! Now, I wonder what I should have you help me with." Freyja was overjoyed.

"Please give those back!" cried the troublesome sage's student.

Sieg safeguarded the preserved twin seeds, while keeping an astute eye out in case Freyja dropped any vouchers so he could pick them up himself.

For some reason, Mariela was extremely embarrassed at having given the vouchers as a present when she was little. She would have preferred such things not to have been hidden in the number one safest place Freyja could've come up with.

In the end, Mariela agreed to honor the promise she'd made on the little tickets. She was already doing everything for her troublesome master anyway.

"I want to eat orc meat fried with general oil!"

The first order Freyja made was for food, unsurprisingly. The particular dish was made by kneading orc lard with orc king lard. The oil produced from this effort could not be created via magic or skills, truly it was the embodiment of effort. Cooking with this rare oil made cheap orc meat as delicious as that of an orc general.

"Yes, ma'aaam."

After completing the blood relation potion, Mariela went to the kitchen to make the substance, as decreed by her master. Was she going to have to make the oil once again by *knead-knead-knead-knead*ing like she did not long after she'd first met Sieg?

Nope. After she put the orc lard in a bowl, she set the bowl under a kneading machine and pressed a switch with a click.

Kneeead-kneeead-kneeead-kneeead, kneeead-kneeead-kneeead-kneeead.

The machine was super convenient. Powerful, too.

As if to say, "This is two hundred years of humankind's progress!", the general oil was ready in the blink of an eye. It was incredibly easy. No Sieg required.

Perhaps Freyja didn't know such a handy magical tool existed, because she stared with dumbfounded shock on her face at the roasted orc meat as it sizzled on the magical heating tool, emitting a delicious smell. Even for Freyja, such an expression was a rare sight.

As if knowing the general oil was made via artificial means, Freyja said a bit dejectedly, "I can't feel my pupil's affection in this..." But she decided she'd let Mariela off the hook this one time. Considering Freyja had—quite literally—dug up the embarrassing service vouchers when Mariela already affectionately looked after the sage every day, it was the least she could have done.

Incidentally, Sieg was the one who collected the service vouchers in exchange for Mariela cooking what her teacher wanted. The young alchemist had insisted that he throw them away, but this time *he* probably hid them somewhere safe in their home.

Appendix

Amber

♀ Age: **29**

A helpful, beautiful, large-chested woman. She tied the knot with Dick after her hardships ended. She prefers not to show affection in public, so Dick feels a little envious every time he sees Voyd and Elmera flirting. Though not appearing very bookish, accounting is her forte; she began working at Sunlight's Canopy right after getting married, and when Mariela is out, Amber manages the shop in her place.

Emily

♀ Age: 10

The poster girl for the inn known as the Yagu Drawbridge Pavilion. She refers to corn soup and tea as "uni-corn" and recommends it enthusiastically. She's a "terrorist" who unknowingly causes Gestaltzerfall on the corn of the people around her...maybe. She's a normal, precocious girl with no combat skills. The holy water in the Labyrinth City has her hair in it. Recently, she seems to be having fun playing with Sherry, Pallois, and Elio in Sunlight's Canopy.

Grandel

⚥ Age: **39**

Shield gentleman of the Black Iron Freight Corps. He has a frail gastrointestinal tract, so meat and fat don't agree with him and he can only eat vegetables in small quantities. Because of this, he's thin and has weak muscles despite being a warrior. Although he has powerful shield skills, he doesn't actually carry a shield. Armor and helmets are too heavy for him to wear, so he resigned from the Labyrinth Suppression Forces and joined the Black Iron Freight Corps. He always carries an umbrella around in place of a shield, and he uses Umbrella Shield Bash to do away with scoundrels. A "legendary hero."

Illuminaria

♀ Age: ?

A sacred tree spirit who guided Mariela to the ley line two hundred years ago. She survived the Stampede and grew next to Sunlight's Canopy. She stored power from the *Drops of Life*–infused water Mariela gave her, and manifested in Sunlight's Canopy to convey the danger Endalsia was in. Like all spirits, she harbors goodwill toward Sieg and shows him favoritism, such as when she dropped more sacred tree leaves for him than for her friend Mariela.

Freyja

♀ Age: ?

An alcohol-loving woman known as the Sage of Calamity due to her outrageously high-ranking spirit magic expertise and her fiery personality. Despite being Mariela's master, she's a rather typical sort of teacher, and her knowledge extends to many different things. As such, her level in precise, bothersome alchemy is surprisingly low. Her words and actions appear whimsical but often contain a deeper point, and she seems to foresee everything. Her identity is shrouded in mystery.

Kunz Marrock

♂ Age: **52**

The representative of the Rock Wheel Autonomous Region. As the term "half dwarf" suggests, he inherited half the disposition of a dwarf, so he possesses both political ability and dwarven dignity. Because he visited the Labyrinth City right around the time of Caroline's kidnapping, he was suspected of being involved in the incident. He seems like a difficult person, but if one cooperates with him in regard to what every dwarf aspires to—the ultimate sword—befriending this simple old man proves rather easy.

Master* Mariela's
Alchemy Recipes

Special-Grade Edition

* Unofficial title

Special-Grade Heal Potion

A miracle that brings you the healing of the ley line!

As long as you're alive, it can heal any injury!
A definite miracle medicine that can help heal lost limbs.

【Ingredients】 Ley-line shard: A physical crystal of the *Drops of Life* dwelling in a monster.

Curique: An unusual herb. Its medicinal components collect in its veins.

Dead dragon shroom: A mushroom that grows on the corpse of a dragon. It feeds on the magical power remaining in the dragon's hide and bones.

Dragon blood: Blood from a member of the dragon species. Removing the toxicants is a must.

Face tree fruit: The fruit of a face tree, an active monster that uses its roots to move around. Use it before it's ripened. When it's ripe, the fruit has a baby's face, which is creepy.

Hot sand scorpion poison: The poison of a scorpion that lives in hot sand. Only a little can be obtained from each creature. It deteriorates if it comes in contact with the air.

Kraken viscous liquid: The viscous liquid of a soft-bodied creature of the sea. Slaken's is acceptable.

【Quantity】 Ley-line shard: 1; Curique: 1 handful; Dead dragon shroom: 1;
(per potion) Dragon blood: 1 teaspoon; Face tree fruit: 1 piece; Hot sand scorpion poison: Several drops; Kraken viscous liquid: 1/2 cup.

Special-Grade Specialized Potion for Eyes

A mysterious medicine that regenerates a lost eye.

It can even heal Sieg's Spirit Eye! The final word on treating peepers!

【Ingredients】 Crystalline lens of a gazer: The crystalline lens of an eye monster that's also called an observer.

Ley-line shard, curique, dead dragon shroom, dragon blood, face tree fruit, hot sand scorpion poison, kraken viscous liquid.

【Quantity】 (per potion) Crystalline lens of a gazer: 1 per eye to be treated; Ley-line shard, curique, dead dragon shroom, dragon blood, face tree fruit, hot sand scorpion poison, kraken viscous liquid: The same amount used in special-grade heal potions.

Secondary Materials for Special-Grade Potions

Indispensable secondary materials for making special-grade potions

Particular secondary materials are required to process special materials.

【Ingredients】 Coal ashes: The ashes of coal that dwarves used to forge steel. Used in separating hot sand scorpion poison.

Caustic slime acidic liquid, slime acidic liquid: The acidic liquid of a lightning slime that was fed salt, and acidic liquid created by dissolving the gas it spits out in water.

Special vinegar: Vinegar made using lynus wheat as a base and combining several varieties of grains and fruit, and dozens of different varieties of nuts. Delicious when aged, but then it's no longer a material for potions.

【Quantity】 (per potion) Coal ashes: 1 cup; Caustic slime acidic liquid: 1 cup; Slime acidic liquid: About 1 teaspoon; Special vinegar: 1/2 cup.

How to Create Special-Grade Potions

《1. Ley-Line Shard Acidic Liquid》

Bring *Drops of Life* to a state that's neither gas nor liquid through extremely high temperature and pressure, then dissolve a ley-line shard into it.

《2. Processing the Hot Sand Scorpion Poison》

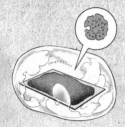

2-1 Mix the ashes from coal that dwarves used to forge steel into a slurry with a caustic slime's acidic liquid, then cure it for a few hours under high temperature and pressure to transform the ash into an adsorbent material with tiny holes in it.

2-2 After soaking the hot sand scorpion poison, slowly rinse with water so the adsorbent isn't washed away. After that, add *Drops of Life* to the caustic slime acidic liquid to separate the poison components from the adsorbent, then neutralize it with slime acidic liquid.

《3. Other Materials》

3-1 At a normal temperature, mix the dragon blood with oil that evaporates at room temperature, liquid oil, and warmed solid oil in that order. Then separate and extract the toxicants.

3-2 Remove the seed from an unripe face tree fruit, make a hole in it, and take out the liquid inside. Put the liquid in a sponge made from daigis fibers, and after you draw out the magical power of the variety of living things that nourished the face tree, extract it with alcohol.

3-3 Dry the dead dragon shrooms at a temperature high enough to make even live trees burst into flames, then finely crush and extract them with water colder than ice. Go ahead and extract or use Crystallize Medicine on the curique and kraken viscous liquid, too.

《4 • Crystalline Lens of a Gazer (Specialized Potion for Eyes)》

4-1 Make the vinegar by using lynus wheat as a base and combining several varieties of grains and fruit, and dozens of varieties of nuts. Freshly made vinegar with a sharp, acrid odor is required.

4-2 After thinly slicing the gazer's crystalline lens, dry it at a constant temperature and pressure, then grind into a powder and dissolve it in the vinegar.

4-3 Warm it at a temperature low enough that it won't boil until the sour odor disappears. Add water containing *Drops of Life* while making sure the total volume doesn't change.

《5 • Putting It All Together》

Add the curique, kraken viscous liquid, face tree fruit, and dead dragon shroom extracts, in that order, to the ley-line shard acidic liquid, and then if you're making a specialized potion, add the processed liquid from the gazer's crystalline lens. Before mixing the whole thing, drip in the hot sand scorpion poison, and the instant it is uniformly mixed, add the dragon blood. Be careful not to lose focus the whole time!

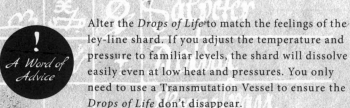

! A Word of Advice

Alter the *Drops of Life* to match the feelings of the ley-line shard. If you adjust the temperature and pressure to familiar levels, the shard will dissolve easily even at low heat and pressures. You only need to use a Transmutation Vessel to ensure the *Drops of Life* don't disappear.

Limit Breaker's Time

Kept ya waiting! This is the start of my story! There are several key words for Volume 5 hidden throughout the Life of Haage. It's a marvelous system where the words in **bold** are hints of the next book. That's what *Limit Breaker's Time's* all about!

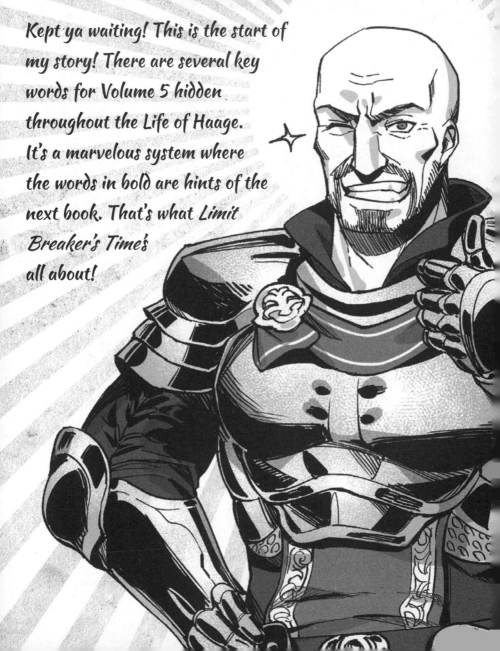

I want to protect what's precious to me. I want to take back what's precious to me. Everything is for the sake of that desire…
Mariela's progress, and Sieg's efforts, are now connected to the wheel of fate.

On that day, the ground in the Labyrinth City rumbled mightily.

"Wh-what's that?! A *stampede*?!"

Haage and Freyja, as well as the bar's customers and the bottles of alcohol, felt a shaking from the lowest stratum of the Labyrinth. Each patron used not only *both hands*, but *both legs* to catch the glasses and bottles that jumped off the shelves. Those who were dexterous enough even used their *stomachs*.

"This is an earthquake caused by an earth-type hibernating catfish. Don't worry."

Of course, Freyja was a font of knowledge. Incidentally, she had *encouraged* and *sought after Edgan* as a substitute for a tray to hold as much of her precious alcohol as he could carry. According to her, earth-type hibernating catfish usually slept deep underground near a water source. They awakened once ever few decades, causing earthquakes, and *crawled out from the depths of the earth* to mate.

"But won't it loosen the earth's crust during this downpour?"

Haage had come to the bar to skip—to gather information. In response to his question, Freyja looked through the window

Limit Breaker's Time!!

at the threat of rain outside and exclaimed "Wuh-oh."

"So it's overlapping with the mating cycle of the water-type hibernating catfish? It's been *two hundred years* since that happened."

The mating cycle of the earth-type's was seventy years, but the water-type's was thirty years. These two cycles overlapped once every 210 years. When only one happened, it didn't cause much damage, but when the two mating cycles occurred together, the damage was greatly amplified, and could be a bit annoying.

"Haage, wait a sec. Here, and here. A *mudslide* might occur in these places. If we don't help people evacuate, we might end up with at least one *dead person* on our hands."

After Freyja, who knew of this situation from when she'd lived in the era of the Kingdom of *Endalsia*, showed him which areas were most prone to disaster. Haage left to extricate the victims.

"Honestly. They should have been on different days. Why'd they have to happen at the same time?"

"That's because there are *links* between the two species. They can crossbreed. For those guys, it's the *beginning of a new world*. Oh yeah, it would be a real headache if a lightning elemental happens to be born in this rain. You should wear a rubber raincoat."

"Got it! I'll prepare to encounter all four elements if I need to!" Haage said, then hurried off to the guild. Talking about all *four elements* was a bit of a *leap* in logic, but the guild probably needed to employ *all members to challenge* the problem.

Thanks to the efforts of Haage and the rest of the Adventurers Guild, the Labyrinth City didn't suffer serious damage and was able to *overcome a disaster that hadn't been seen in two hundred years*. The following day, around noon, they returned to the guild, then immediately began to change clothes, relieved at finally doffing their hot raincoats.

Men in the prime of life had been made to wear rubber raincoats the whole time they'd been working to make sure everyone was safe.

"Welcome b... Gaaah, it stinks!!! **Ventilate!!!** I don't know where you've been, but I don't give *a lick, sir!*"

All the female employees of the guild present greeted Haage and the others, and promptly used ventilation magic that blew away both the stench and the men. The story of the female employees' *defeat of the boss* of the Adventurers Guild was a hot subject among the City for a while afterward.

Limit Breaker's Time!!

AFTERWORD

Volume 4. Freyja's invasion. Fire.

No, Volume 4 wasn't just about her. The pages were jam-packed with as much material as the page count would allow, plus edits. The growth of Mariela and Sieg; the start of potion sales; the complete change of the Labyrinth City's economy; Caroline's kidnapping and romance that completely left out the main character; the oppressive circumstances of Malraux's family; the restoration of Sieg's Spirit Eye; and even the truth behind the Stampede. Yet, if the impression of Mariela's master is the only thing that remains after finishing the book, what does that tell us? I might have made the character a little too extreme.

Now, leaving aside the pretty (itty-bitty?) Freyja of many mysteries, the secret of the Spirit Eye and the truth of two hundred years ago have revealed themselves at last.

Sieg is the successor to the Spirit Eye and heir to the ruined country. During the planning stage of this tale, I considered having Sieg as the main character, but I also wanted to tell a heartwarming story. I decided to have him deal with conflict alone and grow as a person while Mariela was sleeping like a log and dreaming of meat. Sieg's background made him too powerful, so I gave him the handicap of starting as a dying slave. Poor guy.

Although that's how he used to be, he pushed through adversity and grew up reasonably well, so he's going to play a big role in

419

the next volume. Of course, so will Mariela, who's finally able to make special-grade potions.

The Labyrinth City has the Spirit Eye and special-grade potions at its disposal at last, but there's still a heap of problems.

The red dragon, which the Labyrinth Suppression Forces can't do a thing against, is still going strong, and an even stronger enemy lies in wait in a lower stratum. However, with the spirit Endalsia's life in peril, there's no more time to waste.

What kind of potions will Mariela make to help in this crisis?

How will Sieg, Leonhardt, and the people of the Labyrinth City fight and forge their destiny?

Will spring at last arrive for the poorly treated Edgan? Will Freyja get dead-drunk like she always does?

And there's still the matter of the identity of the Labyrinth's boss...

Volume 5 brings us to the finale.

Last but not least, I'd like to express my heartfelt thanks to ox, the illustrator who drew the truly incredible cover art depicting the Labyrinth; Shimizu, the editor I am continually indebted to for helping me with everything from scheduling to sales promotions; everyone else at Kadokawa; and finally, everyone who picked up this book and has followed it to this point, as well as everyone who cheered me on while reading the Internet edition of the story.

Usata Nonohara

HAVE YOU BEEN TURNED ON TO LIGHT NOVELS YET?

SWORD ART ONLINE, VOL. 1–20
SWORD ART ONLINE PROGRESSIVE 1–6

The chart-topping light novel series that spawned the explosively popular anime and manga adaptations!

MANGA ADAPTATION AVAILABLE NOW!

SWORD ART ONLINE © Reki Kawahara ILLUSTRATION: abec
KADOKAWA CORPORATION ASCII MEDIA WORKS

ACCEL WORLD, VOL. 1–22

Prepare to accelerate with an action-packed cyber-thriller from the bestselling author of *Sword Art Online*.

MANGA ADAPTATION AVAILABLE NOW!

ACCEL WORLD © Reki Kawahara ILLUSTRATION: HIMA
KADOKAWA CORPORATION ASCII MEDIA WORKS

SPICE AND WOLF, VOL. 1–21

A disgruntled goddess joins a traveling merchant in this light novel series that inspired the *New York Times* bestselling manga.

MANGA ADAPTATION AVAILABLE NOW!

SPICE AND WOLF © Isuna Hasekura ILLUSTRATION: Jyuu Ayakura
KADOKAWA CORPORATION ASCII MEDIA WORKS

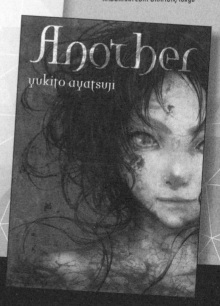

I DON'T INTEND TO BRING HARM TO THIS CITY.

I'M SIMPLY ASKING QUESTIONS SO WE MAY WELCOME YOU AND NOT BE DISCOURTE-OUS...

F-FAR FROM IT.

MY PUPIL'S NAME IS MARIELA.

GII
(CREAK)

MY NAME IS CAPTAIN KYTE OF THE CITY DEFENSE SQUAD.

YOU DON'T WANT TO LET ME IN, DO YOU?

WHO IS YOUR PUPIL?

UGH, I HATE BUREAU-CRACY.

I'M FREYJA. I CAME TO VISIT MY PUPIL.

COULD YOU LET ME IN?

I CAN GATHER FROM YOUR APPEAR-ANCE THAT YOU'RE A FAMOUS ADVENTUR-ER.

I'D LIKE TO HEAR THE REASON FOR YOUR VISIT.

WHAT!?

I WAS SPOTTED...

WHAT IS IT?

TCH!

TO THINK THEY COULD BE DISCERNED AT FIRST GLANCE...

THE SUMMONER'S MAGICAL INSECTS LOOK NO DIFFERENT THAN ORDINARY ONES...

I THINK IT WOULD BE FASTER TO SEE FOR YOURSELF, SIR.

......I SEE. AND WHAT KIND OF PERSON WAS SHE?

SHE SAID "LEAD THE WAY" TO MY INSECT, SO...

IT WASN'T MERELY YOUR IMAGINA-TION?

HEH.

IT'S AN HONOR TO BE WELCOMED. NOW, LEAD THE WAY.

ぷぃーん
PUUUUN (BZZ)

GRRR...

RRRRR...

RRR...

ズ゛ン
ZUN (BOOM)

SHE'S NOT SLACKING OFF IN HER WORK, IS SHE?

THIS CLOSE TO THE CITY...

ヒュッ
HYU (WHOOSH)

WE HAVE CONFIRMED A TREMENDOUSLY POWERFUL MAGICAL REACTION IN THE FELL FOREST!

R-REPORTING IN!

WE HAVEN'T YET DETERMINED THEY'RE AN ENEMY.

WHO COULD IT BE...? ARE THEY EVEN HUMAN...?

YES, SIR. THEIR IDENTITY IS CURRENTLY UNDER INVESTIGATION.

AN UNIDENTIFIED PERSON IS RANDOMLY FIRING OFF HIGH-LEVEL MAGIC AS THEY APPROACH THE LABYRINTH CITY?

SIR!

BA (FWIP)

HE'S TO BE AS DISCREET AS POSSIBLE.

HAVE THE INSECT SUMMONER FIND OUT THIS PERSON'S IDENTITY.

GOOOO
(FWOOOM)

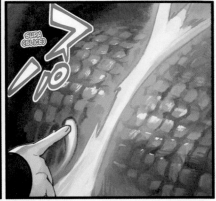

SUPA
(SLICED)

HAAAH...

WHAT THE HECK? HAS THE MONSTER POPULATION EXPLODED RECENTLY?

GRRR...

RRRI

GRRRRR...

GRRR...

ZU
(WHOOSH)

ZU

ZUZUN
(FWOOSH)

HYU
(FLICK)

FLAME PILLAR CHAOS!

GRANT ME NOUR- ISHMENT.

CONSUME AND BURN THE MANY FOES THAT DEFY ME.

GOU
(RUMBLE)

HOW LONG WAS I ASLEEP ......!?

PERFECT TIMING.

ずしん
ZUSHIN (THUD)

OH.

I'M STARVING. MIGHT AS WELL GO HOME AFTER SO LONG!

OH WELL. THAT GIRL'S PROBABLY AWAKE BY NOW TOO.